Praise for

The Girl in the Glass

"*The Girl in the Glass* is possibly the most beautiful book I've ever read. Susan Meissner lifted her book to the level of poetry at the same time she drew me in so deeply to the story that I was lost in the world she created. The story comes in three threads that twist together into a stunning, compelling, enchanting whole. I absolutely loved it."

—MARY CONNEALY, author of The Kincaid Brides series

"*The Girl in the Glass* is a compelling story that left me begging the world to stop long enough to savor its pages. Susan Meissner is a master storyteller who weaves times and characters together with writing that paints perfect images. This time she gifts us with a trip to Florence, home of art and story."

—CARA C. PUTMAN, award-winning author of *A Wedding Transpires on Mackinac Island* and *Stars in the Night*

"Susan Meissner has done it again with this sweeping tale that will have you turning the pages late into the night. Get caught up in the journey of Meg as she finds her life and direction in the beauty and mystery of Italy. You will be cheering *magnifico!*"

—JENNY B. JONES, award-winning author of *Save the Date* and A Charmed Life series

Praise for
Susan Meissner

"Meissner delivers a delightful page-turner that will surely enthrall readers from beginning to end. The antebellum details, lively characters, and overlapping dramas particularly will excite history buffs and romance fans."

—*Publisher's Weekly* starred review

"Meissner transports readers to another time and place to weave her lyrical tale of love, loss, forgiveness, and letting go."

—KAREN WHITE, *New York Times* best-selling author of *The Beach Trees*

"My eyes welled up more than once! A beautiful story of love, loss, and sacrifice, and of the bonds that connect us through time."

—SUSANNA KEARSLEY, *New York Times* best-selling author
of *The Winter Sea*

"How does Susan create characters that stay with me long after I close the book? How does she address the emotions and memories that hold us hostage with such grace? I keep reading, knowing I'll discover a fascinating story and hoping I'll infuse some of the skill and craft that Susan weaves to make it."

—JANE KIRKPATRICK, award-winning author of *The Daughter's Walk*

THE
GIRL
IN THE
GLASS

SUSAN MEISSNER

AUTHOR OF *The Shape of Mercy*

THE GIRL IN THE GLASS

A NOVEL

WaterBrook
PRESS

THE GIRL IN THE GLASS
PUBLISHED BY WATERBROOK PRESS
12265 Oracle Boulevard, Suite 200
Colorado Springs, Colorado 80921

All Scripture quotations are taken from the King James Version.

Apart from well-known real people and real events associated with Medici history, the characters and events in this book are fictional and any resemblance to actual persons or events is coincidental.

ISBN 978-0-307-73042-8
ISBN 978-0-307-73043-5 (electronic)

Cover design by Kelly L. Howard

Published in the United States by WaterBrook Multnomah, an imprint of the Crown Publishing Group, a division of Random House Inc., New York.

WATERBROOK and its deer colophon are registered trademarks of Random House Inc.

Library of Congress Cataloging-in-Publication Data
Meissner, Susan, 1961–
    The girl in the glass : a novel / Susan Meissner. — 1st ed.
      p. cm.
    ISBN 978-0-307-73042-8 — ISBN 978-0-307-73043-5 (electronic)
  I. Title.
    PS3613.E435G57 2012
    813'.6—dc23

                         2012013005

Printed in the United States of America
2012

10 9 8 7 6 5 4 3 2

For Bob, because he promised to take me to Florence. And he did.

*Everything you
can imagine
is real.*

—PABLO PICASSO

Prologue

The sun is setting on my last day in Florence. Tomorrow I will marry the man my uncle has chosen for me and Florence will be at my back, perhaps forever. My soon-to-be husband will have no reason to come here after we marry, and my uncle will not expect to see me again. His responsibilities for me, such as they are, will be done.

My cousin Maria does not understand my melancholy at the prospect of leaving forever the place where my life began. "What has Florence ever brought you but heartache?" she has said more than once.

And if I've any kindred souls in this world besides her, perhaps they would say she is right.

But within my heart so cruelly handled, there are unseen places that have been shaped by Florence's beauty. Florence is a coin with two sides, a room with two doors, a river with two banks. Everything that wounded me happened here. And everything that brought me solace happened here too.

Maria brought me to Rome with her to see me out of Florence, out of the maelstrom of Medici woe that she believes Florence is to me. Maria does not know that Florence alone speaks condolence to me; I couldn't wait to return. Only Florence, in all her vast majesty, assures me that as much as people can create ugliness, they can create splendor. It is all around me in Florence: the ache of loveliness, in every work forged by human hands that can kill as soundly as they heal.

And now it seems I must bid farewell to my very soul.

Maria is calling for me. The carriage is ready. My uncle would have us leave for the Villa dell'Ambrogiana before darkness falls.

As I depart, Florence safeguards my childhood treasures, buried beneath the marble and within the frescoes and in the threads of the canvases. All my longings, whispered on dark nights and gray days, I press them now into the folds of my city, so that as my shadow falls away from Florence forevermore, I shall not be forgotten by her.

Nora Orsini
October 1592

1

When I close my eyes and think of home, I always envision Florence—a place I've never been.

The red and cream hues, remembered from the paintings on my Italian grandmother's walls, speak "home" to me as much as any address where I've ever lived. My grandmother is gone now, and her pictures and paintings have been scattered among my father's family members. But with my eyes shut, I can picture the rosy cap of the cathedral dome, the toast-colored stucco, the lizard-green Arno River as it lazes down its course. I can hear the odd cadence of European emergency sirens, the zipping of Vespas down asymmetrical streets, and the acoustic darts of a language I don't understand beyond simple endearments spoken by my *nonna*. I can smell the cappuccino—because she told me hers smelled just like it—the perfumed doorways of the fashion houses, the dense exhaust of too many cars. And I can feel the cool, silken flesh of *David's* marbled feet if I were allowed to stretch out my hand and touch them.

Even now, so many years later, I can see the canvases on my grandmother's living room walls—the litho of Botticelli's *Primavera,* the oil Nonna had done of a woman walking in the rain in a puddled piazza, the watercolor of rows of Italian cypresses and a young man on a bicycle.

But the one of a young girl reaching toward a beckoning statue is the only one I still dream about. My great-great-grandfather painted it when Nonna was young, before she and her parents immigrated to America. My grandmother was the girl in the painting, and the statue stood in the Florentine background. A palette of russets and burgundy and ocher filled the rest of the painting with depth and elegance, with a hint of blossoms to come.

Nonna used to tell me I was the girl in the painting, just as she had been when she was a little girl, an impossibly wondrous thought that I clung to until well after my eleventh birthday. Nonna, as the young girl, whose back was to my great-great-grandfather as he painted, wears a rosy-pink gown that glistens in the sunlight playing behind her. I used to imagine the statue was speaking to the girl and that's why her hand was extended—as if she were inviting my grandmother to dance, to join her world of joy where anything unexpected was possible. I loved that painting and thought of it often, long after my parents divorced, long after my mother and I moved to San Diego and the visits to Nonna's dwindled. Nonna was going to take me to Florence when I graduated from high school to find the statue, but she died when I was twelve. I never saw that painting again after she died.

My father promised his mother, as she lay dying, that he would take me to Florence in her stead. I wasn't there when he promised her this. My mother and I were in San Diego when we got the call two days after she died that Nonna had had a massive heart attack. But Dad told me of the promise when my passionate grief over Nonna's death left him grappling for words to make me stop crying. Six years later, however, in the summer months following my high-school graduation, Dad had knee surgery. From then until now, the promised trip to Florence has been in a perpetual state of postponement. From time to time he'll remark that we need to take that trip. He hasn't forgotten, but it's almost as if he's waiting for something to happen—or change—before he can make good on that promise.

Eighteen years after Nonna's death, I marvel that the mention of her birthplace still sounds like the name of a matronly soul, kind and sweet. Florence—a woman with ample arms, a soft voice, and silver wisps in her hair. I've been to London and Paris and to Aruba twice for publishing conferences. But the closest I've come to visiting Florence are the phone calls I make to one of my authors who happens to live there.

A phone call to Lorenzo always makes me feel decidedly homesick.

❧

I awoke to early-April coastal fog, frothy white like a bridal veil, and my first thought after remembering I'd be Skyping with Lorenzo before nine, was that my ex-fiancé would marry that evening.

A blanket of mist coddled Bird Rock and the rest of the San Diego coast with a ghostlike embrace as I lay scrunched under the covers, wondering if Miles was feeling nervous or afraid. Was he thinking of me, even just a little? Would the unintended wound I gave him two years ago needle him as he got ready for the day? I hoped not. I didn't want to ruin his wedding day twice.

Coffee drunk, cheese omelet eaten, I gave scant thought as to what to wear to work. I wouldn't be rushing to Balboa Park for twilight nuptials. I chose a denim skirt, red-and-white-striped knit top, black flats. Chrome jewelry. Ponytail.

I was pouring a second cup of coffee into a travel mug when my cell phone rang. My mother's ringtone. I fished the phone out of my purse and answered with a cheerful "Hello, Mom."

"Meg. You don't have to pretend. It's me."

"Good morning to you too."

"You doing okay? Really?" In the background I could hear her pushing buttons on her microwave.

"Really."

"But today is not just any old Friday."

I replaced the carafe on the coffee maker and pressed the Off button. "I'm fine. I'm the one who broke up with Miles, remember?"

"Of course I remember. That doesn't mean you enjoyed having to do it. Or that you are enjoying this. You and Miles dated for two years. He's marrying someone else today."

"But I'm happy for him." I screwed the top on my travel mug.

"Yes, well, I didn't call him to see how he's doing today. I called you."

"And I'm fine."

"Well, if you're sure."

"I am. But thanks."

I heard the sound of the microwave whirring to life.

"So, I was thinking if you're free tonight, we could meet up at the Melting Pot for dinner."

My mother loves fondue restaurants. No one touches your food while it's cooking but you. No one touches it when it's done cooking but you.

"Why? Something up?" I grabbed my car keys and then knelt to unlatch the kitty door for Alex, my borrowed cat. He brushed past me, meowing his thanks, and disappeared through it into the tiny backyard of the cottage that I am caretaker for.

"I just want to have dinner with you. I... There's..." But she didn't continue.

I stood up. "There's what?"

"Nothing. Can you come? Are you busy?"

Since breaking off my engagement with Miles, I'd given myself a year to heal—wounding someone could be just as painful as being wounded by someone—and then had spent the next twelve months slowly reentering the dating life. I'd gone out on a few dates, but I hadn't met anyone I'd wanted to rush into a relationship with. My mother had applauded my caution. Elaine Pomeroy always applauds caution. "Better safe than sorry" would be tattooed on my mother's forearm if she wasn't convinced tattoo artists don't properly clean their needles. She was all for me taking it slow. Gabe, the graphic designer at the same publishing house where I work, is the closest I have come to dating anyone exclusively. We've gone out a few times. The thing is, a dating relationship is always going somewhere. Even nowhere is a place. I didn't want to mess up Gabe's and my workplace friendship with a potential dating destination like nowhere. So I recently backed off—a sublimely cautionary move my mother applauded—and Gabe gallantly retreated. And I am not dating anyone else at the moment.

I had no plans for the evening of Miles's wedding.

"What time?" I asked.

"How about seven thirty? Unless you want to do it earlier. I was thinking we'd miss the worst of the evening traffic."

"Seven thirty is fine." I turned off the kitchen light and reached for my purse. "See you then."

"Oh. And your father is probably going to call you today."

My arm reaching for my purse paused midstretch. It wasn't odd that my father might call. Our amicable relationship includes occasional phone calls and the even more occasional visit. But it seemed odd to me that he'd call today, out of the blue. Dad surely didn't know Miles was getting married that night. He couldn't have known. Unless my mother had called and told him. Nineteen years postdivorce my mother still calls my father to remind him of things she thinks he will forget, as if it still matters what he does and doesn't do.

"I'm telling you I'm fine, Mom."

"It's not about Miles getting married. I'm sure your father couldn't care less about that. I didn't call him. He called me."

"What for?"

"He lost your new cell phone number. All he has is your work number. So I gave it to him. I wasn't going to without asking you first, but he said he needed it to talk to you about something. And he didn't want to call you on your work phone."

As my mother talked, I began to conjure possibilities as to what my father would think important for me to know that he couldn't tell me at work. Maybe at long last he was setting a date for our trip to Florence?

"If he is coming down today and wants to see you, do what you must," my mother continued. "But don't bring him to the Melting Pot."

The tone in my mother's voice was a mix of apprehension and distaste.

"I won't bring him. And I doubt he's coming down. He could tell me that at work."

"There've always been a great many things he could have done and didn't."

Sunlight was peeking through the marine layer outside my kitchen window, reminding me that a full day at work awaited. I was due to talk with Lorenzo in less than fifteen minutes. It could take that long just to get from the cottage in Bird Rock to the office in downtown La Jolla, especially if all the good street parking was taken.

"Hey, Mom. I've got to run. I'm Skyping with one of my authors, and I don't want to keep him waiting."

"Call me if you're going to be late tonight. And tell your father to give you a bit more notice next time."

"I doubt he's coming down. I'll see you tonight." I headed for the front door, travel mug in hand. "Okay?"

"All right. Oh. And it's quite foggy this morning on the coast. Saw it on the morning news. Don't rush out into it. If it's too bad, just go in later."

I hung up and stepped out into the lacy vapor.

Nora

I was the first child born to my mother who lived. When I was little, Nurse liked to tell me that when I was born, I had lips as pink as a Florence sunrise and a howl to set the castle dogs to barking. Such a fine, healthy baby, she said. I didn't know until I was older about my mother's other babies or that rose-hued lips and a throaty cry were the difference between us.

Had I been a boy, my father might have decided to come from Rome to greet the first of his children to survive childbirth. But again, perhaps not. When my brother, Virginio, was born a year after me, it was many days before my father came to Florence to meet his infant heir.

I'm a Medici *principessa,* and my christened name is Francesca Eleonora Orsini, but no one calls me that. All those letters are reduced to *Nora,* which sounds like a breath expelled without hurry or pretense or significance. I like it. It suits me.

Paolo Orsini, my father, was betrothed to my mother, Isabella de' Medici, when she was eleven and he was twelve. They married when my mother was sixteen, and I was born, alive and wailing, thirteen long years later. I was a miracle, Nurse told me time and again. And I believed her; long after my mother was taken from me, certainly after I learned of the other unborn babies, and even for many years after the last time I saw my father. As childhood fancies began to thin and stretch, I was tempted to see the miracle of my being born as something else entirely. But I blew the temptation away, and it floated off like thistledown.

2

When I was little, the crinkly paint tubes in the garage corner where my grandmother painted had beckoned me in a way that seemed almost familial. A visit to her house always meant touching those metal tubes and fingering the horsehair brushes. The artistic gene showed up often on my father's side. He even dabbles in watercolors when he allows himself the luxury of time spent in front of a canvas, which isn't often. I used to tell people that I was going to be an artist too.

But while I favored my dad's side in looks—my one-quarter Italian appears three-quarters when I wear knockoff Gucci and stilettos—I wasn't gifted with the family flair for art. After a less-than-stellar first year in college as an art major, my mother reminded me that my SAT English scores were a better indicator of what I was good at. I changed schools, changed majors, and graduated three years later with a degree in English. An internship at Crowne & Castillo Press led to a job as an editorial assistant after graduation. Four years later, I was named an assistant editor. Four years after that, I was promoted to editor. Crowne & Castillo publishes travel books: how-tos, planning guides, travel essays, and pictorial coffee-table books. It's my personal goal to one day soon produce travel memoirs, but the once-married publishers, Geoffrey Crowne and Beatriz Castillo, have yet to be convinced that a travel memoir has enough commercial appeal for the typical Crowne & Castillo buyer.

"Who really wants to read about one person's cerebral contemplations of a place?" Geoffrey said only a few days ago. I replied that I would want

to. Lots of people would. And that not all memoirs are cerebral contemplations. He said that memoirs don't have photographs to engage the senses
and that's what sells a Crowne & Castillo book—the photos. I said that's
why ours would be different. Ours would have full-color photos. He said
he'd think about it some more.

As I came into the office out of the fog, this recent conversation with
Geoffrey was on my mind, along with my father's imminent phone call,
and Miles, too, and the fact that I was a few minutes late for my Skype ap-
pointment with Lorenzo. I mumbled hello to the front-office staff, rushed
into my office to open my Skype account, and found Lorenzo waiting for me.

Lorenzo DiSantis and his sister, Renata, an Italian brother-and-sister
writing and photography team, have authored five books for Crowne &
Castillo: two on Italy, two on the South of France, and one on the Catalonia
region of Spain. Their sixth project, still in the production stage, is a guide
to planning intimate Italian destination weddings. Lorenzo and Renata
live in a flat in the heart of Florence; no small wonder they are my favorite
Crowne & Castillo authors.

I like talking with Lorenzo, and not just because he and Renata live in
the one place I've always wanted to visit. Lorenzo is the only person who
calls me by my full name—Marguerite. I like the way it sounds falling off
his tongue. When Americans say it, like the woman at the DMV last week,
my full name sounds like a bunch of concrete bricks rolling around in a
wheelbarrow. But Lorenzo says my name the way my grandmother said it,
light and sweet. Everything Lorenzo says sounds a little like my grandmother. Nonna's melodic Italian accent produced an unnecessary yet enchanting *a* sound at the end of every word and so does Lorenzo's. Lorenzo
just turned forty, and Renata's a year older. They are apparently perfectly
happy being single and sharing a flat.

When my Skype account finally connected with his, I could see that he was sitting back in his desk chair, a Florentine evening just beginning to fall on the world outside the window behind him. He was unshaven, a look that went well with his nearly hairless head. Lorenzo told me that when he started to go bald in his twenties, he promptly took matters into his own hands. He bought an electric razor and clipped his hair down to the scalp. Some men can expertly pull off the sophisticated five-o'clock-shadow-on-top look. Lorenzo is one of them.

I apologized for being late.

"Nothing to worry about, Marguerite," he soothed. "Ten minutes is nothing. Fifteen? Nothing."

I checked my watch. "It's only five minutes."

He leaned in and smiled. "Less than nothing!"

The little *a* sound on that end of "nothing" made me laugh.

"Do not worry so much. It puts wrinkles on the face." He stroked his stubbled chin.

"I get that from my mom, I'm afraid."

"Ah. Give it back to her, eh?"

Again, I laughed. "So how was Florence today?"

"Enchanting as always. When are you coming?"

For the last four years I've been telling Lorenzo and Renata that my dad has promised me a trip to Florence, but Lorenzo doesn't fully get why I don't want to come alone. He doesn't understand that when my father and I finally go, it will be more than just a trip to Italy. It will be something special and long awaited, like a lost thing found. I like to imagine that it will happen that way.

"Soon, I hope."

"So. You do not like the photo Renata and I suggested for the cover?"

"I never said that."

"I have your e-mail right here. You say 'Beatriz had pictured Venice or Rome.'"

"Yes. Beatriz was thinking either Venice or Rome."

"And you do not disagree with her?"

I riffled through the photos on my desk and uncovered Lorenzo's shot of a man in a black suit holding a woman's hand as they walked barefoot on the beach on the Amalfi coast. A grove of nodding lemon trees bloomed on the hillside above them. The woman was dressed in a gauzy white strapless gown. The skirt was caught in a breeze that wanted the ocean; its hem reached for the foam. I could almost hear the rush of surf and smell the tangy twin scents of citrus and salt water.

"It's a great shot, Lorenzo. But Beatriz wants the cover photo to be of a city that people will instantly recognize."

"And you think we should give them Venice because everyone will be expecting Venice?"

"Is there something wrong with giving people what they expect?"

He laughed. "You know I like the unexpected, Marguerite. Besides, the Amalfi coast is a lover's bliss. Tell Beatriz that. Venice is for tourists with cameras. The Amalfi coast woos and flatters; it celebrates romance, eh? That is what the bride and the groom will remember when they go back home to wherever their real lives are. The romance of the place. If the romance does not matter, they can marry in a courthouse in Detroit and save a lot of money. It is all about the romance."

A tiny comma of pain poked me. I had loved Miles as a friend. But I had not been *in* love. There is a difference.

"You do not believe me?"

I must have grimaced, and he had seen it. "I believe you."

"So you will sell Beatriz on the Amalfi coast? If she doesn't like that photo, I have others. At Positano, Ravello. Many others."

I nodded. "I will try."

"Good. Now I have something else to ask of you, *cara*. My neighbor, she is writing a book and needs some advice. She asked if I would ask you to look at a chapter or two. I said I would."

I placed the photo of the Amalfi coast in its file. It is usually a bit awkward when a friend says he knows somebody who has written a book— worse when it's the friend who has written the book. I once had an acquaintance at a cocktail party insist on showing me three hundred pages of her poetry, all of it about birds. "What kind of book?" I asked. "If it's not travel related, there's really no point in my giving her advice."

"It is not exactly a travel book. But I think you may want to look at it anyway."

"Why would I want to do that?"

"Because Sofia's book is more like a memoir, cara. Memoir. Like what you told me you wanted to publish."

I reached for my travel mug, interested. "Really? What kind of memoir? Is it related to a place? Beatriz and Geoffrey won't consider anything that doesn't revolve around a travel destination."

"It is set in Florence. Your favorite place." He grinned. "And it's in English. Sofia is fluent. She was married to a British man once. Long time ago."

"But you and Renata have already written a book about Florence. It's only been out a couple years. How can I convince Beatriz and Geoffrey we need another one?"

"Ah, you will find Sofia's book to be very different, I think."

"How? Have you read any of it?"

"Some. Sofia has talent but needs direction, perhaps. But that is what a good editor is for, eh?" He laughed. I didn't.

"So what makes hers different from other travel books about Florence? You know how many are out there. There would have to be something amazingly unique about it. Especially if it's a memoir."

"Oh, that's easy. Sofia says she's one of the last known Medicis."

I heard what Lorenzo said, but it didn't quite register in my head. "What did you say?"

"She says she's one of the last of the Medicis."

I hadn't tanked every art class in my first year in college. I aced art history. I knew the Medici family ruled Florence for three hundred years and then evaporated in the eighteenth century because the last one died childless. The Medicis were extinct and had been for more than two centuries.

"So you're telling me your neighbor's delusional?" I asked, half-laughing.

Lorenzo smiled easily. "Sofia is a very interesting person. Easily the kindest person I know. You would like her, cara. And her story is very out of the ordinary. She is sweet. If she is delusional, we should all sign up for it, no?"

"I didn't mean to sound insulting. But it just sounds a little odd."

Lorenzo shrugged. "I don't think it's so odd that a Medici still lives. Big family. Lots of little Medicis. It's possible."

"Does anyone else believe she's one of the last of the Medicis?"

His smile was conciliatory. "But that is what makes her interesting, Marguerite. So you want me to send the first two chapters to you? I have them on my computer. She e-mailed them to me when she knew I would be talking to you today."

I had nothing to lose by agreeing to look at those two chapters. I could tell it would mean a lot to Lorenzo. And my interest was certainly piqued.

"But you won't promise her anything, right? She can't think that just because I am looking at her chapters, that we will publish her. She can't even think that I will be able to help her get it to the point where some other house will publish it, okay? I don't want her to have false hope."

"Of course. Here they come." Lorenzo tapped on his computer keyboard, then leaned back. "So you will speak to Beatriz about the photo, yes?"

"I will. I promise. And I will try to take a look at uh, Miss Medici-Whatever's chapters this weekend."

"Borelli. Sofia's last name is Borelli."

"She's a Medici with the last name Borelli."

Lorenzo shrugged. "The ladies don't get to keep the family name, do they, Miss Pomeroy?" He winked.

"All right. I will try to take a look at Ms. *Borelli's* chapters this weekend."

"*Buono.* No rush. And now help me choose a tie. Renata is in Greece this week." Lorenzo produced two ties and held them to the webcam. One was solid blue with frenetic silver swirls; the other was a rosy pink with thick, black diagonal stripes.

"Where are you going? Date with Alessandra or business meeting?"

"Alessandra? No. When was the last time we talked? Date with Rosabel."

A tiny Cheshire cat–like grin tugged at the corners of my mouth. It was none of my concern who Lorenzo dated. Yet for no apparent reason other than she'd distracted Lorenzo from meeting a few deadlines, I was glad that fair-haired Alessandra must be out of the picture. I had no idea who Rosabel was, though, and that wasn't any of my business either. I tamped the grin down to a thin line, as though I could barely decide between the ties. "The pink one, then. Rosabel?"

Lorenzo dropped the blue tie and held the rosy one up to his neck and looked down at it. "*Grazie.* She's here from Milan for eight weeks. Met her at a party. And where will you be going tonight?"

"Dinner with my mother."

He lifted his head to stare into the webcam. "Your mother."

"Don't say a word, Lorenzo."

He ignored my command. "Is it her birthday?"

"No."

He clucked his tongue. "If you were in Florence tonight, *cara mia,* you would not be having dinner with your mother."

True.

I'd be having it with my father.

Nora

My mother's sisters died of illness as young maidens, seventeen and sixteen. I believe it was for this reason that my grandfather doted on my mother the way he did and let her live whatever kind of life made her happy. My grandfather, Cosimo de' Medici, loved his daughters. He was fond of his sons as well; for what titled man does not want sons? But oh, the affection toward his daughters! The deaths of my mother's sisters—one before my mother married and one after—devastated him. It is said he turned all his affection toward my mother, lavishly so. What she wanted, my grandfather gave her. What she didn't want, he took.

All this was whispered about my grandfather when people didn't think I was paying attention to them.

I barely remember him. He died when I was three, and all I can remember of him is the feel of his tunic against my skin. It was smooth and warm and smelled of mint and limes.

There is a painting of him in the Uffizi by Master Bronzino. He is young, like me, and he wears armor, and his gaze is off to the right, as though he might have to don the helmet he is holding and rush off to direct a battle. But that is not how I imagine him. I imagine him silverhaired and smiling and ready to chase away the mere shadows of imps and goblins that would conspire to threaten a little girl's dreams.

3

I pushed the photo of the Amalfi coast across Geoffrey's desk. "Lorenzo really wants this photo on the front. People who've the money and motivation for an Italian destination wedding already know about Venice and Rome. He's thinking they've probably even been to those places already. They want a place that is romantic and special. And not crawling with a million tourists."

Geoffrey glanced at the photo. "Yes, but this book isn't just for people who've already decided they want an Italian destination wedding. It's to entice those who've never even considered it to consider it. Those people have never been to Venice and Rome, Meg. And that group of buyers is the bigger group. Exponentially bigger."

He pushed the photo back.

"So it's a no? You want me to tell him it's a no?"

Geoffrey sat back in his chair and rubbed an eyebrow. "Let me talk to Beatriz. I doubt she'll change her mind, but I'll talk to her. In the meantime you need to inspire confidence in that Venice photo. It's a good photo. Or the Florence one. That's the one you like, isn't it? The cover has to sell the book, Meg, not plan the wedding. Big difference."

"I think Lorenzo appreciates that, Geoffrey. He thinks this one *will* sell the book."

"He's a photographer."

"He's a romantic."

Geoffrey laughed lightly. "My point exactly. Photographers and lovers don't sell books." He turned to his computer. "Assure Lorenzo we will make the best decision for the book. We always do. And tell Gabe to start on the cover using the Venice photo for now."

I stepped out of Geoffrey's office. My cell phone in my skirt pocket began to vibrate, and I pulled it out.

My father.

I let the call go to voice mail. Whatever it was my dad wanted to tell me, I didn't want to talk about it in the hallway. When I arrived at Gabe's office, I found him standing over his desk, comparing two cover mock-ups of our latest guide to urban getaways. He smiled at me when I stepped inside.

Gabe is only a few inches taller than I am with short, curly brown hair that would probably grow in ringlets if he let it. He is missing two fingers on his right hand from a motorcycle accident when he was sixteen, but that hasn't hindered his skill. Sometimes I find myself a little jealous of his obvious artistic talent. The walls of his office are covered with his designs; some of them he drew freehand.

"Can't go wrong with Boston," I said, nodding toward the design at Gabe's left.

He pointed to another mock-up featuring a toned-down urban landscape. "Savannah's not on your bucket list?"

I cocked my head to look at the Savannah skyline. "I'd go. I guess I'd go to either."

"Savannah's pretty cool. Great art school there. Almost went to it. Guess we'll just have to see where Beatriz lands on it."

"Speaking of Beatriz, it looks like she wants you to go with the Venice shot for Lorenzo and Renata's book."

He regarded me for a moment. "Not one of Florence, eh?" His smile was subtle and knowing.

My face grew warm. "Everyone knows my secret loves. Not fair."

Gabe gathered the two mock-ups and sat down at his desk. "Everyone thinks you should just go, Meg. What are you waiting for? Just go."

His candor stung a little. And I knew he didn't mean for it to.

"I want my dad to take me. You know that. He said he would. I'm not ready to give up on him. I don't like giving up on people. Hey, want to join me and my mom at the Melting Pot tonight?" The invitation flew out of my mouth before I had a chance to consider it fully. But it was a safe enough request. Not a date. Not with my mom there.

Gabe looked down at the folio in his hands. I had taken him by surprise. "I, uh, can't do it tonight." He looked up. "I've got plans, I'm afraid."

"Oh. Too bad."

"I've a date, actually."

Gabe had a date.

"Oh. Well. That's...that's cool. Anyone I know?" My voice sounded distant in my ears, as if the question came from someone standing behind me.

Gabe shook his head and smiled. "I don't think so. I met her at my sister's party last weekend."

A party Gabe had casually invited me to and which I had casually declined.

"Sounds like fun."

Gabe's smile widened. "Does it? I didn't even say where we're going."

Increased embarrassment warmed my face further. "Legoland, right?" Time to go. I turned to leave. "Have fun."

I heard him laughing behind me. "Another time, Meg?"

"Sure. The Melting Pot with my mother and me. Round two. Check."

More gentle laughter.

I chanced a look back at him, supposing he had returned his attention to the mock-ups on his desk. But he was watching me leave.

My phone vibrated in my pocket, reminding me I had a voice mail waiting. The distraction was a welcome one. I pulled it out as I walked away. "Voice mail," I said.

Gabe nodded thoughtfully.

Back in my office, I slid into my chair, annoyed that Gabe's date bothered me. He had every right to go on a date. So did I, had there been someone I wanted to go on a date with. I pressed the button on my phone for voice mail, ready to hear my dad's message and then get on with the business of the day. I began to read an e-mail message as I listened but stopped when I heard his voice. He sounded tired. Old.

"Meg, it's Dad. Sorry to bother you at work, but I need to talk to you about something. When you have a minute, can you call me back on my cell? Don't wait until tonight. And don't call me at the house. I mean, I'd appreciate it if you could call me back before I go home tonight. Okay. I guess that's it. Talk to you later."

I replayed the message, listening to the tone of my father's voice, the strange ache behind the words. I couldn't remember my father ever sounding so…defeated.

He was definitely not happy about something, and it was something he felt I needed to know about, something that would have some indirect effect on me.

I'd been up to see him and his wife, Allison, only a few months earlier at New Year's. Everything seemed fine. The last phone conversation my father and I had was three weeks ago. Nothing seemed amiss then either. Whatever it was, it was recent, and something he'd been able to mask in his earlier phone call to my mother. She would have said something if she'd detected something was wrong.

I punched the button to call him back. When he answered, he seemed to exhale gently before saying my name.

"Dad, what is it? What's up?" I asked.

He hesitated only a second. "Hey, I'm coming down to San Diego tomorrow. I know it's really short notice, but I'd really like to talk to you. Will you be around? I won't need more than an hour."

My father's voice was calm but thin, as if he was saving the air in his lungs for nobler purposes than a quick phone conversation.

"So you're not going to tell me what this is about?" I laughed nervously.

"How about I bring breakfast over to your place? Around ten?"

He had ignored my first question and now my second. Something was very wrong. Maybe Allison had kicked him out. Maybe he was the one who'd had the affair. It wouldn't be the first time.

"Dad, I think I deserve to know what the urgency is, don't I?" I asked tentatively. "If this is about you and Allison, it's not like it's any of my—"

"I'd rather tell you in person, Meg."

He paused a moment, waiting for me to agree to his terms.

"All right."

"So is ten okay? I'll bring poppy-seed bagels. That's the kind you like, right? The poppy-seed ones?"

"Uh, sure."

"Good. Okay. Then it's all set."

"All right, I'll see you at ten. And Dad, honestly, you could've called me on my work phone to ask me this. Beatriz and Geoffrey wouldn't have cared."

"I…I wanted your new cell phone number. I know you gave it to me already, but I lost it."

I was about to tell him he could've called me at work to get my new cell phone number and I would have been happy to give it to him, but I stopped before the words came out of my mouth. He had wanted to talk to my mother. It's why he called her before calling me. I've always been amazed that my father will still call my mother for advice and that she will still dispense it. But apparently he'd decided not to ask her opinion on whatever it was that was on his mind. Instead, he'd just asked for my cell phone number. The brief conversation with my mother had affected him somehow. Made him change his mind about what he wanted to say.

Poppy-seed bagels were not my favorite. They were my mother's.

Nora

Sometimes when I visit my favorite of the country villas and I look at Master Botticelli's *The Birth of Venus,* I can imagine that before my mother was made to marry and the unraveling began, her life was like that of Venus arriving on her seashell at the dawn of her being. In the painting, the gods of the winds are pushing Venus to shore under a shower of blossoms, and a nymph stands ready with a cape to cover Venus's beauty lest the viewer be undone by it. Venus doesn't appear to know the effect she will have on us. She is unaware of how stunning she is. And if that were not enough, everything in the painting seems to be gently moving, beckoning, and inviting us to step inside the canvas.

But in truth, it is only a painting. It whispers of a realm not meant for earthly eyes. The canvas is a window, not a door. But I thank God it is at least that. If we can't step into that lovelier place, at least we can see that it exists. Sometimes that vista is the only thing that keeps us from collapsing into languid indifference under the weight of our circumstances, unable to appreciate anything truly marvelous.

With my marriage to a man I barely know only hours away, being certain there is grandeur beyond what I can see just now comforts me.

My grandfather chose a husband for my mother for political reasons, as all dukes must. Just as Ferdinando has chosen for me. But when my parents married, my mother did not want to join my father in Rome where his home was. I can't blame her, though I feel badly for my father. She wanted to stay in Florence where she could live in her beloved palace, enjoy the Medici villas, and have my grandfather nearby. And my grandfather, who had what he wanted in my mother's marriage—a useful relationship with the Orsini family—gave her what she wanted: her freedom to live where she wished.

My parents saw each other infrequently. Sometimes my father came to Florence to see her. Sometimes she went to visit him.

Some say that is the only miracle of my being born.

4

A few minutes before seven, I stood on my porch with a cup of green tea. I saluted the sun as it clung coyly to the ocean's horizon and wished Miles and Pamela a long and happy life. The day had been busy at work, and I'd not had time to muse much on the event that had sent Miles looking for another fiancée. Now as I stood watching joggers and surfers return to their cars from the beach two blocks away, the silence of my single life seemed shrill. I wondered what my life would've been like if I had ignored my instincts and married Miles.

I'd been extremely fond of Miles, especially in the beginning. And when he asked me to marry him, his devotion awed me. It wasn't until the multitude of wedding plans were finalized, and I had a distraction-free moment that I realized if Miles suddenly called off the wedding, I wouldn't be devastated. I didn't know what I would be, but I knew *devastated* didn't describe it. *Relief* was the more apt word. At that moment I knew I couldn't go through with marrying him.

Telling him was an agonizing affair. He said little, but the look on his face communicated his hurt and surprise. It was a full week before he was ready to talk with me about how to put the brakes on the wedding machine.

Kara, my best friend from high school, said I broke off my engagement because Miles wasn't like my father.

"Miles just isn't like your dad, so deep down, Miles seems all wrong for you. Lots of women pick men who remind them of their dads," Kara said the evening I called off the wedding. I had gone to her place after breaking the news to Miles, needing moral support and one of Kara's famed herbal teas. Kara's navy pilot husband, Tom, was on a two-week exercise, and their infant son was asleep in his crib. Her house was quiet.

"That doesn't make any sense." I held the hot mug to my forehead to melt the tension headache that was swelling under skin and bone. "Why would I be looking for a man like my dad? He left my mother for another woman."

"But that's just one of only a few things about him that disappointed you—"

"That's a pretty big thing."

Kara leaned in over the kitchen table. "Everything else about him, you kind of admire."

"No, I don't."

"Okay, well, maybe it's not admiration, but it's what you are comfortable with."

I lowered the mug. "One of your psych professors tell you this?"

"Doesn't matter if one of them did. You measure every man against your dad. Even the not-so-great qualities you measure up against your dad's not-so-great qualities. Miles isn't anything like your dad."

"Which is a good thing."

"It actually shouldn't matter, right? It shouldn't be a good or bad thing how much or how little the guy a girl marries compares with her dad. Except for you, it does seem to matter. I've been watching you date since high school, Meg."

I had sat back in my chair, dumbfounded. "Not that I agree with you, but if you had doubts about me marrying Miles, why didn't you say something?"

Kara shrugged. "I thought it was a good thing you decided not to hold Miles to a standard he couldn't meet. And shouldn't have to. But if you don't love him, Meg, you shouldn't marry him. And that's what you're telling me, right? You don't love him?"

I took just a moment before answering, to reassess the reason I'd just called off my wedding. "I don't miss him when he's away. Shouldn't I miss him when he's on a business trip? Don't you miss Tom when he's not here?"

Kara reached out to squeeze my hand. "Like my heart is missing from my body."

I winced now at the memory of those words and drained my tea to wash it away.

I had done the right thing.

I stepped back inside the cottage and set my cup on the kitchen counter next to files I had brought home from work. The printed pages of Sofia Borelli's first two chapters peeked out of the Manila folder I put them in just before leaving. I had originally thought maybe I'd read the chapters before dinner. I stared at the folder now, though not truly seeing it, my thoughts in a jumble. Alex, on the oval throw rug by the back door, stretched and blinked, acknowledging my presence with a closed-mouth murmur. Then he curled back into a wheel of fur and closed his eyes.

I grabbed my keys and purse and left.

A cerulean twilight was falling across the coast as I maneuvered my car up North Torrey Pines Road toward the Melting Pot.

As I waited at the traffic light by the university, I pondered whether or not I should tell my mother that Dad seemed deeply troubled about something. Maybe I should wait until I knew what it was and if he even wanted my mother to know.

The light turned green, and I turned onto La Jolla Village Drive. A cascade of crimson taillights glimmered on the boulevard as it spread downward toward the interstate and the rest of upper La Jolla. As I joined the display of gleaming lights, I had the uncanny feeling that everything was about to change.

Nora

My father never knew his parents. He was born Paolo Orsini, the first and only son, a few months after his father's sudden death. When his mother remarried, as young titled women do, she left behind my father and his older sister. His mother died not long after her second marriage. An uncle, a cardinal my father barely knew, saw to his unbending upbringing as a future duke.

Sometimes I comfort myself with this knowledge of where he came from. When I think of the life my father knew before he became a man, I can imagine why I seldom saw him smile.

Anguish is a tutor, just as privilege is.

5

I handed my keys to the parking valet at the Melting Pot and pulled my linen jacket around my shoulders. A chilling breeze had cooled the air, and I couldn't remember if I had closed the bathroom window. I laughed as I considered how my mother would react if I'd said that out loud and in her hearing. We'd be in the car and headed back to the cottage to make sure. An open window didn't just let chilly air inside; it also provided access for a would-be burglar. Never mind that the window was only big enough for a six-year-old to fit through. A resourceful robber could easily finagle a six-year-old into crawling through the window and opening the front door for him for five bucks. Not that he *would,* but that he *could,* and that made all the difference. She'd be unable to enjoy her fondue until I had made sure the window was closed.

Mom had become cautious after the divorce—about everything. And I guess I became a dreamer. There had been this secure life that I knew, where I lived in a house near my nonna and her Florentine echoes, where I had a mom and a dad, and *custody* was a word only policemen used. After the divorce I liked to dream about my old, safe life, and my mother liked to protect her new one. In that one tiny way, we were the same. At some point I stopped dreaming, but she never seemed to drop her caution. She wore it comfortably like a favorite hairstyle.

My mother's cautious life has kept her looking young; she eats sensibly, watches her weight, wears sunscreen even on rainy days, and gets a good night's sleep every night. I have wondered more than once what my father thinks of how gracefully his former wife has aged in the years since the divorce. She is still very pretty. And they had been in love once.

❧

Inside the restaurant I told the hostess I was meeting my mother and that the reservation was under the name Elaine Pomeroy.

"Yes. They are already seated. Right this way."

They?

I opened my mouth to comment, but the hostess was already walking away. I fell in step behind her, ready to make a course correction. But then I saw my mother's head at a booth near a wall. And another head across from her.

A younger man.

I closed my eyes for a second, incredulous. My careful mother was no fan of blind dates or online pairing. The risk of finding yourself being stalked by a psychopath—or at the very least pestered incessantly—was enough to keep her out of both camps and advising me to do the same. But she wasn't above a little maternal matchmaking from time to time, since eligible men she deemed suitable had obviously already passed her scrutiny. She had offered a time or two to introduce me to so-and-so's nephew or son or personal trainer. I had declined. I don't need or want my mother's assistance in finding a husband, as she puts it. She knows this.

So I opened my eyes to reward my mother with a dagger look before the man turned his head at my approach. But she missed it.

I arrived at the booth, and the man looked up. He was nice looking, a few years older than me. Late thirties, perhaps. Dark hair fashionably cut and gelled into wavy submission. Tufts of premature gray at the temples. Nickel-hued, rimless glasses. Kind face. Ringless left hand. A bit stocky. He smiled at me.

"Here we are," the hostess said, turning her head to me, looking for direction as to which side of the booth to seat me.

"Here, sit by me, Meg." My mother scooted over and patted the empty space next to her.

I hesitated, waiting for my mother to make eye contact and get the full effect of my wordless annoyance. But she just smiled up at me and again patted the seat. She looked calm and elegant in a silky Indian-print blouse and silver jewelry.

I slid into the booth.

"I'm so glad you could come tonight, sweetheart," my mother said brightly. She turned her attention to the man across the table. "Devon, this is my daughter, Meg. Meg, Devon Sheller."

Devon Sheller reached across the table to shake my hand. "It's a pleasure to meet you, Meg. I've heard so much about you." His teeth were perfectly straight and glistening white.

I took his hand and shook it lightly. "Uh, yes. Nice to meet you as well."

"Devon's a pharmacist. He works at Rady Children's Hospital. He's been there for what, five years?" My mother raised a glass of water and took a sip.

"Just about," Devon replied.

"That must be very interesting," I said woodenly. Again I turned to my mother, but she was waving a waitress over.

"Could you bring us a bottle of Pinot Grigio? The one from Australia? I liked that one last time."

The waitress smiled, nodded, and walked away.

"Your mother tells me you're an editor with a publishing house in La Jolla," Devon said.

"Yes. Yes, that's right. Crowne and Castillo. They publish travel books."

"She's quite a wordsmith," my mother said. "They made her an editor after only four years. I'm so proud of her."

"You probably have the more interesting job, then," Devon said politely. "I suppose you get to travel a lot?"

A common misconception. You don't need to go to Morocco to line edit a book about sightseeing in Marrakesh. "Um. Not as much as I'd like, actually."

My mother patted my hand. "I, for one, am glad she doesn't have to travel to all the places her authors write about. The world is so uncertain. Every time you turn around, it seems another nation is at war. I don't think it's very safe to travel these days. Look, here's the wine."

As the waitress poured, I chanced a peek at Devon. He was looking over the rims of his glasses at my mother, a thoughtful look on his face. He had probably just figured out my mother hadn't told me that she had set this up. It was a rather awkward position in which to put a nice man, I thought. Asking him to dinner to meet me and then not telling him that I would have no idea he'd be there.

The waitress walked away, and my mother raised her glass. "To good food and great company!"

Devon smiled at her, a bit uneasily, and raised his glass.

In spite of my frustration with my mother, I felt bad for him. He was clearly sensing the tension in the situation. And he seemed a nice enough guy. She should've told him. She should've told us both.

But, then, of course, I probably wouldn't have come.

"To surprises," I whispered, wondering if he would hear me, hoping he would. A smile, small but genuine this time, cracked across his face.

"What was that, Meg?" my mother asked.

"To Fridays," I said.

"Oh yes. Most definitely. It's only April, and the kids at school are already restless for summer."

We sipped from our glasses and then in unison placed them on the table.

A weighty silence followed.

Devon cleared his throat. "So, I suppose your company has published books on all kinds of places?"

I hesitated, wondering what else I could reply to a question like that except yes.

"That was a dumb thing to say," he said quickly. "Of course you've published books on all kinds of places."

My mother laughed easily. "I said the same thing when she got the job!"

Devon turned back to me. "Okay, how about what's the one place you've published a book about that you want to visit more than any other?"

The moment he asked this, I felt a tingling kinship with him, tiny and subtle. He had detected there was a place that called to me, a place that reminded me of home and family and safety, even though I had never been there. He did not know all this, of course, but he sensed there had to be a place…

Florence was on my lips, a breath away from being said when my mother interrupted.

"Oh, that's easy!" my mother said, smiling. "I know the answer to that."

The tingling sensation stilled. Devon blinked, waited.

"Florence," I said. It fell off my lips somewhat flat.

Devon nodded. "Beautiful place."

"You've been?" I couldn't keep a trace of envy out of my voice. I've met plenty of people who've been to Florence but never on a first date. Or a first date–like evening.

He nodded. "I hope you get to go sometime. You'll love it."

But I already do, I wanted to say.

"She's always wanted to go there, ever since she was little," my mother said. "She had a grandmother who was born and raised there. She had pictures of Florence all over her walls."

"Oh well, then, you must be sure to go." Devon's voice was soft but urgent, as if he understood my longing.

I felt for the stem of my wineglass and tried to pull my gaze away from him. The waitress appeared at our table and asked if we needed more time with the menus, and I nearly thanked her for the well-timed intrusion. Except that we hadn't even opened the menus.

"A few more minutes would be great," Devon said, the take-charge tone of his voice surprising me a little.

The waitress left and awkward silence fell across us again.

Devon folded his arms on the table and cocked his head. "Look, I don't think we started off very well here, Meg. I am sorry about that. Maybe we should back up a little?"

"What do you mean back up?" My mother looked from him to me. "You two only just met!"

Devon's gentleness and honesty calmed me at once. "It's not your fault," I said to him. "And it's not you, Devon. Really it's not. You seem like a very nice person. It's me."

"What do you mean, it's not his fault?" my mother said. "What is not his fault? I'm the one who set this dinner up."

Devon turned to look at my mother. His smile was kind. "I think maybe you should've told Meg I'd be here."

He laughed lightly and so did I. A laugh that was not a laugh. And yet felt nice.

Then, to my thundering surprise, Devon reached out his hand to cover hers. He stroked it tenderly and rubbed her thumb.

The room seemed to squeeze in around me. My eyes couldn't leave those two hands on the table. My mother's and Devon's. My mother hadn't brought me to the Melting Pot to set me up with a polite, eligible pharmacist. She had invited me to meet the man *she* was dating. A much younger man.

My mother, the epitome of safety, convention, and temperance, was dating a man closer to my age than hers.

It took everything in me not to laugh out loud at the absurdity of it. Of me, warming up to what I thought were kind advances. I choked back a chortle.

"I think I need to use the rest room. Excuse me." I exited the booth as Devon half-stood. As I headed to the rest room, I could hear my mother close behind me.

When we were behind the closed door, I braced my hands on the granite counter.

"What was I *thinking*?" I exclaimed to myself, but not to myself, aware that a woman washing her hands at the sink looked at me wide eyed.

"What do you mean?" My mother's face in the mirror above me was wrapped in confusion.

"He's *your* date!"

The bewilderment on her face deepened. "I wanted you to meet him. Why is that so odd?"

"He's *your* date," I said again, incredulous. "And he's *my* age!"

My mother's face blossomed a pale crimson.

The woman washing her hands tiptoed past us with a barely audible "Excuse me." The door closed silently behind her.

"You…you thought I brought him for *you* to meet?"

"How old is he? Thirty-seven? Thirty-six?"

Her flush on her cheeks deepened to scarlet. "Not that it's any of your business, but he's forty-three. He can't help it if he looks younger than that."

Devon's real age set me off balance mentally, but only for a second.

"And you are fifty-six."

She took a step toward me. "In case you hadn't noticed, he doesn't seem to mind that. And for Pete's sake, Meg, we are just dating. It's not like I've run off to Vegas and eloped with a twenty-year-old."

Just dating.

She's was *just* dating a man I thought she was fixing me up with. A kind soul who had, in mere minutes of meeting me, coaxed Florence out of me. A man only thirteen years older than me, thirteen years younger than her.

"We met at a children's health conference in February and became friends. We didn't plan to date. We just started seeing each other and realized we liked each other's company. We like a lot of the same things. And he knows what it's like to have your spouse leave you for someone else. He's been divorced for five years, if you must know."

"You've been dating him since February? And you never said anything?"

"This is exactly why I waited to tell you. You've never encouraged me to date anyone. All these years, you've never asked me if I might want to date again and actually have a life beyond the school and you."

My mouth dropped open. "Are you saying I don't want you to be happy?"

"That is *not* what I am saying. It's just you've never… You've always made it seem like no one but your dad was good enough for me, even though he left me and married someone else."

"That's not true!" I had no idea what she was talking about. "And he didn't leave you; you left him!"

She swallowed. Blinked several times. We had, the two of us, opened something black and ugly. Still.

"He had an affair." She said each word calmly but with effort.

"But he was sorry. He wanted to make it up to you. You wouldn't let him. *You* left him."

"You're not married. You don't know what it's like. He was sleeping with another woman. That is not something a person can just be sorry about. And it's not something you can just forget."

Tears glistened at the corners of her eyes, and I felt wetness in my own eyes. "You can if you want to bad enough."

For a few seconds we just stood there, each flicking glimmers of tears away. I knew I was being unfair to her. But she had gotten what she wanted after my father hurt her and I hadn't.

"This is why you never gave me permission to date, isn't it?" she said. "Because you blame me for what happened."

Caution had kept her single. Not me. "You don't need my permission to date," I answered.

"But that's exactly what you're demanding! Permission!"

I stared at her, wordless.

"You never let me feel like I could date again, that I deserved to date again. And for a very long time, I didn't think I did either. That's why I waited to tell you about Devon. And why I picked a public place and told you nothing before you got here. But you're right about one thing. I *don't* need your permission to date. I'm going back to the table."

She turned, swung open the door, and left.

I stood there for several minutes waiting for the tumbling thoughts in my head to settle. I couldn't make sense of anything she had said, and I knew that wouldn't change by standing there in the ladies' room at the Melting Pot. I needed to go back to the table, collect my things, and offer a suitable excuse to bow out. I needed to be home in the quiet of the cottage to deal with this.

I took several deep breaths and walked back to our booth. The menus lay on the table unopened. My mother had refilled her wineglass. Devon's expression was kind but pensive. I didn't like the lingering wave of attraction that I felt for him. I reached for my purse.

"I am so terribly sorry to do this, but I won't be able to stay for dinner. I'm not feeling very well. Devon, it was a pleasure to meet you. I do mean that. Please stay and enjoy the fondue."

Devon stood and shook my hand. The sheen of concern on his face was nearly paternal. I looked away from him. "Sorry, Mom. Really. Call me tomorrow?"

She nodded and raised her glass to her mouth.

"Can I walk you out?" Devon asked.

"Thanks. I'll be fine."

He touched my elbow. I wavered a bit. "I am really sorry about this," he said.

"Don't be," I said quickly.

"Perhaps another time?" Devon asked.

My mother looked up and waited for me to answer.

"Of course. Another time."

I waved good-bye to my mother, and she blew me a kiss, though her eyes betrayed the hurt she still felt.

I walked away from the booth, passing table after table of patrons happily plunging tiny skewers into sizzling, steaming pots.

Nora

When my father was young, did he lie awake and wonder what it might be like to feel his mother's hand pressed to his cheek? Did he ever envision how his life would have been different had his father lived? Did he know that if he'd been groomed to be an Orsini duke, as he should have been by his father instead of being left to untangle life's hardest lessons on his own, he might've been a different man? I've heard that my father frequented brothels, spent money as though it had no value, and was addicted to having the latest fashion or convenience, whatever it may be. Had he the guidance and discipline of an attentive father, would he have still led an unsatisfied life?

In my lessons I was given the opportunity to learn a variety of instruments, but I wanted to paint. I wanted to see what it was like to create beauty out of nothing. I hadn't the skill of the masters; I knew this. And my tutor was not inclined that I should take up the brush—painting was messy work. But he provided me canvases and colors, nonetheless, and an instructor named Benito who needed the money. For my first work, I painted a picture of how I imagined my father as a child. I painted him standing at his mother's knee, leaning slightly toward her. Her arm is around him, and his papa stands close behind. The three of them are so close the fabrics of their clothes touch. Nurse told me it was quite good for it being my first.

It was not a very good painting. The older I grew, the more I saw the painting's flaws. I thankfully became more adept at form and depth, and my first works were put away, as they should have been, replaced by better pieces, including a self-portrait that my instructor said was the best he'd seen from me as an artist.

But I still remember the peculiar joy that was mine as I gave my father his mama and his papa—an imagined moment, caught in oils, of a satisfied life.

6

A few months before my father met Allison, he took me and Nonna to Disneyland. I was nine. My mother had suffered a miscarriage very early into a surprise pregnancy and needed a day with none of us in it. The loss of that much-wanted child would take my mother to an emotional place my father didn't understand, which begins to explain—though doesn't excuse—why he ended up having an affair. She thought a new baby would fill the holes in their marriage. He didn't know how to handle her grief.

But I didn't know any of that on that day. All I knew was my dad was taking me to Disneyland and my mom couldn't go because she had been to the doctor's a few days before and wasn't feeling well.

Dad took me out of school on a sunny Friday—the most amazing thing a parent can do when you're nine. We went on all the big rides, twice. The Matterhorn, three times. It was the most magical day of my life up to that point. Maybe it still is.

I still remember sitting in a giant, pastel-pink teacup and holding on to the disc in the middle as Dad and I spun and laughed. On the other side of the ride, the world was a kaleidoscope of rushing colors, sounds, and smells: the calliope from the nearby carousel, the aroma of hot popcorn, and Nonna's blurred image under the shade of the Alice in Wonderland ride as she watched us. I was amazed that the world could seem like it was spinning far too fast with the colors of everything familiar slamming together, but it was perfectly fine if you were with your father and you were both laughing. After our tummies recovered, we ate Mickey Mouse–shaped pancakes for dinner. We didn't leave the park until the announcement came over the loudspeakers that the park was closing for the night and guests needed to be making their way to the exits.

On the way home I leaned my head against the car door window in the backseat and closed my eyes, reliving every fabulous moment of the day in my head so that I could tell my mother about it when I got home. Nonna and my father naturally assumed I was asleep. They began to talk about me as if I weren't there, saying things I understood perfectly, like "Meg sure had a good time" and "Wasn't Meg cute talking to Cinderella?" and "Meg sure can put food away." But then they started talking about things I didn't get at all. Not at first.

My father asked Nonna if she'd given any more thought to his idea. Nonna seemed to hesitate before replying that Therese and Bianca didn't think it was a good plan. I didn't know what idea they were talking about. But I knew who Therese and Bianca were. They are my aunts; my dad's older sisters.

"Why did you have to bring them into it?" Dad seemed angry. He kept his voice low, but I could hear the frustration in it. "They don't have anything to do with this. This is between you and me."

Again my nonna waited a second before answering. "You asked me to take out a mortgage on my house—the only thing I have left to leave you children—so it does have something to do with them. You know it does."

"But it isn't going to change anything for you, Ma. I will pay the bill every month. It will be just like it is now. Like the house is paid for. You won't have to pay a thing extra."

This time my nonna did not hesitate. "I admire your optimism, Nick. You know I do. I know you think this idea will work and that nothing stands between you and success. But the world is an uncertain place. And you have had other ideas that never really—"

"But this concept is completely different!" Childlike longing hung in my father's voice. It so surprised me that I opened my eyes. I didn't understand at the time what my father was asking for—the word *mortgage* meant nothing to me—but I knew it was something Nonna could give him and my aunts didn't think it was a good idea for him to have it.

"Yes, this idea is different. But the odds are just the same," Nonna said.

"Is that what Therese and Bianca told you? Did they tell you that?"

"They did not have to. I can see the risk, Nicky. And you haven't paid back the ten thousand you borrowed two years ago. That concerns them."

My father swerved the car a little. "You told them about that?"

"I didn't tell them. They asked. I am not going to lie to my children."

I heard a swear word fall off my father's lips. "They asked? They *asked* if I owed you money?"

"They asked if this was the first time you had asked me for money. I couldn't tell them it was."

My father swore again, and my grandmother shushed him. My magical day was ending, and I couldn't pretend that it wasn't. I wasn't sitting in a pink teacup and laughing. I was in the backseat of my father's aging Volvo listening to adults argue about money. It wasn't the first time I'd heard my father have a conversation with Nonna about money. Nor was it the first time I'd heard him talk that way about his sisters. My aunts had always come across to me as kind of bossy with their immense brown eyes, pointy eyebrows, and stern mouths. I thought my dad didn't care much for his sisters because they were always trying to tell him what to do. That night on the way home from Disneyland, I wondered if maybe the aunts had a reason for being mad at my dad all the time. And it hadn't occurred to me until that moment that Nonna loved Therese and Bianca like she loved my father. The aunts weren't annoyed with Nonna or their husbands or their own children. Or even with me. But they were with him. Almost all the time.

When I was older, I understood that my father was a fabulous idea man but terrible at follow-through. He would see a business for sale, like a little candle store or a sandwich shop, clearly at the end of its rope, and he could vividly imagine hauling it back from the edge of the abyss. But he couldn't forge his noble ideas into reality, and he didn't have the money to keep trying. I would think of that night often, whenever I felt cheated out of a simple desire. I grew up wishing the odds weren't so stacked against people with dreams.

Whatever it was he wanted money for as we drove home from Disneyland, he wasn't going to be getting it from Nonna. He would have to stay at the insurance company doing whatever it was claims adjusters did. I didn't know what he did all day long; I just knew he didn't like it.

"It's none of their business, Ma. When they asked, you could've told them that. You could've—"

I didn't want to hear any more. I closed my eyes again and made a little sound like I was waking up, and my father immediately fell silent.

"Are we home yet?" I asked sleepily.

"No, angel. We're not home." But he said it quietly, as if not to me.

❧

The morning after the epic evening at the Melting Pot, I awoke well before my dad was supposed to be there with poppy-seed bagels. And since I hadn't stayed for dinner with my mother and Devon, nor had I eaten much after I got home cranky and disillusioned, my stomach was growling. I pulled on a pair of sweats and a hoodie, grabbed a Pink Lady from the fruit bowl on the kitchen table, and went for a walk along the beach.

I knew deep down that it shouldn't matter that my mother was dating a man thirteen years younger than she was. In the morning chill off the frothing surf, my face warmed as I remembered liking the idea that Mom had set me up with Devon right about the time I realized he was *her* date, not mine.

It was dumb to relive those stirrings, and yet I did anyway. I hadn't been attracted to a guy that quickly in I don't know how long. It was exhilarating and yet embarrassing since he clearly hadn't felt the same instant attraction for me. After the walk I came back, showered, and waited for my dad to arrive, which he did, half an hour later than he said he would.

My father's blend of mutt American on his dad's side and Nonna's pure Florentine heritage had created for him a nice, light-olive-skinned complexion, an average stature, large brown eyes, and curly hair the color of maple syrup. When he married Allison after my mother divorced him, he became a stepfather to her two sons, who were six and eight at the time. I think in the beginning he liked having boys around him, but it seemed to me, from my safe distance, that he learned soon enough those boys had a father whom they loved very much. The difference was those boys spent an equal amount of time with their real father and with Allison. Michael and Ross never called my father Dad or went to him for advice or money or car keys. Michael is married now with a baby. But it doesn't mean my father is a grandfather. He is Nick to Michael and Ross, and I suppose he will be Nick to their children too. Secretly, I have always been fine with this. When I still lived at home, I was intensely jealous that Allison's boys got to spend way more time with my dad than I did.

Even now, as he stood on my porch with a bag of bagels and whatever news he had to tell me, I was still secretly glad that the attachment to his second marriage didn't extend to the sons. Not that my dad doesn't care for them—I know he does—but he isn't their father. They already have one of those.

"Hey, angel." He stepped into the cottage and took me into his embrace, a white paper sack sandwiched between us. He smelled like morning air, leather, and the sea. I could smell the Pacific Coast Highway on him.

"I'm glad you're here." As soon as I said it, I knew it was true and not just a nice greeting to extend to him. My arms tightened around him.

"Sorry it's been so long." He pulled away and the bag with the bagels made a crunching sound in protest.

I reached for the bag. "I made some coffee to go with these, if you're interested."

"Definitely." He bent to scratch Alex, who was looping himself in and out of my dad's legs.

In the kitchen I grabbed two mugs out of the dish drainer with my free hand.

"I'll pour the coffee." My dad reached for the cups, anxious, it seemed, to be doing something.

"Toasted?" I lifted the bagel bag and he nodded. In the lemon-yellow sunlight dumping into the room from the kitchen window, I saw lines of worry on his face, hidden minutes before. He looked tired as well as anxious.

"Drive down okay?" I asked.

"It was perfect."

"I'm glad to hear that." I sliced a fat bagel in two and shoved the two halves into my toaster. Released poppy seeds fell to the counter like confetti. Out of the corner of my eye, I saw my father take the cups to the table. He pulled out a chair and sat down heavily.

"So how was your week?" he asked nonchalantly, the way you ask someone how they are when you really don't expect them to say anything other than "Fine."

I opened the fridge and pulled out a container of strawberry cream cheese. "Most of it was okay. Yesterday wasn't that great."

I hadn't thought my answer through. I wouldn't have minded talking about Miles getting married yesterday, but I didn't want to tell him about Mom and the boyfriend I'd mistaken for a setup for me.

But he just said, "Yeah. Fridays can be like that." He sipped his coffee.

I said nothing else and waited for the bagels to pop up. The tiny kitchen filled with their fragrance. I heard my dad speak endearments to the cat as I spread the cream cheese and set the bagels on a plate. When I set them down on the table, he smiled at me.

"Poppy-seed bagels."

I smiled back. "Yes."

"They're not your favorite, are they? They're your mom's."

I shrugged. "I like them too."

He laughed and grabbed one. "It didn't occur to me until after I paid for them that it was your mother who used to ask for them, not you."

I reached for the other bagel. "But they're good. That's why she likes them. And I was just happy you were coming. I didn't care."

He took a bite and so did I. We chewed in silence. He wiped the corner of his mouth with his thumb, set the bagel down, and inhaled deeply. I could tell he did not want to begin with small talk, so I decided to make it easy for him.

"So what is it, Dad? Is something up between you and Allison?"

He looked up quickly, relief and surprise both playing across his face. "Not exactly." His voice cracked a little; not like mine would if I was on the verge of crying, but more like a splinter in his resolve to keep things from getting too serious.

"Are you…are you seeing someone else?" I asked.

When he quickly shook his head, I asked if she was.

"No. No, it's nothing like that. It's… I just… Look, I didn't come down here to talk about Allison. I really just wanted to tell you I was sorry, Meggie."

He took a quick sip of coffee and then looked up at me. Regret etched the contours of his face, and I didn't know why.

"Sorry for what?"

"For all of it." He put the mug down. "Not just the divorce but everything that happened afterward. Actually everything that didn't happen afterward. I know I wasn't around much for you. I know I told you I'd take you to Florence. And I know you still want me to. I just could never get that kind of cash together. Allison's got money. Allison's always got money, but she'd never... I mean, I've already spent money she didn't want me to spend, so there's never been any way I could..."

He broke off, and I immediately felt stupid for assuming the reason my father hadn't taken me to Florence yet was that he found it easy to postpone. I've always known he has a hard time managing his money. I should've offered to go dutch long before this. Go dutch to Italy. We could each pay our own way. I actually could've saved up enough for us both to go by now if I had just thought to.

"It's okay, Dad. I can start saving up to pay my own way, and then you—"

He raised his hand. "No. I promised Nonna I'd take you. She'd never forgive me if I let you pay your own way. That's not happening."

I paused for a moment. "But she's not here, Dad. And I just want us to go."

He locked his eyes on mine. "I know you do. I'm working on it. I want you to know that. And I'm thinking it might work out to go this summer."

My first thought was that I'd heard that before. There had been a few other times in the last decade he had said we were going. But it sounded different this time. He sounded a bit less sure, which actually made it sound more like he truly meant it.

"Really?" I finally asked.

"I think it might work."

It was an odd way to say "Yes, let's take that trip to Florence!" but excitement began to build inside me nonetheless, and I struggled a bit to rein it in.

"That's...that's great!" I said. "When? When do you want to go? July is better than August as far as crowds go. And June's better than July. That's what our books say."

"Yeah. Yeah, I think so." His reply was distant and detached, as if he were only half-listening.

"What? You think what?" I said.

He nodded. "The earlier, the better. I'll get back to you on it. Okay? Can you get away?"

The summer months were busy at Crowne & Castillo as we prepped for our winter catalog. By August we were taking infant steps toward spring. But I'd convince Geoffrey and Beatriz to let me go. There was no way I was going to miss out on this.

"Sure," I said.

He held my gaze with intensity, as if he wanted to say more but couldn't or was perhaps at a loss for the right words.

"I mean it this time. I *am* working on it," he finally said.

"I believe you." I needed to say it; he needed to hear it.

He seemed to relax then. And he sat back again in his chair. "Is there anything else I can do for you? Anything at all?"

His tone was strange, as though he owed me a stack of favors and was itching to pay some of them off. I had never seen my father so mindful of his past. He'd always been attracted to the present moment or the dazzling future. "The past is for the History Channel," he was fond of saying. "And let them have it. You've got today and you've got tomorrow. Don't let go of either one to hang on to the past."

Something had changed since the last time I saw him. It worried me a little—this abrupt transformation—even though it seemed like a nice one.

"Is everything okay?"

"It's nothing that you need to worry about, angel. What can I do?"

I didn't believe him, but to press the matter would've been to perhaps break the spell. His eagerness to please me was endearing. I wanted to give him the absolution he was longing for, but I also knew that for him, it had to be something tangible. I couldn't just tell him that I had forgiven him.

I pondered for a moment what I could ask him for that was big enough to let him feel like he had paid a debt but that didn't cost him any money. It took a couple of seconds, but when I came upon it, I knew it would not only give him what he wanted but also fill an emptiness I had carried since Nonna died.

"Do you remember the painting of the little girl and the statue?"

He blinked. "The what?"

"It was one that Nonna had in her living room. Her grandfather had painted it. Remember? The little girl is reaching for the statue, and the statue is holding out its hand to her."

I could see him mentally picturing the placement of the artwork that had been in his mother's living room. Then he frowned, no doubt trying to remember what became of that painting after Nonna died and he and the aunts emptied the house. I don't know what my father inherited from my nonna, but I know it wasn't her art. I never knew what happened to the paintings.

"That's really what you want? That's it?"

I nodded. "I loved that picture. It was my favorite."

He studied me for a moment, brows crinkled. "Why didn't you say something when she died?"

A tiny pain sparked inside me. "I was twelve, remember? And no one asked me what I wanted."

He opened his mouth to say something and then closed it. "I'll find it." The resolute tone of his voice surprised me. He picked up his bagel.

"You will?"

"I'll find it."

"But I take it you don't know where it is."

"I'll find it, Meggie." He bit into his bagel and began to chew with purpose. "I think I'll have another one of these," he said a second later. And I stood to slice another bagel in two. We didn't speak of the painting again. Or the promised trip to Florence. He didn't ask about Mom. I kind of wanted him to and kind of didn't. He asked about work, if I was dating anyone, and if I ever hear from Miles. I told him work was mostly okay, I wasn't dating any one person, and that Miles had gotten married the night before.

He left on his motorcycle half an hour later, saying he needed to get back to LA. He wanted to start looking right away for the painting, starting with talking to his sisters. We hugged good-bye. He assured me that he'd find the painting and that this was the summer I'd see Florence.

Nora

My father was in debt when he married my mother—so I have heard. My grandfather, Cosimo, refused him my mother's dowry, assuming my father would use it to pay for his careless choices prior to the marriage. I don't think my grandfather cared much for my father, even though he chose him. The marriage is never about the man. Or the woman. It's about the binding of families who might otherwise be at war with each other.

There is a painting that still hangs in Lorenzo de' Medici's bedchamber of the Battle of San Romano. I do not like it. I would never hang it in my bedchamber, and I would never paint such a thing myself. Warriors are spearing one another as they battle on horseback. But the horses are the ones who are wounded and dying on the canvas. And they have no quarrel with anyone. They are merely doing as they are told.

War can come any way. If we let it. If we invite it. Not on land with horses and swords. But in our houses. In our bedrooms. In our hearts.

7

It has always filled me with wonder that my father and my aunts sold Nonna's house when she died. Dad and Allison had a house in Santa Monica, and Therese and Bianca and their husbands had houses nearby too. But it just surprised me that when Nonna died, the house was emptied and everything in it was scattered.

"It was just a house," my dad said when I asked him about it once, a long time ago. "In a run-down neighborhood. Who would want it?"

I told him I would have wanted it, and he laughed and said I only remembered the good things about it.

My memory of that house is not the neighborhood it stood in. My memory of that house is my grandmother's presence, the fabric of home and belonging, the feel of arriving at the place where you are safe.

What's there to remember if not the good things?

Dad told me, more than just that one time, that people who are in love with the past only remember what they want to, even if it's not entirely true.

Geoffrey says that's what makes memoirs lousy reading.

I disagree.

Remembering what you want about the past, even if it's not entirely true, keeps you from giving up on the present.

After my father left the cottage, I felt both full and empty at the same time. I was paradoxically full of hope and empty of expectation. My father's strange, new regret for past disappointments teased me to believe he was serious this time.

I wanted to call someone. Gabe. Kara. Lorenzo.

Somebody.

I stepped back into the kitchen and stared at the empty bagel plates. Alex meowed at me, and I told him I had no idea what to think.

I took the plates to the sink. When I turned back to get our mugs, I bumped mine, still half-full, and sent it toppling over. The spilled coffee spread toward the Manila folder I had brought home from the office the night before. I swept it into my arms, and several pages fell out onto the floor. I stepped over the fallen pieces of paper as I grabbed a paper towel. I tossed it onto the coffee puddle and then bent down to get the pages. I turned them over and saw that they were the first few pages of Sofia Borelli's manuscript. I read the first line, and it stilled me.

I read the entire first page before I became aware that the paper towel was sodden and cold coffee was slowly dripping onto the floor.

All That Is Seen
by Sofia Daniela Borelli

Florence wakes up golden every morning, even when it is raining. At daybreak the honey-stone and blushing tangerine tiles seem warm to the touch, even in winter, even in a downpour. I have never lived anywhere else. I have never wanted to. I grew up in a flat six blocks from the Duomo, and I live there still. When I was little, I knew I could never be lost on the streets of Florence. The cathedral's dome and tower rise from the ground like a crown and scepter handed to us by the sun. They are the sky over Florence, and I could always find my way home if I just looked up.

I am a tour guide, just like my father was. Six days a week, I stroll along the downtown sidewalks and piazzas with my pink polka-dot parasol, leading groups of tourists on an excursion of an art lover's paradise. I have stood before Michelangelo's *David* six thousand times, and he still woos me. I know every molecule of his fair body. And I daresay he knows mine. He is in my blood.

I am a Medici. History books say the last of my family, childless Anna Maria Luisa de' Medici, died in 1743. But she was not really the last Medici. She was simply the last of the ruling dynasty. Dear Diana, the Princess of Wales—may she rest in peace—had the blood of Medici women in her veins, as many people no doubt do, only most do not know it. What you do not know, you cannot embrace.

Anna was not the last, and perhaps I am not the last either. But I am the last in my family who knows what I know. I've no brothers or sisters, and my beloved papa, who taught me how to listen for the echoes of the Florence of old, is disappearing into the folds of his mind a little more each day. Soon it will only be me who hears the echoes of my ancestors.

My family ruled Florence for three hundred years, and as patrons of the arts, we gave the world da Vinci, Michelangelo, and Botticelli, to name only a few. The Medicis were bankers who ruled like royalty, but they were not kings and queens. And while they loved the arts, most were not artists. Beauty spoke to them, and they understood its language even though they did not speak it themselves.

We Medici have always been at home in Florence. We may have traveled the length of Italy from its northern alpine mountains to the pebbled coast of Naples, but we always came home to Florence. She lured us back each time. I tell the people on my tours that once you have been to Florence, one of two things will happen to you. You will leave with her fragrance in your very skin and bones where it will haunt or delight you forever, or you will not leave.

Florence, my father told me long ago, is like a dance. It is more than streets and buildings and a steady river; it's a presence you feel, a rhythm you fall in step with. My parents loved to dance. And they did not need records or a band or the radio. My father hummed the music they swayed to—the music of Florence. When I was especially little, I would wake from nightmarish images that would flee the moment I opened my eyes. And in my wailing, my father would come to me and soothe me with these tunes that had no words. They were the songs of the city, he said. He told me to listen very carefully, and I would hear the music in the air and in the paint and in the marble, and the music would chase the bad dreams away. If I listened very carefully, he said, I could hear the beauty all around me and I would know that in Florence I would always be safe.

But when I began to hear it, I was six, and it wasn't music I heard, but a voice, soft and sweet, whispering to me within the paintings and sculptures. Papa was surprised, I think, when I told him that I heard words and not music. But he told me it was because I was Medici, like him, that I could hear it, and he asked me if hearing it made me feel happy and safe inside. When I said yes, the surprised look on his face went away. I asked him if he could hear the whispers. And he said the whispers were meant only for me. I wanted my mother to hear what I could hear. But she was not

Medici. When I told her I wished she could hear the statues and paintings, she just smiled at me with tears pooling, as if she knew her eyes and ears were not meant for it.

My father told me that to speak of such things to anyone but my mother and him would be to set a boundary stone between me and everyone else and I would be alone. He told me when angels come to earth with messages for us from God, they do not speak of how beautiful heaven is because if they did, it would make us languish for it, unsatisfied, all our earthly days.

And so I have kept the dearest charms of my city close to my heart, all these years, just as he told me to. But we Medici are mortal. Soon there will only be me. And then when I am gone, there will be no one who knows what I know, so I will share all of it with you in these pages. I do not care if it means I set a boundary stone between you and me. I do not fear the specter of solitude. I am surrounded by beauty at every turn. I do not know what it is to be lost. And I do not know what it is like to be alone.

I have a story to tell you. It is a story of Florence and a Medici princess that time has all but forgotten.

Hers is the voice I hear in the statues and paintings all around me. Her name was Francesca Eleonora Orsini.

But everyone called her Nora.

The slow, steady dripping of the coffee onto the kitchen floor coaxed me out of Sofia's memoir, pulling me back to my ordinary Saturday. I set the pages down on the counter, grabbed another paper towel, and cleaned up the mess. I was anxious to read the rest of the pages I had printed and was strangely disappointed that Lorenzo had only sent me the first two chapters.

As I tossed the paper towels in the trash, the doorbell rang, and with some irritation I went to answer it.

My mother stood at the threshold with a potted bromeliad in her hands. She was wearing a lime-green-and-white striped shirt and white capris, hoop earrings, and new white Keds. Her hair wasn't pulled back into its usual Saturday pileup but hung curled and sprayed into place. Red Orchid by Oscar de la Renta wafted about her.

She held the plant aloft. "I got this at the farmers' market. It was the last one. Thought you would like it."

I opened the screen door for her. "He's already gone, Mom."

She frowned and stepped inside. "That's not why I'm here."

The door closed behind us, and she turned to face me. "So you're telling me he left already? What kind of visit is that?"

"I thought you said that's not why you're here."

She stepped into the kitchen and set the plant down on the tiled counter, next to the toaster. Poppy seeds were scattered about, and she stared at them. Then she turned to me. "It's not. I thought we needed to talk. About last night. Devon thinks maybe I owe you an apology."

"He said that?"

"Yes." She walked over to my sink and washed her hands, rubbing at a smudge of potting soil on her knuckle with vigor. "I actually think you owe me one, too, but he doesn't think so. But then again, he didn't hear what you said in the ladies' room."

She applied more soap and rubbed harder. "He said it wasn't fair that I didn't tell you I was dating someone and then to have sprung it on you with him sitting right there was a bit inconsiderate. I guess I see his point." She turned off the water and scrutinized my dishtowel hanging off the drainer. "May I have a clean towel?"

I opened a drawer, pulled out a folded towel, and handed it to her.

"He said it was probably a shock for you to see me with a date," she went on. "Especially one younger than me, when I really haven't dated anyone in years. I don't even know how long it's been—"

"It was. A shock, I mean." *You've no idea how much of a shock it was.* "And I am sorry if I offended Devon—"

"Oh heavens. You didn't offend him. He's on your side." She folded the towel neatly and hung it over the oven door handle.

"My side?"

"You know what I mean. He's not offended. He feels bad for you that you weren't given a heads-up. He's very thoughtful toward other people, Meg. It's the first thing I noticed about him."

The rest of Sofia's pages were resting near my arm, calling to me, but I pulled out a kitchen chair. "You want to sit?"

She ignored my question. "Are you still mad at me?"

"I'm not mad. And I'm sorry for what I said about your age. And his."

She paused a moment. "And what about what you said about me and your father? How do you feel about that?"

It seemed like the kitchen was still warm from my father's remorse and kindheartedness, and now here was my mother standing in the dregs of it, asking me how I felt about what had happened between them. "I don't know how I feel about what I said."

"Well, I know how I feel about it. I'm stunned that you still think, after all these years, that it's my fault your father and I divorced. You still blame me for it. Even now, as an adult, when you know darn well what he did to me. To us."

I folded myself into the chair I had pulled out for her. It's amazing, really, how powerful childhood memories are, especially those that involve your parents. You don't realize how small your world is when you are a child. Your parents are your east and west, your sun and moon. In an instant I can summon the memory of how I felt when my parents' marriage ended and my entire universe shifted. I looked up at her.

"I don't blame you for what happened to your marriage, but it wasn't just your marriage that ended, Mom. Your divorce ended my family. You took me away from Dad, brought me here to live, and I hardly ever saw him anymore. And then Nonna died, and it was like everything that I knew had been torn away from underneath me."

A single tear formed in the corner of each of my mother's eyes. One of them oozed out and slid down her cheek. "It's not my fault your father had an affair. And it's not my fault Nonna died and you were here when it happened instead of there. He had an affair, Meg. It wasn't my fault."

"It wasn't my fault either, but the results were the same as if it was. My family disappeared."

She flicked the tears away. "Why are we even talking about this? It was almost twenty years ago. Is it because I am finally dating someone? You can't handle me dating someone?"

I thought back to the few times my mother dated after the divorce. The first time was four or five years after the divorce. The second was another four or five years after that. Neither relationship lasted longer than five or six months. I tried to remember how I felt when I met those men. One had been a sixth-grade teacher with enormous teeth, and the other had been the choir director at church, an older man whose wife had died of cancer a few years earlier. I couldn't remember feeling about those men what I was feeling now.

But this much I knew. The divorce was ancient history to her, but not to me. "Look, I know you are way over the divorce. Of course you should be dating. I'm very sorry I somehow made you feel like I didn't want you to be happy. I understand that Dad hasn't been your husband in a lot of years and you're beyond ready to move on. And I know you don't love him anymore. But he's still my dad. And I do love him."

She stared at me for a moment. Then she pulled out the other chair and slowly sank down into it. It was the same chair Dad had sat in.

"Where is all this coming from? What has he told you? Why was he here?" Her voice was gentle, sad almost.

I shrugged. "He wanted to apologize for all the years he wasn't around. I think he feels bad about the time we didn't have together while I was growing up. Not just because of the divorce but because he didn't make the effort to see me as much as his stepsons' father saw his kids. I think he's realized he and I missed out on a lot. He wanted to apologize."

My mother seemed to need a second to process this. "Apologize. He came down here to apologize?"

"Yes."

"So he said he was sorry, and then he left?"

I pondered for a moment how much I wanted to tell her. I doubted she would even remember Nonna's painting of the little girl and the statue. She would definitely remember the promised trip to Florence, though. And then it just spilled out. "He told me it's looking good for us to go to Florence this year."

Her eyes grew wide. "Florence. He's finally taking you to Florence."

"I said he told me it's looking good for us to go this year. That means we might go."

Up the eyebrows rose, as if she'd thought of something startling and unimaginable. "Is he sick? Is he dying of cancer or something?"

That thought hadn't even crossed my mind. But it suddenly seemed remotely possible. I could see someone with a terminal disease wanting to put things in order before leaving the planet; except I really wanted my dad's contrition to be based on something more noble than just his own mortality. That would make it all about him. Only about him. I refused to consider it.

"He's not sick, Mom! He just wants to set a few things right. Can't a man do that?"

"Sure he can," she said slowly.

We were quiet for a moment.

She finally broke the silence. "When are you going?"

"He said he's working on it. I told him the earlier in the summer, the smaller the crowds will be."

Again, silence.

"Well," she finally said. "I hope he comes through for you, Meg. I really do."

I said nothing.

She cleared her throat as if to clear away the topic. "Devon would like to have coffee with you sometime—just so you can get to know him. Just you and him. He feels you deserve that. And you can say whatever you want because I won't be there."

"That's not necessary." I energetically shook my head for emphasis.

"But he would like to."

"But *it's not necessary.*"

Hurt registered in her eyes. "You won't even give him a chance? Aren't you doing what you are accusing me of doing all those years ago? Making me pay the consequences of your decision? I like him, Meg. I really do. He won't continue to date me if he thinks it will harm my relationship with you."

"He doesn't need my approval!"

"You can't say what other people need or don't need."

"All right, all right. I will meet him for coffee."

Her face melted into a smile of relief. "Really?"

"Really."

"I can give him your e-mail address?"

I nodded.

She reached across the table and squeezed my hand. "Thank you," she murmured. "This means a lot to me."

"All right."

"I know you think he's too young for me, but when you get to be my age, things like that just aren't as important."

"But he's not your age. Only you are. And I have to say this isn't like you, Mom."

She sat back in her chair. "And I have to say this isn't like you. I would think you'd be glad for me. You are always telling me I never take any chances, that I've never done anything spontaneous or reckless."

"I wasn't daring you to."

"It's just thirteen years' difference, Meg. Lighten up."

It seemed at that moment that the scaffolding of my little universe was all akimbo. My father and mother were shifting roles before my very eyes. He was morphing into someone who almost came off attentive and responsible, and she was shaking off years of caution the way a wet dog sheds water after a bath.

My mother pointed to the little white bag sitting by my toaster. "Are there poppy-seed bagels in there?"

I rose to toast her one. Sofia's pages were at my elbow as I spread cream cheese on my mother's bagel. I could see one phrase that peeked from the edge of the folder: *My parents loved to dance.*

Nora

My mother married my father at the villa at Poggio a Caiano where the summer heat was not so severe. There was fine food and madrigals and poetry readings, but it was not the celebration that was her sister Lucrezia's wedding a few months earlier. It was not necessary to impress the Orsini family.

I have seen the dishes on which my parents' wedding feast was served. The borders are etched with Orsini roses and mythical creatures. In the center is the Orsini coat of arms, a shield with a rose above diagonal lines. Whenever I see roses, I think of these dishes. I don't know where they are now.

There is also a lovely portrait of my mother in her wedding dress that I've not seen in many years. It was a beautiful dress. A lacy collar, pearls at her neck, a beautiful netting of jewels on her head, darkest blue velvet bodice and skirt trimmed with gold trim and ermine, and shining white damask sleeves. There is a little dog anxious to be in the painting, and her hand is gently resting on its tawny fur. She holds a flower in the other hand.

I believe my uncle Francesco stowed this painting away somewhere, or perhaps he sold it. Or destroyed it. There were many nights after it was taken down that I would huddle in front of the place where it hung and I would whisper things to her in the blank space. I wish I knew where that painting was. I would ask Francesco, but he is dead, and my uncle Ferdinando doesn't know where it is. He has said he will look for it, but I worry that he will not. It's not important to him. Ferdinando doesn't need reminders of the day my mother wore that dress. He was there. Ferdinando doesn't have devastating moments when he forgets—even just for seconds—what she looked like.

8

The first thing I did after my mother left was toss my cell phone onto my bed where I wouldn't hear it, and then I went out to my munchkin-sized patio with Sofia's pages. I wanted to lose myself in Florence more than ever. Alex followed me. I sat down on a wicker chair, its faded daisy chair pad still clammy from the morning marine layer. I didn't care. Alex jumped into my lap, and I began to read.

When I begin my tours, I tell my guests to close their eyes and whisper the lovely word "renaissance." Isn't it the most elegant word in all the world? Renaissance. A time of renewal. Even those who do not know what *renaissance* means know something beautiful began when this word replaced the Dark Ages. And when God gave the world the Renaissance artists, He gave us artistic genius the likes of which have not been seen since.

Renaissance is a French word with a lovely meaning. It means to be reborn. It is a word with hope infused in every letter. It assures us that what has fallen into pieces can be made whole, what has sagged into ugliness can be made beautiful again, what has died can have life breathed into it once more. My father told me I should never forget this and I never have.

It is widely known that there were many in the Medici family who rocked heaven with immoral, even diabolical, schemes. The Medici were often unjust and unfaithful: they killed, they harmed, they betrayed. And yet their passion for beauty and elegance funded the greatest creations outside the hand of God.

Beauty tamed them as it tames us all, Nora has assured me, if only for the moment.

Nora was the granddaughter of Cosimo I, the first grand duke of Tuscany. Her mother, whose life story is a sad one for another telling, was Isabella de' Medici. When Nora was born, Michelangelo and da Vinci and the other great ones had already come and gone. Nora lived in the echo of their accomplishments, and those echoes kept her from caving in to despair. For, you see, she did not lead the happiest of lives.

I think this is why it is her voice I hear. It is her young woman's voice that emanates from the stone and canvases; that part of her she left in Florence when she married and moved away. She knew sadness here as I have known sadness, but she also found Florence eager to heal the wounds suffered while in her embrace, just as I did.

Florence was established by Julius Caesar as a settlement for his veteran soldiers. It was named Florentia, which means "flourishing," for a reason.

We are not meant to languish here. Even if our situation flattens us. In Florence we are meant to find that which will empower us to live in the caress of what we can imagine. This is what Nora has whispered to me.

It is not a ghost I speak of. It is not a dead Nora who speaks to me. The Nora who died in her sixties in a convent, I do not know her. The Nora who speaks to me is the young woman who had not yet left Florence for good. The one who speaks to me is the one who still knew how to hope.

I read it twice, lingering on Sofia's phrases. At lunch I read both chapters again.

The rest of the day passed slowly. I did laundry. Washed my car. Cleaned out the litter box. Swept the porch. Vacuumed. Read. Hopped onto Facebook to see if anyone had posted pictures of Miles's wedding. And when I saw that someone had, I scrutinized the images, studying Miles's and Pamela's happy, serene faces for clues as to how they managed to get their lives to play out just like they were supposed to.

When that contemplation afforded me no quick answers, I sent a quick message to Lorenzo, telling him that my father was making plans for us to come this summer and that I hoped he and Renata would be around in June. And might he ask Ms. Borelli if I could see a few more chapters? And then I sat around waiting for Lorenzo to reply, as if he'd be awake and loitering on Facebook in the middle of the night.

I stayed up until after midnight watching a dumb movie, then slept poorly. I awoke several times, wondering as I wandered in and out of sleep what exactly Sofia meant when she said the paintings and sculptures spoke to her in the voice of a Medici woman named Nora. In that in-between place of sleep and wakefulness, I imagined I knew what Sofia meant, but only in the smallest of ways. When I was young, sometimes I could hear the music that the girl in my nonna's painting danced to in front of the beckoning statue. At least that is how I remembered it. Perhaps it was only Nonna humming a tune while in the kitchen, a melody that swirled into the hall where the painting hung and where I stood gazing at it.

But when I awoke in the morning, Sofia's claims that she could hear statues and paintings whispering to her needled me. I was a child when I imagined I heard the music. She was an adult who should know better. After reading her chapters over coffee a third time, I texted Gabe and asked if I could go to his church with him instead of my usual rendezvous at my mother's. Gabe attends an artistically minded church that meets in a refurbished warehouse in East Village. They were as likely to paint or dance a sermon as preach one. But he was on his way to Orange County to visit a friend. I asked him how his date was, and his one-word reply was "Okay." I was immediately aware of my selfish desire to keep Gabe right where he was. Available.

I ended up going to church with my mother anyway. She told me in between choruses of "Blessed Assurance" that Devon looked forward to having coffee with me. After eating crepes for lunch with her, I went home and rearranged the furniture that isn't mine.

By Sunday night I had a very clean cottage, no further word from my father, no return message from Lorenzo, and an e-mail from Devon: "Coffee after work on Tuesday?"

Sure.

He asked for my phone number. In case we needed to contact each other. And he gave me his.

❧

I was hungry all day Monday. Hungry to hear back from Lorenzo, hungry for more of Sofia's memoir, hungry to hear back from my father, hungry for Florence. I e-mailed Lorenzo when he still hadn't responded to my Facebook message and then hungered for an e-mail back from him. I was hungry for details of Gabe's okay date, hungry to get Geoffrey and Beatriz on board with the memoir thing, and hungry to not be hungry for anything.

I didn't think it was a good idea to pump Gabe for details on the date, and he didn't offer any. He was happy to hear my dad was at last making plans to take me to Florence, but he was cautious in his enthusiasm. "Let me know when you have the dates," he said. "I'd be happy to take you to the airport." But the tone of his voice sounded more like "Let me know if you actually get an airline ticket out of this guy, and I'd be happy to take you to the airport."

"I think he might be serious this time," I said.

And Gabe said he hoped I was right.

I mentioned to Geoffrey that I might take a week or so off in June, and he grumbled that August would be better and what did I mean by "or so"?

I told him if my dad offered to take me to Florence and said we could stay two weeks, I would be staying two weeks.

But I was thinking it would be more like a week. I told Geoffrey I would let him know.

By Tuesday morning there was still no word from Lorenzo. And nothing further from my dad. The day dragged on with nothing to look forward to but coffee with my mother's boyfriend.

I arrived at the Living Room, an eclectic café on Prospect, and ordered a decaf. I got there early so I could order my drink myself and pick the table. By the time Devon arrived, I had nearly finished my coffee, and he offered to buy me another one. To my relief, he looked slightly less handsome in his just-from-work clothes and soft-soled shoes. And he smelled a little like a hospital. He came back to the table with his first cup of java and my second. I sat back in my chair and slipped one leg over the other as if I were perfectly at home.

When he smiled at me, held up the coffee mug, and said "Cheers," he had a slightly crooked smile that I hadn't noticed before.

I held up my cup, wordless, and waited.

"Thanks for doing this," he said gently.

"I'm barely doing anything." I shrugged and took a sip.

"Do you want me to stop seeing her?"

I set the cup down too quickly, and a tiny wave of coffee sloshed out and burned the tender skin between my thumb and index finger. I shook my hand to chase away the pain. "So we're not going to start with the Padres?"

He laughed and the crooked smile returned. "I just thought the sooner we get to it, the sooner you can get on with the rest of your evening."

I placed a napkin on the minuscule spill on my hand. "Okay. Well, Devon, you don't need to do this. You are both adults, although she's been an adult a lot longer than you have, so you honestly don't need to ask me what I want."

He cocked his head a fraction, the way thoughtful people do right before they say thoughtful things. "Actually, I do. Family is the most important thing there is. It's the most precious thing there is. I'd rather not mess with that."

For the next five seconds, I sat in awe of his virtue. Then an urge to topple his coffee cup swept over me as I realized he must think I have the maturity of a four-year-old. "What kind of person do you think I am that I would disown my mother over who she dates?"

"Wow. That's…that's not what I meant." He grinned uneasily and the lopsided smile crinkled his brow line. "I just meant that if you think she's making a mistake by dating a younger man, I want you to know I respect that. And I'll back off for a while if it's going to put bad feelings between you and her."

I stared at him. He was being completely sincere; there wasn't a hint of audacity there. His concern was both charming and annoying. He had obviously been told what I had said in the ladies' bathroom at the Melting Pot. And how I had said it.

"Look, the way I found out about you and my mom—"

"Not the best way to find out," he interjected. "I feel bad about that. I didn't know she wasn't going to tell you until you got there."

"And you do know she is fifty-six, right?"

The lopsided grin lost a bit of its curve. "I do know that. But I don't think it matters. I mean, it doesn't matter to me. I can see it matters to you. I didn't mean it shouldn't matter to you."

"You don't want to…be with someone your own age?" I said, and I willed myself not to blush.

"Well, I was with someone my age. Just because someone is your age doesn't mean everything will turn out perfectly."

True.

"And I enjoy your mother's company. She is…fun to be around."

This was an interesting concept to me. My mother wouldn't hesitate to give you the shirt off her back—only if she had sunscreen in her purse for after she gave it to you—but I had never thought of this making her fun to be around.

"So her quirks don't drive you nuts?" I said.

The grin disappeared. "What quirks?"

I sat stunned for a second, unable to produce an answer. But then he laughed.

"I'm just kidding. I know what quirks you mean."

A nervous laugh escaped me. He was kind *and* clever.

"I think they're kind of cute," he continued. "And I guess if those are the worst of her quirks, I am pretty lucky. She has to put up with my quirks, too, of course."

But you don't seem to have any. Aside from dating older women.

"Everybody has to put up with something if you're going to be in a relationship with someone, right?" he said. "I mean, there are no perfect people. Even your own quirks might annoy you a little if they showed up in someone else."

He was too good to be true. "I suppose you're right," I managed to murmur.

He took a drink from his mug and set it down. "So. Does this mean we are okay?"

I knew he meant was I okay with him dating my mother, but the question startled me nonetheless.

"You don't need my permission."

"But I want it anyway."

"I don't want you to hurt her. She was hurt once before."

He nodded slowly. "I know she was… And we are a long way off from anything other than just dating," he continued. "If it should get serious, we promise you'll be the first to know. Okay?"

We sat there quietly for a few moments, letting the aura of our understanding settle in around us. At some point he must have decided we could move on.

"Your mother says you might be headed to Florence this summer?"

Florence.

"Yes."

"With your dad?"

"Yes."

"Okay. So when you go, there's a little restaurant in the Piazza della Signoria that makes the best porcini mushroom ravioli in the world. Honestly. The best. Porcini mushrooms are tangy sweet and as soft as marshmallows. You will love them. The restaurant is in the same piazza where the copy of the *David* statue is. But promise me you won't settle for that one. It's just a copy. When you get there, make sure you get tickets to the

Accademia and see the real statue. It's simply the work of a genius. You have to see it."

He didn't say "if." He said "when." No one else had ever talked of my promised trip to Florence that way. Not even my dad. The muscles in my chest tightened.

I looked across the table at the man dating my mother, and a smile involuntarily spread across my face. I felt it lift.

Devon smiled back at me, the gentle hook of his crooked smile softening the lines around his jaw.

I hadn't been even the tiniest bit jealous of my mother in I don't know how long. But in that moment, what I felt inside me was not attraction to her new boyfriend but an odd envy that she had found one so wonderful.

Nora

My mother longed for Florence whenever she was away from it. She told Nurse the Orsini castle in Bracciano hadn't the beauty of Florence and its lifeless corridors bored her. But I don't think it was boredom that made my mother dislike any place that wasn't Florence. It was loneliness. And Rome, though majestic in its own way, could not woo her either. Only Florence charmed her.

When my father came to Florence to see my mother, he would always ask her to join him in Rome, but apparently he did not insist. Nurse thought he asked because he wanted to be heard asking. Sometimes my mother visited him at his family home in Bracciano or in Pisa or at one of the Medici villas in the country. But she hardly ever went to Rome to see him. Two years after their wedding, during a summer when my father had joined her at the Medici palace, my mother found herself with child but miscarried within the same month. Nurse said my mother barely had a moment to consider that she would be a mother before the tiny life was taken from her.

9

Our reason for meeting clearly met, I told Devon I needed to get back to the office to finish something I'd left undone. Devon stood when I stood, reached for my hand to clasp it in thanks for meeting with him, and offered to walk me to my car.

No need, I told him. No need, no need. I said he should enjoy the rest of his coffee.

Five minutes later I slid easily into a parking place in front of the darkened building. I fumbled for my office key, grateful I couldn't see any lighted desk lamps inside. I punched in the alarm code, locked the door behind me, and headed for my office.

I tossed my purse onto the desk and sank into my chair.

This ugly feeling inside me was ridiculous.

Devon was dating my mother. He liked my mother. Liked her in that way men like women. She deserved a guy like him. Of course she deserved a guy like him.

I grabbed my computer mouse, and my computer screen sprang to life. I clicked into a search engine for bargain flights out of LA. Dad would want to leave out of LA. I couldn't type the words fast enough. Los Angeles to Florence. LAX to FLR. From where I was now to somewhere far away.

The results came up quickly. Dad and I could leave on a Monday in late May. There were two seats left at a great price, leaving at three in the afternoon. And arriving the next afternoon. A connection in Paris. And then we'd be there.

In a month or so, I could be in Florence.

I couldn't possibly wait until June.

I e-mailed the suggested itinerary to my dad. And then I texted him.

"Hey, Dad. Just wanted you to know there are two tickets to Florence at a nice price for the end of May. Just sent you the itinerary. Thoughts?"

I pressed Send and waited for ten minutes.

There wasn't a sound in the place except for my own inhaling and exhaling. My phone was silent. And the room around me was silent too.

With less speed this time, I reached for my mouse to open my e-mail inbox. Maybe Lorenzo had responded back to me in the three hours since I had last checked. I chortled cynically at my own childish anticipation and checked anyway.

A handful of messages dropped into the inbox. Nothing from Lorenzo.

But the last one snatched my breath for a second. In the *From* line was a name that made me sit up in my chair: Sofia Borelli. I clicked the message:

Dear Miss Pomeroy,

My dear neighbor Lorenzo tells me you would like to see more of my manuscript! I cannot tell you how thrilled and amazed I am. I know this does not mean you will publish my book, but I am so honored that you wish to see more. I asked Lorenzo if this was a good sign, that you wish to see more, and he said it was.

I have other chapters. Fifteen or twenty, I think. They are not in any kind of order. I write them as the stories come to mind; the ones my father told me and the ones Nora has whispered to me. I am afraid I am not very skilled at putting things in order. I trust that will not spoil the reading for you. I have never written a book before, although I have always wanted to. And my parents always told me I had a gift for writing. It runs in the Medici family, you know.

I am sending you two more chapters. Do you want more?
I hope it is acceptable that I send them to you directly. Lorenzo
thought you would not mind.

He also thought I should tell you a little more about myself.
I am fifty-six. I have been a tour guide here in Florence since I was
nineteen. I am fluent in English. I decided to write the memoir in
English because Lorenzo told me it was a good idea.

I live across the hall from Lorenzo and Renata. They are
wonderful neighbors and have been very good to me.

Thank you for wanting to see more of my manuscript. I hope
very much that you like it. Lorenzo thought perhaps you would like
my contact information to speak with me, so I have included it at
the top of the attached pages. Lorenzo helped me place it there. It
is on every page.

Yours very sincerely,
Sofia Borelli

The awkwardness of the last hour, the frenzied desire to hear back from
my dad on those tickets, and the tomb-like silence of the office at night
faded as I guided the mouse over the little paper clip icon that held Sofia's
attached files. I opened the first one and began to read.

My home in Florence has been in the family since the days of Anna
de' Medici's twilight years. My father has a younger brother, Emilio,
who lives in Rome. I do not see him very often.

The flat is lovely with wood floors, creamy plaster walls, and
arched doorways. There are three bedrooms and a lovely kitchen
with a tiny balcony where I can grow basil and tomatoes most of the
year. The flat, and four others like it, sits above a leather boutique

very close to the Piazza degli Antinori. The only time I did not live here was when I was married and I lived on the other side of the Arno. But that was a long time ago; so long, it sometimes seems to have been someone else's life that I observed.

My mother, Natalia, worked for the owner of the leather shop below us. Leather goods are very popular in Florence and have been since tanners at Via delle Conce provided the leather for the manuscript covers at the Santa Croce monastery in the thirteenth century. The boutique where my mother worked sold beautiful, expensive things, but my mother smelled like a horse at the end of a workday. The three of us would laugh about it: how she could work in a boutique that sold such fine things and yet she would climb the stairs in her high heels after the boutique closed for the day, sounding like a clopping horse and smelling like one. She died when I was just twenty-eight. She had a weak heart, which is why, my father told me, they had no other children after me. She died the same year my marriage ended and the man I loved went back to England without me. When she passed away, my father and I suddenly had this terrible thing in common; it was a blessing and it was a curse. We both lost the loves of our hearts in the sweltering, unforgiving heat of summer; me, twice the loss.

The only cool place to be in August in Florence is inside one of its many churches. And that is where we went, he and I, to beseech heaven for comfort.

My favorite place of solace in those days was the Church of Santa Trinita, just one block from the river. Nora often went to Mass at this church with her mother. When I walk its floor, I am mindful that her feet also brushed the stones more than four hundred years before.

As the heat of that awful summer pressed me to my knees beneath the painting of Saint Francis renouncing all worldly joys, Nora assured me my shattered heart would not be my undoing. I felt her very breath on my neck, as I bent my head in prayer, reminding me that Medici women are resilient. I had only to look backward to see that the Medici passion for beauty stemmed from their passion for life.

Were it not for Nora's whispers reminding me of this day after day after day, I surely would have disappeared into my grief. Grief is a river like the Arno, the depths of its dark bed you cannot see. To swim in it is to tire in it and sink in it and be lost forever in it.

My father, Angelo Borelli III, is an accomplished artist. The walls of our flat are covered with his canvases. He loves trees; there is always a tree in his paintings.

There have always been many talented artists in Florence, from the daybreak of its existence. To this day, countless artists line the piazzas with their creations, selling them to tourists for a handful of euros. Florence has always been a magnet for those who itch to paint, to sculpt, to bestow beauty on a world in need of it.

The concentration of such genius during the Italian Renaissance is staggering. The greatest works of art since ancient times were left to us during the three hundred years of Medici rule. Such talent was absent during the Dark Ages, and its zenith seems to have come and gone in Florence, in the span of three centuries.

A French author who went by the name Stendhal visited Florence in 1817 and was so awestruck at the immense beauty of Florence's art that he suffered heart palpitations and feared he would faint dead away. He was not the first to feel this way, but the first, perhaps, to write of it. Stendahl Syndrome, sometimes called Florence Syndrome, became a byword, and two centuries later, scientists are still curious to know if what Stendahl wrote is true. They ponder his claims with studies and projects. Is the vastness of what the Renaissance artists left to Florence too great for the human soul to fully grasp? Is it truly like a crippling encounter with the Divine?

Doubters call it a psychosomatic illness, this racing heart, dizziness, and confusion in people who've beheld such astonishing artistic achievement, and yet I see it on my tours all the time. The staff at Santa Maria Nuova hospital is accustomed to treating woozy and disoriented tourists after they've seen the *David*. He takes your breath away. Literally. And *David* is just one of thousands of artistic treasures to woo you, though he is the most spectacular. They are everywhere. To have one's breath stolen at every turn is what makes a person swoon. It's that simple.

I can tell you what makes the tourists totter and sway, what makes them grab for tissues and handkerchiefs as unbidden tears begin to flow, what makes them stagger as if struck. Their souls hear the music, the tunes and whispers that Medicis like me can hear, but their ears tell them they hear nothing. The tug of war inside them is what makes them lurch for a handhold, gasping for air. I tell my guests to sit for a moment, to put their heads between their knees, to breathe slowly, in and out, deep cleansing breaths. And while they close their eyes to concentrate on my instructions, I raise my eyes to the statues and faces that stare down at us from the walls, and I press a finger to my lips. Sometimes Nora will agree to my request, but not always.

Bells are for ringing; that's what she says.

Nora

Of my mother's brothers, her favorite was Giovanni. Nurse tells me my mother and Giovanni were like my brother, Virginio, and me, so close in age. They were always together, like kindred friends. My mother and Giovanni hunted together, played card games, and spent long summers at the villas, and it was Giovanni who worried over my mother when her pregnancies ended in empty bassinets.

And because Giovanni was a cardinal, he was the all-important Medici representative in the Vatican. My grandfather favored him as well.

When Giovanni fell ill and died when my mother was twenty, Nurse told me it was as if the sun stopped shining in Florence. And while the family still grieved, a younger brother, Garzia, also fell ill to the same fever and died just three weeks later.

The losses of these sons, together with the previous losses of my mother's sisters, proved too much for my grandmother. Five days after Garzia died, Eleonora, the duchess for whom I was named, flew to heaven too.

10

Three good things happened in the days immediately following the meeting with Devon at the coffee shop.

Lorenzo e-mailed me back and said he and Renata would find a way to be around whenever my dad settled on the dates. He asked if we knew where we'd be staying or if we needed help with that. I wondered if that meant would Dad and I like to stay with them, which I thought was a great idea, considering my dad's finances. I e-mailed him back and said I didn't think my dad had made any plans yet, hoping Lorenzo would reply with what he had in mind for "help."

The second good thing was Dad called to tell me he was getting close to finalizing the dates and that he'd be checking on those tickets I had found. I asked him how many days he thought we'd be staying. That didn't seem to matter much to him, which was weird since he would be paying for it. I suggested maybe eight to ten days. He said fine and asked me if I could get a ride to LAX. It was nice to be able to say I already had that. We didn't talk long; he said he was driving without his Bluetooth. He sounded like he was on his way somewhere and was late.

The third good thing was that I mentioned to Beatriz that I'd read some interesting chapters of a travel memoir written by a friend of Lorenzo and Renata's and that I thought the writer had some potential. She said I could tell her more about it at the next idea meeting.

Three not-so-good things also happened.

In his phone call, Dad had said nothing about the missing painting. I figured he hadn't had much luck with his sisters and stalled on asking any of his cousins. But I rationalized that we would be spending time together in Florence looking for the statue that inspired it. I could then ask him how the search was going, and he'd be reminded that he had promised to find it. It was surprising how much I wanted the painting now that he'd promised he'd get it for me.

Second, the idea of introducing Sofia Borelli's book at the next idea meeting was a little intimidating. Her manuscript pulled me as if magnetized, but the voice of reason kept reminding me that statues and paintings don't actually talk. Would Geoffrey and Beatriz think I was insane for even suggesting we look at it? Quite possibly. Was Sofia's the best book to launch a memoir line? It didn't seem like a safe pick in so many ways, but her chapters fascinated me, as a good memoir should.

Third, I couldn't squash the blossoming jealousy I had toward my mother's and Devon's newfound happiness in each other. The envy, though somewhat flimsy, nevertheless made me feel ugly inside. Gabe caught on that something distracted me beyond the details of the Florence trip and Sofia's odd memoir. He asked what was bothering me, and I couldn't tell him.

I didn't want to tell anyone what was bothering me, but it flopped out of my mouth a week after the coffee shop incident when Kara and I were catching a movie on a girls' night out. Before the previews started, she asked me how my mom was, and the next thing I knew, I was confessing to her that my mom had a new boyfriend and I was practically wishing he was mine, instead of hers. Like I was infatuated with him. With the idea of him.

"That's probably not what it is," she said, when I came up for air.

I was very quick to tell her that's exactly what it was.

And she said, "I'm thinking infatuation is what it feels like, but that's probably not what it is."

I told her that was not helpful. If it feels like it is, it may as well be. But then the previews started. Two hours later, when we were headed out of the theater, she asked if I wanted to talk about it.

No, I didn't. I just wanted to stop thinking about it.

She looked at me sympathetically. She didn't say "Good luck with that," because she's too good a friend. But I could see she was thinking it'd be a lot easier to figure out my feelings for my mother's boyfriend if I talked the matter over with someone who had nothing to lose by my being completely honest.

Don't ever reveal the confounding mysteries of your soul to a friend who was a psych major unless you are prepared for a look like that.

"Be good to keep some distance between you and him," she said softly, and before I could tell her I had no plans to see him at all, she suggested we go to the cupcake place near her house for a snack.

My mother hadn't asked for a minute-by-minute play-by-play of coffee night; it had been enough for her that Devon told her our visit had gone very well. He apparently hadn't told her I had left in a casual rush five seconds after we started talking about Florence. And why would he? My mom was pleased there was nothing awkward between Devon and me anymore. That's exactly how she said it. And since she now had a new focus for her evenings, her calls to me were fewer and didn't last as long.

Hearing her sound so happy poked at me. Of course she was happy. She had Devon.

I distracted myself with making elaborate plans for every day that my dad and I would be in Florence, heartily assuming that we were, in fact, going. I e-mailed Sofia Borelli and told her I had tentative plans to be in Florence in late May and asked her if she'd consider being our guide for a few of those days, hoping she wasn't out of my price range. I knew from Lorenzo and Renata's first book on Florence how much to expect to pay for a basic, private tour guide. I didn't get the impression Sofia was a guide only for the rich. And since I told her we'd be able to talk more about her book while I was there, I hoped she would perhaps be our guide for a reduced rate.

She e-mailed me back within the day, telling me she would be happy to show us all of Florence and we weren't to think of giving her so much as a euro for it. It would be her gift to us, and I would not be obligated in any way with regard to her book. She just wanted to show me her beautiful city. She asked if I had enjoyed the other two chapters she'd sent, and in my reply, I told her they intrigued me very much. I didn't tell her I planned to soft pitch her idea to Geoffrey and Beatriz later that day.

I hadn't heard from Dad since the day he called and said I could decide how many days we'd be gone. So I called him to tell him we had a free tour guide for our trip as a way of nailing him down. He didn't answer, and I had to leave him a message.

I lunched with Gabe outside overlooking the cove before the idea meeting. As we ate, I let him skim Sofia's chapters, which I had e-mailed the day before to the other editorial staff, interested to hear what an artistic man would think of them.

I watched his face as he moved through the pages, noticing when he smiled or raised an eyebrow, wondering if he found her amazingly interesting or plainly unhinged.

When he was done, he handed the pages back to me. "Well, it's certainly not like anything else we've ever done."

"You think she's crazy."

"She doesn't write like she's crazy. It's very interesting, inventive even. Travelers may not get into her style, but artists will. I've heard of Stendhal Syndrome. She's not making that up. We studied it in art history."

I frowned. "That probably won't be good enough for Geoffrey. He won't care if artists will like it. He'll say that's not our market."

Gabe tossed the fragmented remains of his sandwich into the trash can next to our bench. "It's not, technically."

"But can't you see this appealing to the traveler who has been to Florence before? The one who loves it, and loves going back because the way Sofia writes about it is the same way they feel about it? Or, think of this. What if it's for those who've never been and will probably never get to go, even though they want to very much? A book like this will make them feel like they've been there. What other kind of travel book is like that? For the person who will never go but wishes they could?"

He was quiet for a moment. "So you want to make it up to them by giving it to them in a book?"

"Sometimes that's as real as it's going to get. And that has to be enough."

He stood up and reached for my hand and pulled me to my feet. "Then that's what you'll tell Geoffrey and Beatriz."

Half an hour later, I felt confident when I walked into the meeting and saw that Geoffrey and Beatriz had Sofia's pages in front of them. The two other editors did too.

As soon as Gabe and I sat down, Geoffrey poked the pages. "So what exactly are you thinking with this?"

I told him and everyone else around the table what I'd told Gabe— Sofia's memoir was for the traveler who is more than just a tourist; we'd be expanding our audience as opposed to shrinking it because we would be offering something not only for the person who was planning a trip to Florence, but also for the person who had already been and fallen in love with it; and more important, for the thousands upon thousands who will never be able to go and who would feel like they had been after reading Sofia's book.

Gabe, sitting at the end of the table, smiled kindheartedly when I was done. It was not a smile of triumph. He knew before I did that Geoffrey hadn't thought much of it.

"The paintings and statues tell her things? Come on," Geoffrey said.

Beatriz, resplendent in a fuchsia suit, tapped the tabletop with manicured fingernails. "Can she prove she is a Medici descendent?" Her accent clipped her words short, as did her tone.

"What difference does that make? She's a nut!" Geoffrey pushed the pages back to me.

"But if she could prove she is Medici"—Beatriz's tone was softer than it had been a minute ago—"and we get her to take out the talking statues…"

Geoffrey shook his head. "I'm not interested in working with a writer who is delusional."

"We do it all the time. They all start out thinking they can buy a vacation home with their first book's royalties," Beatriz quipped. Gentle laughter rippled across the table.

"Okay, fine," Geoffrey said. "I'm not interested in working with a writer who sees dead people."

"Hears them," I said. More laughter.

"But you know, if we take the crazy out, maybe she has a good book inside her. I like her style," Beatriz said. Then she turned to me. "How much does she have finished?"

"I'm going to see her when my dad and I go to Florence next month," I said. "I think after I've met her and have seen the rest of the manuscript, I will have a better idea of what we're working with."

"We're working with a nut job," Geoffrey mumbled.

"She has a nice way with words, Geoff," Beatriz said.

No one else calls Geoffrey that. It amazes me how they get along as business partners even though they are divorced.

She continued, "I think we should see if Meg can authenticate Ms. Borelli's ancestral claims and then convince her to downplay the voice.

Then Meg can bring the manuscript back to us, and we can talk about it again."

"I would never buy a book like this." Geoffrey waved his hand across Sofia's pages.

"You wouldn't buy a book on destination weddings in Italy either, and we're publishing one," I said quickly, and Beatriz, who hardly ever laughs, guffawed loudly.

"I think it's got a whole new vibe to it," Gabe said from the far end of the table. "Meg's right. We'll be expanding our readership not only to people who like memoirs but also to those who wish they could see Florence but probably won't have the opportunity."

Beatriz turned to me. "When are you going?"

"Um. Maybe next month." I hesitated. "My dad and I are finalizing the details."

"Next month is in a couple weeks," Geoffrey said. "You're still finalizing the dates?"

"End of the month." I forced myself to sound resolute.

"Don't promise Ms. Borelli anything, but do see if you can authenticate this claim, hmm?" Beatriz placed the chapters I had given her in her folio, and Geoffrey sighed loudly and retrieved his. "And see if she has more chapters ready to send."

Feeling rather triumphant, I headed back to my office after thanking Gabe for sticking up for me. I wanted to e-mail Sofia to ask for additional chapters while Beatriz was still interested. When I got back to my desk, I saw that I had two missed calls on my cell phone. One from my mother and one from Dad's phone at home, not his cell phone. I quickly sent Sofia an e-mail asking for two more chapters, and then I punched the button on my phone to call my father on his landline.

On the fourth ring, the call was picked up. I was so certain it would be him who answered, I nearly said "Dad" before realizing it was a woman's voice who'd answered on the other end. Allison.

"You called back." Her voice sounded odd.

"*You* called me?" I couldn't hide the surprise in my voice. Allison and I are not close. We are cordial to each other when I visit my dad at his and Allison's home, but there is no wealth of affection between us. We never talk by phone. It hit me with a sickening force that something terrible must've happened and that is why she'd called me. Before I could summon the courage to ask her, she asked *me* a question.

"Are you going to tell me where he is or not?"

Allison didn't sound worried or afraid. She sounded angry.

"What?"

"Are you going to tell me where he is?"

She didn't know where my dad was, and she was darn sure that I did. "Allison, I haven't the slightest idea what you are talking about."

"So that's the way it's going to be?"

I had never heard her sound so incredibly ticked off. What on earth had my dad done?

"What has happened? Where's my dad?" The second question was out of my mouth before I could yank it back in. She hadn't the foggiest where my dad was. That's why she'd called.

"I know he was planning a trip to Europe with you," Allison snapped. "Is that where he is? Are you going to meet him there?"

"Allison, I haven't heard from him in several days. I don't know where he is! Are you sure he's okay? Should we call the police?"

"Oh, I'm definitely calling the police! He stole fifty thousand dollars from me! And my car! And my jewelry. You can bet I am calling the police!"

Oh, Lord.

Instantly I felt Florence slipping away from me. A thick ache spilled inside as four words seemed to strike up a dirge in my head. *Not going to Florence. Not going to Florence.* Dad has left Allison. He has left me. He has left all of us.

There is no trip to Florence.

A sound escaped me; a single, strangled moan.

Allison either did not hear it or just refused to acknowledge it. "His passport is gone. His clothes are gone. And fifty thousand dollars of my money is gone! And you were the last one to talk to him!"

"I swear to you, I don't know where he is."

"Sure you don't."

The line clicked dead.

I tossed my phone onto my desk, and I tried very hard to rein it in. But my resolve was crumbling. Years of little-girl disappointment flooded up from a deep place inside me.

The tears started to fall despite frantic attempts to rub them away.

The sound of my door closing made me snap my head up. Gabe.

He moved closer to me, concern etched in his face. "What's happened?"

At first I couldn't bring myself to say it, because saying something somehow makes it more real. I eked out the words "He left."

And somehow Gabe knew exactly what I meant.

Nora

That terrible time when Giovanni died, my poor mother lost not only her favorite brother, a second brother, and her beloved mother all in less than a month, but she lost another baby as well.

I know what it is like to lose so much all at once. It's as if you've been shattered into a million fragments. I wonder who she turned to then for solace. I do not mean who she took to her bed. I am not yet married, but I'm of the mind that balm for the soul is not found in the bedchamber. Physical relations, near as I can tell, can distract you from your troubles, but they do not solve any of them. I should like to be proven wrong about that in the days to come.

What does one do with a heart that has been broken? One might look for a bonding agent that will fuse the pieces back together. Or one might learn to live among the shards.

Or one might be tempted to sweep up the bits and toss them and be done with hearts.

11

The rest of my day was tedious and torturous. Right after I'd summoned the words to explain to Gabe my dad had run out on Allison—and me—Geoffrey appeared at my door, looking for Gabe.

There had been no time to fix my makeup or even blow my nose. It took all of half a second for Geoffrey to realize I'd been crying.

He frowned at Gabe. "What on earth did you say to her?"

Gabe opened his mouth to, no doubt, assure Geoffrey he'd said nothing, but he hesitated, and I filled the space.

"He didn't say anything," I said, sniffling.

Geoffrey swiveled his head back to stare at me. "Beatriz practically said yes to you. Didn't you get that? It was more yes than no to those chapters, although I'm still trying to figure out why."

"This has nothing to do with the meeting," Gabe said gently. "Did you need something from me, Geoffrey?"

"Is something going on between the two of you?" Geoffrey looked from me to Gabe and back to me again.

"No." I dabbed at my eyes with a crumpled napkin. "It's nothing like that. I'm… I don't…"

My voice fell away and Gabe stepped in. "You were looking for me, right?" He took a step toward Geoffrey.

"Is he giving you trouble?" Geoffrey jerked his head toward Gabe, creasing his brow line sternly and ignoring Gabe's question completely.

Geoffrey's gruff, paternal tone both amused me and raked against my father's fresh wounding.

"Gabe's been great," I murmured. I blotted my nose. "It's my dad who's giving me trouble."

"Why? What? What's he done?"

I sighed heavily. "I'm not sure I'm going to Florence next month, after all. I think my dad might've skipped out on my stepmother. She doesn't know where he is, and he apparently stole fifty thousand dollars from her."

"What do you mean he stole fifty thousand dollars from her? They're married. This is California. What's hers is his."

I shrugged. "That's what she told me. And she thinks I know where he is. I don't."

Geoffrey stared at me. "He walked out on his wife, emptied their bank account, and left you hanging on to your suitcase? And this is the guy you want to go to Florence with?"

Gabe shot me a look of compassion.

"It's complicated," I said.

"No it's not," Geoffrey replied. "The heck with him. You don't need your father to go to Florence. Just go. Don't waste another minute moaning over it." He turned to Gabe. "I need that mock-up of the Machu Picchu cover."

Geoffrey left my office, assuming Gabe would follow.

"You going to be okay?" Gabe said.

My phone began to ring before I could answer. On the screen I could see it was my mother, trying a second time to reach me. I nodded and he left.

I answered the phone.

Mom wasted no time getting right to the point. "Did you get a call from her?"

"You mean Allison?"

"Please tell me you're not hiding him from her."

"Mom."

"I told her she was crazy to think you knew anything about this. I'm so sure."

She sounded just like one of her junior-high students.

"So she called you thinking I was hiding him?" I asked.

"She actually thought *I* was hiding him. Can you imagine? He took a bunch of money. And some of her jewelry. And their nice car. She drives the nice car, if you'll remember."

I was suddenly very tired. I didn't want to talk to my mother about what my father had done to his second wife or what he had taken that apparently didn't belong to him. I just wanted to go home. To my little borrowed cottage and my borrowed cat and my quiet borrowed life.

"Was she rude to you?" my mother continued. "She was rude to me."

"I don't know. She hung up on me. I guess you could say that was rude."

"I have to say I am floored that he just left her like that. Taking all that money and just up and leaving her. No note or anything. I'll bet she thinks it's another woman, because, you know, once upon a time she *was* the other woman. But I don't think so this time. I think maybe he owed some money somewhere; that's what I think. It's about money this time."

"I need to go, Mom."

"Wait! I want to make sure you're okay. Are you okay? I know he promised he'd take you to Florence this summer. That's probably not going to happen now."

My next words fell out of my mouth with crisp speed. Sharp as tacks. "He's been promising that since I was a teenager, Mom. I'm used to it."

A divot of silence hung between us as I recovered from the indictment of my own sentence and she processed it on the other end.

"So...so, you're okay?"

Okay with what? I wanted to say. What does *okay* really mean, anyway? Less than marvelous? Better than miserable?

"I really need to go."

"Do you want me to call Allison back and assure her you don't know where he is? If she hung up on you, she probably thinks you know and aren't telling. I could—"

"Don't call her, Mom. She's going to think what she wants. I've got to go."

"Well, okay—"

I pressed the Off button while she was in midsentence. It was only a little after two, but I began to gather my things. I was going home. As I shuffled papers on my desk, my eyes met Sofia's pages and a skewer of deep disappointment rippled through me. This was the closest we had ever come to taking the trip. It seemed like it was really going to happen this time. He practically had the tickets. I was so looking forward to meeting Sofia and letting her usher me into the heart of Florence to meet her talking statues and paintings. I knew just what I wanted to ask her. *Do you know the statue of a young maiden kneeling with her hand stretched out?* And I'd already imagined Sofia saying, "Yes. I know it."

I stuffed her pages into my book bag and tapped out a quick e-mail to Geoffrey and Beatriz that I was leaving for the day with a massive headache. Geoffrey would know why I was really leaving, but he would also know magnificent disappointment can produce a magnificent headache.

Just as I hit Send, my cell phone began to vibrate. A Los Angeles area code shone in the screen. A number I didn't know. I grabbed for it, hoping my dad was calling me from a pay phone somewhere in LA.

"Meg. This is Therese. I need to talk to you."

It'd been at least six or seven years since I had spoken to my father's oldest sister. The last time had been at a post-Christmas gathering when I had driven up to spend some time with my dad over the holidays. Therese and her husband and three children were there when I arrived and stayed the better part of the day. The moment I heard Therese's voice over the phone, I remembered that she actually got along with Allison. After my parents' divorce, Allison was no longer the other woman, but my dad's new wife, and then simply his wife. Therese liked Allison. Allison was a successful businesswoman who didn't take bull from anyone, and she made smart investment decisions. Of course Therese liked her. They were two peas in a pod.

I knew before she said another word why she had called.

"I don't know where he is, Therese. I haven't talked to him in several days."

Therese didn't say anything for a few long seconds. When she did speak, I could tell she didn't believe me.

"What he did was wrong, Meg. The money he took was what Allison had been given from her grandfather's estate. It didn't belong to him. Neither did the car or the earrings and necklaces he took."

"I don't know where he is." I said it plainly and without a hint of emotion.

"Do you hear what I am saying? He took money that her grandfather had left her."

I was seconds away from hanging up on her, but I wanted to get out of the office with her as a distraction as I walked out. I grabbed my purse, Sofia's pages, and my book bag.

"And do you hear what I am saying? I don't know anything."

"You were planning a trip to Italy with him. I'd say that's knowing something."

I pulled my office door shut and headed down the hall at a brisk pace, hoping that Gabe was still with Geoffrey and I could just walk out. Get away. "Apparently you know just as much as I do."

"Why are you protecting him?" Therese shouted.

"Why do you care what he does or doesn't do?" I yelled back. I could see heads in the reception area turning toward me as I pushed open the front door and emerged into April sunshine. "He's not your husband. He's not your problem."

"He's my brother! I promised my mother I wouldn't let him bury himself in debt. And for your information, Allison doesn't deserve this!"

I clacked my way to my car, wanting to run to it and feeling imprisoned by the heels I had decided to wear that day. "Oh yes. Let's do talk about what Allison deserves. Goodbye, Therese." I was ready to hang up on her, but she yelled at me not to.

"Look, I don't know what he's promised you, but you've got to know he's stringing you along, like he always has. You think he wants to do right by you, but he's got you fooled, Meg. You know I am right about this. He's in trouble. Big trouble. He owes money all over the place. He's not taking you to Florence. I'm sure he never planned to."

I stopped in the middle of the street as her arrow hit home and buried itself in my chest. "How dare you say that?"

"It's true. I've known him all my life. I'm sorry to say it, but this is just the way he is."

A car whooshed past me, honking. For a second I wavered. I nearly gave in to her, but then I remembered the morning Dad brought the poppy-seed bagels and he apologized to me. Something had changed inside him; he was different. He desperately wanted to make things right between us.

He begged for me to come up with a way to let him show me how much.

He promised to find the painting.

I took another step toward the curb and then stopped. My dad left the last morning I saw him, impatient to find it. He said he was going to start looking for it that very day.

He was going to start with Therese and Bianca.

With one question, I could gauge my father's new intentions toward me. One answer to one question would let me know if he'd been sincere the day he drove down to see me or if he was still who Therese said he was.

"Did my dad ask you about the painting of the little girl and the statue?"

There was a momentary pause. "The *what*?"

I closed the distance between myself and my car. I steeled myself against it and asked her again. "Did my dad ask you about a painting? It was Nonna's."

"What painting? I haven't talked to your dad in over a month. Why are we even talking about this?"

The ache that had begun at losing Florence intensified as I fought now to calmly remind Therese which painting of Nonna's I was talking about. "The one of the little girl and the statue."

A second of silence.

"I have no idea where that painting is." Exasperation laced her voice. "I haven't seen it since my mother died. What has this got to do with *anything*?"

No idea where that painting is.

No idea.

He hadn't even asked her.

He hadn't even asked.

"Are you still there?" Therese's question was wrapped in impatience.

Oh yes. I was still there.

Nothing had changed.

Nora

I was in my eighth year when I asked Nurse what my father was like, for I could not remember him. I had seen him only once after my mother died. And it was only for a moment. He came to Florence to discuss financial matters, not to see Virginio and me. There was no caress on the cheek during that visit.

Nurse and I were outside taking in the fresh air on a warm spring day. I was watching my cousin Maria with my uncle Francesco, observing how he spoke to her as he held the reins of his horse with Maria on the animal's back. Two years younger than I, she still seemed little more than a baby. There was an urgency to my uncle's words as he told Maria how to sit on his horse, as if she had only that day to learn and all would be lost if she could not make the horse obey her that very afternoon. His attention on her was intense, in a way that interested me, even though I was afraid of him. He was the closest thing to a father that I had, and he never spoke to me. I think he saw my mother in me, and that made him look away from me whenever I was near. He was not fond of my mother.

Maria did not seem to be enjoying the lesson very much. I saw the sparkle of tears on her cheek. I never envied her having Francesco for a father. But a curling tendril of something akin to envy began to wrap itself around my heart as I watched her being the center of her father's attention in that moment.

I allowed the little vine to stay. Even then, though I did not know it yet, I was nurturing my budding belief that envy can transform into something nobler when watered with hope.

12

When I moved into the cottage last year, Findlay Wyndham, an old family friend on my mother's side, told me I was to think of it as my home. I was to eat on the good dishes, burn his candles, use the seashell-shaped soaps, and play his vintage LPs on his old-school turntable as much as I wanted. The lifelong bachelor was off to spend three years sailing around the world at a minnow's pace, and I was his happy answer to needing a house sitter.

I eat off my own open-stock stoneware, and I forget to burn even my own candles. The seashell soaps are still in their packaging, and I hardly ever turn on his old stereo.

But on days when I am feeling particularly disappointed with the state of the universe, I pull out his B. B. King albums, switch on the stereo, and fill the cottage with the blues.

Fifteen minutes after I hung up with Therese, I was sitting on Findlay's leather sofa, sipping a Merlot at three o'clock in the afternoon with Alex on my lap and BB belting out "Worry, Worry."

Therese had figured out, within seconds of my asking, that Dad had promised to find a painting that meant a lot to me and he hadn't even asked her about it.

But the cruelest of his injuries was letting me think he was taking me to Florence when apparently his only plan of late had been figuring out how to run out on his wife with as much cash as he could. What was the purpose of his so-called plans to go to Florence with me? Had it been a distraction for Allison so that she wouldn't wonder why he was making travel plans, airing out his suitcases, and pulling his passport out of the safe?

He knew how much I wanted to see Florence, how much I've always wanted to see Florence. He had to know how much this would hurt.

My phone vibrated as I sat there sipping, musing, and pondering; a text from Gabe.

"You all right?"

I texted back that I would be okay. I would. Eventually.

"Want to do something tmro? Helping friend move but can come over when done."

I texted back that he could let me know when he was finished and I would see where I was at emotionally. I wanted to think that by tomorrow late afternoon, I'd be up for frozen yogurt and company instead of tissues and pity.

I finished the glass of wine, BB moved on to a happier tune, and I got up, dumping Alex on his black-and-white feet.

A sense of finality seemed to spread over me as I took the glass to the sink and rinsed it out. I was finished with waiting.

Done.

I walked over to my kitchen table where my laptop rested, opened it, and powered it on. A minute later I was transferring two hundred dollars from my checking account into my savings account. The following month I would do it again. And again the next month. And the next. By the same time next spring I would have more than two-thousand dollars saved. If that wasn't enough for the plane ticket and food and cheap lodging, I'd beg Lorenzo to let me sleep on his kitchen floor. I wouldn't care. I wouldn't care if I slept on tile and ate bread and water for a week straight. I would see Florence. I would let Sofia Borelli take me wherever she wanted. And I would stop at any painting or sculpture or doorknob in a church that spoke to her and ask her to tell me what Nora wanted to say about it. And I would find the statue with the beckoning hand. I would take a picture of it and have it printed on canvas when I got home, and I'd hang it over Findlay's fireplace. I wouldn't have Nonna's painting, but I would have this.

⚘

Saturday dawned brilliantly sunny, a rare treat for a coastal dweller, but I pulled the covers over my head and slept like a moody teenager until eleven. I'd missed a call from my mother while I slept. Her voice mail made it easy for me not to call her back. She wanted to know how I was doing.

I changed into yoga pants and a cotton hoodie and medicated my smarting emotional aches with a long walk on the beach. There is a calming aura at the ocean's edge, despite the frothing foam, crashing waves, and roaring white noise. The ocean looks the same on your good days and your bad days. Nice to know on the worst of days that there are a few things you can utterly count on.

After a late lunch of fish tacos at a sidewalk café and then a long walk back, I finally returned to the cottage a little before two, my feet aching. A purple, orange, and white envelope was leaning up against my front door when I stepped onto the porch and opened the screen door.

A FedEx envelope.

I scanned the *From* label as I unlocked the door.

Premier Travel out of Los Angeles. My breath caught in the back of my throat.

I threw my keys onto the little table by the door and tore open the envelope. Inside was a folded piece of paper, an American Express cash card, and an airline ticket in my name. With a quickening pulse, I zeroed in on the destination.

Florence, Italy.

A tiny gasp burst past my lips.

The date? A red-eye out of Los Angeles. That left that night. In five hours.

I leaned back against the wall, dazed. It had to be a mistake. I reread the date and time. Twice. Three times.

The ticket in my name was for that night, leaving out of Los Angeles at seven.

I roared something unintelligible.

How could he do this? How could he do it like this?

I unfolded the piece of paper, and my eyes met my father's handwriting.

Angel,

I hope you can forgive me for not giving you any notice. I know we were talking about later in May. I am sorry. It has to be like this, or I won't be able to pull it off at all. Don't let anyone talk you out of getting on that plane. Just pack your bags and get to the airport. You deserve this trip. You deserve so much more than this trip. I am a rotten husband and skunk of a man, but I don't want to be a terrible father. You deserve this trip. My mother always wanted you to be able to go, angel. Please get on the plane. Bring the cash card.

I love you,

Dad

I read the note twice, my heart pounding in double time the second go-around. I tipped my head back against the wall, the fish tacos feeling very near to my throat.

"This is insane!" I moaned toward heaven.

How could I even get to Los Angeles by seven? I wasn't packed. I had no one lined up to take care of Alex. Geoffrey and Beatriz were expecting me to be at work on Monday. It was impossible. How could I even think of just leaving work unannounced for… I looked at the ticket to see for how long my father had booked our trip. The return date was open ended.

Open ended.

I was perplexed for only a moment.

Dad was letting me decide how long I would stay because he wasn't planning on coming back with me. He was staying in Florence. I would be coming home alone, just like I was leaving alone.

He wasn't coming back.

My father had taken Allison's money and gone to Florence ahead of me, and he wasn't coming back.

God, what should I do?

And this time it really was a prayer.

I stood there, my back against the firm wall, weighing my options. If I wasn't on that plane, he would be standing at the airport in Florence tomorrow, waiting for no one. I had no way to get ahold of him.

He was expecting me.

He knew other people would talk me out of going. He must've also thought that if I waited, Allison would find a way to cancel the ticket, especially if my father had bought it with one of their jointly held credit cards.

Plus, if I didn't get on that plane, when would I see him again? When would any of us see him again? He was in trouble, and he was running away from it. I shuddered.

I needed to pack.

And I would have to find a way to LA. I dashed into the bedroom, grabbing my cell phone from my purse as I swept past the kitchen table. I pressed Gabe's number hoping I would catch him before he left to help his friend move, but there was no answer. Next I tried Kara. Again, I had to leave a quick voice mail. Who else could I impose upon to drive me to LAX on no notice? I cringed at the audacity of it. It's a two-and-half-hour drive to LAX from La Jolla.

I yanked a suitcase out of my closet and pressed the speed dial for my mother. She'd think it unwise, but she'd take me.

Again, no answer.

"Come on!" I railed against heaven, wanting to blame someone in charge for everyone having other plans that afternoon.

I scrolled through my contacts. I didn't feel comfortable asking anyone else to do this. It was madness.

Where was my mother, for Pete's sake? It was a Saturday afternoon!

"She should be home!" I yelled to Alex.

And then it dawned on me that she might be with Devon. Maybe she had her phone on silent because they were out somewhere. I ran back to the kitchen and dumped the contents of my purse onto the table. I rummaged through the mess, looking for the folded Post-it note where I'd scribbled Devon's number from his e-mail regarding the evening we had coffee. I snagged it and punched in the numbers. On the third ring, he answered. He had a soothing voice, even when just saying "Hello."

"Devon, it's Meg. I am so sorry to bother you, but is my mother with you?"

"Oh. No, she's not. I think she has a baby shower this afternoon. Is something the matter? Are you okay?"

He just had to sound so kind and fatherly.

"I…I just really need to talk to her. Is the shower at someone's house? Is it close?"

"Uh, I think it's at a restaurant. I'm not sure where. Meg, what is it? What's wrong?"

It seemed the very walls of my cozy borrowed house were pressing in on me, forcing me to realize the situation was too big and too complicated. I couldn't find a way to make it work. The next set of words spilled out of my mouth like air out of a balloon.

"I need to get to LAX. I need to be on a plane."

"Los Angeles? Today?"

"Yes, today." I sank onto a kitchen chair.

"Does this have anything to do with your dad going missing?"

My mother had told him about Allison's phone call. And probably her own phone call with me. "He sent me a ticket. I got it in a FedEx envelope ten minutes ago. The flight leaves for Florence at seven."

"Italy?"

"Yes, Italy."

"And you're going to go." He didn't phrase it like a question. His tone was indistinguishable. Did he think I was irresponsible or crazy or daring? I couldn't tell.

"I think my dad might be in trouble. He took a bunch of money from his wife. From her grandfather's estate or something. And his sister called me yesterday. He apparently owes money everywhere."

"So is he meeting you at the airport?"

"He sent me a cash card and told me to get to the plane. I think he might already be there. And that he's not planning to come back with me."

Seconds of silence.

"I've got to find out where my mom is. Did she say anything about where she was going?" I rested my forehead in my hand to knead my temple.

"No. No, she didn't."

"Great."

Now what? I was thinking. *Would Geoffrey take me? No, no. He was going to hit the roof when he opened the e-mail he'd get Monday morning. Who else could I impose upon?*

As I pondered, Devon spoke. "I can take you."

I stopped kneading. "What was that?"

"I'll take you to the airport. When do you need to leave?"

I needed a ride. He was willing. The perfect man, who held family in high regard, understood why I had to go. "I also have a cat," I blurted out of nowhere, as Alex wove his warm body between my ankles.

"Your mom and I can figure out a way to take care of your cat. When do you need to leave?"

"Like, now."

"Can you be ready to go in half an hour?"

"Yes." I rose to my feet in a rush and Alex darted away.

I had thirty minutes to get ready to go to the one place I'd wanted to go to my whole life.

❧

It's amazing how productive a person can be when she has no choice. Twenty-eight minutes after I hung up with Devon, I was pulling my zipped suitcase and a carry-on to the door. I'd no plan for what I tossed in for clothes. What was easiest to grab was what I threw in. Skirts and cotton blouses. Thin sweaters with three-quarter-length sleeves. Rosette-studded knit tops. The one clean pair of jeans I had left. A pair of black flats, white sandals, honey-leather slip-ons. An extra bra. Underwear. A handful of jewelry. Purse-sized perfume bottles, a quick assortment of makeup, and a pink shawl. I shoved my laptop into my carry-on, as well as my camera, the charger, my passport and purse, and the two hundred dollars I keep in my sock drawer for emergencies. As Devon knocked on my door, I remembered the FedEx envelope with the ticket, the note, and the cash card.

I was ready.

I opened the door, and Devon stood on the welcome mat with the afternoon sun casting a haloed glow on his head. He smiled and the curve of his grin revealed an unspoken reluctance.

"All set?" he said.

I stood there, frozen for a second. "Not having second thoughts about taking me, are you?" I don't know why, but his opinion suddenly mattered to me.

"Are you?" He held my gaze, as a kind friend would, while I weighed my options one last time.

"I don't know when I'll see him again if I don't go," I said, certain now that that was my greatest fear.

He nodded and reached for my suitcase. "Let's hit the road then."

My hands were shaking as I locked my front door and followed Devon out to his car. He pulled away from the curb, and I watched the cottage fall away behind us.

Our eyes met as he watched for traffic, and his crooked smile cracked across his face. "Think she will hate me for this?" he said.

"Only for a moment or two. Then she will hate herself for not hearing her phone when I tried to call her."

"Would she have taken you to the airport?"

I could see he was searching for affirmation that he was doing right by my mother. Mom would've put up a momentary fuss, but she would've quickly seen my side of things. "She would've," I said.

"But she'll be worried about you traveling solo on an international flight." He laughed, no doubt thinking of my mom and her addiction to safety.

"You'll have to promise me you won't get into a taxicab alone," he continued. "Make sure your dad is with you if you take a cab anywhere. Otherwise stick to public transportation. And don't walk past any parked vans if your dad's not with you."

I grinned. "You sound just like her."

He laughed as well. "I know what she will worry about. And she'll worry less if I tell her I reminded you to be careful."

My admiration for this man tumbled about inside me, and I wished we were just on our way to San Diego's airport, a fifteen-minute trip.

"Thanks for doing this," I said quickly. "You probably have better things to do than drive to LA and back tonight."

He shrugged. "Not really. I don't have better things to do than this. I know this is important to you." He turned to me to give me an affirming nod, and his sweet empathy for the sojourning daughter off to Europe on a moment's notice sent me diving into my purse for the *Wicked* CD I'd shoved inside for the drive up.

"Well, still," I mumbled. "It's quite an imposition, and don't tell me it's not. Mind if I put in some music?"

"Of course not."

I slid it in.

"I love this soundtrack." I sank into my seat, and he cranked up the volume.

"Me too," he said.

We fell into silence as he drove, and the music careened around the car. I pulled out my phone and e-mailed my mother, Geoffrey, Gabe, and Kara, telling each one a slightly different version of where I was headed and why.

An hour and a half later on the 405, traffic snarled a bit, and I began to panic that I would miss my flight.

"We've still got plenty of time, don't worry," Devon said more than once, kind and calming.

When at last he pulled up curbside at the terminal, I told him I didn't need help getting my bags. He could just stay put behind the wheel and drop me off, and I could avoid any kind of warm, paternal hug or awkward handshake. I wanted so much to express my gratitude to Devon for bringing me and risking my mother's annoyance, for not saying so much as one unkind word about my father, for knowing small talk on the drive up was not what I needed, for offering to take care of my cat, for soothing words and compassionate glances. But what came out of my mouth didn't reflect any of that.

"Thanks a lot," I said, and I reached for the door handle to dash out, grab my bags from his backseat, and send him on his way. But he reached out his arm and laid his hand on my wrist.

"Hold on just a second." With his other hand, he drew out folded-over bills from his chest pocket. Money. The one on top was a one-hundred-dollar bill. He held them out to me. I made no move to take them.

"Please?" he said.

"I…I have some cash on me. And my credit card. And I've got the cash card my dad stuck in the envelope with the plane ticket. I'll be fine."

"Yes, but…but I think it's been too crazy an afternoon for you to be able to think about that cash card and how your dad was able to get it. I think it would bother you tomorrow if you had to use it. If he really took it from his wife's inheritance, then from the little I know about you, I think that would bother you. Am I right?"

He was exactly right. There was no way I could use that cash card if it really was Allison's inheritance from her grandfather. Tomorrow I would think of it and cringe if I had to use it. Devon never ceased to be too good to be true.

"Yes," I murmured.

"Then please take the cash. Your mom would want you to. And you can pay me back when the trip is over, if that will make you feel better. It's just a couple hundred bucks."

The airport unloading and loading recording was blasting in my ears as I sat there with the car door open and one foot outside Devon's car. I couldn't sit there pondering the options. I reached for the money.

"I'll pay you back." I stuffed the bills in my purse. On impulse I reached into the FedEx envelope, pulled out the cash card, and handed it to him. "Can you give this to my mother? Tell her to send it back to Allison. Tell her to put a little note on it that we think this probably belongs to her."

Devon nodded wordlessly and slipped the cash card into his shirt pocket. Then he smiled. "I probably don't need to tell you to find a way to e-mail your mom when you get there."

I stepped fully out of the car. "As soon as I land."

I yanked open his back door, pulled out my suitcase and carry-on, and pushed the door shut. The world around me was ablaze with taillights, headlights, blinking turn signals, shiny chrome and glass, all against a bronzed, pre-twilight sky. People at the curb toted their suitcases like pull-toys, dashing away from parked cars after quick kisses, to be on their way to distant places. No one leaves LAX after five unless you are headed somewhere far away.

I leaned in the still-open passenger-side front door. I wanted to quip something like, "I owe you one," but I surprised myself by looking straight into Devon's kind face and telling him he had been a godsend to me.

"Be careful. Be safe," he said.

"I will."

"You're sure he's there?"

"He's there."

"Oh! And the key to your house?"

I stared at him, flabbergasted. He wanted the key to the cottage?

"Your cat," he said.

For Pete's sake. Alex. The cat. I pulled my keys out of my purse and handed them to him. "Yikes. Thanks," I said.

As I grabbed hold of the car door to close it, he called my name, and I ducked my head in.

"Just one more thing. He… You may not be able to convince him to come back with you."

I swallowed. "I know."

"Try to enjoy Florence, anyway. It's so beautiful."

I probably would have kissed his cheek had he been standing next to me saying good-bye. As it was, I could only nod and give him a thumbs-up.

I pushed the door shut, waved, and then stepped into the flow of people bound for the skies.

Nora

Nurse told me, that spring morning as we watched Maria ride, that my father was like a fine horse no one had tamed. I thought she meant my father was like a happy, wild horse that no one had yet caught, one that could run free in the countryside with the wind in his mane and never had a rider tugging him this way and that, telling him which way to go.

"I like wild horses," I had said. I'd never actually seen a wild horse, but I knew that before a horse had been broken into submission, it was its own master. The unbroken horse was more like a soaring eagle than a beast to carry us here and there. This image of my father running through fields of dewy grass with his arms stretched wide, with no reins, no whip, no crop, made me smile. So I said it again.

"I like wild horses!"

And Nurse, who would shield me from the truth for yet a little while longer, told me we'd been outside long enough. It was time for lessons.

13

I have flown internationally a few times, and I knew getting to the gate might take a while, but the line through security moved quickly; a gift from the heavens. I arrived breathless at my gate just as coach was boarding. I felt like throwing some confetti in the air. A mere five hours earlier, I had been eating fish tacos at a sidewalk café, expecting to do a load of laundry when I got home, and now I was boarding a plane for Europe.

It wasn't until I had my seat belt around my waist that I fully grasped that if I slept at all in the next few hours, I would awaken in Paris; at an airport like this one, with intercom voices I wouldn't understand and directional signs that would take me by pictures to the second plane I would board—the one that would take me to Florence.

Florence.

I pressed my head against the glass of my little window, missing my nonna like I hadn't missed her since I was a little girl. My dad was finally taking me to Florence, but he wasn't with me on the plane, and I wasn't sure he would be on the return flight either. Our days and nights would be shadowed by what he had done.

When we were airborne and cruising far above the dark land below us, I pulled out my laptop, willing to pay to use the plane's Wi-Fi so that I could see if my mother or Gabe had a chance to see my e-mail yet.

My mother had, and her reaction was what I'd expected: shock that my father would leave for Florence ahead of me and force me to travel alone, followed by prognostications of bad weather, cancelled flights, missing luggage, a stolen passport, and food poisoning. She told me to e-mail her when I'd arrived, and I assured her I would. Gabe seemed genuinely disappointed that he'd been out when I needed the ride to LAX that he'd promised. He, too, asked me to e-mail back or text him when I got there.

I checked the weather in Florence, used my credit card to buy an international data plan for my phone for the next several days—gasping audibly at the price but knowing I had to have it—and sent an e-mail to Lorenzo telling him I was on my way and hoping with all my heart he and Renata weren't off on a research trip to Portugal or something. I couldn't imagine making this trip after all this time and not even seeing him. I was about to log out and attempt to sleep when a new e-mail deposited itself into my inbox.

From Sofia Borelli.

I hastily opened it. She had sent me two additional chapters, as I had asked. Excited, I opened the documents to have them ready to read before attempting to nap. Then I e-mailed her back and told her my trip to Florence had been bumped up and I was actually on my way there. I asked if she'd be available in the next few days to meet, offering up a tiny prayer that she had at least some free time this week.

Then I logged off the Wi-Fi and settled into my seat to read what Sofia had sent me.

Florence, when you come to visit her, will not welcome you with showers of greetings. It will not matter to her that you are there, nor will she notice when you leave. She is not one for sentiment, and she does not need you to love her. If no more tourists came, the vendors and café owners and artists on the piazzas would miss the tourists, but Florence would not. She is indifferent to the visitor. What you take from Florence when you leave, you take for yourself; she does

not give it to you. That might seem cold to you, but to a Medici, it is
not so hard to understand. Your life is what you make of it, not what
happens to you. Papa told me this. And he told me that's what
Florence is and her people are.

It's not as if the city is uncaring or unfriendly. I had an American man tell me once that people in Florence weren't friendly to
him. They wouldn't give him directions when he was lost or present
him with the check for his meal or offer a table to sit at though he
stood for many long minutes just inside the door of a restaurant.

I told him, as my father told me a very long time ago, that here
in Florence it is customary to discover for yourself what it is you
think you need. Asking for directions is not discovery. This same
man told me, in a rather terse tone, that asking for directions is how
you find your way. But I told him gently that asking for directions is
how you rob yourself of finding your way yourself. In Florence you
do not wait for your check; you request it. And you do not wait to be
seated. You decide for yourself where you will sit. It is not that way
in America, he said. Florentines are rude and unhelpful. He did not
tip me.

It is all about perspective, isn't it? It is how you see something
that you decide what it is. And in Florence, perspective is celebrated,
not reprimanded. Always.

In the time of the Renaissance, art and science were not separate
views on life, but one and the same. Today, science is studied at one
college and art at another, but the two disciplines were entwined in
the days of old. The great artists insisted on correct proportions, and
they were masters of perspective. Perspective is what the heart sees.
Nora whispered this to me. Perspective is mathematical and precise,
but it is also artistic and unfixed. I think she meant that we see all

the time what the great masters of the Renaissance saw; we just don't know it. When you look at two parallel lines, they seem to converge in the distance, like a long stretch of highway that melts into the sky at the very end of what you are capable of seeing. Your head tells you these lines do not converge, but your eye tells you they do. And because your eyes tell you they do, you can imagine they do. This is what is called the vanishing point. Florence's Leonardo da Vinci and Donato di Niccolò di Betto Bardi—you know him as Donatello— were the first to use it. Brunelleschi, the brilliant architect of the Duomo, was a master of linear perspective. Some say he invented it. Wise Brunelleschi merely discovered what God had already set across man's path to stumble upon. And that is, what we see is not always what is. And what is, we often cannot see until we train our eyes to see it.

When Papa was teaching me how to paint, he said I must first imagine my drawing as an open window through which to see the painted world beyond. He drew a straight line to represent the horizon and then rays connecting my eye to a point in the distance, the vanishing point. The horizon, he told me, is where the sky meets the ground. I told him the sky never meets the ground. But Papa said, "But you can imagine that it does."

In the Uffizi, once the Medici offices but now a gallery of the Medici art collection, there is a painting by da Vinci called *The Annunciation*. There are many paintings of the Annunciation and the Crucifixion in Florence. So many, I lose count. Christ is coming! Christ is leaving! as if nothing in the middle of His extraordinary life is worth capturing in paint.

If you look at da Vinci's *The Annunciation* and don't rush past, you will see the vanishing point. And you will see where the horizon meets the ground. On the left side of the painting, an angel holds out a lily. On the right side, the Virgin Mary responds in graceful surprise and awe to the greeting. In between the angel and the Virgin is the horizon, the rest of the world. Da Vinci painted her calm and composed, as if she saw angels every day and had just been told only that the kitchen was fresh out of figs for breakfast.

The hills in the distance—beyond the tiny coastal city and the boats in the water that everyone in a hurry misses—represent all that is beyond the moment in time when the angel told the Virgin she would bear the Savior of the world. That is the vanishing point. Without it, there would be no sense that this moment is a slice of time.

When my father first showed me *The Annunciation*, he showed me the place in the painting where this moment in time and the rest of eternity collide. I was seven. And I stood there for many long minutes transfixed by the unseen dot on the canvas that held my gaze. Then Nora called to me, rewarding me for finding the place where the painting began and ended. She told me a secret that I share with you now.

The Virgin's slender hand, the one not raised in astonishment at the angel's words, rests on an open page of Scripture. The verses are in shades of red and black ink, like patterned stripes on wallpaper. The letters seem to be neither Latin nor Hebrew, nor any alphabet we might recognize. But the canvas whispered to me that the Virgin was reading from the book of Isaiah.

"But he was wounded for our transgressions, he was bruised for our iniquities: the chastisement of our peace was upon him; and with his stripes we are healed. All we like sheep have gone astray; we have turned every one to his own way; and the LORD hath laid on him the iniquity of us all."

The stripes. The red and black rows.

I began to cry when I heard this because I knew then the Virgin had to know what lay ahead. What lay ahead was written under her own fingers, and she was reading it. And I also knew why the angel carried a lily. It was the kind I had seen at a funeral procession, a flower that spoke of love and loss.

My father leaned down and asked me what was the matter, and I told him the painting had whispered to me what the Virgin was reading.

Papa always knew when to say absolutely nothing. He just put his arm over my shoulders and waited. After a while Nora's whispering ceased, and the painting was quiet again.

Now that day we were there was my father's day off, but a lady at the Uffizi knew he was a guide, and she sent a couple over to him because they had a question about the painting.

When they came close to us, Papa stood and I wiped my eyes. The couple looked down at me, eyebrows arched, thinking perhaps I had just been scolded for running in the museum. They asked Papa if another artist had begun *The Annunciation* and da Vinci just finished it, because that is what they had heard. Papa told them yes, it's believed da Vinci's mentor, Verrocchio, began the painting and instructed da Vinci to complete it as part of his training. They said, "Oh." And they glanced at the painting and walked away.

They did not see the vanishing point. They did not see where the horizon meets the ground, where a moment in time meets the rest of eternity. If they had stayed longer than five seconds, my father might've told them to look for it. He might've even told them, by the way, that da Vinci's contribution to another painting, the *Baptism of Christ,* was so magnificent, it was rumored that this very same Verrocchio threatened to stop painting.

When they were gone, I asked Papa why they walked away so quickly. He said it happens all the time and not to let it bother me.

But it did bother me. And he kissed my head and said, "That's because of who you are."

Da Vinci once said, "Perspective is the rein and rudder of painting." That sad couple walked away, oblivious that the painting wished to take them somewhere.

You don't have to be a Medici to understand a painting is never just about who painted it. It's also what you see when you look at it.

When I take people to visit the Basilica di San Lorenzo, I sense within me, still, after all these years, a tug of melancholy. The basilica is the burial place of most of the Medici family.

It is older than the Medici family itself. Historians say it was consecrated in the fourth century after Christ, but it has been rebuilt many times. History tends to be hard on the church. The one we see today is mostly the work of Brunelleschi in the fifteenth century.

The Medici Chapels at the Sagrestia Nuova, the New Sacristy, are showcased by Michelangelo's tomb of Giuliano de' Medici— watched over by the statues *Night* and *Day*—and the tomb of his brother, Lorenzo the Magnificent—graced with *Dusk* and *Dawn.* People ask me why *Dawn* and *Night* are female and *Dusk* and *Day* are male. Their genders were assigned to them based on Italian nouns, but there is more to it than that. I will tell you in a moment what Nora told me.

Giuliano de' Medici was brutally assassinated in 1478 in front of parishioners celebrating the Mass at the Duomo. Right there in the cathedral, by murderers masquerading as comrades. The Pazzi Rebellion was designed to send both Medici brothers, bloody and dead, to their Maker. Whenever there is a family in power, there is always another family that wants to take its place. Lorenzo, who was very fond of his brother, narrowly escaped.

The Medici fortunes dwindled under the rule of Lorenzo the Magnificent, just one of the reasons he is not my favorite ancestor. He was most certainly unfaithful to his wife, though when she died of tuberculosis, he wrote of his great sorrow. Still, Lorenzo funded the school that Michelangelo attended as a young apprentice and was patron to Botticelli, whose work I love. And Lorenzo was a poet, though an odd one. He would write lovely poems of devotion to God and then dreadful parodies that my parents would not let me read. Here is a bit of the poem of his I like best:

I saw my Lady by a purling brook
With laughing maidens, where green
     branches twined;
O never since that primal, passionate look
Have I beheld her face so soft and kind
(Sonnet 1)

It is most likely my favorite because it was my papa's favorite. He would recite the whole piece to my mother while she washed dishes, and he would pretend the sink was the brook and I was the laughing maiden. I had to be told what a purling brook was, because I thought, of course, it was pearling brook, and I asked my papa how the oysters got there since oysters are only in the sea. Then he told me purling is a way of describing a brook that twirls and twists, like a dance. The tiny loops along the edge of lacy braid are its purling. Knitters know what purling is. That image seemed prettier to me than a pearl and sweeter than an oyster. A pearl is a lovely thing, but an oyster is not. Sometimes pretty things got lost in oyster-stink. A lacy braid never does.

The statue known as *Night,* my tour people are always quick to note, is supposed to be sleeping, but she looks like she is having anguished nightmares. *Day* does not appear to be enjoying the blessings of another day on earth either. They are both in postures that, were you to attempt to mimic them, would have you quickly experiencing muscle spasms and other little agonies.

Turn your eye to *Dusk* and *Dawn,* and you will see that *Dawn,* beautiful in feminine form, wears the face of grief. *Dusk,* with his relaxed, partially finished face, sits cross-legged with his chin dipped to his chest, as if there is nothing he can do to change what the next day will bring.

Despite their muscular anatomy and marbled austerity, the four faces appear robbed of peace and strength.

In the agony of my grief at the loss of my mother and my marriage, Nora whispered to me that *Night* and *Dawn,* as female, reveal our guaranteed mortality. They are life-givers only during the time their bodies can create and sustain life. Resigned *Day* and *Dusk* know they cannot change that fact. But, Nora told me, do not forget that the day that ends at nightfall is given back to you on the morrow. You get it back. And you keep getting it back, so it is up to you to decide what you will do with it.

❧

The bong of the aircraft's intercom pulled me from a strange place of sleep. We were about to land at Charles de Gaulle where I would have two hours to convince myself it was not the middle of the night but two thirty in the afternoon. I forced myself to eat a roast beef sandwich during the layover, even though what I really wanted was a bowl of Cheerios. I found the gate for my connecting Air France flight, pulled out my laptop, and checked my e-mail again, relieved to see a response from Lorenzo. He had written his answer in a hurry on his phone, but he told me he and Renata were in town, he was thrilled that I was coming, and he wanted me to call when I got there. He included his cell phone number. There was no new e-mail from Sofia. I put my laptop away and let my head fall forward to rest. Twenty minutes later when my flight began to board, a young Indian woman with a scarlet drop on her forehead woke me and gestured that our flight was boarding. I thanked her and made my way onto the plane. Just two more hours and I'd be there.

I gave in to another nap on the flight from Paris to Florence. It seemed I had no sooner buckled myself into my seat than I was being told we were beginning our descent into Florence. I didn't have a window seat this time, and I couldn't see much. But the day was turning amber as we made our approach, and I itched to see more.

The line through customs seemed to take far too long. As I waited, I tried texting my dad that I had arrived, but the message failed. Then I even tried calling him, but I got a voice message that the person I was trying to reach was unavailable. Finally I was on my way to baggage claim. Big-city airports differ only in the choice of tile on the floor, names of the coffee shops inside the terminal, and the language of the relaxed-voice announcer over the loudspeakers. I sped toward baggage claim, eager to meet up with my father and get outside.

But I didn't see him in baggage claim.

People run late, I told myself. *It's Italy. Give him a minute.*

I retrieved my suitcase and searched the sea of faces for my father. All around me reunions and meet-ups were taking place with hugs and hand-shakes, double kisses on cheeks, and happy, loud greetings. A few people stared at me, wondering perhaps who I was looking for. One gentleman, older than me, with his shirt half-tucked into frayed pants and carrying a single duffel bag, asked me something in rapid Italian. He smiled at me, and then his gaze traveled down my body.

"No Italiano," I said as I moved away from him.

I checked my phone. I walked up and down the baggage claim area. I checked my phone again. Outside, the day was giving over to night. Inside, my excitement was giving over to panic.

I was alone in Florence.

And my dad wasn't coming for me.

Nora

My favorite of Master da Vinci's paintings is *The Annunciation*. It has always been my favorite. There is such calm beauty in the brush strokes; you could hardly know that the angel bending to the Virgin Mother is giving her news that will change her life. The Virgin's face is so serene. Surely she knew the hard road that she was to walk as one betrothed yet pregnant. Surely she knew she could be stoned for being with child and not yet married.

Her life would forever be tied to scandal.

The looks she had to endure. The sneers. The unkind words. The whispers of some and the derisive comments of others.

Surely she knew what lay before her.

It was a kindness that the Virgin was sent an angel to prepare her for what was to come.

Sometimes I wonder what I would have done if I had known beforehand what would befall me. But then I remember that the Virgin simply did as she was asked. Knowing what was to come, she was equipped for the assignment she was given. It did not afford her a choice of changing it.

14

I remember getting separated from my parents just once when I was little. I was six and we were at an outdoor shopping mall in LA. There were little kiosks in between the stores, and at one of them, a woman was selling silk butterflies the size of dinner plates. They sparkled as if they were made of pixie dust, and the breeze caught their gauzy wings, coaxing them into gentle movement on the pitched sides of her sandwich-board displays.

I stopped to look at them, transfixed by their elegance and enormity. My parents, deep into a conversation that had them both ticked at each other and which neither could remember later, didn't realize I was no longer at their side. They kept walking into a press of other shoppers, declaring their differences, while I stood as one enchanted, unaware that minutes later I would be alone.

When a child realizes she is lost, the first emotion that rises is panic that this is the beginning of a nightmarish life forevermore without parents. I remember the swell of fear rising up from my stomach, the speed with which tears formed at my eyes, and the quirky assessment that the beautiful butterflies were malevolent creatures who'd connived with evil forces to steal my parents from me. My mother had told me if I ever got lost and I couldn't find a policeman, to look for a mother with little kids. She told me I could probably trust a mother with little kids to help me, but I probably couldn't trust anyone else.

Even though panic tore through me, this is exactly what I did. I ran to a woman pushing a stroller with a squealing toddler inside it and wailed to her that my parents had disappeared. My mother had been right about mothers with little kids. That mother knew just what to do. We waited, she and I, at the place where I'd last seen my mom and dad. At the butterflies kiosk. "They will come for you," this mother said. And sure enough, my parents returned to me, as terrified as I was, within five minutes.

As I stood there in baggage claim, I felt my gaze being tugged to mothers with little kids. I watched as mothers grabbed for hands, shushed the tired and too-traveled, cuddled infants, and toted off toddlers who babbled and pointed. I wanted to hail one of those mothers and be rescued the way I had been when I was six.

I'd given no thought to what I would do if my dad wasn't there to meet me. It hadn't occurred to me that he wouldn't be there. How long could I wait for him? Half an hour? An hour? It would be dark in an hour.

What if he wasn't here in Florence at all?

In my mind I could hear Devon asking me, *"Are you sure he's already there?"* and me answering, *"He's there."*

I had been so sure my dad would want to be here with me I hadn't considered that he never said he would be.

And now I was alone in Florence with a suitcase, a credit card, my sock-drawer money and two hundred dollars in borrowed cash. I couldn't waste time considering how immensely disappointed I was in my dad; I had to figure out what to do. I yanked my phone out of my purse and keyed in Lorenzo's number, thanking God I had it. I texted that I was stranded at the airport. My dad wasn't there to meet me. And I needed help. I waited twenty minutes for him to text me back, knowing that every minute he didn't, the sun was sinking lower into the western sky.

I was going to have to find a place to stay on my own, and I couldn't wait any longer. I reached into my carry-on for my laptop, hoping I could find an airport café with Wi-Fi to browse for hotels near the city center and wracking my brain to remember what street Lorenzo and Renata lived on, so that I could find a place close to them. As I reached, my fingers felt the pages of Sofia's printed pages.

Sofia.

She lived in a flat in the same building as Lorenzo.

And she had printed her address in the header of every page of her chapters. I pulled out one of her pages and made a beeline for a kiosk to change my dollars into euros. Ten minutes later I was outside on the curb in the last remnants of the day, getting into a taxi, alone. I could hear Devon's request echoing in my ears that I should not do this very thing. But what else could I do? I showed the driver the address, and he nodded, zooming off with such speed that my head rocked into the back of the seat as he pulled away.

Despite the headache from lack of sleep and utter disillusionment with all things related to my father, my eyes drank in the scenery outside the taxi window as the driver zipped along at a dizzying speed, tailgating buses, tiny smart cars, and even Vespas and pedestrians. The crush of movement all around us was almost suffocating, even though the taxi windows were closed. I felt small and expendable as he dove in and out of lanes of traffic. I wasn't a true part of the daily count of people and cars and scooters and bicycles, just an unnumbered spectator. But as the buildings and storefronts that dripped modernity began to give way to old stone and tile, and as the streets grew narrower, I began to sense an underlying calm. Not in the press of people outside the windows, but in the steady ancientness of the buildings we passed. The people in the other cars and on bikes and even walking—to what seemed their certain peril—seemed unaware of where they were, and I was superaware of where I was.

The trepidation inside me was real, but below the worry was a calming layer, like the voice of my grandmother, or the voice of the long-ago mother with the stroller, or the voice of Devon driving me to LAX in traffic, assuring me that everything was going to be okay.

Honey-stone walls, ancient and beautiful, rose up on either side of me as the driver turned onto a narrow street, passed a quiet piazza, and sped to a stop in front of a leather boutique. The driver pointed with his thumb to a door next to the store and rattled off something in Italian. Dark was gathering, and the street was lit only by the headlights of other cars and the interior security lights of the now-closed store.

The driver turned to me, and repeated whatever it was he'd said, and pointed to the door. Then he said what surely was Italian for, "You might want to get out. This is it."

He hopped out to get my bag and a better tip. I paid him twenty euro, and in seconds he was gone and I was standing at the door that led to Sofia's and Lorenzo and Renata's apartments. I knew before trying that the entry door would be locked. But I tried it anyway. Then I saw a series of six call buttons and two names I instantly recognized. I pressed the button for DiSantis and waited. Nothing. I pressed it again and again. Then I pressed Borelli.

"Please be home," I whispered.

But there was no answer.

I pulled out my phone and texted Lorenzo: "Outside your apartment. It's dark out here. Where are you?"

I waited. He didn't text me back.

Night was shrinking my field of vision, and I didn't know what I was going to do. I had to find a hotel. But how would I find it? I needed Wi-Fi or a policeman or an angel from God. I leaned against the old stone around the heavy wooden door and willed myself to remain calm.

"Help," I whispered to the cool rock, exhausted from sleep deprivation and sensory overload. I wasn't sure if I could summon the energy to find another taxi and communicate my need to find an available hotel room that I could afford. Several people brushed past me, nearly knocking over my suitcase, on their way home to their supper and cozy beds.

Then I felt a hand on my elbow.

"Posso aiutare?"

I turned toward the voice, which was soft and melodic, and saw a woman my mother's age grasping a closed pink polka-dot umbrella in her other hand. I knew before I even said the words that help had come.

"Sofia Borelli?"

The woman smiled wide. *"Si."*

I nearly fell into that smile. "I'm Meg Pomeroy."

Her smiled wavered and I felt a tremor of unease.

Then she grasped me as if we were long lost classmates. "Marguerite!"

Yes. I nodded.

"You are here!" she exclaimed. "In *Firenze*! Lorenzo did not tell me you were coming!"

Her voice was like my nonna's. Chewy and sweet like taffy. I shook my head. "I don't think he knows I've arrived yet. I've tried texting him. I don't think he's gotten my messages."

"I thought you were coming next month!"

"There's been a change in plans," I said, as brightly as I could. As if I always drop everything and jump on a plane to Europe when the mood strikes.

She noticed my suitcase, and then she looked past me. "And you are here with your papa, no?"

A tiny sigh escaped me. "No. Actually I'm not."

This perplexed her, as an hour ago it had also baffled me. But for different reasons. "I thought he was going to meet me here in Florence," I went on. "But I don't think he's meeting me here after all." I did not intend to sound like a little lost child, but that's what I sounded like.

She frowned slightly. "You are alone?"

Yes. Alone. "Looks that way."

Her frown deepened.

"Ms. Borelli—" I began.

"Sofia."

"Sofia, could I impose upon you to help me find a hotel? I...I guess I thought my dad would take care of those arrangements, and I don't think he did." I thought of the cash card I'd given to Devon. That piece of plastic was my dad's arrangements.

"No, no." She shook her head gently, and I felt my heart sag. Weariness crept in like a purse snatcher, robbing me of the tiny bit of strength I had left.

"You will stay with me." She reached for the handle of my suitcase. "You will stay with me. Please."

Surprise mixed with equal parts relief and apprehension spread over me. I knew next to nothing about Sofia other than she claimed she was the last of the Medicis and that statues and paintings spoke to her in the voice of a young woman long dead. But I also knew Lorenzo liked her. Said she was one of the kindest people he knew. And where else was I going to find a place to stay? Still, it seemed too big an imposition. "Oh. I couldn't. You weren't expecting me."

Sofia pulled my suitcase closer to her. "I am expecting you now. Stay with me. I have a nice little guest room. And please. I know this does not mean you will publish my book, eh? Not to worry. You stay with me, I will show you Firenze. Florence. Yes?"

"It's too much to ask," I said. "I'm not sure how long I will be staying."

"You are not asking. I am. And it does not matter how long you will be staying." She reached into her pocket for a key ring and slid a key into the lock on the door. "I was just at church praying to God about wanting to be of use to Him today. And see? Here you are. I ask; He sends."

Church. I forgot it was Sunday.

She pushed the door open. *"Benvenuto!"*

Welcome.

Nora

There are moments when I can imagine an angel was sent to me. In every painting and statue in Florence where angelic hosts are going about their sacred business, I picture one of them was the very one sent to me, when I was too little to properly stow away the memory, preparing me for what lay in store.

I can imagine it.

Florence is full of angels on canvas and in stone. I can imagine them bending toward me, telling me to be brave. I listen and listen and whisper to them that I shall try.

15

Sofia had mentioned in her manuscript that the flat she lived in had been in her family for more than a century, but I was rendered speechless nonetheless when she opened the door to her building and I stepped into antiquity. The wide marble steps to her second-floor flat, subdued with use and age, and the banister, thick as a gymnast's balance beam, all bore marks and nicks from a hundred moving days. And I could smell the past on the coral plaster walls as I climbed the steps. It was the aroma not of age but of history.

She pointed to a door next to the landing on the second floor. "That's where Lorenzo and Renata live. And there's a retired teacher at the end there. Three more flats on the third floor." We turned toward a matching door across from Lorenzo's. "And here's my flat."

Sofia unlocked the door and led me inside. The wooden floors creaked shyly under our feet, shushed by a thin carpet runner of Persian design. She moved ahead of me to turn on lights. The narrow entry led to an open room. The walls were covered in paintings, too many to be aesthetically pleasing, although the canvases were beautifully done. Trees, river landscapes, cobblestone piazzas, fruit on vines—and the same dark-haired woman over and over. Sofia's mother, perhaps? The furniture was at least forty or fifty years old but in good repair, though a bit threadbare in places. The main room featured crowded bookshelves, a tiny television set, and windows that looked out onto the street. A small dining room lay just off the main room, and a kitchen was to our right. An arched hallway led to the bedrooms.

"Let's just put your suitcase in the guest room," she said.

I followed her, passing a room on the left filled with easels and canvases. A long table with art supplies strewn over it was the most prominent feature in the room. On the right, the bathroom was a throwback to the fifties—tiny black-and-white tiles; cream porcelain sink, commode and open tub; and minimal shelving. At the end of the hall, she pointed to a half-open door, where in the spill of streetlight invading from the window, I could see a four-poster bed and a kidney-shaped vanity with a burgundy skirt.

"I am just in there," she said. Then she turned to the room across from hers. "And here's the guest room."

She smiled at me. "This was my room practically my whole life, until my papa became ill. And of course, when I was married, I didn't live here."

We stepped inside and she flipped on a light switch. The room was no bigger than ten by ten, with a tall, twin-sized bed fluffed high with a feather mattress and pillows, matching dresser and nightstand, and a wardrobe with climbing roses painted on its sides and front. The paintings on the wall were of flowers and an outdoor flower market and a little girl gathering blooms in her arms.

I suddenly felt like I was ten. I hadn't slept in a twin bed since junior high, but at that moment it didn't matter. I'd been feeling like I was a kid since the airport.

"Will you be all right in here?" she said. "The bed is a single, but it's very cozy. You will be surprised how much. I sleep in here sometimes just to remind myself how cozy it is."

"I'm sure I will be fine," I said. The bed looked delicious to one who'd only slept a few hours and had missed a night of sleep. I pointed to the paintings. "Your father painted those?"

She smiled brightly. "Yes. The little girl is me!"

"They are beautiful."

She pushed the suitcase to the corner. "And now we eat a little something, yes? Are you hungry? Did you have supper already?"

I couldn't answer her at first. I couldn't recall what meal I'd had and when. There had been a sandwich in Paris, whenever that was. "I don't think I've eaten since lunch," I said.

She clapped her hands together. "I am so pleased I get to make you your first meal in Firenze. Come! We have a glass of wine, and I make you supper!"

She fairly skipped back to the kitchen, and I followed, bringing my purse with me so that I could keep my promise to my mother and Gabe to let them know when I had arrived. Sofia directed me to a tiny table covered in a lemon-patterned tablecloth. A closed laptop lay on it covered with a folded newspaper and a saucer with a curl of toasted bread on top of that. No wonder my presence on her doorstop surprised Sofia. Likely she hadn't looked at her e-mail since the day before when she sent me the last two chapters.

"Sorry about my plate." She grabbed the saucer and took it to the sink.

"Not at all." I took a seat at the little table. "I'm just going to let my family know I made it here."

I quickly tapped a text message to my mother. I could just imagine what she would think when she read Dad wasn't in Florence and I had to call upon a writer friend Lorenzo knew to house me. I left out the part that the same writer friend believes a dead Medici talks to her.

Sofia brought two glasses to the table and poured dark red wine from an unmarked bottle. She saw me looking for a label as she poured.

"Florence is in Tuscany; this you probably know. Many vineyards in the countryside. In the city you can take your empty bottle to any local *vino sfuso*, and they will fill it for you. You have to remember what you have them put in or make your own label. *Vino sfuso* wines are made from grapes that are what you might say, common. Not fancy, yes? Ordinary. You have to drink it soon after you buy."

She placed a plate of sliced bread and basil-flecked mozzarella balls before me. "A little snack for you while I make us supper."

I sipped the wine, and its robust warmth was soothing.

Sofia opened a fridge no taller than either one of us. "So I have some pancetta and onions. Tomatoes. I throw together with some pasta and pecorino. Some basil. You will like it?"

"Sounds wonderful."

Sofia poured olive oil into a skillet and tossed some chopped garlic into it. Then she began to brown the pancetta and onions. The little kitchen began to smell like a corner of heaven. She turned from her cookstove, a spatula in hand.

"I am just so pleased you are here," she said. "I have to pinch myself to know I am not imagining this, that I am talking to you in my kitchen."

"I can hardly believe it myself." I took another sip. "Yesterday—I think it was yesterday—I thought it would be next year before I'd finally see Florence."

She stirred and then stopped. "Next year?"

Perhaps it was the wine or the length of time I had been up, but I told Sofia exactly how I came to be at her doorstep.

"He didn't come," Sofia murmured when I was finished, speaking of my father, her voice soft with compassion.

"No. No, he didn't." I popped a mozzarella ball into my mouth. Smooth and creamy as butter.

She set a pot of water on the stove. "We will have to talk about something else, Marguerite. I do not know what to say to that."

Fine with me. I didn't know what to say to that either. My phone vibrated next to me, and I thought for sure my mother had just read my text.

But it was Lorenzo, at last. "Cara! Where are you?"

I knew it would cost me a buck a text probably, but I decided to have some fun with him.

"Where are you?" I texted back.

"At home! Where are you?"

"You always ignore people you call 'my treasure'?"

"Playing bocce ball! Left phone at flat! Just got home. Where are you?"

"Was alone on your doorstep. In the dark."

"I looked up and down the street for you!"

"Not on the street anymore."

"Tell me where you are."

"Your polizia cars are smaller than police cars in America."

"You torture me!"

I'd had my fun.

"I am next-door. At Sofia's."

I looked up at Sofia who was slicing ruby-red tomatoes. "I think we might be hearing Lorenzo knocking on your door in about two seconds."

But I was wrong. He didn't knock. He just came swooping into the room.

I'd seen Lorenzo only in head shots and Skype screens where I could see his upper body. Geoffrey and Beatriz had met Lorenzo and Renata in person at a conference in New York a couple of years back, but I hadn't been on that trip. Lorenzo had been mostly a floating head, five o'clock shadow, tanned skin, coffee-brown eyes—for four years. For some reason I was unprepared to see him with legs, moving toward me. I stood slowly from the table as he barreled into the little kitchen and swept me up in his arms to kiss me on both cheeks.

His muscled arms, the scent of his cologne, and his height and physical strength covering my body overwhelmed me. I had not been hugged by a

man since I fell into my dad's embrace on Poppy-Seed Day. I was tired from
jet lag, from suppressing my odd feelings toward Devon, from the emotional duress of the last twenty-four hours, from yet another crushing disappointment from my father. There in Lorenzo's strong arms, the brave front
I had constructed crumbled. As he laughed his way through our hug, my
defenses evaporated and traitorous tears began to ooze out of my eyes.

I wanted to stop them, but they wouldn't be stopped. He started to pull
away after he had planted his kisses, and I would not let him.

I drew my arms tighter around his neck, wanting to squeeze the manly
strength out of him, wanting to feel safe and wanted. It seemed I couldn't
hold him tight enough, and my skinny arms were like a cheap vice around
him. I was aware of the second he understood that something was wrong
about why and how I was there. He startled at that moment of clarity, but
then a second later, he brought his hand up to the back of my head and
began to stroke my hair, whispering soothing Italian words. I buried my
head in his chest, refusing to cry out loud but letting the tears fall since I
couldn't stop them anyway.

After a moment he began to sway with me, like a parent might comfort
an addled infant, and I was surprised at how quickly that lullaby motion
coaxed my tears into submission. It was like a dance with no steps, and soon
I was swaying too. He was still whispering something. And I was vaguely
aware that Sofia had turned her attention back to what she was cooking.

"I'm sorry," I muttered.

"You do not need to be sorry about anything. What happened, cara?"

I would've liked to have had a one-sentence answer for that question.
When someone sees a bandage on your arm and they ask "What happened?" usually you can answer in a sentence how you got hurt. *I cut myself
in the kitchen. I fell playing soccer. My neighbor's dog bit me.* But I didn't know
how to tell Lorenzo what had happened to make me fall apart in his arms.

It wasn't one thing; it was everything.

I could sense him looking at Sofia. She said something softly to him that sounded like this: *Suo padre ha rotto il suo cuore.*

The only two words I knew were *suo* and *padre.* Her father.

ॐ

Lorenzo stayed for dinner. Sofia added more pasta to the pot, and the three of us crammed around her little table, eating from wide ceramic bowls and finishing off the anonymous bottle of wine.

When we were done, Lorenzo grabbed my hand and told Sofia he would have me back pronto, that he just wanted to walk me to the river and back.

"The Arno by moonlight is the only time it looks pretty," he said.

Sofia said she'd clear away the dishes while we were gone and she'd make coffee to have with some anisette cookies she had made the day before.

I could barely keep my eyes open, but I left with Lorenzo.

On the stairs, with my hand firmly in Lorenzo's, I told him I didn't want to talk about my dad.

"I don't want to talk about him either," he said.

We emerged onto the street, calmer now than it had been earlier but still electric with motion.

"Did you see the Duomo when you came in?" he asked as we turned west onto the narrow street.

"My taxi driver didn't exactly point out any highlights."

He laughed and pointed behind us. "It's just over there. I am sure you will see it tomorrow. Very pretty in the sun."

The night air was fragrant with exhaust, warm stone, and dinner plates from open kitchen windows in the flats above the stores. I could close my eyes and pretend for a moment that I was back in San Diego, except that in the distance, I could hear the seesaw siren of a European ambulance. "Sorry to spring this trip on you like this," I said.

"No matter. You are here at last. Renata is gone until Tuesday. But we will take you to dinner. She will want to take you to her favorite place."

Tuesday. Did that mean I wouldn't see either one of them again until Tuesday evening? "You have a busy week?"

He pulled me across the street. "Not too busy for you, cara. We make time for you."

We turned down a second street lined with shops all shuttered for the night. A sandal-maker. Stationers. A pharmacy. A clothing store for children. A candle shop. A little store that seemed to sell nothing but olive oil. A sweet shop. Cars and scooters zipped past us as we crossed another street, and then another and another. Then suddenly we were at the river. A line of Vespas, parked like dominoes ready to fall, lined the street that overlooked the water. Bridges stretched across the Arno at well-placed intervals, looking like bracelets.

Lorenzo pointed across the water. "The Pitti Palace is just on the other side, and the Boboli Gardens. Very beautiful. And that"—he pointed to a bridge with windowed-structures all along its length—"is the Ponte Vecchio. Old Bridge. The Germans didn't bomb that one. Long ago, butchers had their shops there, and they tossed all the carcasses into the Arno to drift down to Pisa, a place no one liked. Funny, no? The Medicis didn't like the smell, though. Tossed the butchers out and put goldsmiths on the bridge. They are still there."

I waited to see what it was that Lorenzo had wanted to tell me by bringing me out to the river's edge. I thought maybe he'd ask if I was all right staying with Sofia since I had only just met her. Or if I thought her memoir had a chance. Or if I'd changed my mind about why I had cried like a schoolgirl in his arms and did I want to talk about it after all. Because all those things were on my mind, and I was surprisingly ready to talk about all of them.

But apparently he really did just want to show me the Arno under moonlight.

❧

We walked back to the flat, me at a sauntering pace, and I nearly gave in to Lorenzo's laughing offer to carry me up the stairs when we returned. Sofia's coffee was the best I'd ever had, and there were no worries that it would keep me awake. I could barely finish my cookie, my eyelids were so heavy.

"Ha bisogno di dormire," Sofia said to Lorenzo, as we sat in her living room and my head kept lolling back on the cushions behind me.

I didn't understand all the words, but *dormire* meant sleep. I knew that from my nonna.

It suddenly occurred to me that I hadn't packed a nightgown. And I guess I said this out loud. Sofia told me not to worry, she'd loan me one. She stood, took our cups to the sink, and then disappeared down the hall.

Lorenzo leaned in and kissed my forehead. "I'll see you tomorrow. Have fun with Sofia. I've a photo shoot during the day, but I should be home in the evening. We can sit outside on my balcony and have a drink."

I snuggled into him like a child and he laughed. Then he leaned in closer, as if to kiss me again, somewhere different than on my forehead. I was too tired, too emotionally bankrupt to process why Lorenzo would want to kiss me and would I want him to, but his lips brushed against my ear nonetheless, and I gasped.

But he was not kissing me. He was whispering something in my ear.

"It is good you are here with Sofia. Do not think you need to get a hotel room. She will love having you here. She's a kind soul. But be careful with her book and with what matters to her, eh? She is a bit fragile."

My response was lightning swift. "Aren't we all?"

Then he did kiss me. At the curly place on my ear. *"Ragazza buffa,"* he said, laughing.

He sprang up from the couch and yelled something to Sofia. I caught the word *domani.* Tomorrow. And she yelled something back.

He turned to me and winked. *"Ciao, cara mia."*

Then he was out the door.

Sofia appeared a moment later, and in her arms was a pink cotton nightgown frothing lace everywhere.

I was too tired to ask for just a pair of sweats and a T-shirt. I stood and took it from her.

"Thank you, Sofia. For everything."

Her eyes glistened. "It is my pleasure."

As we walked down the hall, I asked her what *ragazza buffa* meant.

She grinned. "Funny girl."

Lorenzo thought I had been kidding.

Nora

I have some of my parents' letters written when they were away from each other, which was nearly all the time. They spoke of missing each other and wishing the time would pass until they were reunited again. I read those words, and I hear what is said about my parents, and I wonder if it is truly possible to live two lives.

I know what people say happened to my mother when I was five. And I know what I want to believe happened to my mother when I was five.

If life is a series of choices and consequences of what you choose, then shouldn't I choose carefully what I will believe?

When nothing else about your life is yours to orchestrate, shouldn't you at the very least decide to believe the good that is possible? Especially if that is all you remember?

16

I awoke in Sofia's childhood bed, disoriented, disheveled, and desperately thirsty. A brilliant sun was streaming in through a slender opening in the curtains like a knife blade, and I knew before even looking at my phone that it was late morning.

I sat up slowly, rubbing sleep from my face. I reached for my phone at the bedside table and saw that it was ten thirty and that I had two text messages from my mother and one from a number I didn't recognize. I opened that one first, instantly hopeful that it was my father wondering where I was.

The text was indeed from him, but his short message was not the explanation I had hoped for.

Please forgive me, angel. Someday I will explain. I am borrowing someone's phone. He doesn't know it. Please don't text. I won't have his phone anymore when you get this. Plenty of money for you on the card. Enjoy Florence. Pls don't come home until after Friday. Love you.

Enjoy Florence and don't come home until after Friday? Don't come home until after Friday? It was the most inexplicable thing my father had ever said to me. I read the message three times and finally switched to read my mother's texts to see if she had also heard from him. But her first text was an angry lament about my being epically stood up in a place I'd never been before. The second was a rant that Allison had contacted her yesterday and she now assumed I was again protecting my father's whereabouts by pretending I hadn't met up with him in Florence. I was going to have to e-mail my mother not to text me unless it was an emergency.

I could certainly manage to stay in Florence well beyond Friday, but why should it matter? Unless he was going to drop another bombshell on Allison she'd somehow blame me for.

I rose from the bed, listening for any sounds in the flat. I heard nothing. I opened the door and stepped into the hall. From the hallway I could see Sofia's bed, freshly made.

"Sofia?" I called out. No answer.

I headed into the little bathroom and then made my way to the kitchen for a glass of water. On the kitchen table was a note, a plate of knobby rolls and round slices of blood orange, and a brown file folder.

Dear Marguerite,

I am canceling my tours this week so that I can show you Florence! I am just making arrangements for us, and then I will be back. Then this afternoon, I am taking you to the Accademia to see the statue of *David*. Lorenzo popped over this morning, but I told him to let you sleep. He will stop over later tonight. I printed some more pages of my book for you, if you would like to read them while you have your breakfast. And maybe after the Accademia, you can tell me what you think? You can use my bathroom to shower if you want.

Help yourself to anything in the kitchen. If you need to use the Internet, the wireless network password for the building is topo27&.

See you soon. I hope you didn't have other plans for today!
Sofia

P.S. My little balcony is a lovely place to drink coffee and read!

I didn't have other plans for the day.

I found bottled water in her fridge and unashamedly took one, down-ing the whole thing in one long guzzle. She had made coffee earlier, and I touched the carafe gingerly, hoping it was still warm, and was overjoyed that it was. I poured a cup, grabbed a slice of bread, and headed to her bathroom first and then to her balcony.

To study the history of my family is to acquaint yourself with the best and worst that mankind has to offer. Nora told me at Genga's painting of the martyrdom of Saint Sebastian never to spend too much time thinking about how terrible some people can be. Most are terrible not because of who they are; they are terrible because of what they had or did not have. I've heard it said that love drives people to jealousy. But I don't think that can be true. Fear drives people to jealousy, not love, Nora said. Fear drives people to do a lot of things in the name of something else.

There are but a few reasons that people kill one another. Revenge, of course, is one. Greed, a second. Jealousy, a third. Envy and jealousy are not the same thing. Envy sets you to obsessing about the thing you want; jealousy sets you to obsessing about the person who has it. And jealousy like that can lead to murder. It did. Within my own family. What I learned about Nora's parents, I learned from Papa and the history books. It is not something Nora ever speaks about. And why should she?

I don't know if it was jealousy or revenge or greed that drove Nora's father to kill Isabella, her mother. Some say it is because she refused to move to his home in Rome when she married him. Some say his longtime lover in Rome wished to take Isabella's place as duchess. Some say he was jealous of Isabella's longstanding affair with his cousin. Some say her older brother, Francesco, wanted her out of the picture after their father died. Nora was just five and her little brother four when their father murdered their mother and then abandoned them. So little is written about Nora; she all but disappeared when her mother died. History books tell us that when she grew up, Nora married a man named Alessandro Sforza, that she played music, and that she bore him several children. But history does not tell us how she coped with losing her mother at the hands of a father who cared nothing for her. That is of more interest to me than anything. And while Nora speaks to me in ribbons of whispers, we do not have conversations. It's not as if she hears anything I say back to her. It's more like her words have been pressed into the stone and paint and have been waiting for someone like me, all these years, to bend to hear them.

I asked my parents once how a little girl so young could survive what Nora Orsini survived. Mama never knew what to say when I asked the hard questions. But I know this bothered her, too, what happened to little Nora. Because her eyes welled up with tears, and she looked at my father so that he could answer. My mother was always tender-hearted that way.

Papa said Nora found a way. Perhaps it was through her music. Or maybe art. Or writing. She was Medici, after all. Everyone whose heart is broken will eventually find the one thing that will mend it if they do not shut their eyes. "What happens when you shut your eyes?" I asked. And he smiled and said, "Close your eyes." So I did. "What do you see?" he said. I laughed and said, "Nothing." A moment later he said it again. "What do you see?" And again, a moment later. "Papa, I can't see anything! It's all dark!" I said finally. And then he said, "Open your eyes."

When I did, I saw that he had put a chocolate bar in front of me and a pink rose from the vase on the windowsill behind him. And a shiny five-hundred-lire coin.

He pushed them toward me. "Shut your eyes to the world of pain, and you also shut your eyes to the world of delight." I laughed and reached for the chocolate first.

My mother tsk-tsked him for giving me candy just before supper. But he smiled and told her there were worse things than sweets before a meal.

I kept that five-hundred-lire coin. Four decades later I still have it. In 2002, Italy went the way of the euro; no one uses lire anymore. I could have turned it in for the cash value of the euro, but I had no desire to do that.

I didn't want to ever forget what my papa told me. There have been many times over the years when I might've forgotten if I hadn't had the coin to remind me not to shut my eyes.

I set the pages down on my lap and just sat there on Sofia's balcony, looking over the rooftops of Florence, captivated by Sofia's prose. In my mind's eye, I could see the chocolate bar, the rose, the coin, and even the little girl who found a way to keep her eyes open though her heart was broken. I was falling in love with Sofia's book, and it scared me a little how much.

It was not a travel book.

It was not even a travel memoir.

I didn't know what it was. But I wanted it. I wanted Crowne & Castillo to be the ones to publish it. And I had no idea how to convince Geoffrey and Beatriz to take a chance on it.

I had to find a way to verify her ancestral claims. She had mentioned that she was a descendent of Gian Gastone de' Medici, the last grand duke of the Medici dynasty. Sofia said there had been an illegitimate child born to Gian Gastone's mistress, or one of his mistresses. I was beginning to think all Medici men had multiple mistresses. Which mistress was it? What was her name? And how did Sofia's family come to learn of their heritage? If I could validate her claim, I knew Beatriz would be more easily convinced.

I didn't know if that would change things for Geoffrey.

Geoffrey.

Southern California wasn't awake yet, but soon it would be. Geoffrey would get to the office in a few hours, and he'd see that I wasn't there. Then he would open his e-mail and discover why.

I stood up and went back into the flat to shower and dress for the Accademia. I didn't want to think about what Geoffrey would say. He wouldn't be furious, since I hardly ever miss a day of work, but he'd be ticked that I had dropped everything because my dad asked me to. The sooner I made headway on Sofia's book, the sooner I'd have something interesting to report back to Geoffrey that had nothing to do with my dad.

Nora

When I look at Master Michelangelo's *David,* I am struck by his sheer and utter completion. There is nothing about the giant-slayer that is un-done or masked or hidden, nothing that leaves you pondering. Every-thing about the shepherd man in the stone is laid bare, shining white as new snow and solid as the ground beneath your feet. No one wonders what *David* might look like were he to breathe or should blood start flowing to his limbs, because he stands there with air in his lungs and veins pulsing under the marble. You don't have to imagine anything. He is all there, in naked totality. There is nothing hidden.

Words skip away from me when I look at *David.* Indeed, I must look away from that stark completeness where nothing is left to my imagination. If we cannot suppose and dream and wonder, are we not doomed?

My mother had in the garden of her favorite villa a statue of Adonis. I remember it because it gave me nightmares. In the statue, Adonis is dying, and a wild boar sent by Diana the goddess is tormenting him. Adonis did not love Diana; he loved Venus.

I told my mother once that I didn't like that statue and that it scared me. We were approaching the statue as we walked in the garden in the cooling afternoon. "Don't look at it, then," she said. "Find something you like to look at, and fix your eyes on that, Nora."

I can remember her saying this to me as clearly as if she said it to me yesterday, though I had only just had my fifth birthday. She said it as if it is just a small matter to pull your gaze away from that which frightens you.

"I feel like it wants me to look at it," I whispered as we passed the statue, and I simply had to turn my head and peek at it. She followed my gaze, seeming to look at the tormented Adonis for the first time.

"That doesn't mean you have to do what it wants," she said. And she quickened her step so that I had to run to keep up with her. I asked her if it frightened her, and she said it did not. "Figures in stone cannot harm me," she said.

But I did not walk past that statue again for a very long time. When I saw it again many years later, my childhood fears had given way to understanding. Statues do not harm, but they can speak to us of what can.

And better still, they speak to us of what we are capable of overcoming.

17

When Sofia returned, I was back on the balcony, refreshed by a shower and clean clothes, and reading again the chapter about Isabella and Nora. A hesitant smile snuck across her face when she found me sipping the last of the coffee and reading the pages.

"Do you like it?"

I recognized the tone of someone unsure of her writing. When I meet prospective authors, I often hear the tiny tremors of self-doubt, which I much prefer over arrogance.

"I actually like your writing very much," I said.

"You do?" Her smile intensified, then quickly sagged. "All of it or just that chapter?" Her gaze dropped to the pages in my hands.

"I mean all of it." I set down the pages and the cup of coffee. "But I need to see the rest, of course. And we need to find a way to tie everything together so that it's less a history book and more a memoir about Florence and what this city meant to you growing up. Does that make sense?"

Her brows crinkled in doubt. "Yes. No. What do you mean?"

I wasn't sure what I meant. But I had a thin idea of what I was trying to say. "Well, it's like your father and Nora are to you what Florence will be to the rest of us. Your dad can't be my dad. And none of us will understand Nora like you do. But your Florence can be my Florence. The way you talk about your father is the way you talk about Florence. It comes across that way in your prose. We need to punch up that idea that they are one and the same."

She nodded slowly. "Ah, it's because I am Medici that it comes across that way."

And that Medici thing.

"So, Sofia, if you don't mind my asking, how can we prove that you're, you know, a Medici?"

She blinked. "Prove it?"

"You know, like do you have family records that show the ancestry? Birth records, baptismal records, things like that."

"Well, I don't know. I've just always been told that's what we were." I had offended her, but she was too gracious to say it.

"I don't doubt you, Sofia. But if we're going to talk about publishing your book, we need to have this discussion. My publisher has asked that we have it. It's a valid question, don't you think?"

She pulled the corner of her bottom lip into her mouth. "I suppose."

"Did your father have a family Bible or family records or anything?"

"Maybe. I can ask him."

I had pictured her father as already being in the nether world of Alzheimer's the way she described him in her first chapter.

"Or your uncle in Rome?"

She shook her head. "He won't be any help."

"Why not?"

"He's…he's different. Grouchy. All the time. It's…it's not nice for me to talk about him that way."

A cloud seemed to pass over her, and I decided now wasn't the time to press it. I waited until the moment passed. "Let's come back to this another time, okay? I want to see *David*."

The veil lifted from her face. "Yes, you do!"

I stood and gathered the papers and my coffee cup. She reached for them both. "I'll take those. Did…did you like this chapter? It's kind of sad, this one."

"I did, but yes, it was sad."

"I've always had a tender place in my heart for Nora. And not just because she speaks to me." Sofia looked off in the distance, over the cream and salmon rooftops, into the vanishing point off her own balcony. "Papa said it was because I wished for her to have a mama and papa who loved her like mine loved me." She turned her gaze back to me. "It's that, but something else too." Then she shrugged, as if I wouldn't understand or wouldn't care. But I did care.

"What is it? What's the something else?" I asked.

She frowned slightly, pondering perhaps how to describe what she meant. "I don't know why, but I feel that I'm connected to her beyond family ties. I've always felt that way. Some of my childhood memories are wrapped in a fog of fear that I can't quite understand. I remember having terrible nightmares when I was little. But I had the happiest of childhoods, so I don't know why it is that I would think I have anything in common with Nora Orsini. But I've always felt that we were kindred souls. Funny, isn't it?"

She smiled thoughtfully and then looked at her watch.

"We'd better go. We have some walking to do, and you will need to eat something more than bread and oranges. And I have our tickets already for this afternoon, so we will not have to wait."

It suddenly occurred to me that not only had she gone to some trouble to get tickets to the Accademia for us but that she had rearranged her entire week to accommodate me.

"Will your boss be angry that you're taking off all this time for me? I will feel bad if this is going to be a problem for you."

She laughed lightly and touched my arm. "You are sweet. My boss will not be angry with me!"

"You're sure?"

"Oh, I am sure. I am the boss. It's my company. My father's and mine. But you are sweet."

"Really?" I didn't mean to sound so surprised. But I was surprised. Sofia had not come across to me as a business owner.

"Papa started it. We have other guides. Part time, most of them. Many of them students at the university."

I excused myself to go inside to put on comfortable shoes—Sofia said we'd be on our feet most of the day—and to grab my purse and camera, though Sofia told me I wouldn't be allowed to photograph anything inside the Accademia.

"But don't be too sad," she said, as we headed out her door. "Once you've seen him, you won't be satisfied with a picture."

A moment later we stepped out onto her street, alive with Monday activity. I drank in the sound of activity and purpose. We turned left on Via Porta Rossa and began walking east; at least I think it was east. Based on where Lorenzo had taken me last night, I imagined the banks of the Arno were a few blocks away on my right.

"First I take you to the Piazza della Signoria. The fake *David* is there. When the real one was brought indoors, they put the copy in its place. Many tourists think they have seen Michelangelo's *David* when they see that one. But it is like thinking you have seen heaven when you've only seen a cloud."

Devon had mentioned the name of that piazza. And something about mushrooms. I hadn't thought about Devon since the day before, but as soon as I tied his name with the piazza we were headed toward, I remembered.

"My mother's… A friend of mine mentioned there's a restaurant in the piazza where you can get ravioli with por…por-something mushrooms," I said. "He said I had to try it."

"Ah, porcini mushrooms. Yes, they are lovely. But the restaurants on the piazza cater to the tourists, Marguerite. None of the locals will pay what they charge."

I imagined going home and telling Devon I didn't eat at the restaurant he recommended. I thought of the money I had in my purse that he gave me. "Can we go anyway? My treat."

She smiled at me. "Of course we will go. First we will see fake *David*. Then you shall have your ravioli with porcini mushrooms."

We continued down the narrow street, past golden-stone buildings and little shops and merchants with the wares on tables that faced us. And while we walked, Sofia told me more about the piazza.

Soon we turned on Via dei Calzaiuoli, and before me was an expansive courtyard filled with camera-toting tourists, locals on their way to somewhere else, and dark-skinned gypsies selling scarves and sunglasses and leather purses. Sofia shooed the gypsies away and grabbed my hand. From the center of the piazza, I could see that it was filled with statues, grand and immense. The courtyard was flanked on one side by a stone building and a soaring clock tower that looked ancient, and I could see the copy of *David* standing in front of it. To the right was a three-arched canopy of carved stone over a group of statues that Sofia let me take my time gazing at and taking pictures of. Then she pointed to the ancient building.

"Palazzo Vecchio," Sofia said. "It means 'old palace.' The first stone was laid in 1294. Come. I want you to meet someone."

We started to walk past the fake *David*, but I stopped to take a picture— if nothing else than to compare him to the real one. And I wasn't the only one. Other tourists were snapping pictures of him. The fake was certainly impressive. If someone came to Florence and couldn't squeeze in a trip to the Accademia, they would want to at least see this. But I was guessing that if I said as much to Sofia, she would say how can you come to Florence and not see Michelangelo's *David*? It would be like visiting Paris and not seeing the Eiffel Tower. Or visiting heaven and not seeing God.

Sofia waited patiently for me to take the shot, and then she led me to an immense fountain of Neptune. Sofia stopped so I could take a picture.

"A few years ago, a young man who'd had far too much to drink climbed onto Neptune and smashed the hand to bits," Sofia said. "It was very sad. Twenty-three private sponsors donated the eleven thousand euro it took to repair it. It had been shattered into thirty pieces. They had to use stainless-steel pins to reconstruct it."

"Yikes. I suppose if this statue could talk, he'd say it hurt like the dickens."

Sofia smiled at me and leaned in close. "That's pretty much just how he described it."

I spun my head around.

Sofia's smile broadened. "Marguerite, I am just kidding." She laughed and so did I. "It's only Nora's voice I hear." She nodded toward Neptune. "He probably talks to someone else."

She pulled me to the bronze statue of a man on a horse, aged by the elements to a shade of creamy green.

"Here is who I wanted you to meet. Giambologna sculpted this. This is Cosimo I. He was Isabella de' Medici's father. Nora's grandfather. She wouldn't have remembered him since she was only three when he died. He created the Uffizi and the Boboli Gardens, and he finished the Pitti Palace." She turned to me. "And of all the Medicis, he and his wife, Eleonora, were one of the few couples that actually loved each other. They had an arranged marriage, you know. But they loved each other. Sometimes it works out."

We walked to the southern end of the piazza to a restaurant with umbrellaed tables and waitstaff beckoning.

"They have porcini mushroom ravioli here," Sofia told me as we settled into chairs. "It's quite good. Despite the price."

Devon was right.

Porcini mushrooms are as sweet and soft as marshmallows.

After our meal, which Sofia refused to let me pay for, we headed back out to the Via dei Calzaiuoli. Sofia told me at lunch we'd be walking past the Duomo and while I would want to stop and gape at it, we would need to keep walking to meet our ticket time to the Accademia. We turned on Via del Corso, which would take us to the backside of the magnificent cathedral so it wouldn't be as difficult for me to pass by.

Even so, the moment we rounded the corner and the south side of the Duomo stretched before me—four city blocks long and piercing the sky in a kaleidoscope of pink, white, and green marble—I did stop and gape. Sofia let me. I took a few pictures, lame as they were, for no one can capture the depth and breadth of it—even its backside—with a lens. I hadn't sensed my nonna's presence yet, but I felt her when I stood at the edge of the cathedral she said was the most beautiful in the world. Or maybe it was just awe speaking to me, sounding like someone I loved.

"The long name is the Basilica di Santa Maria del Fiore, the church of Saint Mary of the Flower," Sofia said, pulling me along. "But everyone calls it the Duomo because of Brunelleschi's dome. We will come back."

Reluctantly, I followed her.

Less than ten minutes later, we were at the Accademia and waiting for our slot to step inside what looked more like an apartment building than an

academy. Sofia told me Cosimo I founded it, and that it was the first drawing school in all of Europe. The lines to get in were thick all around us, and
I was infinitely glad Sofia had her connections to get us in.

Once inside we made our way into the hallway where Michelangelo's
unfinished statues lined the aisle like sentinels, leading to the room that
would reveal the statue of *David*. I had seen pictures of what Michelangelo
called the *Prisoners,* but I was astounded by their tortured poses. Chunky
marble monoliths stood erect with torsos of men writhing out of them, half-
formed, some with arms or pieces of arms, some with a neck but no head,
all of them with their muscles flexed in agony or perhaps defeat, as if someone had poured concrete on them while they begged to be shown mercy.

"What a terrible way to die," I whispered.

She cocked her head. "I've never thought of them that way. I've always
thought that was a terrible way to live."

I was so appalled by the *Prisoners* that I hadn't looked ahead of us as we
walked.

"Marguerite," Sofia was saying gently.

I turned and the seventeen-foot statue was before me, white like snow
under moonlight and shining with his sinewy legs, tensed arms, a full chest
of air, and pulsing veins in his neck. His skin looked warm and soft. His
Adam's apple seemed to bob after a swallow. He was a giant of a man about
to slay a giant, with the sling nearly swaying behind his back. I staggered
back a step, and Sofia reached to steady me, as I am sure she has done with
others a thousand times before.

"No one was meant to see him this close," she murmured to me, the
way a mother might say to a child, "It's okay, it was just a dream."

She patted my arm. "He was meant to be atop the roof of the cathedral.
But the statue was too heavy. You weren't meant to be this close to him.
This is why you stagger. Why everyone does."

Sofia took my arm, and slowly we made the circle around the pedestal. I was vaguely aware of other people in the room, some standing in awe, some reading their guidebooks, giving their eyes a momentary rest from the magnificence in front of them. I was also only slightly aware that the statue in front of me, clearly portraying a young man about to kill a giant, hadn't a stitch of clothes on. I was transfixed by its perfection no matter where I looked. And I shivered as I saw that the statue's expression seemed to change as my angle of vision changed. Courageous. Then hesitant. Then calculating. Then determined. And then courageous again.

"Michelangelo was only twenty-six when he took this commission," Sofia said. "The marble had been sitting in a courtyard for twenty-five years after several ill-inspired attempts to hew something out of it. It's amazing, isn't it? It's facing Rome! How's that for attitude?"

I appreciated the comic relief and smiled. "What did you think when you first saw it?"

She shook her head. "I can't remember the first time I saw it. Papa brought me here from the time I was little." She looked up at the statue. "I have always known him."

The next question out of my mouth fell away from me without forethought or reason. "Do you hear Nora's voice in here?"

"Sometimes it seems like I can hear her saying my name in here. Just that. Just my name. Or maybe it's the statue itself saying my name. This is the one place where I'm not sure if it's Nora I hear or something or someone else."

"Do…do you hear it right now?"

She tipped her head, unfazed by my question. "Not today."

I knew we would be heading back out onto the street and my grand moment with the statue would be over. I stood as close as I could and looked up at his face, high above me. I opened my mouth, not caring who heard me or what anyone would think.

"Hello, my name is Meg. I mean, Marguerite. Marguerite. That's my name."

A few people next to me whispered to one another, but I didn't care.

I just wanted that statue, if indeed it were even remotely possible that it had a soul, to know my name.

Nora

My mother loved Carnival. In the gallery of my mind, in one of the images I have of her, she is dressed in Carnival regalia, as beautiful as a fairy princess—all glitter and diamonds and feathers. She is showing me her dress in this memory, and I am asking her if I can come with her to the theater where she has staged a play. She is bending down to place an errant, downy feather on my head. Then she kisses me and says, "When you are older, Nora." And I ask her if I can have a dress just like that one, and she says, "You can have this one. I'll save it for you."

I never saw the dress again. I looked. I asked. But by the time I asked about it, several years had passed since I had last seen it. No one knew which dress it was. She had many beautiful dresses, and they'd been given away or sold. I only wanted that one because she twirled in that dress when I asked her to. She hummed a little tune, and it made me laugh.

She also loved music. There is a painting of her holding a piece of sheet music that looks very much like the portrait of her in her wedding dress. But there is no little dog in this one. It soothes me to know she loved music and that she staged concerts and plays at her villa and the palace, even though she did not play for me. Music is the language of the soul. Music captures our prayers and hopes and joys—and yes, our sorrows—and gives them voice, just as the paintings and the statues give them dimension.

Nurse told me my mother was fond of games too.

Her face was sad when she said this, as if she wished to warn me that some games are too dangerous to be played. I understand now that unlike music and art, games do not give voice and dimension to our dreams and desires. Games exist to make sport of them, for our entertainment. Games produce victors.

And wherever there is a winner, there is by necessity, the one who lost.

18

Sofia and I spent the rest of the afternoon at the Duomo. She encouraged me to climb the stairs to the top to see Florence from the sky above it.

"You don't want to come with me?" I asked her as we made our way to the northern exterior of the basilica.

Sofia shook her head. "The underside of the Duomo is beautifully painted, but Vasari's fresco of *The Last Judgment* is too much for me. I know people deserve what they get for the terrible things they do against God and one another, but I do not want to see it." She leaned her head back and looked at the outside of the dome. "It gives me nightmares. I don't go that close anymore."

She stood in line with me while I waited, sharing with me Brunelleschi's genius in completing a dome no one believed was possible to build.

The cathedral preceded the dome, of course. Arnolfo di Cambio designed the basilica, but the design for the cupola itself—the architectural term for the dome—was the subject of endless arguments. Arnolfo envisioned a cupola over the massive cathedral, but he could not come up with a way to execute the dome; there didn't seem to be a way to build it with scaffolding. And there certainly was no way it could be built without it.

A competition was arranged in 1418 so that masters all over Italy could propose a solution. Filippo Brunelleschi proposed raising a dome that wouldn't need a centring, the wooden structure that arches are built upon and is removed upon completion. No one believed he could pull it off. Brunelleschi proposed that whoever could make an egg stand upright on a slab of marble should win the competition. No one could do it. Brunelleschi took the egg, brought it down on the marble hard enough to make the shell on the underside come up inside itself, distributing the weight between inside shell and outside shell. That was his proposal. A double cupola—an outside shell and an inside shell—indistinguishable unless you looked at the dome outside and then ran into the cathedral and compared what you saw. The exterior would appear bigger than its interior.

Sofia said when Vasari wrote of how beautiful the Duomo was, he began with a list of its mathematical measurements.

When the line I was in entered the building, Sofia waved good-bye to me and told me she would meet me outside by the Baptistery doors. There were people ahead of me and behind me, but I felt alone as I began to climb the 463 stairs that would take me to the top.

There was no one I could comment to about the seemingly endless steps or the breathless exertion it took to burst out onto the top.

As I stood looking over all of Florence, I felt invisible. I took some pictures, amazed by my view but unable to share that amazement with anyone. I saw a man and wife and their teenage daughters laughing and taking photos. They were British, or Australian, perhaps. And I was envious of what they were experiencing together. My father should have been standing there with me.

A young couple, obviously in love, walked past me, cuddling each other as if it were a frigid forty degrees up there instead of a balmy seventy-something. My gaze fell again on the girls. One of them noticed me staring.

It took me a moment to look away.

She smiled at me. "Would you like me to take your picture for you?"

Her kind offer surprised me and I hesitated.

"Do you speak English?"

"Yes. Yes, I do. Thanks. That's very kind of you."

I handed her my camera.

"Right, then," she said, holding the camera up. Her family assembled around her to wait for her to take the shot.

"That's a great view, right there," the other sister said. "Take mine next, Gemma."

She snapped the photo. "How about you smile on this next one?" I produced the commanded smile.

"There's a good one," the mother said.

"You a student here?" the dad said as his daughter handed my camera back to me.

I am invisible here, is what first sprang to mind, but I reined it in. "Sort of. I do feel like I am supposed to be learning something while I'm here." They all laughed. Then they waited for the real answer.

"I work for a company that publishes travel books." It wasn't a lie by any stretch of the imagination, but I felt like I was deceiving them nonetheless.

"Oh, how lucky you are," said the daughter who had taken my picture. "To be able to travel the world like that."

Guess I had succeeded in deceiving them.

"I actually don't get to travel that often. Most of our authors don't need us to come visit them. The Internet makes communicating internationally pretty easy."

"So you're publishing a book on Florence, then?" the dad said.

"Considering it."

"We love coming here," the mum chimed in.

"My favorite place too," I said. I hoped the mother wouldn't ask me how many times I had been. I'd been a hundred times in my mind.

But she didn't. They said good-bye and I thanked them for taking my picture. The daughter who wanted her picture taken where I had been standing got what she wanted, and then they headed for the stairs that would take them back to the pavement far below us.

A few minutes later, when I was sure they were many steps ahead of me, I headed down as well.

Sofia had been right about the fresco.

From the floor of the cathedral, the spray of colors and scenery looked beautiful. Up close, the demons that reached for unrepentant souls were the size of swimming pools and clearly overly fond of their work.

Some things you just aren't meant to see that close.

After I reunited with Sofia, she showed me the Baptistery doors—beautiful—and then I proceeded to try to take the cathedral's photo from its front side. Again, not easy to do. The massive front of the basilica spills over every camera frame.

Sofia leaned in close. "The bell tower was begun by Giotto in 1334. When he was being considered as its architect, the pope wished to know if he had the credentials to build it. He drew a perfect circle—freehand—and sent it to Rome. A perfect circle. That's all he sent. He got the commission."

It was late afternoon when we started to walk back to her flat, but Sofia must have sensed I was getting weary and needed a pick-me-up.

"Let's get a cappuccino," she said, and she led me down a few streets to another piazza where an ancient-looking church, plain and monochrome to me after having just seen the Duomo, dominated the view.

"Basilica di San Lorenzo," Sofia said, nodding toward it. "Very old. Consecrated by Saint Ambrose in 393. Brunelleschi made adaptations in 1423. There was supposed to be a marble facade added, but it never came about. Very pretty and peaceful inside, though."

We walked toward a café, and she told me to take a seat at one of the tables under an awning and she would be back with the cappuccino.

A few minutes later, she returned with our drinks, and I sipped the frothy concoction, at once smitten with it.

"I will never be able to be content with American coffee again," I said, not even half-kidding.

She laughed. Then her tone turned thoughtful. "I was in America once. In Maryland. My husband took me along for a business trip."

A dozen questions swirled about in my head. I didn't know which one to ask first.

"But your husband wasn't American, right?"

"British. I met him here, though. He was teaching a business class at the university. I was taking it."

"Love at first sight?" I asked gently, not sure if she would want to say more.

She smiled the kind of smile you have for events that took you to the crucible but that you survived to tell about. "I don't know what it was. I was simply drawn to him like a moth to a flame. And I couldn't shake it. I thought that was love when I was young. But love isn't like that. Desire is. Can be. But love is not like that. It is not obsessive and fearful. Papa tried to warn me. He could see that Thomas would break my heart. He saw it from the very beginning."

She paused and sipped from her cup. Her hand shook a little.

"We don't have to talk about this," I said.

"It's all right. It was ages ago. I was young. Only twenty-four." She looked beyond me to the ancient church she had shown me moments before. "He asked me to marry him inside San Lorenzo."

I said nothing. A second later she pulled her gaze away to focus on the cup in front of her. "He hadn't asked my father first. If he had, Papa would've told him no. In a nice way, of course. Because Papa was always gracious to everyone. Even people who didn't deserve grace. But Thomas and I both knew my father wouldn't approve, and my mother was already sick with cancer by then. So I convinced myself that I would be doing them both a favor by eloping with Thomas. So that's what I did. We went to Rome, got married, and I was Mrs. Thomas Burnside when I came back."

Sofia sighed, not loudly, but with effort, as if she needed extra oxygen to tell me the rest. "Papa wept when we returned. Not in front of Thomas, though. He was as civil as he could be to Thomas, but Thomas knew my father didn't trust him. They barely talked to each other. I think my mother already knew the cancer would beat her, even though she lived another four years, so her reaction was quiet resignation. It was as if she knew she couldn't undo what I had done. So what purpose was there in wishing she could? There are things you just can't wish away, no matter how hard you try."

I nodded. I knew this to be true too.

"I kept thinking at some point Thomas would want to return to England, not to live there because he told me he loved Italy, but to see his parents and his brothers. To introduce me to them. But he never wanted to go. I think he let me go to Maryland with him that one time to get me to stop asking him when we would go to England. And for a while I did stop.

"After we'd been married for two years, I wanted a baby, but Thomas said no. We couldn't afford one yet. We were living on the other side of the Arno, and I was still working for my father, though he spent much of his time caring for my mother. I would stop in and see them every Monday and Friday afternoon. Thomas and I were renting a flat, and he didn't want to even talk about having children until we could buy our own place. In the country. So I started saving every lire I could get my hands on. I would take on extra tours, and I saved all my tips, thinking that if I could put away a small deposit, we could buy a little place and finally start a family.

"We had been married four years when he said he had to make a business trip to Paris. He was gone for a month. When he got back, he told me he had really gone to England and that he had something to tell me. I thought he had a surprise for me. I thought he had bought a little house for us in England, and though I was sad to think of leaving Florence, I knew this meant we could finally have a baby. At last I would have a child, and I could be to that child what my parents had been to me. I would bring the baby to Florence for a visit, and maybe the baby would give my mother a reason to fight the cancer and she would get better. A baby would change everything.

"I thought of all of these things in just a handful of seconds. I was still thinking of them when he said he needed to tell me something he should've told me when he first met me. He looked troubled, and I put my hand out to caress his face, and he...he pulled away from my touch."

Sofia paused to gather some inner strength, and I used the quiet moment to seek some for myself to be able to hear what she was going to say. I knew it couldn't be good.

"He told me he was already married when he met me four years ago. That he had left his wife and infant son because he thought she had been cheating on him. And he took a teaching post here to get away from her and married me so that he could stay in Italy." Twin bubbles of silvery tears peeked out of Sofia's eyes, and she fingered them away. "But apparently she hadn't cheated on him. She had somehow finally been able to convince him, and he realized he still loved her and that he wanted to be a father to the child he already had.

"So he left me. And went back to England alone."

I felt hot tears at my own eyes, and I daubed them away with a napkin. "I'm so sorry that happened to you, Sofia."

She shook her head. "I was sorry too. Sorry enough to want to throw myself off Giotto's bell tower. I knew I could probably have taken Thomas to court for having lied to me about his marriage. But I didn't have the wits about me to be livid enough to do that; I was too full of anguish. I went back to my parents' house, and Papa drew me into his arms and into the home I had grown up in. My mother was nearly gone by then, and when she understood what had happened to me, I think that was the thing that sent her skipping toward heaven, far away from this terrible planet. She died a week later."

By this time I was wiping my nose with my napkin and searching my purse for a clean Kleenex to replace it.

Sofia reached across the table and squeezed my other hand. "It was a long time ago, Marguerite."

I thought of my own losses that seemed tiny compared to hers, and I shook my head. "How…how did you recover from all of that?"

She smiled, patted my hand, and then sat back in her chair. "It took a while. Took a long while. But I had my papa to travel the road of grief with. It's not as scary when you have someone who walks it with you. He would remind me, at my darkest moments, that I had the blood of the Medici running in my veins. I was strong. I was resilient. I was able to stand under the crushing weight of this double sorrow. I told him one day that I just wanted to close my eyes and never wake up again. And he went into my old bedroom, found that five-hundred-lire coin, and pressed it into my palm. 'That is not your way,' he said to me. 'That is not your way.'"

She paused and drank the last of her cappuccino.

"Was…was there ever anyone else?" I asked. "I mean, did you ever think of getting married again?"

"No. I never met anyone who could love me the way my papa loved my mama, and that's what I wanted. Love like that. The other isn't really love. If the Medici know anything about love, it is that there is no substitute for the real. I have no regrets, Marguerite. My papa and I found happiness after our sorrows. Until he became ill a couple years ago, we had a lovely home together in the flat. I wish sometimes that I'd had a child, just one. I am the last. There are no more Medici after me, at least none that can hear what my father and I can hear."

I thought of what Geoffrey had said to me when I first told him about Sofia's claim. "But aren't there others out there who can trace their lineage back to the Medici? I mean, it was a big family, and they were always marrying their children into royal families of other nations, right? Aren't there little Medicis running around the royal houses of England and Spain and France?"

Sofia laughed. It was good to hear her laugh.

"Sure there are. But no one seems to consider that it matters. The family name is dead to them. What does it matter who you are if you don't care that's who you are?"

She stood. "Let's stop by the market and get some veal for supper. I will show you how to make *Vitello alla Fiorentina.*"

I stood too, crumpled the napkin I had been crying into, and shoved it into my pocket.

Nora

During those long years of my youth, as I tried to comprehend what happened the summer my mother died, I went to Nurse for answers and advice. She knew all the answers to my questions, and she had more advice for me than anyone—not because she was amazingly wise, but because no one else was interested in giving me counsel.

When people whispered of my mother's death, the name Troilo Orsini often appeared in the same breath. The more I began to understand the way of men with women, the more I understood Troilo was my mother's undoing. He was my father's cousin and was a very handsome man. I remember him in snatches of memory. Tall, muscular, and with laughing eyes the color of polished wood. Nurse told me that my father and Troilo were born the same year, but my father grew in girth as he aged, and Troilo grew only more beautiful. Troilo came to Florence after my parents were married—long before I was born—to impress my grandfather, win his favor, and improve his financial prospects. Many people came to Florence to impress Cosimo de' Medici. And since he was family, Troilo was welcomed.

Troilo was handsome, brave, ambitious. My father was not really any of those things. And he was not in Florence.

19

When we returned to Sofia's flat, the exertions of the day had caught up with me. It was a few minutes before five, but I needed to lie down for just a few minutes to pacify my annoyed body clock. Sofia promised not to let me sleep longer than an hour.

I don't nap often during the day because when I do, I almost always sabotage the rest I might've gotten with disturbing dreams that leave me feeling worn out when I wake. On top of Sofia's fluffy featherbed, I dreamed I was back at the cottage, but it wasn't exactly Findlay's cottage, of course. I kept walking into rooms that hadn't been there before, but I was pretending that they had been. I awoke with a start.

I sat up quickly, unsure where I was and groggy from interrupted sleep. I must've cried out because Sofia appeared at the door with a wooden spoon in her hand. "You all right?"

I swung my legs over the side of the bed. "Weird dream. Probably just jet lag messing with my imagination."

"Want to help me make supper? You said not to let you sleep too long."

"Sure." I followed her back out to the kitchen. I realized as the dream was fading that I hadn't yet mentioned the statue in my grandmother's painting. "Say, Sofia, when my grandmother was little, my great-great-grandfather painted her with a statue of a young woman. The real statue is somewhere here in Florence. I would like to try to find it, if I could. My grandmother thought it was in the Uffizi, perhaps. She wasn't sure. She doesn't remember posing for the painting."

Sofia was pleased to hear this. "We can go to the Uffizi tomorrow. There are a number of female statues at the Uffizi. And many more at the Pitti Palace if we don't find her there. You can tell me what the statue looks like, and I can tell you if I've seen it."

Her doorbell rang at the moment, and she went to answer it.

A conversation at her threshold began that I could not make heads or tails of. I decided to take a seat on the sofa while she talked in rapid Italian with a gray-haired woman wearing a yellow rain bonnet. The woman who had rung the bell was obviously upset about something. Sofia, it seemed, was doing her best to calm her. A minute later she turned to me.

"Marguerite, could you move the garlic off the flame on the stove for me? I need to run upstairs for a moment or two. I won't be long."

I nodded. The two women left, and I carried out my simple task. I turned the stove off and moved the golden garlic bits off to the side. Sofia's wall clock in her kitchen told me it was twenty minutes to seven. I did the quick math and knew that it was nine forty in the morning in San Diego. The office had been open almost two hours.

I knew I probably had an e-mail waiting for me from Geoffrey. I needed to know to what degree he was mad so that I could figure out how long I could stay, assuming it would make no difference to Sofia. And I certainly wanted to stay past Friday, as my dad had inexplicably asked me. Could I stay the week? Ten days? Would Geoffrey flip if I said I'd be gone ten days? Beatriz would be concerned and surprised about my sudden departure but not mad. Geoffrey, however, disliked surprises.

I found Sofia's note from breakfast with the Wi-Fi password, and I settled onto her sofa with my laptop. I logged on to my webmail. Geoffrey had e-mailed me twice. Beatriz, once. My mother, three times.

Geoffrey's first reply was short and terse. He wanted to know how long I'd be gone, and he wanted to know who was in charge of what until I got back. The tone of his second one—sent forty-five minutes after the first one—was noticeably different. He wanted me to make sure I connected with Sofia Borelli to find out how many finished chapters she had. And he wanted to know if she had records to prove she was in the Medici bloodline. Beatriz's e-mail was like Geoffrey's second one, only more polite and more to the point. She told me she had mentioned Sofia's premise sans the ghost to a major book distributor in New York and they were now quite interested in a destination memoir written by a Medici descendent. She, too, asked me to please authenticate Sofia's ancestry claims—as soon as possible—and to make sure Sofia wasn't crazy regarding the talking statues bit. And Beatriz also asked me to make sure I connected with Sofia to see what her total word count was. If it was less than forty thousand, Beatriz asked me to help her identify enough content to punch it up to at least fifty. There was nothing to talk about yet if it was less than fifty.

She also asked me to enjoy the time I was spending with my father. And to please be back in the office, if at all possible, in eight to ten days. She would only charge me five vacation days because of the connection she was hoping I would make with Sofia. But they couldn't spare me any longer with such short notice.

Nervous anticipation rippled through me as I considered that Sofia's book idea had gone from a crazed clunker of an idea to one that clearly Beatriz was enthused about, and which Geoffrey apparently wasn't going to continue to ridicule. There was interest. A major distributor was interested. But I didn't know how to prove Sofia was who she said she was.

And I didn't know if I could convince her to take a more subtle approach regarding Nora's whispers.

I also didn't know how much of her manuscript she had finished.

Still, Sofia's project was making my surprise trip to Florence not a complete waste of time for Geoffrey and Beatriz. That was a good thing.

I e-mailed them back jointly and got them up to speed regarding who I was spending my time in Florence with; that is, not my father. And since I was with Sofia in her apartment, I'd have ample opportunity to address the questions they had.

I told them I would give them an update in a couple of days. Then I logged on to the Air France website and found a flight that left the following Monday, one week from today; the next available after that wasn't for fifteen days. I secured the last available seat.

My mother's e-mails were next. The subject line of the one in the middle read "Your father." I opened that one first.

Meggie,

So Allison's decided to get a lawyer, and she's hired a private investigator. She wanted to file a missing person's report, but I don't think the police believe there's been any foul play. It looks like your father just took off on her. Although that's not a nice thing to do, it's not illegal. The money he took was in a jointly held account, so taking it wasn't illegal either, just in very poor taste. She said the private investigator thinks he probably went to Mexico. And some not very nice men came to the house looking for him. She thinks they were loan sharks. I don't know why she keeps calling me to tell me the latest. It's like she thinks we now have this gigantic thing in common.

She doesn't think he's in Florence with you anymore.

Just thought you'd want to know.

You don't have to stay there, Meg. He's not going to show.

You can come home, if you want.

I opened the first and third one before constructing a reply. The first one:

Meg,

I am just not comfortable with you staying with a woman you
hardly know. I hope you brought your doorstop with you. Be sure
you put it against the door when you go to bed at night. And sleep
with your passport on you. And watch out for juvenile pickpockets.
Devon said they work in teams. A cute little boy will create a di-
version, and other little boys will laugh and joke with him. And
while you take their picture, two other little boys who've not even
caught your attention will rob you blind. Be careful.

And the third:

Devon fixed the hinge on your screen door. He went over to your
place last night to take care of the litter box and cat food because I had
a church thing I couldn't get out of. You know how it used to catch
and then not close all the way? Well, now it doesn't do that anymore.

And don't forget to use the doorstop tonight. Love you.

Mom

Picturing Devon fixing my screen door and in my house taking care of
Alex made me frown.

I liked it and disliked it, that image. I wished I felt nothing but simple
gratitude that my borrowed cat was being properly cared for.

Sofia came back into the flat, and the image skittered away.

"Sorry about that!" she said brightly. "Now we can get on with dinner!"

"No problem," I said. I wrote a quick reply to my mother.

I am staying until next Monday. Geoffrey and Beatriz have some
things they want me to do here. I got a very short text message from

Dad on a borrowed phone. He apologized for not being here in Florence and said he would explain someday. I have no idea where he is now. The area code was Los Angeles, but he said he'd be gone by the time I read it. You can call Allison and tell her, if you want. She might like to know that one day ago he might have been in Los Angeles.

Forgot the doorstop at home. Sorry.

Tell Devon thanks for fixing my screen door.

More tomorrow, maybe.

Meg

I closed my laptop and joined Sofia in the kitchen. She turned from the sink where she was washing her hands.

"Everything okay?"

I guess I looked like everything wasn't.

"Everyone seems to think my dad has probably fled to Mexico with his second wife's money." Saying it out loud made it seem more real somehow.

"Oh, Marguerite. I am sorry. He's not coming to Florence at all, then?"

"No."

"I can see you love your father very much," Sofia said. "Even though he has hurt you. And this is not the first time, no? Still, I think you will see him again."

She turned to a cabinet, opened it, and began pulling out little jars of herbs. I wanted to slowly digest each of her four proclamations—that I loved my father, even though he hurt me, and has hurt me before, and despite where he was right now, I would see him again—but Sofia swiveled and extended a little jar toward me and jostled me from these thoughts.

"Here. Smell this. *Herbes de Provence.* My favorite thing to cook with. It's a lovely mixture of many herbs."

I took the jar and inhaled.

I remembered that fragrance. Nonna cooked with this. She had done the same thing once. Lowered a jar of it to me and told me to smell it.

Memories crowded in of those childhood years when I had no idea things were falling apart. I don't remember much of the years before I was six; I don't think many people do. But the years when I was seven, eight, nine—those years were the happiest for me. And yet those were the same years my parents' marriage was disintegrating, and I didn't even know it.

I backed away from the scent. "Say, Sofia. I just had an e-mail from my publishers. They are actually really glad I'm here with you. They are interested in your book, but there are some things we need to work out."

The delight on her face was childlike. "Really? They like it?"

"They like the concept. And they do like your writing style. But really, when it comes to getting a book published, the concept is key. And you've got a great concept."

"I do?"

"Sure. You are writing a destination memoir about Florence from the vantage point of a Medici descendant. It's a great concept. And you have a great writing style. Lovely, really."

This appeared to be more than she could take. She turned to the sink, set the little jar down, and laughed. "You've no idea how I've needed to hear that. My father always said I could write, but you know how fathers are. They tell you things because they love you." She looked up. "I think you know what I mean."

I couldn't think of an appropriate response. So I just continued with what we needed to talk about. "Well, what my publishers would like from you are all your finished chapters and a word count. And a few other things."

"Word count?"

"Your total word count. If you put all the chapters together that you've written to this point, what would the total word count be?"

"Oh." Sofia stared off into the window above her sink. "I don't know."

"No problem. We can figure that out. Are all your chapters about the same length? You know, the same number of pages when you print them out?"

"Oh! That! Yes. They are all about the same."

"Great. And how many chapters do you have that are finished?"

"Twenty. No, twenty-one. I have twenty-one."

We had a problem. Sofia's chapters averaged a thousand words each. She didn't have even half the amount we needed completed. I framed my next question carefully so as not to scare her off.

"And how many more do you think you could write?"

She seemed pleased by this, not taken aback. "You want more? I have hundreds of stories to tell. You want ten more? Fifteen more?"

"How about thirty more? Could you write thirty more?"

She grasped me by the shoulders and laughed. "This is wonderful! Yes! Yes, I can write more."

"That's great. Sometime this week let's sit down and see what each new chapter would be about, okay? We'll make a list, and I can send that to my publishers. Maybe Wednesday?"

"Yes, yes!" She turned to the little oil painting by her window and kissed it.

My gaze turned to the painting too. It was of a woman holding a baby in her arms. She was sitting under the shade of leafy boughs.

"Your mother?" I nodded toward the canvas.

"And me. I love this painting of her. It's the smallest one my papa ever did of her and me together. But I love it anyway."

"It's very pretty."

"The painting is more my father than my mother, yes? He painted it. All the love that he has for her is in every stroke. And he painted her—and me—while we posed for him. This canvas is like a fragment of real time, fixed here, forever. That's how it is when I hear Nora whispering to me. She left her imprint everywhere. I think we all do."

I sensed a pulling sadness that this part of her manuscript might have to be scrubbed, or at the very least toned down. There had to be a way to keep it without destroying her credibility or reducing her to a delusional freak.

"Do you hear any other voices besides Nora's? Do you hear her in every piece of art?" I asked.

She laughed lightly. "No, no, no! And I am very glad I don't. No, the ones that speak to me with Nora's voice are the ones that she and I are both a part of. Like, she can't speak to me through my father's paintings because she never saw them. She wasn't there to leave her imprint. It's different with the art we both have shared. But if all the art in Florence spoke to me, could you imagine? I would be a lunatic. Never a moment's peace."

Ah, yes. The specter of being thought something of a lunatic. I had to address it. "You wrote that your father told you not to share with people this ability you have because it would distance you from them. You do understand, don't you, that there will be people who will not believe this part of your story? That you can hear Nora Orsini talking to you."

Sofia shrugged. She unwrapped the parcel of veal she had bought on our walk back. "People are too quick to count as unbelievable anything they haven't been gifted to be able to do themselves. It's how they deal with the disappointment of not being able to."

"But sometimes people will come along saying something is true when it's not. You do know there are delusional people in the world, Sofia, right? I am not saying you are one of them. But other people probably might. I think maybe that's why your father asked you to keep it to yourself all these years."

She slowly turned her head to look at me. A frown crisscrossed her face. "What are you saying?"

"Just that we need to figure out how we could publish your book without making you a target for people who will not believe you have this ability. There's no way to prove you have it. Someone else could come along and say paintings and statues talk to them too. No one could prove that they are lying or delusional, because they can't prove that you aren't either."

"Someone else wouldn't have Medici blood. I do."

"That's why we need to authenticate that, Sofia. The publishers are pretty clear on that."

She smirked. "Why is everyone so unable to believe something without proof? I am an honest person. I don't lie. Look at my life. I have never lied."

"But even a liar can say they have never lied. Proof doesn't mean you are who you say you are. It means we can believe that you are who you say you are."

She shook her head. "A person's word should be enough."

"I agree. But you know the world we live in. We need to give people the confidence they need to put their trust in your story. It's a trust issue, Sofia. It matters."

Sofia set the pieces of veal down. She looked out over the rooftops from her kitchen window. "I guess I can understand that. Maybe we should go visit my father and see what he says. Maybe he knows where the records are." This new thought seemed to change her disposition. She whirled to face me. "I would love for you to meet my father. Perhaps after the Uffizi we can go see him? Would that be all right? I usually see him on Tuesdays."

"Well, sure. If you think he would like meeting me."

"Of course he would!" She retrieved the pieces of veal and laid them out on a marble cutting board. She grabbed a mallet from a canister. "He hardly ever gets visitors anymore."

I wanted to ask her why, but I couldn't find the words. I would see soon enough if her father would be able to help us track down the family records.

She handed the mallet to me. "First we need to pound out the attitude. That's what my mama always said. We make the veal tender by treating it harshly. Crazy, isn't it?"

"Very." I took the mallet and brought it down onto the meat.

"Harder, Marguerite."

And I obeyed.

Nora

Among my family there aren't many who can paint, but my mother was an exception. She painted a portrait of me and little Virginio to send to our father in Rome, even though she had the means to hire any Florentine artist to paint us. When I began to paint, my tutor and the instructor he hired no doubt wondered if I had been gifted with any of her talent. Even using her brushes, which I still have in my possession and which are very dear to me, I could not match her natural skill. My few canvases pale in comparison to the few I have of hers.

Nurse tells me Virginio would hardly sit still for her, and the painting took many months, but my mother did not mind. She loved spending her day with us. I remember her scent lingering on my bedclothes, dresses, and wraps because she was always near me.

She often took me to Santa Trinita for Mass. I remember sitting with her, running my finger along the trim of her sleeves and the jewels on her skirt.

Sometimes we went out on the balcony at night to look at the stars. My mother loved the night sky. She told me once she wished she could paint it, but the heavens, she said, refuse to be painted.

And yet it wasn't always just the three of us. I remember Troilo Orsini being there on occasion. Sometimes on the balcony with us. Sometimes in the gardens. Sometimes in our games room, playing with Virginio and me. I remember he had a loud voice, but it wasn't frightening. He wore blue. He had shiny shoes. He was too jovial to be thought of as a father figure. He was more like a court entertainer sent to us to make my mother laugh.

I was too young to think anything of it.

20

After supper, and while I waited for Lorenzo to return from his photo shoot, Sofia and I sketched an outline of the other chapters she had written that I hadn't read yet and ideas for the new chapters she would need to start writing right away. She already had chapters on the Palazzo Vecchio, the Baptistery doors, *David* and the *Prisoners,* the ceiling of the Salone dei Cinquecento, the statue of *Judith* with her sword held high, the Bargello, and a dozen other landmarks. They were in various stages of near completion. She asked if she could have a week or two to polish them.

When we began to brainstorm ideas for thirty new chapters, I asked Sofia to choose must-sees that were personal to her so that she could dovetail a personal story with the landmark. She told me everything in Florence was personal to her.

When Lorenzo knocked on her door a few minutes before nine, the list of new chapters was at twenty-two. Sofia sent me off to visit with Lorenzo while she completed the list herself. I think she was glad to be alone while she finished it.

Lorenzo kissed me on both cheeks at Sofia's door, a greeting I know is standard with everyone he meets, but his kisses felt personal and intimate and I blushed. He didn't seem to notice. He shut Sofia's door behind us.

"A good day?" He led me across the hall to the front door to his flat.

"I'd say so. Saw *David* and the Duomo. And I climbed the steps to the top of the dome. About killed me, but so worth it."

"Ah, you would not be able to leave Florence without having climbed those steps. Good for you."

We stepped into his apartment, which was similar in floor plan to Sofia's, but a little bigger. The décor was modern, unlike Sofia's, and seemed oddly out of place with the character of the building. The furniture reminded me of an Ikea catalog page, except the aesthetic here was top-of-the-line, designer minimalist, not bargain price. Lorenzo and Renata's books had done well.

"Wow," I remarked, taking in the soft and hard edges, whites and blacks and taupes, and the aroma of leather everywhere. "Your taste or Renata's?"

He laughed. "If the decorating were left to Renata, there would be crates and patio furniture in here. Renata is not a homebody. She likes to be out and about. She only comes here to sleep and change shoes! You are lucky you will be able to see her tomorrow night."

He showed me their writing room, paneled in dark wood. Two desks faced each other with matching laptops, neat on his side, messy on hers.

He pointed out the bedrooms as we made our way back to the front of the flat. His was minimal, but clean. Even the camera equipment in the corner was arranged nicely. Renata's bedroom was a tousled frenzy of fabric—clothes, bedding, and pajamas.

As we walked back to the main room, Lorenzo placed his hand on the small of my back, a tender touch. "Shall we sit on the balcony? I want to hear all about your day."

He led me to a balcony off the kitchen, one that was twice the size of Sofia's. Upholstered chairs and a sofa sat facing the blip of violet-orange where the sun had been. A decanter of red wine and two stemless glasses rested on a low table. I sank into one of the chairs.

"Your balcony's quite a bit bigger than Sofia's, or is it just my imagination?" I asked.

He poured a glass of wine. "Ours is the biggest one in the building. You'd think her family would have chosen this flat for themselves."

"You mean they had their choice?"

He handed me the glass. "It's their building, so I'd say they had a choice. If I owned the building, I'd want the flat with the biggest balcony."

Surprise walloped me and I nearly fumbled the glass. "Her family owns this building?"

"Her father. And his brother, Emilio. It's been in her father's family for generations. I told Angelo once how lucky he was to own this place, and he said I was the lucky one because I got to live in it and didn't have to worry about the upkeep."

"Sofia owns this place?"

"Her father and his brother do. Didn't you just hear what I said?"

I remembered the older woman who had come to the door earlier in the evening. A tenant, surely. She had come to Sofia's flat because Sofia was the landlord's daughter. Sofia was probably handling the building's affairs since her father became ill.

"How long has her father been in the nursing home?"

"A couple years, I think. Why?"

"I don't know. It just seems like a huge responsibility for someone like Sofia to have."

He sipped his wine and then echoed my words. "Someone like Sofia."

"Yes. Someone like Sofia. She seems a little naive, Lorenzo. It just seems like a lot for someone like her to handle. You said yourself she was fragile."

"I meant with her book. She loves her book. I didn't want you to tell her it was terrible or anything. I did not mean she was fragile about everything. And her father left this building in great shape. He has all the maintenance contracted out. Sofia doesn't even have to collect the rent. A company does that for her. And why do you think she is naive?"

"Well, because...because of the way she talks about Nora Orsini communicating with her. It seems kind of...juvenile. And she insists she's a Medici and yet doesn't seem to understand why people would want proof of that."

"Who wants proof?" He tossed the words out as if I were the silly one.

"Well, Beatriz and Geoffrey, for starters. They like what they've seen of her book. A lot. But they won't publish someone who claims to be the last Medici but who also can't produce a single document that authenticates that claim."

Lorenzo smiled. "They want to publish Sofia's book?"

"I said they like it a lot. They like the concept. Some distributor in New York does too. It's because she's a Medici that there's this interest. So naturally, some family records are going to be required."

"Well, they probably aren't that hard to find, no?"

"I don't know." I sipped from my glass. The wine was smooth and robust and smelled of pepper and cherries. "We're talking three hundred years of Sofia's ancestry that she says begins with an illegitimate son. I have no idea how hard it will be. I was hoping there were family records right here in the flat. Wouldn't you think there would be if Sofia's family is Medici? How would they all know this if there weren't records?"

Lorenzo shrugged. "Pieces of paper. Records. Not that important."

"Well, money is pieces of paper, too, Lorenzo. And it's pretty important."

He laughed loudly but didn't comment.

"She's taking me to see her father tomorrow to see if he knows if there are family records in the flat," I continued.

Lorenzo's jovial tone slid to something more thoughtful. I could see in his eyes that he already suspected our visit to Sofia's father wasn't going to yield anything. "Really?"

"Yes."

"You know what I think?"

I shook my head.

"I think we need music." He lifted himself out of his chair and disappeared inside. Apparently we were done talking about Sofia's ancestry. Smooth acoustic guitar music, Mediterranean in style, floated out to me. Lorenzo reappeared.

"That's better," he said. Then he held out his hand to me.

"What?" I said.

"It's a beautiful night in Florence. Let's dance."

"I don't know how to dance."

He reached for my hand and pulled me to my feet. "There is no how, cara. You *feel* a dance." He put one arm around my waist and brought me close enough to smell his cologne. Spicy and sweet. He took my other hand and bent our elbows so that our arms rested against his chest. He hummed the tune that the guitar was strumming and swirled me about the little balcony. I stepped on his foot. Not on purpose, but he didn't seem to care.

"I told you I couldn't dance," I said. And he laughed and said something in Italian that meant nothing to me. "You might want to try that again in English."

He laughed louder and twirled me away from him and then pulled me back.

"You saw the *David*?"

"Yes."

"And?"

"And he knocked me off my feet." This pleased him and he twirled me again and brought me back close.

"Not so hard to imagine a statue could talk to you, eh?"

I've only been in the arms of a dancing man a few times in my life. My father used to dance with me, but it's different when you are a little girl standing on your father's shoes as he sways to old Sinatra tunes. Prom doesn't count because no one really dances at prom. You just bounce around on the fast songs and schlep a shuffled circle on the slow ones. I'm talking about dancing the way Lorenzo was dancing with me at that moment. Even polite Miles couldn't dance like this, like it was as easy and effortless as breathing. I relaxed into that graceful movement, and soon I wasn't stepping on Lorenzo's feet anymore. My eyes were closed, my head was nestled against his chest, and I was feeling the dance, just like he told me I should.

"Look at you, cara mia," he whispered into my hair. "You are dancing."

"Look at you," I whispered back. "You've got bruises on your toes."

He laughed, said something in Italian, and I again had to remind him that if he wanted to discuss anything with me, he had to use the language of all us lazy unilinguals.

"I said, you are sweet and fun and lovely. Why aren't you married?"

When you're thirty and single, the last thing you want to hear is "Why aren't you married?" It sounds an awful lot like "What is wrong with you?"

"Why aren't you married?" I shot back.

He rubbed the small of my back with his thumb. "I tried it once. Not very good at it."

"Maybe you didn't try hard enough."

He rested his head on top of my head. "Maybe. You'd be good at it, though."

"And how would you know that?"

"I just do."

We were quiet for a moment. I didn't know what to say to that comment. So I said nothing.

"Do you have a special someone, cara?"

I bristled a little. "You know I don't. You ask me this every time we Skype."

He drew me closer, perhaps thinking I was going to pull away. "I meant is there someone who is special to you. And perhaps he does not know it?"

I felt heat rise to my cheeks, and I tipped my chin downward in case there was some physiological way for him to feel the warmth on my face through his clothes.

"Marguerite?"

"I don't know," I mumbled into the fabric of his shirt.

"What?"

Who knows why I lifted my head and spouted what I did next. Perhaps I am at my most honest when I am in the embrace of strong arms.

"There are moments when I think I am in love with the man my mother is dating."

Lorenzo arched back a little. "Truly?" He was smiling. Sort of.

My face was burning with embarrassment, but it had felt so good to say it out loud and for someone to hear it. Even so, I thumped my forehead onto his chest.

"No. I don't know. I just met him. He's only thirteen years older than me. And the day I met him, I thought she was setting me up with him. But she wasn't. She just wanted me to meet the man she was dating. Who just happens to be a younger man."

"Tell me what you like about him."

"I barely know him," I muttered.

"But you are drawn to him. What is it about him that draws you?"

And as we swayed to the music, I listed the things I liked about Devon, starting with his kind heart toward my mother. His gentle manner toward me. His compassion. His quick response to need. His perceptive thinking. His kind eyes, soft voice.

"He's just such a genuinely nice person," I concluded. "It's...it's very attractive."

Lorenzo began to stroke the back of my head. He held me the exact same way the day before when I fell apart in his arms after being stood up at the airport.

"Those are all wonderful reasons to be attracted to someone, cara."

"But he's my mother's boyfriend!" I looked up at Lorenzo, daring him to find something good to say about that.

But he didn't say anything. He leaned down and kissed my forehead. "If he chooses your mother over you, he has a huge check in the minus column, Marguerite."

I couldn't help but laugh. It was funny, really. But also not funny. The fact was, he *had* chosen my mother over me. I hadn't thought of it quite that way yet. Devon wasn't doing mental gymnastics after meeting me like I was after meeting him. He already had chosen her over me.

The laugh in my throat died away, and Lorenzo must have sensed I hadn't thought this through. He kissed my cheek and whispered something in Italian.

"English, please," I whispered back.

"You deserve more than he will give you."

I knew if I tipped my head up, Lorenzo would probably kiss me. I hadn't been kissed in over a year. I was aware of how dangerous it was to be kiss deprived, hurting, and in the arms of an attractive male friend. But I tipped my head up anyway. Lorenzo wasted not a second. It was as if he had pulled the lever himself that brought my chin up to his. His lips on mine were warm and sweet from laughter and wine. He brought his other hand down around my waist so that I all but disappeared into his embrace. Into that kiss.

I was lost in it for several seconds, in that dreamlike place that your mind takes you when physical sensation is so powerful it is nearly your undoing.

To Lorenzo, it was probably an enjoyable, throwaway kiss. I was quite sure he liked kissing women. He liked bocce ball. He liked to dance. He liked wowing people with his photography.

But I had no place in my brain or heart for throwaway kisses. I pulled away.

"Lorenzo." I said his name gently.

"Yes," he said, kissing my neck.

"I want…some gelato."

He looked at me, eyes sparkling with amusement. "You want…gelato?"

I knew why he was kissing me. He probably thought he was doing me a huge favor, romancing away my troubles with distracting kisses. But surely he wasn't in love with me. I was someone he was fond of. I could think of nothing good that could happen from allowing him to continue.

"You know any good gelato places around here?"

"You really want gelato? That's what you want?"

"I do."

He raised my hand to his lips and kissed it like a Victorian gentleman. "Well, then. I know a wonderful place to get gelato."

His kiss was still warm on my lips when we headed downstairs, my hand in his, as if I were a child who needed help on the stairs.

Nora

I remember my mother talking about my grandfather once, with tears in her eyes, telling me what a kind nonno he was. I have the vaguest memory of him bending down to kiss my cheek. Or maybe I was bending to kiss his.

He remarried after my grandmother died, but I have no memory of the woman who was his second wife. She was not liked among the family.

When Cosimo died, it is said, my mother lost more than her beloved father. She lost the apparatus of her freedom. Not only that, but the matter of my dowry, as well as my future and Virginio's, was now to be left to my uncle Francesco, who succeeded my grandfather as Grand Duke of Tuscany.

When my grandfather died, everything was placed in Francesco's hands.

He was not like Cosimo. He did not dote on my mother. And he did not like Troilo Orsini.

21

Tuesday morning dawned bright and warm. Sofia and I enjoyed breakfast on her balcony while she updated me on the last eight chapters she planned to write to bring her word count up to fifty thousand. She was confident she could have the new chapters done by mid-July. I felt good about the proposed chapters and was fairly sure Beatriz and Geoffrey would be okay with having all the content done by the middle of the summer. The first hurdle to cross in getting Sofia's book published was taken care of. There would be at least fifty thousand words.

Next we had to establish that she was who she said she was. Perhaps I would be surprised by her father's condition when we saw him later that afternoon and he'd be able to easily direct us to older family records. Sofia could only go as far back as the late eighteen hundreds with information she found in her father's family Bible. There was another one hundred years we needed to cover. If her father couldn't bridge the gap, I was going to have to start looking on my own.

And I still had to find a way to somehow let Sofia be Sofia in the pages of her book, ethereal voice and all.

As we sipped a second cup of coffee, Sofia asked me to describe the statue I hoped to find at the Uffizi that morning. I hadn't seen my nonna's painting in almost twenty years. I attempted to describe how I remembered it.

"The statue has her arm bent in either welcome or request; I'm not sure which. It's like she's reaching out to the little girl in the painting who was my grandmother."

"The statue has her hand like this?" Sofia raised her arm and bent it slightly at the elbow, turning her palm upward in supplication.

"Yes."

"And is she seated on a rock in water?"

I couldn't remember. I closed my eyes to picture it, but all I could see in my memory was the little dancing girl and the statue reaching out to her.

"I don't know." I shook my head. "I don't think there was water."

Sofia nodded. "Maybe there was water, but your nonna's grandfather chose not to paint it, eh?"

"Why? You know this statue?"

"I think I do. But she's not at the Uffizi."

My heart sank a little. Just a little. Sofia still looked quite pleased.

"She's not?"

"No. If it's the one I'm thinking of, she's in the Boboli Gardens at the Pitti Palace."

Sofia stood, stepped into the flat, and came back out a moment later with a heavy book in her hands. "All the Boboli statues are pictured in this book. She's in here." Sofia sat back down and leafed through the book's colorful pages. She landed on one and spread it out before me, "That's her, right? Andromeda?"

My long-ago vision of what the statue looked like wobbled for a moment as I compared it with the photograph now in front of me. The statue, erected in the middle of a fountain, knelt on rocks surrounded by water. The snowy-gray hue of her robe-like dress made her look cold and damp. Her expressionless face was not how I remembered it. But her arm and hand lifted toward heaven was just as I had seen it a thousand times in my head. For the first time since I landed in Florence, I felt unweighted by the troubles I had brought with me. The beckoning statue was right here in Florence just as Nonna said it was. And she had a name: Andromeda.

I whispered the name.

"Do you remember the legend?" Sofia asked.

I shook my head.

Sofia ran her finger over Andromeda's bent knees. "Andromeda's mother, Queen Cassiopeia, boasted that Andromeda was more beautiful than the daughters of the sea god Nereus. To punish Cassiopeia, and because he was married to one of the daughters of Nereus, Poseidon sent a sea monster to ravage the kingdom's coastline. Desperate, the king consulted an oracle who told him the attacks would not stop until he sacrificed Andromeda to the sea monster. She was chained to the rock where the sea meets land." Sofia pointed to the marbled chain around the statue's ankles.

I suddenly remembered this myth from high-school lit class and reruns on Saturday afternoons of *Clash of the Titans*. "Great parents she had," I mumbled.

Sofia smoothed the page. "They didn't know what else to do. Sometimes you just don't."

"Sometimes you do and just don't want to do it."

"True. But help can come from another way." She turned the page and pointed to a second statue of a man rising out of the water on a winged horse. "See? This is Perseus returning from having killed Medusa. He rescues Andromeda and kills the sea monster. He saves her. They fall in love and marry. Everything works out in the end. Most of the time it does." She paused a moment before going on. "These weren't here when Nora was here. They were moved here after she left Florence. I think she would have liked this statue too, just like you do."

"Well, that's her." I looked up. "When can we go see her?"

"I don't have tickets for the Pitti Palace for today. I have them for Sunday. But if you want me to change them, I will."

I leaned back in my chair to contemplate. Part of me wanted to grab my shoes and camera and run across the first bridge that would take me across the Arno to the Pitti Palace. Part of me wanted to hold off seeing the statue until the end of my trip so that it would be one of the last things I saw. Seeing it would either be climactic or the exact opposite.

"I'm not sure what I want."

"It is important to you, this statue?"

When she said this, I knew it was not so much the statue itself that mattered to me. It was an echo of the life I knew when Nonna was alive. The life that felt good and right and safe and that had been taken from me.

"Kind of silly, I suppose, but yes."

"I don't think it's silly at all. We will do whatever you want. You don't have to decide now."

I have always been the kind of girl who didn't want Christmas to come too soon. I wanted to enjoy the anticipation of what was to come. The days before Christmas were always more enjoyable and magical than the day itself. And I never cared for the day after Christmas. I still don't. "Let's keep the Sunday tickets," I said.

She nodded, apparently neither pleased nor displeased with my decision, perhaps because it really was just mine to make.

"Then shall we make our way to the Uffizi? I have so much to show you."

There is something to be said for the ancient motto "Everything in moderation." I'd never been exposed to so much artistic genius in such a short two hours' time as I saw in the Uffizi. I was mentally and spiritually unprepared for it.

Walking its halls was like walking through a corner of the Creator's mind.

Canvas after canvas, statue after statue; there was too much for my eyes to take in, and I was quickly fatigued by beauty. But it was exhilarating to see so many works by Italian greats whose last names everyone knows.

Nonna loved Botticelli's *Primavera* the way I loved the painting of her and Andromeda. The *Primavera* print she had hanging in her house seemed immense when I was a child. Perhaps it was. She told me the frame and mat cost twenty times more than the print itself. But she hadn't cared. By the time she was in her midthirties, well before I was born, she was convinced it would be years before she could get back to Florence to see the original again, if at all. The *Primavera* was like her portal home for years. When she promised me the trip to Florence for my high-school graduation, she was gifting herself as much as me. She hadn't been back since her twenties.

"See all the faces?" Nonna said to me once, when I was looking at her *Primavera,* trying to figure it out. "Every emotion is here. Life is hard, but spring always comes. Sometimes she is late, but she comes."

So when Sofia ushered me into the gallery where the *Primavera* hung, as if it had been waiting for me, I had to swallow a dozen emotions.

"The *Primavera* was commissioned as a wedding gift to Lorenzo di Pierfrancesco de' Medici, who married in 1482," Sofia said to me, either unaware of my emotional state or endeavoring to distract me from it. "In the Second World War, it was moved to Montegufoni Castle to protect it from the bombing. It is the most studied of Botticelli's work. You read it from right to left, like a story. See? Zephyrus, the wind of dying winter, takes Chloris and marries her, transforming her into a goddess. Now she is Spring, and she is tossing roses onto the ground. And she is looking at you. As is the caped woman in the center. And the three Graces? They do not see Cupid pointing his arrow at them. Some say Botticelli painted it as companion to *Pallas and the Centaur.* They say Mercury on the end there is looking out of his painting and into the scene where Pallas, in the other painting, triumphs with love over lust. See?"

"And what do you say?" I asked her, as my eyes swept over the canvas.

"There's five hundred species of plant life painted there. Nora and I think this painting just wants to be outside."

After two hours of unimaginable artistry and Sofia's colorful commentary, I was ready to take a little break from sightseeing to go visit her father. I was eager to see what he could tell us, and I needed to reenergize my ability to appreciate beauty.

We bought sandwiches from a food vendor in a little *mercato* and then walked to a bus stop. Sofia told me she had found little use for a car and hadn't owned or driven one in more than twenty years.

It was nine kilometers to the *casa di riposo,* the care home where Angelo Borelli had been living the last couple of years. Getting there involved two buses and forty minutes of travel and transfer time. Sofia was quiet as we traveled out of the older part of the city and across the river into the newer section. I imagined that seeing her father every Tuesday was something she looked forward to—and dreaded—at least a little. I was okay with the silence between us as we traveled since I had my own inner thoughts to wrestle with.

When we stepped off the second bus at a little after one thirty in the afternoon, Sofia's demeanor brightened, as if she had used the last half hour to bolster herself for the visit.

"It's just down the street and around the corner," she said as the bus pulled away. I saw that we were on a fairly quiet street on the outskirts of downtown. Buildings rose up on either side with retail shops on the ground floor and apartments above, none higher than four stories. There were trees on the avenue and patches of flower beds here and there.

"My father knew he was becoming… He was getting ill," Sofia said as we headed down Via Torcicoda. "He picked out this place himself. He wanted to pick it. And he wanted to move in before he really needed to. He knew there would come a time when he would forget this is what he wanted."

I said I was sorry. I didn't know what else to say.

She smiled. "My father has always been such a kind man. Even now, when he has forgotten so much, he has not forgotten that he is a kind man."

We turned a corner.

"It is not a terrible place, but it is not home." She stopped. "Here we are."

We now stood in front of a beige building with wood-trim windows— all of them with closed blinds. The front door was heavy oak, graced on either side by squat urns of red scraggly geraniums. At least they were real.

Sofia stepped inside, and I followed her onto a tiled entry that smelled faintly of burned toast and pine.

"He will be in the common room. They always dress him in street clothes and bring him down to the common room when I come. He asked them to do that. Back when he remembered that's what he wanted."

She said something in Italian to a black-haired woman sitting behind a reception desk. The woman said something back and waved to me. I waved back.

Sofia signed our names to a register, and we proceeded down the hall, past a woman in a wheelchair who said something angrily to me as I passed her, to a set of arched and opened double doors. We went inside. Armchairs and sofas in different shades of rust and russet vinyl were placed about the room. A large television stood in one corner of the room, broadcasting a soccer match watched by three men in bathrobes. Several round tables with half-finished puzzles on their tops were in another corner. A woman in a red housecoat stood at a large picture window, watching birds in a tree that shaded a small courtyard. In another corner, a man wearing khaki slacks and a powder-blue cardigan sat straight-backed in an armchair. One hand rested on each knee.

I knew without Sofia saying a word that this man was her father.

We began to walk toward him. He watched us approach with no hint of recognition. Sofia greeted him cheerfully in Italian and bent to kiss him.

His eyes were wide as she stepped back from him. Surprise was etched in every wrinkle on his face. He blinked several times, and his left hand began to rub his knee as if there were a spill there.

Sofia knelt to look at him at eye level. I don't know what she whispered to him, but after a moment, the surprised look was replaced by one of calm. "Sofia…" he whispered.

She laughed, leaned forward, and kissed him again.

He said something and she laughed again.

I felt like an intruder. I backed a few steps away and sat in an armchair identical to his a few feet away.

Sofia spoke to her father for a few moments before turning toward me and motioning me to come.

When I reached them, Sofia introduced me. I heard her say my name, and I extended my hand. But her father did not do likewise. Instead, he rattled off something and patted the chair next to him.

I turned to Sofia. "What did he say?"

She looked troubled. "He…he'd like you to sit next to him."

"Um. Okay." I took the chair next to Angelo Borelli and crossed my feet at the ankles, assuming as casual a pose as I could, but I felt anything but relaxed.

Angelo turned to me and said something and laughed lightly. I eked out a complementary laugh and turned to Sofia. "Sofia, I don't know what he's saying."

She chewed on her lower lip before answering. "You remind him of my mother."

"I do?"

She sighed. "He…he thinks—for the moment at least—that you are."

"What?"

"He thinks you're my mother." She sighed a little.

"What do you want me to do?"

Before she could answer, Angelo leaned closer to me. His eyes were watery with age and illness. He said something else and nodded toward Sofia.

"I don't know what to do here," I said to Sofia.

"I don't either." Sofia looked troubled. "Maybe I should come back alone later this week."

My first thought was that sounded pretty good to me, but we hadn't even asked him about the family ancestry. Beatriz and Geoffrey were expecting an update.

"Do you think you could ask him about the family records?" I asked.

She hesitated a moment. "I will tell him again who you are, and then I'll ask him. I'll tell him you're helping me write the book."

Sofia knelt down and said a long sentence in Italian. Angelo listened, and his expression grew more pensive as she talked.

He said something to her and she stood up.

I looked from him to her. "What did he say?"

"He asked me to go find him a cup of coffee."

"That's all he said?"

Sofia nodded and then turned to me. "Will you stay with him while I get him one? Maybe if he has what he wants, he will be able to give us what we want."

I said I would, but I knew I would be counting the seconds she'd be gone.

As soon as Sofia was out of the room, Angelo turned to me. He began to speak, in the kindest of voices, sounding so much like Nonna. He patted my arm with one hand and touched his chest with the other. Whatever he was saying, it was something he thought he was sharing with a wife he loved. He asked me a question and waited for my answer. He asked it again, and his eyes were begging for me to say yes.

It was one of the few Italian words I knew. So I said it.

"*Sì*."

This filled him with such pleasure. He smiled at me. Patted my hand again. And said more. I've no idea what it was. None of the words were words I knew. But I had clearly made him happy by saying yes.

A few minutes later, Sofia returned with a cup of coffee on a saucer. He thanked her and sipped from it.

"I'll try again," she said to me. She knelt down and said something to him. He shook his head. She repeated what she had said. And this time he just said no.

Sofia hesitated a moment before standing. "I don't think we're going to get anywhere with him today. I'm sorry, Marguerite. Some days he is in a fog. Today is a foggy day."

She pulled up a third chair and sat with him for a while longer. I assume Sofia was trying to make small talk with him, but he just kept looking at me and saying things to me that Sofia didn't want to translate. When his coffee was done, he handed the cup to Sofia and said something to her this time.

She took the cup. "He says he needs to get back to work."

But Angelo made no move. He just sat there looking straight ahead, as if the place where he worked were inside his brain.

Sofia leaned down and kissed him, murmuring a good-bye. When she stepped away from him, he looked at me, said something, and pointed to his cheek. He wanted a kiss from me too.

"You don't have to," Sofia said.

But Angelo was looking at me with a sheen of serenity on his face, fully expecting a kiss from the woman he thought was his wife. I leaned in and touched his papery-skinned face with my lips.

"Arrivederci, mie belle ragazze," he said. Good-bye, my beautiful girls.

We didn't say much to each other as we waited for the bus. Sofia seemed sad and somewhat surprised by her father's condition. She apologized for him, and I told her not to worry about it.

When we were on the bus back to her flat, Sofia asked what Beatriz and Geoffrey would say about us not having had any luck with her father.

"We'll have to do some research on our own. There are websites to help with ancestry searches. And city records. And there's your uncle."

She shook her head. "He won't help me. He doesn't like me."

"What do you mean?" I couldn't imagine anyone not liking Sofia.

"I don't know. He just never has." She rested her head against the glass window of the bus.

"Do he and your father not get along?"

She shrugged. "Emilio doesn't get along with anybody. He won't help me."

"Maybe he would help me," I suggested.

Sofia shook her head. She said nothing else, and I let the matter go.

For the moment.

We got back to the flat at four thirty. Sofia said she had things she needed to do at the travel office and asked if I would be okay on my own for a while. I wondered if perhaps she needed to be alone. I told her I'd be fine. I had e-mails to take care of.

And I reminded her I was having dinner with Renata and Lorenzo that evening. She visibly relaxed when I said this.

The afternoon had been hard for her.

Nora

When you are young, you do not know the way of men with women. But when you are nine years, maybe ten, you begin to wonder when you see lovers embrace, or you hear a coarse joke and you don't know why you blush. Sometimes you hear someone whisper something about your parents, and you are struggling to remember what they were like as husband and wife, and you hear a name that your mind stumbles over because you don't know how that name fits in the equation.

Nurse explained as delicately as she could what transpired between my mother and Troilo Orsini when I began to voice my questions.

Nurse had to explain everything to me with regard to men and women; no one else did. When I asked her why my mother took Troilo into her bedchamber when she wasn't supposed to, Nurse said my mother didn't know what it was like to be denied what she wanted. And when I asked Nurse if my father took another woman into his bedchamber, she told me plainly, because she said I needed to know, that my father had many women in his bedchamber.

My cousin Maria and I had been taught the Ten Commandments from our earliest days with our tutors. When Nurse told me this, I thought this was why people whispered around me and gave me sideways glances and wrinkled their brows in consternation when I was near. "They didn't keep their promises," I remember saying.

And Nurse shook her head. "No," she said. "They didn't."

22

Lorenzo came for me a few minutes before eight. I had been able to take care of my e-mails while Sofia was at the travel office, including an update for Geoffrey and Beatriz and one for my mother. There was still no word from my father, and Alex was apparently missing me. I doubt that Findlay's cat was truly pining for my companionship. That was just my mom's way of communicating that all was well at home but that she was concerned for me. She didn't mention Devon, but why would she? I kept forgetting it was only Tuesday. I had only been gone for four days.

The last e-mail I answered before Lorenzo rang for me was from Gabe. He just wanted me to know he was thinking of me and he hoped I was having a good time. And he told me to be sure I had some Illy coffee while I was there. I made a mental note to bring some back for him.

Lorenzo's greeting was as effusive as ever, as if he hadn't seen me in years. His kisses on both cheeks warmed me and made me feel regal.

We said good-bye to Sofia, who was making an omelet for herself and humming. It was nice to see she had apparently recovered from the visit to her father.

We crossed the landing to the other flat, and Lorenzo opened his front door, calling out to his sister that I was there. Renata shouted back something from a back room, cheerful but loud.

In the four years I've worked with the DiSantis brother-sister team, I've never been able to become as close to Renata as I have to her brother. Most of my phone calls, even the editorial ones that deal with the writing, I have with Lorenzo, though he leaves most of the writing to her. I asked Lorenzo once if Renata didn't like working with me because she always deferred to him on the phone calls. He had seemed surprised by my question.

"She knows I like talking with you," he had said. "And she trusts you and me to decide what is best for the books. She likes you very much, cara. If she didn't, she'd be on the phone all the time making you squirm."

Lorenzo poured us each a glass of wine, and he led me out to the balcony. The night air was a little chilly, and I had left the only sweater I brought in Sofia's flat. I shivered, and Lorenzo's arm was at once around me. To keep me warm, of course; that is all. But his closeness felt wonderful and dangerous.

He called out something to Renata, still inside the flat. And she shouted back an answer. Then he held his glass toward me.

"*Salute.*" He touched his glass to mine.

"*Mazel tov,*" I replied, and he tossed his head back and laughed.

He sipped his wine and I sipped mine. It wasn't the same bottle as last night's. This one was sweeter, but not overly so. I tasted blackberries and leather on my tongue.

"And how was your third day in Florence?" he asked.

"Sensory overload, like the first one and the second one. We went to the Uffizi."

"Ah. I should've told you to look with just one eye." He winked and took another sip.

His closeness was keeping me warm, but it was also keeping me distracted from the loveliness of the evening. I wondered if he knew he had that effect on women. Maybe he did. Or maybe I was the one with the heightened sense of awareness, not him. He was just being accommodating. Like with last night's kiss.

I didn't have to contemplate it for long. Renata soon joined us on the balcony, sweeping past the doors with urgency that made the gauzy curtains flounce like waves on the ocean. She had a glass of wine too and a shawl in her arms. She looked just like her head shot on the back cover of their books. Shining hair, expertly tinted with reddish highlights, smoky eye shadow and lots of it. Voluminous eyelashes, perfectly arched eyebrows, flawless skin, gleaming lips, sparkling gold jewelry. She wore a honey-brown silk blouse and creamy-white pants. A spicy fragrance wafted about her as she pulled me out of Lorenzo's one-armed embrace to kiss me on both cheeks.

She said something in Italian. And then quickly switched to English; hers was a little bumpy compared to Lorenzo's and Sofia's. The extra *a*'s at the end of every word made me smile.

"How do you like Firenze, Meg? After all these years, you finally come. See, she has been waiting for you!"

"It's everything I thought it would be." It was a nice thing to say about the city I knew Lorenzo and Renata loved, but as soon as I said it, I knew it wasn't merely a polite answer. I felt at home here, just as I always imagined I would.

"Here. Lorenzo said you need this." She handed me the shawl. It smelled sweetly of a past day's spray of perfume.

"Oh. Thanks. That's very kind."

"You keep it while you're here. Nighttime is sometimes chilly in the spring. You come in the summer, and you'll wish never to see a shawl again."

The shawl felt warm and soft over my shoulders, and I thanked her again.

Renata sat down on one of the chairs and put her feet up on the little table between them. Her taupe leather stilettos would probably cost three hundred dollars in the States.

"Sit!" she said. "Drink first. Then we'll eat. My treat."

I took a seat on the sofa, and Lorenzo sat down beside me. She asked me what I had seen of the city, and I told her the sites Sofia had taken me to so far.

Renata nodded, mentally checking off the landmarks in her head, it seemed. "And the Boboli Gardens and the Pitti Palace? When will you see these?"

"Sunday."

"Good, good. The Boboli Gardens are very beautiful in the spring. Too hot in the summer."

"Renata does not care for the heat," Lorenzo said. "She wilts like a flower. Complains like a squeaky door."

Renata shot back a reply in Italian and Lorenzo laughed.

She turned to me. "So how goes the book?"

I told her that Sofia had some more writing to do but it was looking good that we might be able to publish it if we could clear a few more hurdles.

Renata's lovely eyebrows crinkled. "What?"

"She thought you meant Sofia's book," Lorenzo said to his sister, coming to my aid.

Renata said something in Italian back to Lorenzo; probably, "Why would I ask about Sofia's book?" Or maybe "Sofia's writing a book?" Or "What the heck is Meg talking about?"

"Sorry. Wrong book. Of course you meant your book," I said, practically stumbling on the words to get them out. "It's going well. Right on schedule."

"You talked to Beatriz about the photo for the cover? We don't want *Venezia* on the front. Not the Venice one. That is not the best one for the front."

"I'm working on it," I said. "Geoffrey and Beatriz both like the one of Venice. A lot. It's really a nice photo."

"But it's not the one we want," Renata said, calmly and easily, as if I had already managed to change Beatriz's and Geoffrey's minds. She sipped her wine and waited for me to nod that I had indeed done just that.

"I'm working on it," I said again.

Lorenzo said something to her, and she said something back.

"So what is this with Sofia's book?" Renata asked.

I wasn't sure how much Renata knew about Sofia and her book. I turned to Lorenzo for some affirmation and he nodded. I answered as if she knew plenty. "The writing part is going well. We have a couple of snags, though."

She turned to Lorenzo, and I heard her say the English word "snags" surrounded by a clutch of Italian words.

He smiled at me and answered in English, bless him. "Snags are like little troubles."

Renata faced me. "What little troubles?"

"Well, there are the parts about the talking paintings and statues. Beatriz and Geoffrey aren't sure if their readership can handle that. They've never published anything quite so—"

"Odd." Renata tipped her glass toward me. "Sofia told me once she hears them speak. Like there's a ghost inside them. It is odd."

"Yes. Odd."

"Odd is sometimes good. Odd is sometimes what sells a book, no?"

Renata had a point. Odd can sell a book. Odd can tank a book. I half-nodded in half agreement.

"What other little troubles?" Renata continued.

"Well, Beatriz and Geoffrey want to authenticate Sofia's claim that she's of the Medici line. We might need to do some digging."

"What?" Renata's face was a blank stare.

I looked at Lorenzo. He rubbed his stubbled chin in thought. I knew Sofia hadn't told very many people she was a Medici. I just figured if Lorenzo knew, then Renata did. But it was obvious she didn't.

"Oops," I whispered.

Lorenzo shook his head gently as if to say it wasn't that big a deal. He turned to his sister. "Sofia says her family is in the Medici bloodline. Direct descendant."

"Verità?" Renata looked from Lorenzo to me and then back to her brother. "Why has she and her papa not told anyone?"

Lorenzo shrugged. "I don't know. Sofia only just shared this with me. When I read her first chapters before I sent them to Marguerite; that is the first I heard of it."

"It's why she says she can hear some of the paintings and statues talking to her," I said. "It's because she's a Medici. She hears a Medici ancestor inside them: Nora Orsini."

"Who is Nora Orsini?"

"Isabella de' Medici's daughter. *Isabella.*" Lorenzo drew a finger across his neck.

"Oh, her." Renata appeared to ruminate on that for a moment. "So what is the little trouble with that?"

"We need to authenticate her claim that she's a Medici. Geoffrey and Beatriz want me to get the records that prove it."

Renata frowned slightly. "Why? So they will believe she hears statues? That's what will make them believe she hears statues?"

"Do you believe she hears statues?" I asked.

Renata shrugged. "I like thinking she does. Don't you?"

I hesitated before nodding. "Yes. I do." I did.

"I think Beatriz and Geoffrey find it compelling that Sofia is a Medici," Lorenzo chimed in. "It is a selling point. Right, cara?"

Of course it was a selling point. "Yes. Yes it is."

"And Sofia doesn't have proof?" Renata asked.

"No. And we went to see her father today, and he…he won't be able to be of much help. He's not… He won't be of much help. I think we're going to have to do the digging on our own with city records and ancestry websites."

"What about Emilio? Why doesn't she just ask him?"

"I asked her about her uncle. She said he won't help her."

Again, Renata's lovely eyebrows puckered. "Of course he will help her. Why wouldn't he help her? He is family. If Sofia is a Medici, then so is he."

"Sofia told me that he doesn't like her. That he doesn't like anybody. And she said he wouldn't help me either."

Renata set her empty wineglass down on the table by her feet. "Sofia is like a little child sometimes. Emilio is not like her father. But that does not mean he does not care for her. He is not all smiles and sunshine, but that does not mean he doesn't like her. He is a businessman. He likes solitude. He doesn't need people the way Sofia does."

I was taken aback by how much Renata seemed to know about Sofia's uncle. She must have read my surprise on my face.

"I dealt with Emilio when Lorenzo and I wanted to take out the wall between the kitchen and the living room. He handles all of that, you know. The management of the building. I never got the—what do you call it?—*impression* he does not like his niece. He just does not need closeness. Not important to him. I think he would help you."

Hope began to percolate in me. I really didn't want to have to spend hours on Italian websites that I could barely read trying to piece together Sofia's family ancestry. But I didn't know how to convince Sofia we should give her uncle a try. And I couldn't call him myself unless he knew English. I said as much to Renata.

"He speaks only a little English," she answered but then quickly followed with, "Want me to call him for you? I have his number in Rome."

"Yes!" I answered, without hesitation.

"You should ask Sofia first," Lorenzo said. We looked at him, and he took a sip of wine.

"Why?" said Renata. "Sofia is a child about this. If Meg asks and Sofia says no, what then? Meg can't have me ask? Stupid. That is stupid. Besides, I will ask Emilio. Not Meg. This will be between me and Emilio."

"I think you should ask."

Renata frowned at him. "And what if she says no?"

Lorenzo shrugged. He had no good answer.

"I really need to get to the bottom of this, Lorenzo," I said. "I'm not asking Emilio for any dark family secrets, just if he knows how we can verify that his family is in the Medici line. That's all."

"This is silly. I will call him right now." Renata stood and sailed back into the flat. Lorenzo and I followed her.

She pulled her cell phone out of a leather purse on the dining table, scrolled through her contacts, and landed on the one she wanted. She held the phone to her ear.

I looked at Lorenzo. He looked unconvinced that Renata should be doing what she was doing. But he said nothing.

A moment later Renata spoke into her phone. She was leaving a message. I don't know what she was saying, but I heard the word *Medici* and the word *Sofia*.

"Ciao." Renata slipped the phone back into the purse and then slung it over her shoulder. "Had to leave a message. Maybe he will call back while we eat. Let's go. I'm hungry."

Lorenzo was quiet as he closed the balcony doors and locked them.

Renata began to describe the trattoria we were walking to even before we were out the door. With the front door locked, we headed for the stairs that would take us out into the night. Renata fairly ran down them.

"You really think I should ask Sofia before Renata talks to Emilio?" I whispered to Lorenzo.

He inhaled a contemplative breath. "It is too late to think about that now, cara. Renata has already talked to Emilio." He smiled at me, but it was a loose smile, the kind you tend to offer when someone naively asks you to predict the future.

Nora

I don't know what happened between my mother and my uncle Francesco that made him turn against her. My cousin Maria has told me her father was always jealous of Cosimo's affection for Isabella and Giovanni, the favorite son who died. She said she saw bits of a letter my mother wrote to her father concerning Virginio and me and her own financial welfare. Something that Francesco had promised at my grandfather's deathbed, he was now taking back. And apparently Francesco had no such desire to see my mother, Virginio, or me remain in Florence, and he expected my mother to at last join my father in Rome. But Nurse was never instructed to pack my things or Virginio's. My mother kept putting it off, as she had for many years, but this time, Nurse said, it was for more reasons than just wanting to stay in Florence; she needed to win over Francesco.

In the late summer of 1575, I fell ill. I remember only that Nurse held me while I lay hot with fever and my mother paced the floor as Virginio cried outside my door. He was not allowed in.

After I recovered, everything changed.

23

The food at Renata's favorite restaurant was insanely delicious. For our anti-pastos we had prosciutto and honey-roasted pears that had been filled with goat cheese and drizzled with a balsamic glaze, then grilled octopus with a saffron aioli. The pasta course was *pappardella* with leeks and sausages, and the main dish, beef Carpaccio with parmesan and truffle oil. Renata insisted on ordering the chocolate *panna cotta* with orange and candied hazelnuts for dessert, though I could barely breathe by this point, my stomach was so full.

I thought Renata and Lorenzo would want to talk about ideas for future books, but Renata said from the get-go that she didn't want to talk Crowne & Castillo business at her favorite restaurant. Instead, she seemed intensely interested in me, asking me a thousand questions about my life and dreams and hopes and fears. She found it peculiar that I had waited until now to come to Florence when I've wanted to come since I was twelve.

"My father kept promising he'd take me, and I just kept thinking he would," I answered.

"And so you waited—all this time?"

I nodded.

Renata shook her head. "If my papa promised me something, I wouldn't let him rest until he came through for me. You are too patient."

"You probably grew up with your father right in the next room. Mine was always a hundred miles away," I said. "When your parents are divorced and your father lives two hours away, you learn to expect distance between what you want and what you have."

She thought about this for a moment. "I wouldn't let him rest." She slid a spoonful of panna cotta into her mouth.

"Renata is not one for compromise," Lorenzo said to me, but loud enough for his sister to hear.

"Renata is not one for nonsense." Renata toasted the air in front of her with her cappuccino.

I sipped my own cappuccino, letting its frothy smoothness linger in my throat. I wanted to be done talking about my father. And we were.

When Renata got up to use the rest room, I asked Lorenzo what was up with all the questions. He merely shrugged my concern away by reminding me that his sister was the research half of their writing team; she was filling her mind with details. I was a fresh resource.

When she returned from the rest room, Renata moved on to my love life.

"So you haven't been married before, no?" Renata asked.

"Um, no." I set my cup down. "Just engaged."

Stupid answer. She might've forgotten that detail if I hadn't said anything.

"Ah, yes. You didn't marry him. I remember this."

Lorenzo, who had appeared mildly interested in our conversation to that point, turned his attention fully onto me.

Lorenzo knew what had happened between me and Miles. I hadn't made it a point to bring it up with him; it had just come up after I'd broken my engagement. A few months had passed since Lorenzo and I had talked, and he remembered I was supposed to be married at that point. I had sent him an e-mail about some edits we needed to make on the book he and Renata were writing, and he responded by congratulating me on my marriage and asking me why I hadn't changed my last name. I had to tell him that I had called off the wedding. I suppose professional courtesy prevented him from asking for the pathetic particulars. Or perhaps he really did only care about me—as a friend—and not the details. He asked me how I was, not what happened. And I had told him I was going to be okay, that I had done the right thing, and soon I would feel only relief, not the crushing weight of having hurt someone.

Renata now asked the next logical question—the kind of question a research addict would ask.

"Why didn't you marry him?"

I thought perhaps Lorenzo might say something like, "That's kind of a personal question, don't you think?" But he said nothing. His attention was on me as he waited for me to answer. I had seen that waiting look often. When a wedding is called off, sympathies and curiosities are aroused like you wouldn't believe.

"I knew I didn't love Miles as much as he loved me," I answered. "He deserved someone who did. It was the right thing to do."

"But you accepted his proposal." She didn't frame it as a question but waited for an answer as if she had. Lorenzo did too. And as I sat there in the middle of the noisy restaurant with words flying about me that I didn't understand, I realized no one had ever asked me why I said yes when Miles proposed.

"I wanted to be engaged to him. Later I realized I just didn't want to be married to him. It wouldn't have been right."

"Because you didn't love him."

It still hurt a little to hear my own indictment thrown back on me. "Not enough."

"This is why I have never married." Renata sat back with her cup. "Too complicated, no? Love should be easy."

Lorenzo laughed. "Who says love should be easy?"

"I say so."

Lorenzo's grin widened. "And you make the rules?"

She jabbed her thumb at him. "I make the rules when it comes to me. Just like you make them for you."

"I make no rules for love."

Renata pointed a jeweled finger at her brother. "Oh, but you do. How long did your marriage last? Two years? Your expectations were not met. You ended it. Your rules; your decision."

"Expectations are not the same thing as rules." Lorenzo's tone remained calm and unruffled. I could tell they bantered easily and often with each other.

"But your expectations come from the rules you have set."

"My expectations come from me. The rules for love are outside of me. Where they should be."

She said something in Italian and tossed up her hand for emphasis.

"English, for our dear Marguerite." Lorenzo smiled at me.

"I said, 'Where the hell are these rules, then?'" Renata glared at Lorenzo, but she was smiling, clearly enjoying their argument.

"They are not *in* hell." Lorenzo picked up his own cappuccino, sipped it, and placed it back on its saucer. "Heaven is where the rules for love are, everyone knows that."

"Oh, now we have Lorenzo the theologian." Renata turned to me. "When he was little, Lorenzo wanted to be a priest."

"Really?" I was incredulous. I had never imagined Lorenzo as a priest.

He nodded easily. "But then I changed my mind. I wanted to be a race-car driver. And then an astronaut. And then a model for Armani."

I laughed, but Renata jumped right back in. "You are changing the subject."

"The rules for love are in heaven," he said again, like a volley to his sister.

"But we don't *live* in heaven. We live here." She tossed it back.

"And here is a place where the rules of heaven are needed, don't you think?"

"Those rules do not work here. I have tried them. So have you."

Lorenzo sipped his cup. "I could not live up to the rules. And you could not. The rules are fine. It's us who are broken."

Renata signaled for the check. "You are going to have Meg thinking you are a pious man."

He laughed loudly. "Oh, I think she knows I am not. Just because I don't live by the rules doesn't mean I don't know what they are. And by the way, Marguerite, I think you did the right thing with the man you did not marry. Marrying the wrong person is not good for the heart. It makes it tough."

"It makes it soft, like fruit too ripe," Renata countered. "Look at Sofia. She marries the wrong man when she's very young; he breaks her heart and takes all the pieces with him when he goes. And now she's going gray, and still her heart is jelly." The waiter brought the check to her, and for a second or two, there was silence between us as she gave him a credit card and he walked away.

"I would much prefer the Sofia we have now compared to a hard one. I'm sure Marguerite would agree," Lorenzo said, inviting me into the conversation.

Only I didn't know what to say.

"So do you believe in the rules of heaven, Meg?" Renata asked when I failed to come up with a comment.

I wasn't entirely sure what she was asking me. "Do you mean do I believe God makes the rules about love?"

"Okay," Renata said. "Do you believe God makes the rules about love?"

A Sunday school answer sprang to my mind, and I knew it was true even though I also knew I didn't stop to consider it often enough. "Doesn't God make the rules about everything?"

"Another theologian," Renata muttered, and Lorenzo laughed.

I suddenly remembered something Nonna had told me, something I had forgotten but that this conversation had unearthed inside me. It swelled up from within, and I could hear her voice as plain as any voice in the crowded restaurant.

"My grandmother told me heaven's rules don't just tell us what to do and not do," I said. "They tell us what God is like. People searching for God only need to look at what God says is important. I think love is important to Him. So there are rules about it. Not to make us feel bad about how far we fall short, but to show us how wonderful the real thing is."

Lorenzo and Renata were both silent for a moment, in quiet contemplation.

"The real thing is complicated and dangerous," Renata said, frowning in disagreement.

"And that is what makes it wonderful," Lorenzo said, looking at me and not at her.

❧

We walked slowly back to the flat, Lorenzo and I. Renata rushed ahead to write a magazine article that was due in the morning. Emilio had not returned her call. It was now after ten. She did not think he would call that night.

Her heels tapped a staccato beat as she walked away from us, and Lorenzo turned to me. "It's hard for Renata to understand what made you wait so long for your father to bring you here. Don't feel like you owe her a better explanation. She sees black and white, not so much gray. Even with love, she sees black and white. She doesn't imagine things as how they might be. She sees things as they are."

"Or how they appear," I said. "I don't know if any of us can see things exactly how they are."

He took my arm and laced it through his as we walked. "Smart girl. That is true."

"And I don't see how you can live in a black-and-white world without becoming...uncreative. You can't make anything new. Everything already is what it is."

Renata was far ahead of us now, purpose in every step. I looked up at Lorenzo, whose gaze was on his sister. "You are not a black-and-white person," I said.

He smiled. "No. No, I am not. The best black-and-white photo I have taken is not just black and white. Many shades of gray made it beautiful."

That image made me relax into his nearness.

"But you have to become what you already are. My nonna said that to *me*." He laughed easily. "Renata cannot suddenly be someone she is not. I can't. You can't."

"But people change all the time, Lorenzo."

He was thoughtful for a moment. "People change what they do and how they think. But I don't think they can change who they are. Renata and I were raised by the same parents in the same home with the same opportunities. And look how different we are. It is good that some people see things in black and white and some people, like you and me, cara, can see infinite shades of gray. We carry hope."

"Hope sometimes disappoints you," I said, missing my father at that moment and fully appreciating the fact that we might never see Florence together.

"That's why there are black-and-white people. To remind us of what stays the same, no matter what."

Nora

After I recovered from my illness, my mother's sister-in-law Leonora, unhappily married to my uncle Pietro, mysteriously died at the villa in Caffaggiolo after she and Pietro arrived for a short stay in the country. Nurse told me years later she had been suffocated.

I did not know this had just happened when my father arrived in Florence and hastily arranged a hunting party for him and my mother at the villa at Cerreto Guidi. I saw him for a few moments the day they left for the villa. Virginio and I were playing in the fountains at the palace gardens because it was so hot. Mama was with us. I remember her asking him why he didn't write that he was coming as she would have had us properly attired to greet him. I don't remember what he replied. Or maybe he didn't answer. Virginio and I ran to him, wet and tousled. He touched my damp curls and placed his hand under my chin, lifting it so that my eyes met his. For a moment I thought he was angry that I was sporting about the gardens in wet clothes. His eyes were hard on mine as if he were looking inside me to see if my soul was wet and tousled too. And for a moment, I thought surely he would find that indeed it was. But then his penetrating stare lifted, and he stroked the line of my jaw with his thumb and flicked away a bit of grass—almost a caress. In my memory it feels like a caress. And while he looked at me, he told my mother she and he were to leave as soon as she was packed. Mama asked if Virginio and I were to come along. Virginio was bending down beside us to touch a grasshopper tucked into the blades of grass. With his hand still under my chin, my father said no.

My parents were expected to return within a few days. I waved good-bye to them as though they would. In the folds of my memory, I can see them walking away from me, side by side, as the summer sun beat down on them. Mama was wearing gray. The color of tears.

24

When I arrived back at Sofia's flat after dinner with Lorenzo and Renata, I found her sitting in her father's painting room at a little writing desk, tapping away at her laptop. She told me she was working on one of the new chapters and asked me if I wouldn't mind letting her just keep at it. I wished her a good night, got ready for bed, and climbed into her guest bed. My full stomach kept me from drifting into the sleep my tired body wanted, and it was after midnight before sleep finally overcame me.

In the morning I woke to find Sofia still in bed. The makings of my breakfast were out—bread, Nutella, strawberries, and coffee in the pot—I just needed to press a button to brew it. I found a note from Sofia. She had been up until two, writing. She asked if I wouldn't mind seeing to my breakfast while she slept in. And then we'd go tour the Santa Croce. I made the coffee, toasted the bread, and slathered it with Nutella and sliced strawberries.

An hour later, Sofia joined me on her balcony with her own toast and coffee, sleep still in her eyes. She looked tired. The amount of writing she was trying to accomplish was taxing her. I was glad we were leaving the flat and she'd be away from her desk for a while. We left at ten thirty to walk to the Santa Croce.

"You will love the Basilica di Santa Croce," she said as we walked, and she seemed to gain strength as we made our way down the busy streets. "The tomb of Michelangelo is there, right in front. They say he chose his burial spot himself so that the first thing he would see on the last day, when the graves of the dead burst open, would be Brunelleschi's dome through the open front doors. The tomb of Galileo is there and Machiavelli's. Ghiberti's too. He was the creator of the Baptistery doors. But it's Giotto's frescoes that will leave you awestruck."

She told me the frescoes were recently restored and visitors had been allowed on the scaffolding to see up close the frescoes' intricacies while the restorers worked.

"The site chosen for the Santa Croce was once a marshland outside the city walls," Sofia said. "But Saint Francis himself could see the basilica for what it could be. The frescoes tell his story. And so beautifully. Michelangelo studied those frescoes before he painted the Sistine Chapel. He was inspired by them. It is just like my father said. Out of the marshland arose this beautiful sanctuary. Out of the ugliness, something beautiful."

We turned a corner and the shining facade of the Santa Croce loomed above me, seven hundred years high.

The basilica brimmed with tourists; jaw-dropping Anglos like me who struggled under the weight of visual assault and the enormity of this house of God.

"Does everything in here echo with Nora's voice?" I whispered wearily to Sofia after two hours of gazing at Santa Croce's generous offerings.

"I'd be a dead woman if that were true," she said, smiling, but completely serious.

"Do you walk into a place like this and hear her?"

She took a moment before answering. I either had intruded where she wasn't prepared to welcome me, or she didn't quite know how to explain it to a non-Medici.

"No. It's not like that. I hear her when I am very close to the painting or statue. And only after I have stood there for a few moments. It is sort of like walking into a throne room and you wait for the king to notice you and extend his scepter toward you."

"So, like, she senses when you are near?" I found that notion a little creepy.

"Noooo," she said slowly. "I am just finally able to hear. It's like this. Close your eyes."

I obeyed.

"Tell me what you hear."

I heard the footsteps of shoes on ancient flooring. Low voices carried to the ceiling on a band of echoes as the tourists inside spoke quietly to one another. Someone coughed. A door far off to my right opened. I told Sofia all of this.

"Anything else?"

I strained to listen. The rest of the noise around me was just a soup of indiscriminate resonance. "No."

"Do you not hear the prayers of the woman sitting behind us?"

I was about to open my eyes involuntarily, but Sofia put her hand on my arm. "Keep your eyes closed. Listen for her."

I screwed my eyes shut, thinking that would help, and Sofia whispered to me to relax and listen.

So I did. I breathed in and out, deep cleansing breaths to calm me. It seemed as if many long minutes passed, and I would have grown restless if Sofia had not been at my side, coaxing me to tune everything else out.

And then I seemed to hear the faintest of whispers, carried about as if on a ribbon of air, words that made no sense to me and which sounded only half-formed because of the distance between me and their source.

But I could hear them. I felt a smile crack across my face.

"I hear her!" I whispered.

The moment I said this, the auditory connection was lost. I snapped my eyes open and turned to see the praying woman, and when I did, I nearly staggered. There was no one in the pew behind us. No one.

I turned to see if she had somehow gotten up and walked away already, although I knew that was impossible. The nearest woman was twenty feet away from us.

"I don't understand." I turned to Sofia.

"Sound never disappears. It floats on the air on which it was born and swirls there for all eternity. The prayers you heard were spoken in another time. Maybe yesterday; maybe a hundred yesterdays ago."

"That's not possible," I breathed. "I heard her."

"Yes. You did. But the words were spoken at some time in the past. You heard the echo because I told you to listen for it. I was hearing it too. That's how it is with Nora. What I hear her saying is what she has been saying for centuries. The air about us is woven with her words, the music of her dreams and wishes."

I needed time and space to decide if I had actually heard what I thought I heard or if I had let the power of suggestion woo me. For the sake of her book, I had to understand what she was suggesting so that we could find a way to rationalize it somehow. "Do you ever talk back to her?"

The widening grin on her face suggested I had asked a naive question. "My papa told me that's not what she is here for."

"What?"

"That's not what she is here for," she repeated. "She is here to tutor me, not listen to me. She's here to remind me that art is the artist giving voice to creation. Art speaks words for the heart. In our hearts we hear it."

The desire to see Andromeda was suddenly overpowering. I wanted to believe there was an echo swirling about her as well, an echo that I needed to hear because I had been drawn to her all my life. I didn't want to wait until Sunday anymore.

"Can we change our tickets for the Pitti Palace and go tomorrow?"

"Of course." Sofia neither smiled nor frowned; she just answered me as if I'd asked if there was a nice restaurant nearby for lunch.

Which there was.

❧

When Sofia and I came back from Santa Croce after a leisurely afternoon window-shopping, cappuccino-sipping, and a wonderful meal, it was a little before seven. Sofia was eager to write another chapter, and I told her I was going to pop over to Lorenzo and Renata's and say hello.

I was hoping, of course, that Renata had heard something from Emilio, but that was only half of it. I liked the way Lorenzo made me feel when I was around him, and I wanted to tell him about my strange experience in the Santa Croce. It had floored me and thrilled me. I wanted his perspective, and I hungered for his nearness.

But there was no answer when I knocked on their door.

I went back to Sofia's flat, and I could immediately sense that she was a bit disappointed I had returned so quickly. She probably liked solitude to write; I usually did. She was sitting on her couch with her laptop when I walked in, looking a tad crestfallen.

"I think I will grab my laptop and go find a café with Wi-Fi," I said.

"You don't have to do that," she said quickly.

"I want to. You gave me a lot to think about today. And I won't always have the opportunity to sit in a café in Florence on a lovely evening and watch the world go by."

She didn't try to talk me out of it. Instead, she recommended a place two blocks away with great espresso and free Wi-Fi. And she gave me her door key so that I could get back into the building without having to buzz her.

The evening was cloudy and breezy and smelled faintly of impending rain. I found the café Sofia had recommended and took a corner table near a window. I ordered an espresso, to which I added two packets of raw sugar. I had never tasted coffee that opinionated before.

An e-mail from Beatriz told me she was okay with a July completion date for the rest of Sofia's book, but June would be better. Geoffrey's latest e-mail was a bulleted list of questions he had about other projects I had left in the lurch when I took off without notice. I then sent an e-mail to my mother about where Sofia and I had been today and what we had for dinner and that we'd be seeing the statue that inspired Nonna's painting tomorrow.

There was an e-mail from Gabe, too, about the inside design of a book we were getting ready to publish on road-tripping with dogs. I answered his question and then told him I had been to the Santa Croce and seen the frescoes.

I knew he'd be glad I had found them so remarkable, and as I described my experience, I found myself spilling to him what had happened when Sofia asked me to close my eyes. Even as I wrote to Gabe about it, I could still hear the consonants of a prayer, in a language I didn't understand, on the very air that I was breathing.

I read what I had written to Gabe, and it sounded like I was high on something illegal. I nearly deleted it, but the fact was I *had* heard something. And I had to tell someone about it. I pressed Send before I could change my mind.

It was too early to go back to the flat. I spent the next hour Googling Gian Gastone de' Medici, the man whom Sofia believed was her direct ancestor.

I came up with details of a sad life. He liked booze, gambling, and even other men. He had physical afflictions, didn't take care of himself, and was known for excelling at crudeness. He was nothing at all like Sofia or what I knew of her father. And there was nothing on any of the biographical sites that suggested he had fathered a child.

I was about to close the Google search engine when on impulse I Googled my dad's name to see if it would pop up on a police report or some other kind of headline. I was both relieved and disappointed to get back nothing in the results but his high-school reunion page and the last company he had worked for. I packed up my laptop, paid my bill, and left the café.

I walked for a few blocks just to clear my head, but keeping track of where I was. The last thing I wanted to do was get lost on Florence's asymmetrical streets.

When I got back to the building, I let myself in and climbed the stairs to the second floor. I heard voices from within Lorenzo and Renata's flat.

Good. They were home. Since I had been gone less than two hours, I knew Sofia would appreciate a little more quiet time.

I knocked on the door, and within seconds Renata opened it.

"Meg! Wonderful. Come in."

She pulled me into the flat and shut the door behind me.

She said something in Italian, and I turned, expecting to see Lorenzo.

But it wasn't him. Instead, I was facing a man about Lorenzo's height and build but with a full head of wavy hair that nibbled at his collar. He was quite handsome.

Renata rattled off something else—I heard my name in the mix—and the man stepped forward and put out his right hand to shake mine.

"This is Carlo," she said to me.

"Pleased to meet," Carlo said. "Sorry, English is not so good."

I shook his hand. "My Italian is not so good either."

He laughed lightly. A gold incisor shone back at me.

"Come have a drink with us."

Renata pulled me to the balcony, grabbing three wineglasses along the way. Outside on the balcony, candles were lit and a dark bottle was resting on a tipped apparatus that allowed the uncorked wine to breathe. The tableau looked very romantic.

"I won't stay," I said.

"Of course you will stay." Renata patted a chair and I sat down. She and Carlo settled into chairs across from me, and Renata poured the wine.

"Lorenzo isn't here?" I felt out of place and hoped Renata would tell me he was just in the other room finishing up a phone call.

"No. He had a date." She handed me my glass.

It should not have felt like a slap, not even a little one, but it did for some reason. Lorenzo had a date. He had a date. Four words that felt like a slap from myself to myself. I sipped the wine to quench the tiny sting.

"So where did you go today?" Renata turned to Carlo, handed him a glass, and said something in Italian to him. Then she turned back to me. "I told him you work for my publisher here and are visiting Florence for the first time."

"Oh. We saw Santa Croce." *And I heard the prayers of a woman who wasn't there.*

"Ah. Santa Croce is very old. Very beautiful. You saw the tomb of Michelangelo, yes?"

I nodded and sipped.

She said something to Carlo. I don't think it was about Santa Croce. I didn't think we'd be talking about it anymore. The Santa Croce to Renata was probably like the San Diego Zoo to me. Amazing place, all too familiar.

I decided it was okay to change the subject.

"Have you heard anything from Emilio?"

She nodded while swallowing a sip of wine. "Yes. He texted me."

"He did?"

Renata frowned a bit. "My message to him confused him a bit. He wants to talk to me on the phone, but he's in Portugal for a business trip. He gets back Friday."

"Confused him?"

"I don't think he knows Sofia is writing a book. That part confused him, I think. He might be wondering what she will say. About him, maybe."

I felt a thread of regret weave through me. It had not occurred to me that Emilio wouldn't know Sofia was writing a book. A memoir to be exact. It was stupid of me not to consider she would want to be in charge of him finding out.

This was probably an additional reason Lorenzo had cautioned us about talking to Emilio without asking Sofia first.

I groaned a little in remorse.

"What?" Renata looked at me. "You don't like the wine?"

"I think maybe Lorenzo was right. We should've waited and asked Sofia if she minded us getting in touch with Emilio. Now he knows about the book."

"What's wrong with that?"

"Well, he's probably concerned it's a memoir about his family."

Renata shrugged. "But isn't the book about Florence and the Medicis? They are all dead. Their ancestors are all dead. Who can she offend? They're all dead."

I knew I wouldn't win an argument with black-and-white Renata on this. I said a silent prayer that Emilio wouldn't cause trouble for Sofia. And that Sofia wouldn't be mad at me for very long. Beatriz was not going to like it if Sofia was angry with me.

"It is not going to be a big thing," Renata assured me. "Do not worry. Emilio and I will talk on Friday. I will set him straight. Do not worry."

I tried not to worry, but I did a little. We talked about other things for a while, Renata and I, and occasionally Carlo would toss in a comment or two in broken English. I was nearly done with my glass and ready to head back over to Sofia's when we all heard the front door open. Lorenzo was home.

And he had brought his date with him.

I watched in what can only be described as junior-high jealousy as he came out onto the balcony with a lithe brunette on his arm. Her shining brown hair hung halfway down her back in thick, luxurious curls, and she wore a flowing, off-white dress that complemented her bronze skin. Gold jewelry sparkled in the moonlight.

"Marguerite! How lovely you are here." Lorenzo came toward me, date in tow. He bent down to kiss me on both cheeks, while the girl on his arm blinked languidly. Her eyelashes could shut a door with one swipe.

When he stood back up, she leaned into him and said something. Her voice was velvet deep. She was definitely an alto. He said something back to her, and she laughed and kissed his cheek.

I swallowed the last of my wine and held up my empty glass as I stood. "I was just leaving, actually."

"No, no!" Lorenzo said. "Stay!" He turned to his date. "Bianca, this is Marguerite. She is with my publisher."

Bianca smiled. Professionally whitened and perfectly straight teeth saluted me. "Hallo, Marguerite. Very nice to meet you."

"Nice to meet you too. But I really should be going."

I set the glass down on the little table between the chairs. "Wonderful to meet you, Carlo. Thanks for the wine, Renata."

"I will find you on Friday after I talk to Emilio." Renata rose from her chair and kissed my cheek good night. "You look tired."

I never know what to say when someone says I look tired. Thank you? Sorry? Back atcha?

I smiled and said good night to all of them, my gaze lingering on Lorenzo, who looked disappointed that I was leaving.

"I will see you out," he said. He brought Bianca's hand to his lips, kissed it, and then peeled himself away from her.

"I'm fine; you don't have to," I said, making my way through the open living room to the front door. But he was right behind me.

He put his hand on my arm. "Is everything all right, cara? Did you hear something bad about your father?"

"No. And yes, everything is all right."

Lorenzo frowned. "But you look sad."

"I am fine. Thanks."

Bianca poked her head through the open balcony doors and said something to Lorenzo.

I turned the knob on the door.

"Where are you going tomorrow?" he asked.

To see if I can hear a statue. "The Pitti Palace."

"How about you and Sofia come for dinner here afterward?"

"We have supper with Lauro and Pepe tomorrow!" Renata called from the balcony.

"Certo!" Lorenzo tapped his forehead. "Friday? You and Sofia come Friday?"

"Sure."

From the balcony I heard laughter. It was starting to rain. Renata, Carlo, and Bianca came inside, smiling and shaking rain out of their hair.

"Buona notte." Lorenzo leaned in and kissed me on the cheek.

"Good night." I stepped out into the foyer and closed the door behind me.

Nora

I have long known that death is a robber. The statue of Adonis in torment, the many depictions of the suffering of the Christ, and the frescoes of the Last Judgment have long whispered to me that death steals, and not just a little here and there. It takes everything. And its sweeping hand is expertly skilled. It knows how to accomplish its task.

But when you are five, death seems an ignorant brute who makes terrible mistakes.

Some have wondered why my mother, so shrewd in other matters, did not see what was coming and why she did not flee to Livorno to board a ship for some safer place the minute she got word her sister-in-law Leonora was dead. That is easy. I can answer that in three words. Virginio and me. We were back in Florence. She wouldn't leave Florence without us.

I didn't know for a very long time what happened after my parents left for the villa and Virginio and I returned to laughing as we splashed about in the fountain.

All I knew then is that my parents went on a hunting trip into the country. Mama had kissed me good-bye, told me to mind Nurse and not to quarrel with Virginio and to dream of her while I slept. I did. I still do.

My mother died at the villa. Unexpectedly, so the death notifications read, while washing her hair. Nurse, in tears, had to tell Virginio and me that our parents would not be returning to the palace after all. Papa had gone back to Rome. And Mama was in heaven with the angels.

25

We awoke to rain. Sofia said we could either take umbrellas with us on our half-mile walk to the Pitti Palace or she could call for a taxi, but I didn't mind the gentle sprinkle that would fall on us as we walked the shining streets. I told her I was fine with walking.

She showed me her latest pages as we ate yogurt and toast for breakfast. Sofia's new chapter was about the four Medici popes. She had struggled with the writing of it. Some of them had not been particularly admirable holy fathers, she said.

Lorenzo stopped over just before we left to tell us we could not have dinner together on Friday either. He had forgotten he had other plans. Could we come for breakfast on Saturday instead? Sofia offered him a cup of coffee and a piece of toast, but he had camera equipment strapped to his body and was clearly late for wherever it was he had to go.

"It's raining," I told him.

And he just smiled and said his camera bags had been rained on before.

"Breakfast on Saturday!" he yelled as he took to the stairs.

We watched him descend.

"Shall we?" Sofia asked.

A few minutes later, we stepped out into the rain. As we walked across the Ponte Vecchio, I lingered at the windows of the goldsmiths' shops. Sofia let me look but told me not to buy there. The jewelry on the bridge is priced for the tourist, she said. And that's not what I was. She told me she would take me to a few of her favorite stores later to get some things to take home with me.

By the time we were in sight of the massive Pitti Palace, the rain had stopped, and a weak sun was pushing its way through a bank of clouds. I was glad for the patchy sun to brighten my spirits. Lorenzo's change of plans had irked me a little.

Sofia guided me into the expansive garden from the palace courtyard, past a stone amphitheater behind the palace, and up the hill to a fountain of Neptune. I was anxious to see my statue and she knew it. The garden was beautiful and big and hilly, and had it been any other garden, I would have wanted to take my time strolling about its lawns and landscaping. But my goal was the fountain where Andromeda waited for me. We walked down a sweeping hill, past groves and gardens on either side, down the Viottolone—a grand avenue of cypresses—that would lead us to the Isolotto Basin at the bottom of the decline, and my Andromeda.

"Some of these trees are more than three hundred years old," Sofia said as we walked.

I mumbled a comment about that being pretty darn ancient for a tree.

Her next question came out of nowhere.

"Are you in love with Lorenzo?"

I turned to her. "Are you serious?"

"Of course I'm serious."

"What makes you ask?" I half laughed.

"I saw the way you looked at him this morning. And the way your face changed when he told you he couldn't have dinner with us tomorrow. I saw that too. I'm not saying it's bad if you are."

"I am not in love with Lorenzo."

"Okay," Sofia said.

A couple of seconds of silence passed as we walked under the trees.

"That's it?" I asked. "Just, 'Okay'?" Again I laughed, halfheartedly.

"You said you are not," she said. "I will believe you."

"I am not in love with Lorenzo."

"But there is something, yes? Something there. You're not sure what it is."

I was ready to disagree with her, but I felt a tingling sensation up and down my spine convincing me she was partially right.

"Maybe. Sort of. I don't know."

And she simply nodded, silently inviting me to continue.

"I'm a little mixed up right now. There's a man who's incredibly kind to me, and we get along well. And I like him. Then there's my mother's new boyfriend who is this perfect guy, and I so want to meet a guy like that. At least I think I do. I...I don't know."

"Sometimes it's not about what we know. It's about what we are willing to trust." She was looking at the trees and sky above us when she said this, as if searching for a peephole into heaven from which Nora might be looking down on her as Sofia gave me counsel.

"I'm not sure what you mean."

"Which one of them would make you the most sad if you had to live your life without him?"

I had no answer to such a question. "I have no idea."

She pulled her gaze away from the treetops. "Deep down, you probably do. But you are afraid to trust your choice. It's risky. That's why it's about what you are willing to trust."

I thought about what she had told me about the man she loved, who left her. I chanced the question that rose to my lips.

"Don't you have regrets about who you decided to trust?"

Sofia took a moment before answering. "I don't regret loving Thomas. Those were the happiest years of my life."

I couldn't help but ask the obvious. "But then he left and handed you the worst years of your life, right?"

She shuddered. "Yes. They were terrible years." For a moment Sofia seemed to disappear into a dark corner of her mind. A thin, veil-like shadow fell across her face and a flicker of fear sputtered inside me. I had asked too much.

But then the veil seemed to lift. She inhaled and closed her eyes, recentering her thoughts, it seemed, on what she had learned to lean on.

"But the terrible years didn't make the wonderful years disappear," she said. "I still have them." She looked at me and smiled. "They will always be mine. And the wonderful years are worth having."

I smiled back at her. "How long did it take for you to figure that out?"

She laughed lightly. "I actually didn't have to figure it out. Nora had been whispering it to me all along. I had just stopped listening."

I suddenly hungered to know where Nora had imparted such lofty wisdom, nearly paternal in its beauty. Which statue, which painting, had whispered this to her?

"Where did she tell you this?"

"Everywhere."

Sofia stopped then and grasped my arm. "It was worth it, Meg. It was worth the risk."

Sofia said nothing else and we kept walking. I was glad to again be alone with my thoughts. And the reality that Sofia seemed to think lay before me.

Devon, a man I hardly knew, had already chosen my mother over me. How could I even think of him as part of my dilemma? He surely had to be a representation to me of some kind of security that was missing from my life. Gabe, my office confidant, was a kindred soul at the sweetest friendship level; I liked him. But affection for him felt almost obligatory, as if I must feel a romantic attraction toward him because he was single and I was single and we got along so well. Lorenzo. Lorenzo pulled at some deep part of me that even Miles hadn't been able to rouse. The way I felt when I was near him was new and striking and powerful. But Lorenzo couldn't possibly feel the same way about me. He was a product of his intensely romantic culture, one that captivated me and led my foolish heart to believe something that was not meant just for me. Loving him would crush me. In almost the same way as loving my father had left me broken.

But Sofia hadn't asked me which one I felt most attracted to. She asked which one of them, if he were completely absent from my life, would leave me the most devastated.

I pushed the question away. I didn't want to think about it anymore. It was too complicated. Or too simple. Either way, I wasn't ready to ponder what Sofia said I'd already subconsciously decided.

We were at the end of the cypress lane, and before us was the oval basin and Giambologna's Oceanus fountain. Even before I could clearly make out the other figures in the water, I could see Andromeda's outstretched arms and Perseus, her rescuer rising from the sea on Pegasus, determined to set her free.

There were a number of people sitting on benches arranged all around the oval, looking at maps, taking pictures, and posing with the statuary in the background. I wanted to shoo them all away. It took effort not to. I wanted to be alone with the statue that was all mine.

"Well?" Sofia asked softly. "Is she the one?"

"Yes."

We neared the fountain's edge, and I positioned myself to gaze at Andromeda, many feet away from me, from the vantage point where my great-great-grandfather would have painted her.

Sofia took a few steps back from me, gifting me with the chance to experience finding the statue on more intimate terms.

Andromeda seemed too far away, sitting there in the water, in her weathered-marbled pose. The expression on her face was unfamiliar to me and too hard to distinguish. Water weeds had sprouted up on the rocks she was chained to, and two ducks perched at her feet like irreverent bystanders. One of them pecked at a feather on its back. Bird droppings had slid down her face, and her knees were yellow-green with furred patches of moss. The outstretched hand that was lifted toward heaven was missing two fingers. More bird droppings littered the other hand that she held across her breast in hopeful anticipation of rescue.

A wave of disappointment crept over me.

My great-great-grandfather had painted her far differently. He had endowed his Andromeda with such elegance and beauty that it was easy to believe Perseus would battle a monster no one else had been able to kill—just to rescue her. And my great-great-grandfather's perspective had placed the statue not yards away in a watered prison, but close to the form of my young grandmother who held her own hand toward Andromeda's in a mirrored pose.

He had reimagined Andromeda as beautiful and still hopeful. I turned toward Sofia.

"She's not how I pictured her." Disappointment tugged heavily at my words. "She looks so beaten down."

Sofia nodded sympathetically. "The elements are hard on outdoor statuary. There are other statues of Andromeda. And paintings too. I can show you those."

"But this is the one that mattered to me." I raised my camera, but then lowered it. I suddenly didn't want a picture of the way the statue really looked. I did not want to remember her this way, my beloved, beckoning Andromeda. As if in sympathy for me, the sun edged behind a lingering cloud. I turned away from the statue. "I like the one I see in my memory so much better."

"Then that's the one you hang on to, Marguerite. That's the one you keep."

We turned around and began to walk out of the cypress alley back toward the palace. Sofia shared with me the storied details of the Pitti Palace and the Medicis who had lived there, a kind distraction from the disappointment still swirling inside me.

Clouds were again gathering overhead, and a breeze began to pick up. We were still a few minutes' walk from the palace's front doors.

We quickened our steps.

Finally the palace was in front of us, but it looked plain and homely to me, void of outside decoration, just cube after cube of enormous wheat-colored stone, three stories high.

As we prepared to go in, Sofia told me there was much to see inside, especially in the more than twenty-eight rooms in the Palatine Gallery. But she told me there was a painting she wanted to show me first that hung in the corner between one salon and another.

The opulence inside was staggering, and I kept my eyes trained ahead as we made our way to the left wing of the first floor. We were headed for the farthest corner, bypassing salon after salon of canvas-filled rooms.

We arrived at an alcove of sorts where several statues dominated the visual landscape. At the corner where two walls came together, three paintings hung in a seemingly forgotten place.

The one in the middle, not much bigger than the spread of my outstretched arms, drew me in. I knew in an instant the young girl who stared back at me from within the paint strokes was Nora Orsini.

The girl looked to be twelve or thirteen. Her brown hair was pulled away from her face, revealing deep brown eyes that bore into mine. Her caramel-hued dress was cut tight across her bodice, sucking her into it, it seemed. A pearl necklace circled her neck. Her closed mouth was slightly upturned in the makings of a subtle smile. She held two paintbrushes in her hand.

"Nora painted?"

Sofia smiled. "She did. This was her self-portrait. It's not signed. No one else attributes it to her. But I know she painted it. She whispers that she did. It's the only painting of hers there is."

"Why is it here in the corner like this?"

"Everyone thinks it was painted by a nameless art student in the late fifteen hundreds. It is still a valuable painting based on its age, but the curators here don't know who painted it. How could they know? She didn't sign it."

Up to that moment, every work of art I had seen in Florence had been created by a man. I uttered something of this notion as I stood there staring at Nora's image.

"All the great Renaissance painters were men," Sofia said, "but that does not mean that Renaissance women could not paint or didn't have the aptitude for it. Some had it, but they were not encouraged to pursue it as anything but parlor entertainments. They appreciated beauty in the arts just as much as the men did. They knew the arts' ability to redeem, just like the men did. They probably needed that loveliness more than the men did."

Sofia took a step toward the painting so that her body touched the velvet rope that kept spectators at a safe distance. She was as close to the painting as she could legally get.

"If you can imagine your life is peaceful and good, that your father and mother care for each other, and you are as sure of their affection for each other as their unchanging love for you, then you can paint yourself like this. You can paint what you believe. If you can imagine it, you can paint it."

I started to ask her what she meant, but before I could, she continued.

"And if you could escape to that painted place in your dreams, the time when life had been wonderful, because the truth is, your father murdered your mother and did not care if he ever saw you again, then of course you would."

"I guess you would."

"The first time I saw this painting, I was unable to walk away from it; it pulled me so. I asked my papa why. He said he wanted me to discover for myself why Nora Orsini's portrait tugged at me. Papa told me to close my eyes and listen; just like I had you close yours in the chapel. To shut everything else out and listen, inviting her, by my silence, to speak. You see, Marguerite? She painted herself happy. She created a place in her mind where she could have her wonderful years. No one could take them from her."

At that moment I had a sudden influx of memories of my parents and me when we were still whole; those magical years before the divorce, before my perception of family had been swept away from me. Before the miscarriage, before my dad met Allison, there had been wonderful years. I was a child; I saw the wonderful, more than the terrible. A child's vision is geared to see the wonderful.

My father had confessed to me on Poppy-Seed Day that he felt like he had failed me as a father in my growing-up years, but the truth was, I never felt he had. Even after the divorce, I wanted him to be my Perseus. What I needed now was a new kind of rescuer. I wasn't a little girl anymore. Little girls in distress are rescued by their fathers. Grown girls in distress want to be rescued by someone else.

I wanted a prince to show up, not my dad.

I pulled out my camera, made sure the flash was off, and took a picture of the canvas in front of us. This would be the picture I took home from today. Not a shot of a decaying statue.

Nora Orsini wanted to imagine that a different life could be hers.

So she did.

She looked at herself in a mirror and painted the girl she wanted to see.

Nora

I remember lying in my bed in the suffocating heat and calling for my mother. Nurse told me she couldn't come; she was in heaven with the angels. I told Nurse to go fetch her for me.

And Nurse said heaven is not a place with a door.

"I want her," I said.

"She is with the angels," said Nurse.

For a while I hated every angel in every painting and statue and tapestry, for they had my mother and were keeping her from me. I wouldn't look at them, and I said terrible things under my breath when I passed them.

And then I began to fear them. Would they hurt my mother because I hated them? I wasn't sure. After a while my hatred was exhausting; it sapped me of breath and strength and sleep.

In my weariness I began to be drawn to the angels for solace. They had my mother. If I could be close to them, I could be close to her.

And then I began to cherish them. I wandered the halls and gazed up at them in their paintings and in stone, in reverent devotion like a lovesick maiden.

And then I began to listen to them.

26

Sofia was up before me the next morning, tapping away at her laptop. Later we would see the Medici Chapels and the Basilica of Santa Maria Novella, but we had planned a quiet morning working on Sofia's book before stepping out. I had her other finished chapters to read and send to Beatriz, and she wanted to spend the morning hours writing.

I knew at some point that day, Renata would be talking to Emilio. Emilio had not called Sofia to find out what the heck was going on; she would have said something if he had. As I sat reading her chapter on Lucrezia Tornabuoni de' Medici—finally a Medici with merit—I decided to pave the way for a later conversation about Emilio. I was pretty sure there would be one. She was going to have to know at some point that we had contacted him, especially if he was the one to help us authenticate Sofia's ancestry.

When she got up from her laptop to refill her coffee cup, I asked her as casually as I could if she had any other family on her father's side besides Emilio. Cousins, perhaps?

"No. Emilio never married." She set the carafe back in the coffee maker.

I hurriedly dashed out another question. "Does Emilio ever come to Florence?"

She nodded slowly. "Sometimes. He prefers Rome."

"But I suppose with the building to co-manage, he has to come sometimes."

A tiny frown crossed her face. She was trying to figure out where I was going with this conversation. "I already told you he won't help me with this." She nodded toward the pages I was reading.

"What if we just ask him?" I kept my tone light and casual.

She shook her head. "I know you mean well, Meg. But I do not trust Emilio. My father does not trust him. I know they are brothers and he should not feel that way. But he does. Emilio only cares about money. He would love to sell this building right out from under my father and me. Nothing matters to him but getting what he wants. I do not trust him."

Cold apprehension poked at me. I didn't know what to say next, and since I said nothing, Sofia walked back to her laptop and sat down.

I waited a few minutes and then announced I was going to take a little walk to stretch my legs and that I wouldn't be long.

I sauntered out of the flat and then dashed across the landing to Renata and Lorenzo's door. I had to tell her we needed to nix the call with Emilio for now. I would find some other way to get what we needed.

But there was no answer at the door. I didn't have Renata's cell phone number, but I knew I had Lorenzo's. I pulled my phone out of my pocket and texted him to tell Renata to text me as soon as possible. It was urgent.

I went downstairs and then out the front door to take the walk I said I was going to take, holding my cell phone in my hand and waiting to hear back. After ten minutes Lorenzo texted me that he had left a message for Renata to call him. She was in a meeting with the editors of the magazine she often writes for. He also asked what had happened.

"We need to drop the call to Emilio today," I texted.

A few minutes later, he texted me back.

"She already talked to him."

My heart sank.

"What did he say?"

"I left before she hung up. On a shoot."

My mind began to race with how I would be able to convince Sofia that we had contacted Emilio before she told me she didn't trust him. It was too late to think we wouldn't have that conversation. My phone vibrated in my hand. Lorenzo had sent me another text.

"She just texted me."

And then another text.

"Come over tonight after 9:30."

"Good news or bad news?" I texted.

It was several minutes before he texted me back.

"Neither."

How could it be neither? If Emilio could help us and would help us, that was good news. If he wouldn't or couldn't, that was bad.

How could black-and-white Renata say it was neither?

I walked slowly back to the flat, at a snail's pace, to convince myself "neither" surely had to be more good than bad.

❧

I pushed my upcoming rendezvous with Renata far out of my mind so that I could enjoy seeing the Medici Chapels and the stunning beauty of the Santa Maria Novella. The afternoon was resplendent with grace and beauty, as all my Florentine afternoons had been.

We stopped for cappuccinos on the walk back to the flat, and I bought a couple of unframed paintings—one for my mother and one for Beatriz—from one of the many artists painting and selling their work in the piazza of the coffee shop.

Sofia was making headway with her chapters and wanted to get back to them as the day began to edge toward twilight. I wasn't looking forward to three hours in her flat waiting for the clock to read 9:30 p.m. I told her I wanted to explore on foot a little bit and that I'd get a bite to eat and be back later that evening. She was visibly grateful for the privacy and again gave me her entry key. I took with me a volume of Lord Byron's poetry, which I found on one of her bookshelves, in English, so that I figuratively wouldn't have to eat alone.

I was starting to know my way around and confidently ventured farther away from the flat. A little riverside restaurant caught my eye, but I couldn't figure out how to get down to it. I found a valet at a nearby hotel who spoke English and asked him if he knew how to get to the little restaurant on the river. His English wasn't perfect, but he told me to look for the "green door on the left." I went back to where I could see the restaurant's patio, found the green door, and rang the buzzer, not sure what I was going to do if someone answered in Italian. Instead of a voice, I heard a buzz to let me in. I opened the door and found a set of winding marble steps that led to an area below the street.

I passed empty rooms and a hallway full of trophies and pictures of men rowing and arrived at a counter where a thin man with spurts of gray hair stood bent over a ledger.

"Is this the right place for the restaurant down by the water?" I asked, sincerely hoping he spoke English.

To my joy, he did. He told me I was in the building of the Florence rowing society, and this was an exclusive restaurant for rowing-club members only, but as they were uncharacteristically not busy for a Friday night, I was invited inside.

I was shown to a table on the patio, under a canopy of ivy-like vines with only a handful of other guests, no doubt all members of Florence's rowing club.

After an appetizer of *stracchino* cheese and prosciutto, I had a salami-and-fig pasta dish that my English-speaking waiter recommended, paired with a Tuscan white wine. He also recommended the tiramisu for dessert, which he promised would be better than anything I had ever had in the States. And he was right.

The amazing meal and Byron's poetry were a welcome distraction, and when I left by the way I had come, it was twenty minutes after nine.

By the time I got back to Sofia's building, it was a few minutes after nine thirty. I came up the stairs virtually on tiptoe and quietly knocked on Renata and Lorenzo's door. I didn't want Sofia to hear that I was back and decide to join me.

Renata called from within her flat, welcoming me in.

I stepped inside. She was sifting through mail at the island counter that separated her kitchen from the main room. I didn't see Lorenzo.

"Come in, come in," she said.

I closed the door behind me.

"Wine?" She lifted a decanter.

"No thanks."

She poured herself a glass and motioned for me to follow her into the living room.

We took seats. Me on a chair; she on the couch. She kicked off her pumps and pulled her legs up onto the couch. Her toenails were painted a vibrant orange.

She had a strange look on her face, as if she didn't know how to begin.

"What is it?" I said. "Just tell me what he said. Is he mad? Is he going to make trouble for Sofia?"

Renata crossed her brows in surprise. "No, he's not mad. Why should he be mad?"

"Because... I don't know. Sofia says that's the kind of person he is. That he's mad all the time."

She took a sip of her wine and then set it down on an end table. "I wouldn't say that. He is not outgoing. He does not like silliness or foolish talk. He's…serious. But not mad."

"Is he upset about the book? Is he going to make trouble for her? She told me she doesn't trust him. That he only cares about money. And that he'd sell this building out from underneath her and her father if he could."

It had all tumbled out of my mouth before I could consider whether I should say any of it.

Again, Renata's brow creased in consternation. "She said all that?"

"Yes."

Renata shrugged. "That's not how he comes across to me. Yes, he's rich. Yes, he's done well for himself. But I don't think he'd sell this building unless Angelo wanted to. He couldn't. It's only half his."

"Well, then, what is it? What is neither good nor bad? Are they not Medici? Is that it? Did Emilio tell you his family is not Medici?"

I wasn't sure what we were going to do if Emilio had said outright that the family ancestry did not include Medicis. Would Beatriz put the brakes on the whole thing?

"He says it's possible. But he doesn't have any proof."

So we were back to square one and having to do the digging ourselves. I thought of the hours I had spent that day telling myself to relax and enjoy the sights. "You couldn't have told me that this morning when Lorenzo texted you?"

Renata fingered a dangling earring. "This is not all he told me."

"What, then? What else did he say?"

"Even if his family was related to the Medicis, it wouldn't matter, Meg." That made no sense.

Renata swung her legs around so that she could look at me fully.

"Sofia is adopted."

Nora

I wandered the palace, seeking out my angels, inclining an ear to them to hear if they had words of comfort for me. Sometimes I could hear them telling me my mother missed me and spoke of me and sang songs about me. Sometimes I took Virginio by the hand to show him the angels in the paintings and statues, and I would tell him the angels were with Mama and they could take messages to her from us.

But after a while, he stopped wanting to come with me. He couldn't hear them. And he didn't like it that I could hear the angels and he couldn't.

As the year ended, Nurse thought Virginio and I would be leaving for Rome because that's where our father lived and Uncle Francesco said that's where we belonged. She set about getting everything ready, but he never sent for us.

He misses Mama, I told Virginio. That's why he doesn't send for us.

27

The three words fell easily off Renata's lips but landed hard on my ears.

"She's *what*?" I gasped.

"She's adopted. And she doesn't know it. And it wasn't legal. Emilio said this is a huge reason he and Angelo don't get along. They don't agree on this. Angelo never told Sofia. Natalia never told her. She doesn't know. And Emilio thinks that is wrong."

Oh, Lord. Lord, Lord. "Are you sure this isn't just something Emilio is making up because he doesn't like her?"

Renata looked intently at me. "Meg, what Sofia told you is not true. Emilio told me Angelo is the one who put distance between them. Emilio did not like what Angelo and Natalia did. It wasn't right."

"Are you telling me they kidnapped her or something?"

Renata shook her head. "No. Not exactly. But they didn't adopt her the way most children are adopted. I am not sure it is even recorded anywhere."

"Oh my gosh." I was floored. "Tell me everything he told you."

"Angelo was a night guard at the Uffizi many years ago, back when their father was still alive and he still owned the building. Emilio was still in Florence then. Angelo found Sofia and her real mother attempting to spend the night in one of the Uffizi bathrooms. Sofia was only four. Her mother begged Angelo not to send them away or call the police because her husband was a policeman and he would beat her for running away. He would beat their daughter too, whom the mother called Serafina. She told him her husband said if she ever tried to run away, he'd kill her and their daughter. He often beat them. All she wanted was to get away from him.

"So Angelo brought the mother and the girl, Serafina, to the flat and kept them there for several weeks. The mother was introduced as Natalia's cousin, and the little girl was introduced as Sofia. The mother knew she couldn't stay there forever so she began to come up with a plan to escape to the United States. She was sneaking back to her house to get things. Money. Papers. One day she went back and the husband was there waiting for her. He shot her, killing her, and then he disappeared. The newspapers said he was a model police officer and his coworkers could not understand why he had shot his wife. Everyone believed he took his daughter and fled the country out of remorse over what he had done."

I sat spellbound by what Renata was telling me. She took a sip from her wineglass and continued.

"Emilio said Angelo knew when he read the papers about the murder that Sofia's mother was dead. And the father probably would not return to Florence to look for his daughter. By this time a month had passed, and he and Natalia had both grown fond of the little girl, and they knew she needed them. She was prone to night terrors, and she'd spend hours in Natalia's and Angelo's arms, trembling and unable to speak. Natalia didn't want to let the police know they had the dead woman's daughter because they would take her and put her in some foster home. And because Natalia only ever had miscarriages and wanted a child so badly, Angelo agreed they wouldn't tell the authorities. They just continued the story to the other renters in the building that Sofia was Natalia's niece and they were adopting her because her unwed mother could not keep her. After a while people forgot that Sofia was a niece. There is nobody here in this neighborhood now who remembers her being anyone other than Angelo and Natalia's daughter."

"And all this business about them being Medici? Are they?"

"Emilio said there was this great-uncle on their father's side who used to say the Borellis were Medici from way back—that's why they were so smart with their money and had all the pretty women. But Emilio said it was just something the uncle joked about. No one ever really believed him."

"Angelo did." But as soon as I said it, I knew that wasn't necessarily true. I knew enough about Angelo to be convinced he had a compassionate heart, even if his compassion was to the extreme. If he thought telling young Sofia she was a Medici would imbue her with the resilience she needed to recover from her father's abuse and her mother's absence, then that's what he would do.

In fact, everything Sofia had told me to that point about her father revealed his desire to equip her to deal with the terrible hand she'd been dealt, from the lire coin to telling her the statues and paintings would whisper to her if she listened very carefully.

That's why he told her not to tell anyone; not to keep her from distancing herself from people, but to keep her coping mechanism safe. If it was ridiculed out of her, what would happen then?

Angelo had empowered Sofia to believe Nora Orsini, a long-ago relative, spoke to her through statues and paintings. It wasn't because she was a Medici that she could hear them. It was because she imagined she could. She needed to imagine that she could.

"There's more," Renata said. "There are things Emilio says you should know. Because he doesn't want you to publish the book."

It took me a second to ask what that something was. For a moment I had forgotten about the book.

"You know Sofia was married once. You know the bum she married already had a wife, yes?"

I nodded.

"Well, when she found out and the bum left her, Sofia had a breakdown. She tried to commit suicide twice and had to be institutionalized. She was shouting all the time for Nora to shut up and leave her alone. Emilio said she was finally released seven years later. Her doctor apparently wouldn't let her leave until she would admit Nora Orsini wasn't communicating with her from within statues and paintings. Emilio knows Angelo let Sofia believe Nora talked to her. He didn't like that either. When Sofia was released, Angelo told Emilio that Sofia did not hear Nora's voice anymore. Emilio had no idea she thinks she still hears it."

"What is so terrible about thinking you can hear a statue or painting speak to you?" I huffed.

"It's not terrible until someone thinks you're crazy. She can't prove she is a Medici—even if she was Angelo's daughter, she could not prove this. And if she comes under a firestorm of criticism, even in just the little niche world of travel memoirs, what will that do to her? This is what Emilio is concerned about. And, Meg, so am I."

I lowered my forehead into my upturned hand, kneading my temple. This was a mess. I could probably put the brakes on the project by just telling Beatriz and Geoffrey the family could offer no proof of Medici ancestry. But I was already dreading telling Sofia that the project was pretty much dead in the water. I didn't want to be the one to tell her we'd contacted Emilio and he had said there wasn't an ounce of proof they shared Medici blood, that it was far more likely it was a family joke.

She wouldn't believe me, for one thing. She could hear Nora speaking to her. Of course she was a Medici. How dare I suggest she wasn't?

She'd be mad at me for going behind her back and contacting Emilio.

She'd be devastated at losing the book deal because I believed Emilio and not her.

It was a boatload of multiple disappointments that I was about to hand her.

Maybe we didn't have to tell her we'd contacted Emilio. Maybe I could have Renata call him back and tell him I wouldn't be publishing the book, so he didn't have to worry about it, and we could just pretend we never brought it up.

I could just tell Sofia I wasn't finding any ancestral connection to Gian Gastone de' Medici and, as I had told her earlier, Beatriz was pretty clear on verified ancestry. We needed documentation.

I would encourage her to keep writing to finish the book for herself. I would tell her that she was a fabulous writer and that I could help her turn her chapters into magazine articles for travel magazines. We would just stick to the facts and edit the Medici stuff we couldn't prove and the talking statues that people wouldn't understand.

And if I could convince Sofia to do that, maybe I could convince Beatriz to look at Sofia's chapters as insights from a Florentine native who has been a tour guide all her life. We could keep the references to her wise father intact but just ease up a little on the Medici content and include more non-Medici people. Like Raphael. And Donatello. And Michelangelo.

This could work.

This didn't have to end with Sofia having the carpet pulled out from underneath her.

I started to spill my hastily concocted plan. "We don't have to tell Sofia we contacted Emilio. We can just tell him not to say anything, and I won't publish the book."

Renata was already shaking her head. "It's too late. He's coming."

"Here?"

She nodded.

"Well, tell him it's no big deal. He doesn't have to come. I'm not publishing it."

"It's not just that, Meg. Emilio told me Angelo sold the tour agency to pay for his place at the facility. He doesn't own it anymore. He put the money he made from the sale into an account that pays for his place at the facility and a generous monthly stipend for Sofia. Sofia doesn't work there anymore. The new owners didn't want to keep her on staff. She hasn't worked there in over a year. But she has been able to pretend, even in front of her closest neighbors, that she is still employed there. She's not well, Meg."

Stunned, I groped for words. "She told me she took the week off. She told me she left the college students to take her tours. She…" I didn't finish. I was beginning to connect the dots. Sofia was the queen of being able to imagine that what you want to be true is true. How hard would it be for her to imagine she went to work every day leading eager tourists around the city she loved? She walked around in her illusions every day of her simple and happy life. She wasn't just holding tight the memory of wonderful years, she was inventing wonderful where it didn't exist. "What is Emilio going to do?"

"Emilio wants to sell the building. He has a buyer. He says he can stipulate that Sofia gets to stay in her flat, if that's what she wants. And he will put his half of the proceeds into a trust for her. He is a rich man. It's not like he needs the money. This building is worth a lot. She wouldn't have to worry about finances. Ever."

"And he said that? He said he would give her his half?" My words bristled with frustration and fear at what I had set in motion. "You believe him?"

"I do."

"She doesn't trust him!"

"She thinks she still works at the tour agency, Marguerite."

I sprang to my feet to pace the room. I wanted Lorenzo. Where was he? Why wasn't he here?

"We didn't do anything wrong," Renata said.

"She was happy before I came here. And I come and her whole world is about to crumble."

"Just because she was happy doesn't mean everything was right. You have done her a favor. Sooner or later Emilio would have found out Sofia needed help. And what if her delusions worsen? She needs professional help. She could never pay for that kind of care with all her money tied up in this building. While Angelo is still alive, he can sign the bill of sale. Once he's gone, his half will go to Sofia, and she will never sign it."

I turned around. "Angelo can't sign anything."

"Of course he can."

"I mean, he won't know what he's signing."

"Who cares? It's the right thing to do."

"It's the black-and-white thing to do!"

"What?" Her face was awash in confusion.

I sank back into my chair. "Nothing."

My thoughts were a tumbled mess. "Where's Lorenzo? Does he know about this?"

"We talked before we met our friends at the restaurant. He feels as I do."

"And what if you lose your flat?"

She laughed lightly. "What idiot is going to buy a building and evict all his tenants? And besides, there are many flats in Florence. This is not the first I've lived in. It won't be the last."

I sighed heavily. "What am I supposed to do now?"

Renata shrugged. "Nothing. Emilio is coming tomorrow. He has every right to come. He owns the building."

"What's he going to say to her? Is he going to tell her we called him?"

"Tomorrow at breakfast I am going to tell her I called him. You didn't. I did. I called to see if he could tell me about his family's ties to the Medici. You are visiting Sofia about the book she is writing, and she told you she was related to the Medici family, and I was curious. That's all."

"That's a lot."

"He doesn't care that she's writing a book. He only cares that you don't publish it."

"Okay, but then why is he coming? She's going to want to know why he's coming."

"He's coming because my call simply reminded him he needed to make a trip out to visit. The rest of it is none of our business."

Several weighty moments of silence hung between us. "I think I might take that glass of wine," I said.

She stood, took her glass to the kitchen, and came back with two glasses. Hers and mine.

Renata folded herself back onto the couch.

I took a sip. The wine was robust and ruddy, and I tasted earth and chocolate. "When will he be here?" I asked.

"He said he was leaving Rome a little after eight. He has a car. If traffic is not bad, he will be here before noon."

"I just don't think it's going to be as easy as you are making it sound."

"Stop worrying so much."

I stayed until nearly eleven, partly because I hoped Lorenzo would return and I could talk to him myself about all these new developments and partly because I wanted Sofia to tire and go to bed so that I wouldn't have to talk to her and pretend everything was just peachy.

I got one of my wishes.

As I rose to leave, Renata reminded me Lorenzo was making breakfast and that Sofia and I were to come over at ten. As soon as we were done eating, Renata would tell her about Emilio's impending visit.

I made my way back to Sofia's. The flat was quiet. The door to her bedroom door was closed, and no light shone through.

Nora

Nurse was careful to keep gossipers and unkind courtiers from repeating in my hearing what was whispered in the dining halls and courtyards about my mother's death. And it was easy enough to keep Virginio and me on the fringe of activity in the palace when we were young. Uncle Francesco never came to see us, even though our care had been relegated to him. But the day finally arrived when I came to Nurse with this terrible thing I had heard. It was the day before my tenth birthday. One servant had told another that my father had strangled Mama at the villa and that Francesco knew about it and had said nothing because he'd always been jealous of her.

It could not possibly be true. Could not. I ran to Nurse and told her what I had heard. She sat me down as if she had rehearsed a thousand times the conversation we were to have.

"You can't be listening to what people say, Nora, especially when they talk about things that are none of their affair."

"But that servant said my father had help killing her," I wailed. "Other men waited in the room and dropped ropes from the ceiling. Why would they say a thing like that?"

She told me not to waste time wondering why other people say what they say. It is enough to pay attention to my own words.

"Is it true?" I said. "Is what they say true?"

Nurse said only the Lord God Almighty knows what really happened. The choice before me was not what did I know, but how did I want to live the rest of my life? Did I want to live the rest of my life as if it was true or as if it wasn't?

How does one live as if something is not true when everything suggests that it is?

I am still learning that on the canvas of my heart, I can paint what I will. The brushes are mine. The paint is mine.

My heart is mine.

28

I heard Sofia up and moving about in the morning, but I delayed getting up until after nine. I don't possess a great poker face. If I had to pretend for more than an hour that I didn't know Emilio was on his way to Florence, I would give myself away through pure sheepishness.

I logged on to my e-mail before even getting out of bed, took care of a few work-related matters, posted my pictures from the last couple of days, and lingered over an e-mail from Gabe. He had responded to my telling him about hearing the woman praying in Santa Croce.

He told me I had to consider the amount of sensory overload I was dealing with. It wasn't that odd that I could hear a woman praying in a six-hundred-year-old church full of breathtaking beauty. Someone I trusted suggested I could.

It was that last line I kept rereading. It was a concept I kept falling up against. When we trust someone, we believe what they tell us is true. We experience it as being true. It's not the experience itself that empowers us to believe it. It is the trust. I composed a reply, just to thank him for that insight, but I was soon spilling everything that was happening with Sofia. I could not lay to rest the fear that today was going to be a really hard day for her and it was all my fault. I asked him to pray for the day I was about to step into, knowing that by the time he read it, the day would be over unless he happened to be up at midnight.

I had no sooner sent the e-mail when the reply quickly came back to me. Gabe was up.

Of course I will pray for you and Sofia. I think she needs to hear it straight, Meg, as far as the book goes. And I honestly don't know if she needs to be told everything her uncle told Renata. I wouldn't lie to her to make the day easier for the day's sake. Know what I mean? The truth, while sometimes hard to hear, is not usually hard to bear. You can collapse under it, and it will still hold you up. You don't usually get the same deal with the opposite.

Miss you.

Gabe

I missed him too.

It felt good to realize that.

And he was right. There's a time to imagine you can hear the woman praying, and there's a time to admit she's not there anymore. Or never was.

I got out of bed.

❧

Sofia wanted to bring a fresh bouquet of flowers to Renata, so at nine thirty we headed down to the street and her favorite outdoor *mercato*. She bought a fat bunch of daisies, a little net bag of blood oranges, and a loaf of bread that was still steaming. I found a few leather items to bring home: a billfold for Geoffrey and a folio that I added to my purchase of a tin of Illy coffee for Gabe. The market was noisy and busy, and it would've been impossible to have much of a conversation with Sofia, which suited me fine.

We walked back to the flat and dropped off the gifts I had bought and the bread and oranges. Then we rang the bell at Lorenzo and Renata's.

Renata, dressed in a long gauzy gown of peacock blue, opened the door, and we were immediately enveloped by the aroma of cheese and garlic and spinach. She pecked us each on the cheek, and Sofia handed her the bouquet. She said something in Italian and Sofia smiled wide.

Lorenzo called out a hello to us from behind the kitchen counter. He was wearing a black apron and arranging melon slices and strawberries on a cobalt-blue platter.

"Good morning, *principesse*!" He strode over to us, kissing Sofia on both cheeks and then me. He smelled like spice and the ocean. "I have a frittata in the oven. She's almost done. And I have melon and strawberries, some Greek yogurt, and lovely figs. And coffee!"

"We are eating out on the balcony," Renata said. "I'll just get these flowers into some water and take them outside."

Renata in her flowing dress floated into the kitchen and Sofia followed, both of them easing into their native tongue.

"Help me take the fruit and yogurt outside, cara?" Lorenzo was now extending a bowl of creamy white yogurt toward me. I took it and he grabbed the platter of fruit. I followed him out to the balcony where a carafe of coffee and painted stoneware dishes waited on the table between the padded chairs and sofa.

"Did Renata tell you everything?" I said in as low a voice as I could.

"She did." He set the platter down and did not look at me.

"And?"

"And what needs to happen needs to happen, cara. It's not up to us."

"But we're part of the problem," I whispered.

Now he looked up at me and caught my gaze. "But we are not part of the solution."

"I don't want to ruin everything for her," I murmured, but my voice was urgent.

His face was close to mine, and he touched my cheek with his hand. "She is already broken. We just didn't know."

"You never minded the talking statues before," I said softly.

"There was never a reason to mind. Now we have several. Here she comes."

Several minutes later we were eating Lorenzo's savory frittata, drinking coffee, and enjoying a lovely meal on a sunny balcony. When the plates were empty, our small talk drifted toward books. Sofia asked a question about Renata and Lorenzo's upcoming book on destination weddings, which Lorenzo answered. And then Sofia turned to me and said she was having such an easy time writing the additional chapters; she thought she would be done well before July. She asked me when Beatriz and Geoffrey would decide if what she had was good enough.

I remembered what Gabe said about being truthful. I turned to Renata for a silent vote of confidence, which she gave to me with a nod. Sofia had given us a perfect segue into a conversation about where we stood on the book and how we had gotten there. I could sense that the three of us knew it.

"Actually, Sofia, it's not a question about whether or not you're a good enough writer. You're a great writer. The problem we're having is proving your premise."

"My premise?"

"Right now, one of the primary selling points of your book is that you maintain you are directly descended from the Medici family. It's what would set your book apart from any other book on Florence that's out there, including Renata and Lorenzo's book. And it's not looking like we can prove it. It's a flimsy premise if we can't prove it."

Sofia looked from me to Lorenzo to Renata, and I could tell she understood Renata and Lorenzo were in on this. They were part of the "we." This seemed to surprise her.

"But we only just started looking," she said. "Just because my father wasn't able to help us, that doesn't mean there aren't records out there somewhere."

"Yes, but it's not just that we are going to have trouble finding the records. It's more like there are no records."

Her eyes widened. "What do you mean, there are no records? If we haven't looked for them, how do we know they aren't there?"

"Because..." I didn't know where to begin. "Well, you said you were descended from Gian Gastone de' Medici; but there's nothing recorded to suggest he fathered a child or was even, you know, interested in women. And besides all that, it's quite likely that..."

My voice fell away, and I turned to Renata.

"Sofia, when Meg told me she needed to verify your ancestry to be able to publish your book, I called Emilio to ask him."

"You called Emilio?"

I heard dread in Sofia's voice.

"It was totally my idea. Meg had nothing to do with it. I thought if he knew where any of the family records were, then it would help you both."

"You called Emilio? About this?"

"He's your uncle, Sofia. If you're a Medici, then he's a Medici. So yes, I called him."

Sofia repositioned herself in her chair, restless. "And?"

Renata shook her head sympathetically. "Your great-great-uncle was the one who started telling everyone your family was related to the Medicis. He didn't have any proof; it was just something he said. But—"

"That's not true!"

Renata continued as if Sofia hadn't interrupted. "And your father and Emilio were little when they first heard it, so it felt more real to them. And it was kind of fun to pretend."

"My father told me," Sofia began, carefully enunciating each word, "that we are direct descendants of Gian Gastone de' Medici. He told me there were eight generations between Gian Gastone and him. He told me—"

This time Renata cut in. "Gian Gastone preferred other men, Sofia! It was just a fun story your father told."

Sofia blinked back glistening tears. "It was not just a *fun* story! This is who I am."

All this time Lorenzo had sat next to me on the sofa, quietly staring at his coffee cup. He leaned forward now and put his hand on Renata's arm to gently quiet her.

"This is not between you and Sofia. This thing with the book is between Sofia and Meg," he said.

"Did you tell Emilio I was writing a book?" Sofia asked Renata, her tone incredulous.

"You never told me it was a secret," Renata said defensively.

"You never asked!"

Renata pursed her lips together, obviously ready to say more but swallowing back her words.

Lorenzo said something under his breath in Italian. I didn't think Sofia heard him. She turned to me.

"Are you saying you will not publish the book because of what Emilio said?"

"It's not so much what he said as what we cannot prove. I am thinking we may need to change the focus of the book from your being a Medici to your having this wonderful relationship with your father that makes Florence come alive. And maybe you can write that he told you that you were a Medici when you were little and how it affected you growing up and how it bound you to Florence. It could still be a really good book. We just can't... We can't have you saying you're a Medici who hears...who hears..."

"A dead Medici talking to her." She finished the sentence in a cynical tone I had not yet heard her use. "So that's what this is about. You think I am crazy? Is that what you think?"

"No," I said quickly. "I don't. But it doesn't matter what I think. It matters what people who might buy your book will think."

"I don't care what people think!" Sofia exclaimed.

"Of course you care," Renata said, matching Sofia decibel for decibel. "If you didn't care what people thought, you wouldn't be writing a book."

Lorenzo cleared his throat. "Let's get back to the situation at hand, yes? You need to tell her the rest."

Surely Lorenzo didn't mean *all* the rest.

"The rest? The rest of what?" Sofia said.

Renata looked out over the rooftops. "He's coming here today."

Sofia said nothing. It seemed as though she hadn't heard. But I knew she had.

Renata turned to her. *"Emilio viene qui oggi."*

Sofia blinked slowly. *"Perché viene qui?"*

When Renata didn't answer, Sofia said it again louder. *"Perché viene qui?"*

"It's none of our business why he is coming," Lorenzo said softly, bringing the conversation back to English. "We have already said and done too much. It's none of our business why he is coming. But he is coming."

"Is it because of the book?" Sofia said evenly.

"The book is between you and me, Sofia," I said. "If we can get it to the point where it is publishable, then we will publish it; I promise you. He doesn't have a say in it."

This didn't seem to satisfy her.

"Why is he coming, Renata?" Sofia's eyes flashed anger.

Renata jumped up, grabbed the stack of dishes, and pushed her way past us. "Ask him yourself. He will be here in half an hour."

Renata went into the flat, leaving Lorenzo, Sofia, and me sitting in the brilliant sunshine. After a moment, Sofia stood calmly and slowly. "Meg, I would like privacy when I speak to my uncle. Perhaps you could stay here with Lorenzo for a while until after Emilio arrives and he and I are finished? I will come for you."

"I am so sorry about all of this," I said, but she was already past me, and she didn't look back.

Sofia walked back into the living room without a word, opened the front door, and then closed it quietly behind her.

I turned to Lorenzo. "I feel terrible."

"It's not your fault, cara. She wanted to publish this book. This thing about her not being a Medici was bound to come out. If she had approached a different publisher, it was still bound to come out. She opened herself up to this when she decided to write a book that she wanted to see published. It's not your fault."

"I still feel terrible." My voice caught in my throat.

He smiled, opened his arms to me, and I slid into his embrace.

Nora

Sometime later that day, when I was still nine, I overheard two courtiers talking about why my father never sent for Virginio and me after our mother died. One said to the other that it was because he did not think we were truly his children because of my mother's indiscretions with Troilo Orsini. Again I went to Nurse, and again she told me not to pay heed to people who've nothing better to do than talk about matters that aren't their own.

"They are saying I am not his daughter," I said. And I remember my voice breaking into pieces as I said this. I didn't know exactly what this might mean, but it felt like it meant I was no one.

She took me to the looking glass in my room and stood me in front of it. "You see that girl in the glass?" she said to me. "You are the one who will say who she is, Nora. You decide who she will be and whose daughter she is and the kind of parents she has. You are the girl in the glass."

29

The breakfast dishes were done, Renata was at the dining room table with her laptop, and Lorenzo was showing me the photos he had taken at a vineyard wedding when we heard voices on the other side of their front door.

The three of us looked up.

I heard a man's voice. And then Sofia's. A door closed. All was quiet again.

"Is it Emilio?" I asked.

Lorenzo nodded.

For several minutes none of us moved.

Renata said something in Italian and got up from the table.

I turned to Lorenzo.

"She said she wonders if Sofia has her kitchen window open," he translated.

Renata opened the balcony doors and stepped outside. I followed her. And a second later, Lorenzo did too.

The noise of the city crowded in all around us, but we could hear faintly two voices from a nearby window. There was a flat in between Lorenzo and Renata's place and Sofia's, and an L-shaped wall. Both made it difficult to hear. Renata moved as close as she could to the railing.

"He is saying the time to sell the building has come. She is not employed anymore. The rent checks alone are not enough to cover the upkeep. Sofia is saying something, but I can't hear her... He is saying again the decision is not hers. It is his and her father's, and they will do what is best."

An ambulance or police car on the street below filled the air with its punched wail. We could hear nothing from Sofia's kitchen window for several long seconds.

Then I heard Emilio say a word that even I understood.

Medici.

I could hear Sofia yell something.

"What is she saying?" I asked Lorenzo.

"I think she is saying her papa would not lie to her."

Renata leaned farther over the railing.

"Oh, *mama mia.* He is telling her Angelo lied whenever he didn't want to deal with the truth. That he has lied to her about a lot of things."

Sofia yelled at Emilio a word I knew. *Andare!* Go!

But Emilio kept at it.

"He is saying Angelo did nothing but lie to her her whole life." Renata turned to Lorenzo and me. "This is not going so well."

Sofia said something else, and Renata shook her head. She couldn't make it out.

Emilio seemed to have moved closer to a window. Perhaps Sofia had moved into the kitchen and he had followed her. He said something and this time it was loud enough for Lorenzo to hear it. I could hear it too, but I didn't know what he said.

"He says Angelo lied to her because he thought it was what he should do, but it was still a lie," Lorenzo said. "Again he is saying her father lied to her about many things."

Sofia said something we could not fully hear. It sounded like *non fare.* Don't.

"He is saying it is time to stop living this way. That she needs to face truth if she is going to live without Angelo. That she needs help," Lorenzo said. "He is saying he knows the tour agency has been sold and that she pretends she still works there."

Sofia shouted a word I didn't know. I looked to Lorenzo. *Mostro.* Monster. And then she said something else.

"She is saying he is the liar," Renata said. "Oh! He is telling her to look around and see who is telling the truth. He is asking her where are the records that say she is a Medici? Where does it say a Medici can hear statues talk? Where are her baby pictures?"

At this, the three of us fell stone silent. My mouth dropped open. So did Lorenzo's. Renata whispered a word I didn't know.

"Tell me he is not asking her what I think he is asking?" I said.

Emilio said it again.

"Dove sono le tue foto di quando eri un bebè?" Where are your baby pictures?

"This can't be happening!" I said.

Lorenzo sank into one of the chairs. *"Non buono, non buono."*

"Sofia is asking him what he means," Renata said. "He says there are no baby pictures of her. 'What do you think *this* is,' she says. He says, 'That is just a painting of you. It is not a photograph of you. There are no photographs of you. You weren't born in this house. You were four years old when you came to live with my brother and his wife!'"

I could picture what Sofia was doing at the moment Emilio was saying these terrible words. She was showing him the painting of her and her mother, the one that shows her as a baby in her mother's arms. The little painting on the wall by the sink. The one Sofia kissed.

"Why in the world is he doing this?" I groaned.

Renata whirled around. "I'm going over there."

As she tried to move past him, Lorenzo grabbed her arm. "So you are going to tell him you've been listening to their conversation from the balcony and you have a few things *you'd* like to say?"

She shook her arm out of his grasp. "No, that is not what I am going to say! I am going to invite them over for lunch." She stormed into the flat, and we heard her wrench the front door open.

Emilio's voice punctuated the air. He was very close to the kitchen window now.

"He is saying it is time to live in the real world," Lorenzo said. "The building needs to be sold, and she needs to come to terms with that. She needs to come to terms with everything."

Emilio's voice stilled and we guessed that he heard knocking at Sofia's front door.

We heard no more of their conversation after that.

It seemed like a long time before the front door opened and Renata returned, bringing someone with her.

Lorenzo and I went back into the living room. With Renata was a man who looked very much like Angelo Borelli. Emilio had a few pounds on his older brother and less hair, but the eyes, chin, and nose were the same.

"Emilio needs to talk to you, Meg," Renata said.

She said something in Italian to the man next to her. I heard her say my name. Emilio put out his hand to shake mine.

"He doesn't speak English very well. But he wants to ask you about Angelo. Sofia told him you and she were just there visiting him. He wants to know if you think he is capable of signing the bill of sale for the building."

I looked at the man in front of me, and I wanted more than anything to know why he had said what he did. I didn't care if he knew we had been listening. I wanted to know why Sofia had to be told her father lied to her.

"Tell him we could hear them on the balcony. Ask him why he

had to tell Sofia she has no baby pictures." My voice sounded thick with frustration.

Renata translated my words to Emilio. When she was done, he turned to me and spoke without raising his voice. Renata translated as he talked.

"She cannot live anymore in the dream world her father created. Angelo is not here to keep that world spinning. She must live in the world that is, the one that you and I are in, not in the world he made up. That world is gone. She must know that he created that world with lies. She will not believe me until she realizes this. You tell me how else I can convince her that I am the one telling the truth?"

"Isn't it enough that she had to hear she's not a Medici after all?"

"This is not your concern. I will do what I must to get her to open her eyes. And if you care about her as much as it appears you do, you wouldn't let her live another day thinking she is a Medici who hears paintings and statues talking to her and who thinks she has a job as a tour guide when she doesn't. And please, for the love of God, tell me you will not publish this book she is writing."

He waited for me to answer, and Renata waited to translate it. But I suddenly didn't know what it meant to choose reality over fantasy, as though one couldn't exist if the other were present.

Emilio clearly saw everything black and white, just as Renata did. Just as my mother did. Lorenzo was like me; Gabe was like me; Devon was like me. My dad was like me. We were the ones who saw the countless shades of gray. We didn't choose reality over fantasy; we chose reality *and* fantasy. We saw the beauty in believing some things can be imagined and also the security that some things can be counted on. The things we counted on made the things we imagined possible. And those possibilities made life wonderful and wild.

In my dream world, my father loved me my way. In my real world, he loved me his way. Either way, he loved me.

I didn't need to find a man like my dad to love me. I had a dad who loved me. And at those times when his way of loving confused me, I could imagine his love was one of the many shades of gray that gave depth to my world.

The reality was I had a dad who could not be trusted with my expectations. In the amber light of my dreams, I had a dad who sent me to Florence rather than go with me, who brought me poppy-seed bagels, who called me angel, who took me out of school to go to Disneyland, who let me stand on his shoes while he danced with me. Who never meant to hurt me. If I wanted to list his flaws, it would be easy to do. But I didn't want to list them.

Sofia didn't have to live without all her dreams. None of us did. She needed to face reality, but she didn't need to turn her back on everything extraordinary that gave her life depth. It wasn't a black-and-white world.

I looked up at Emilio, and I spoke carefully while Renata translated. "If I publish anything by Sofia, it will be something she and I and my publishing house will be proud of. And as for your other question, Angelo barely recognized Sofia when we were there on Tuesday. She had to talk with him for several minutes before he remembered who she was. And he didn't know he was at a care facility. He thought he was at work."

Emilio looked away, mumbling something. Renata said something back. I looked to Lorenzo standing next to me.

"He is thinking he will have to get a lawyer. Declare them both mentally unfit."

No.

No, no, no.

"Emilio!" I said the man's name with such force that he took a step backward.

I turned to Renata. "Tell him I know how to get Angelo to sign the bill of sale. Tell him I will help him if he will promise me no lawyers."

She said this to him and he nodded, a pensive look on his face.

"And tell him he needs to help Sofia find someone who can help her manage what she thinks she hears, not someone who will tell her she's crazy."

He frowned, paused, nodded.

"And he needs to let her think she's a Medici, if that's what she wants."

He sighed and nodded.

"And tell him he must tell her he meant nothing by telling her there are no pictures of her as a baby. It was just a silly thing he said."

Emilio raised a hand and pointed a finger at me. He rattled off something, and I turned to Renata.

"He says he won't do it."

"Tell him after all these years, and all Sofia has lost—her parents, her husband, any promise of ever having a child of her own—that she deserves to have at least this. It is such a small thing. It will cost him nothing."

Renata repeated what I said.

Emilio stood unconvinced, a black-and-white man.

I reached out my hand. He flinched. I gently took his. *"Per favore?"*

He tried to pull his hand away, but I wouldn't let go.

"Per favore?"

He said something to Renata.

"Before he agrees to anything, he wants to know how it is that you can help."

"Tell him to take me with him to the facility where Angelo is. And to bring the bill of sale. I can get him to sign it."

Renata looked bewildered. "How?"

"Because he thinks I am Natalia."

❧

In the next five minutes, we formulated a plan. Lorenzo would come with Emilio and me to translate for me and to whisper in my ear what I would say to convince Angelo he needed to sign the document. And to be a witness. We decided it might be best if Lorenzo and I went in alone and Emilio waited in the car until we had what he needed. He would visit his brother another time, under different circumstances.

Renata said she would go over to Sofia's to sit with her while Lorenzo and I took Emilio out to lunch to get him out of the flat and give her time to digest what he was proposing for the building. Emilio would go over with us while I got my purse and apologize to Sofia for saying what he did about the baby pictures. Then we would leave. Renata would stay.

Sofia wouldn't need to know that the building had been sold until she had had more time to get used to the idea. It would be a month or more before the transaction would be complete. By then Emilio would have made arrangements for Sofia to see a therapist who could help her dial in to what was real and what was imaginary. She could have both. She just needed to know which was which.

Lorenzo grabbed his keys and cell phone, and Renata did the same. The four of us made our way across the hall to Sofia's. I knocked and waited.

"Sofia?" I called.

No answer.

"See if it's locked," Renata said.

I put my hand on the knob and it turned. We stepped inside.

"Sofia?" I called out again.

Renata strode down the hallway calling Sofia's name. No answer. She came back to the main room.

"She's not here!"

Sofia's purse and cell phone were on the kitchen table, but Sofia was gone.

Nora

I did not see my father again. He married his mistress, Vittoria, after the suspicious death of her husband. They fled north when the Vatican heard of the marriage, since Vittoria's husband had been the pope's nephew.

The spring I turned fourteen, when word came that my father had died, I brought the letter to Nurse, though she was now in the employ of my uncle Francesco as my cousin Maria's nurse.

Nurse already knew that my father had died. The letter had come to Francesco first. It was she who suggested to him that Virginio and I be told.

It had been five years since she had stood me in front of my looking glass. As I sat there now with the letter between us, she tipped my head toward the glass in Maria's room and told me that I was not like fair Andromeda, chained to the rock of my parents' choices.

In that sad moment of weakness, I told her she was wrong. "But I am," I told her. "I am chained."

She grabbed hold of my shoulders. "Outside, it may look that way, but not in here," she said, and she tapped my chest, where under the folds of my bodice, my troubled heart was beating. And then she pointed to my reflection in the glass. "And not in there."

30

Renata turned to Emilio and spoke to him words I could not understand. Lorenzo started to translate, but then he got drawn into the heated conversation. Tempers were rising. Even Lorenzo raised his voice. Three sets of arms began waving about my face.

I could do nothing but stand there and listen, hoping to catch a snatch of a word here and there.

"Can somebody please speak in English!" I finally yelled.

The three voices fell silent.

Emilio stepped away and shook his head, apparently not having won any part of the conversation. Lorenzo turned to me.

"Emilio thinks maybe we should call the police. He doesn't think Sofia is in her right mind. Renata and I think it is too premature for that."

Emilio rattled off a long sentence of disgruntled words, punching the air with his open hand.

"You should've thought of that before you starting shooting bullets into everything she believes in!" Renata said, in English.

Emilio just stared at her.

"I think Marguerite and Emilio and I should do what we said we would do," Lorenzo said. "We will go see Angelo. We will have him sign the documents. Renata can stay here and wait for Sofia to come home. When we get back, Emilio will go back to Rome. Today. Tomorrow we can help Sofia decide what to do next."

"I'm for that," Renata declared.

Emilio muttered something and Renata turned to him and, I assume, told him he had been overruled.

He brushed past us, mumbling words that meant nothing to me and waving to Lorenzo and me to follow him.

"I'll just get my purse." I retrieved my purse from Sofia's guest room and returned to the living room. Lorenzo was waiting for me. Emilio was gone.

"He's gone to get his car. He had to park a couple blocks away. We will meet him on the street."

I nodded and then turned to Renata. "Sofia will be all right, won't she?"

Renata smiled, but there was an edge of nervousness there. "I think she will be fine. Go. I will watch for her."

I left with Lorenzo.

A few minutes later, I was seated inside Emilio's silver Fiat and we were making our way to the river's edge to cross the Arno. It would take us only fifteen minutes or less to get there. Emilio had entered the address into his GPS, and traffic was relatively quiet for a Saturday at lunchtime.

Lorenzo turned to me from his seat in the front. "What will you say?"

I had no idea.

Assuming Angelo still thought I was Natalia, I figured I wouldn't have to say much.

I have some papers here for you to sign, Angelo.

And he would sign.

"I don't know. How do I say 'Sign these papers, please'?"

"Firmar questi documenti, per favore."

I repeated the line several times.

"And if he asks why?" Lorenzo said.

I thought for a moment how Angelo himself would answer that question. What reason would explain this compassionate thing we were doing for a person who would not understand it as compassion? This was something he was familiar with.

A reason that was half truth and half imagination. He would understand that. He would want that.

"I will tell him it's a present for Sofia. A surprise."

Lorenzo smiled, a knowing half smile. *È un regalo per Sofia. Una sorpresa.*

I repeated the three sentences Lorenzo had given me over and over. I asked Lorenzo how to say "You look well today" and "How are you today?" and "Can I get you anything?" I knew I wouldn't remember all his answers, but I practiced them anyway so that when he whispered them to me, I would be able to repeat them that much quicker.

We pulled up alongside a curb, and Emilio cut the motor. We had arrived.

Emilio handed Lorenzo the sale documents and showed him all the places where Angelo needed to sign.

"I wait," Emilio said.

It was the only bit of English I would hear from him.

Lorenzo and I got out of the car. While we walked up the steps of the facility, I practiced my phrases.

Inside the lobby an older woman sat behind the reception desk. "I will ask her what room he's in," Lorenzo whispered.

He walked confidently up to the desk and spoke to the woman. She nodded sleepily, muttered something, and pointed to the ledger with her pencil. He said something else while he signed the book, and she mumbled, *"Venti quattro."*

Twenty-four.

Lorenzo handed the pen to me, and I signed my name.

"He's in his room. He just had lunch."

Our shoes made clacking noises on the tiles as we passed open-doored rooms with gray-headed people sitting in forgotten poses. Some had their TVs on. Some were stretched on their beds ready for a postlunch nap. Some stared from their wheelchairs at the entrances to their rooms as if waiting for someone to collect them.

We stopped a few feet from a door marked 24, and Lorenzo asked me if I was ready. I nodded. He handed me the sale papers.

I edged to the frame of the door and poked my head in. Angelo was standing at his window, looking out over the alley on the other side.

I knocked on the frame. "Angelo?"

He turned slowly and looked at me.

I took one step inside. I could sense Lorenzo hovering near.

"Angelo?" I said again.

He cocked his head slightly.

"*Possiamo entrare?*" Lorenzo whispered behind me. I repeated it and Angelo nodded slowly.

"Go in," Lorenzo whispered. I obeyed and he stepped in behind me. But Angelo's eyes were on me only. For several seconds he said nothing.

"*Che giorno è?*" Angelo said, his intense gaze toward me softening.

"*È sabato,*" Lorenzo said, and then I said it too. It is Saturday.

A strange silence rested between us. I took a breath for confidence and then walked close enough to Angelo to kiss him on the cheek. I let my lips linger a little. Lorenzo was close behind me.

When I stepped back, Angelo's eyes were glistening. "Natalia."

My voice caught in my throat. I could not speak.

"*Chi è quello?*" Angelo tipped his head toward Lorenzo.

I cleared my throat and my voice returned to me. "Lorenzo."

I waited to see if Angelo would ask who Lorenzo was or why he was there, but he didn't. He seemed to have trouble remembering what it was he should ask next. I took his hand and led him to an armchair in the corner of his room. He sat down willingly. I pulled a folding chair from the other side of his dresser and sat next to him. Lorenzo moved in behind me, close.

"Come stai?" I said. How are you?

He patted my hand as it rested on the arm of his chair. He said something, softly. I waited for Lorenzo to whisper to me what he said.

"He said he can't find his paintbrushes. Tell him you will find them, but first there are papers to sign. *Li troverò. Ma prima ci sono dei documenti da firmare.*"

I struggled with the words, and Lorenzo murmured them in echo. Angelo didn't seem to notice. I reached for a TV tray just on the other side of his chair and pulled it toward him. I placed the papers on the tray and flattened them. Lorenzo handed me a pen from his shirt pocket and whispered the words, *"Firma, Angelo?"* Sign your name, Angelo?

I handed him the pen.

"Questi non miei," he said. These are not mine.

"Sono tuoi. Ecco qui." They are yours. Here.

I guided the pen in his hand to the first place he needed to sign.

"Per Sofia," I said.

"Sofia." Angelo stared at the paper.

I looked up at Lorenzo behind me, suddenly wanting different words. "To keep her safe," I said, barely above a whisper.

"Per tenerla al sicuro." The whispered words floated down to me and I repeated them.

Angelo brought a hand, shaking, up to his temple and rubbed it. *"Non dovrebbe essere con lui. È no buono."* She shouldn't be with him. He's no good.

I knew he spoke of Sofia's long-ago husband. "He will not hurt her anymore," I whispered to Lorenzo.

"Non le farà più del male."

This seemed to satisfy Angelo. He put the pen to the paper and began to sign his name; slowly at first, and then it was as if he suddenly remembered how to release his signature from his hand to the pen.

I turned to the second page and pointed to the line he needed to sign. And then the third page. After he dotted the last *i* in his name, he held the pen aloft. *"Abbiamo finito?"* Are we done?

"Si. Finito."

He sighed then. *"Dove vado adesso?"* Where do I go now?

I looked up at Lorenzo and he shrugged. "Nap?" he mouthed. I nodded.

"Ti vuoi riposare?" Would you like to rest?

Angelo turned to his window but held his hand out to me. I took it tentatively. He brought it to his lips and kissed it, never taking his eyes off the scene outside his window; cars going by, a nun on a Vespa, a silver-haired woman pushing a shopping cart, a young man walking a dog.

"Non trovo i miei pennelli," he said. I cannot find my paintbrushes.

"We have the signatures. Let's go." Lorenzo's whispered tone was gently urgent.

"We just got here," I said.

"It won't seem that way to him. And I don't like this pretending anymore. We have what we need."

I stood, but Angelo still had my hand in his.

"I know where your paintbrushes are," I murmured over my shoulder, and Lorenzo fed me the line.

"Io so dove sono i tuoi pennelli." I stood and kissed Angelo's cheek, pulling my hand out from within his.

I reached for the papers and waited to see if he would ask me where the paintbrushes were. But he didn't. He just nodded and closed his eyes.

"Ciao, Angelo," I murmured, and he seemed not to hear me.

I put the papers in my purse and we left.

I hadn't pretended anything. His signature would keep Sofia safe.

And I did know where his paintbrushes were.

Right where he left them.

Nora

My dear nurse took ill that winter, and my angels bore her away to heaven. I held on to her words in the years that followed, drawing strength from them and in the beauty that lay all around me, reminding me what the imagination is capable of.

I can imagine my mother wouldn't have left Florence without me.

I can imagine my father would have been a different man if he had known a different childhood.

I can imagine he had no part in planning what befell my mother.

I can imagine that the last time I saw him, my father touched my wet curls because there was a part of him that knew I wanted him to love me.

I can imagine the beautiful because I've seen it, in spite of every terrible thing that has happened.

Tomorrow I marry, and I fear I shall not see Florence again, but I will carry her with me in every beautiful image she bestowed on me.

31

Emilio and Lorenzo talked the entire time it took to drive back to the building. I tried to catch a word here and there that I could understand. I knew they were talking about Sofia, perhaps striking some kind of agreement with regard to her care. I heard Emilio say the Italian words for "doctor" and "institution"—they sound nearly like the English words—but I also heard Lorenzo respond with words I didn't know but that seemed to pacify Emilio. I was anxious for Emilio to get us back to the flat and for him to leave so that Lorenzo could tell me what the future held for Sofia.

I didn't want Emilio orchestrating that future and deciding how many delusions Sofia was allowed to have. I didn't think black-and-white people should be allowed to answer that. They have no experience with fantasy.

When we got back to the building, Emilio pulled up alongside the curb. He said something to Lorenzo and pointed to the windows above us, specifically Sofia's living room window. Lorenzo patted Emilio on the shoulder and said something in soothing tones.

"Approvazione?" Lorenzo said.

Emilio looked at me and then back to Lorenzo. He nodded.

Lorenzo said "Grazie" and got out of the car. I followed him. We had barely closed the Fiat's doors when Emilio zoomed off.

"What's he going to do?" I asked as we watched him drive away.

"He said for now he will allow Renata and me to look for a psychologist here in Florence. If we can get Sofia to agree to see this person, then Emilio will leave the situation alone. Renata will be able to convince her, I think. It's not healthy that Sofia thinks she goes to work every day."

"And what about the sale of the building? What about Sofia's home? She's never really lived anywhere else."

"Emilio says his buyer is a friend who has wanted this building for years. He will agree to let Sofia stay in her flat and pay a fixed rate for rent with the condition that she can live there as long as she wants. The rent will be taken from the proceeds of the sale. She won't ever have to write a check."

"And Sofia's book? Does he have conditions about that too?"

Lorenzo looked at me. "You have conditions about that, cara. You're the one who will need to decide what to do. He is already certain you will not publish it the way it is."

Emilio's car turned a corner, heading south out of the city toward Rome. Lorenzo and I went inside.

Minutes later we found Renata sitting in the doorway of their flat with a clear view of Sofia's front door, tapping away on her laptop.

Sofia hadn't returned.

"It's only been an hour," she said, verbally whisking away my worry.

"Maybe we should go look for her, no?" Lorenzo said.

I agreed.

"Where do you think she went?" Renata got up and moved the dining room chair she'd been sitting in back to the table where it belonged.

"A favorite place?" Lorenzo suggested.

Renata frowned. "This is Florence! Everywhere is her favorite place!"

"A place where she feels peaceful, then."

"A place where she is used to getting good advice," I said, as the places she'd taken me to the last five days filled my head. She would go somewhere where Nora's echoes would be the most prominent, where she'd heard whispered words meant for Medici descendants to hear, words that affirmed who she was. And what she was capable of surviving.

If I were Sofia, where would I go?

I was pretty sure I knew.

Lorenzo turned to me. "Which places, Marguerite? We can split up. The Accademia? The Uffizi, the Duomo, San Lorenzo, the Pitti Palace?"

"I'll take the Pitti Palace," I said. "You split up and take the other places. But don't go to San Lorenzo. She doesn't care too much for San Lorenzo. The scumbag proposed to her there."

"Let's go, then." Renata grabbed her cell phone and wallet from her bag on the kitchen counter.

As we turned to leave their flat, I thought of something I wanted to bring with me. "You didn't lock her front door, did you?"

Renata answered that she hadn't. Sofia had left without her keys.

"I'll be right back."

I stepped back into Sofia's flat and made my way to her bedroom, asking the heavens for forgiveness in advance for the snooping I was about to do. Sofia had several jewelry boxes on the kidney-shaped vanity. I opened the first one and scanned its contents. Pendants and beads. And then another one. Earrings and bracelets. And then another one. Brooches and old name badges.

I turned to her dresser. A mirrored tray held little bottles of perfume and hand lotion. Next to that was a small wooden box inlayed with the design of a lily. I opened it and fingered the trinkets inside. And then I saw it.

The five-hundred-lire coin.

I put it in my pants pocket and replaced the lid.

A moment later I rejoined Renata and Lorenzo, and we made our way down the stairs to disperse on the street.

❦

As I walked the half mile to the Pitti Palace, I contemplated what I might say to convince Sofia that all would be well, that nothing had shattered that couldn't somehow be pieced back together. I was fairly sure I would find her at Nora's self-portrait. It's where I would go if I lived where she did and now faced the crumbling of my carefully constructed world.

It's what I was already doing.

As I paid for my ticket inside, I still wasn't sure what I would say. What would the people I looked up to tell her? All my shades-of-gray people. What would they say?

My father would tell Sofia to believe what she wanted. It was her life. If she wanted to believe she was a Medici who could hear the wisdom and woes of the ancients, who were we to say she couldn't?

Devon, who I barely knew and yet knew, would probably tell her what matters is the relationships you have with the people who love you most.

Lorenzo would tell her to find a place where she could manage the dreams of her heart and the waking moments of her days. That place existed for every artist. She would find it if she risked a bit of her handhold on the part of her world that was the most dear to her.

And Gabe would tell her the imagination is boundless, but truth and hope have boundaries we can trust.

As I walked the echoing halls where Medicis had walked before me, I realized I could only know these things because they were what I also had needed to hear.

When we walk away from the canvas of our imaginations to live in the world of ache and wonder and beauty and sorrow, what do we take with us from the edges of the painting?

Everything we brought to it.

❧

I found Sofia kneeling on the tiled floor, her body up against the wall in the posture of the weary. She sat with her eyes on the brown-eyed girl with paintbrushes in her hand. A couple in front of a painting nearby were staring at her and whispering. I walked past them and then knelt to sit beside her on the ancient ground of her ancestors.

"Hi," I murmured.

No response. I went on, praying for wisdom.

"When I was little, my grandmother would take care of me on those weekends my parents spent trying to glue their marriage back together. I used to sit in front of her painting of Andromeda. You know, I fell in love with Florence looking at that painting. It seemed like a place where anything was possible. Every kid needs to believe there's a magic place like that. Even when I got off the plane a week ago, I still believed it was."

She turned her head slowly to look at me. "And now you don't?"

I trained my eyes to the painting, searching for words to express what I had come to realize. "No. I still do. Magic influences how we see reality, makes us step back in wonder. That can happen anywhere, Sofia. And I'm really glad it does."

She was quiet for several seconds. Then she spoke.

"Emilio told me my father lied to me about many things. That I am not a Medici. That there's a reason there are no baby pictures of me."

"Sofia—"

She faced me. "Papa told me my baby pictures were stolen. He said a thief came into our flat and took all my baby things. Papa said the thief was probably a desperate father who needed my baby clothes and toys and books. He didn't want the pictures, of course, but thieves don't have time to sort through what they can use and what they can't."

"I…I suppose they don't."

"There was no thief, Meg. Thieves take money and jewelry and silver. They don't take toys and baby clothes. Only a child would believe that."

"But—"

"There was no thief."

Sofia turned her head to gaze up at Nora. She was quiet for several seconds. In the moments of silence, her eyes grew misty. She shook her head gently. "For the longest time, I thought…something wasn't quite right with me. A woman appeared in my dreams and in my memory. A mother." Sofia's voice tapered to a whisper. "And…and there was a man. A father. I remember being afraid of that man. I remember this mother had bruises. I remember her sad face. I remember hiding in a museum. And I remember the day she kissed me and told me she'd be right back."

Again Sofia turned to face me, her eyes imploring me to listen. "I've always remembered those things, Meg. And I have never known what to do with them. They didn't fit anywhere in my mind. Who remembers a different mother? A different father? I couldn't ask my papa or my mama about it. I was afraid they would think that I didn't love them or that something was wrong with me. I thought something was wrong with me! I had such terrible nightmares for such a long time. But they gradually eased away when Papa told me that if I let her, the beauty of Florence would speak healing to me."

Sofia leaned toward me, pulling my gaze into hers as though she was about to divulge a long-kept secret. "The first time I heard Nora whisper to me, I actually felt the shattered parts begin to pull together. When I learned Nora's father had killed her mother, in my heart I knew something powerful bound us together. I didn't know why then, but I think maybe now I do. I think something terrible happened to the mother who bore me. I think my parents tried to help that mother that I see in the haze of my earliest memories and they couldn't. But they could help me. Papa and Mama rescued me by pretending I was theirs."

Tears that had welled up on Sofia's eyes spilled down her cheeks and dotted her knees. I wiped my own eyes.

I didn't know what to say to her.

"I think Emilio knows who that other man and other woman were," Sofia said, after a long pause.

"I think he does too," I murmured.

"And I think I know why my papa and mama said what they did. Why my papa never told me I had another mother and another father. He was such a good papa. He didn't know I remembered. He was like the thief who stole my baby clothes for his little girl. When you are a desperate man who loves his little girl, you will do whatever you must to protect her."

In my mind I could hear Angelo saying this to Sofia. And I could see her as a young girl taking it all in. "Of course that's what you do," I said.

Her shoulders slumped then, and she inhaled heavily, pondering something new. "But if I am not Angelo Borelli's biological daughter, I guess I am not a Medici."

For a moment I thought perhaps she would collapse into despair, the words sounded so final and hopeless. I quickly spoke. "There are thousands of Medici descendants, Sofia. You told me that. They just don't know it. Right?"

The corners of her mouth lifted slightly. "Princess Diana was a Medici descendant."

I smiled too. "So you said."

"I could still be one also, couldn't I?"

"Yes. Why not? Nora speaks to you, doesn't she?"

"Ah. That. Emilio says statues and paintings don't speak. He…he thinks I am… That I need help. That I don't know what's real and what isn't."

"Everybody needs help with that sometimes," I said gently. "I know I do. We all do." I took a deep breath for extra courage to fill me. "Maybe you do need some help. Not with everything. Maybe not about Nora. About some other things."

She blinked back tears and frowned slightly. "What other things?"

"Your father's tour agency has been sold, Sofia. He sold it a year ago. To pay for his place at the rest home. Remember?"

Sofia opened her mouth in obvious protest but closed it again just as quickly. She looked down at her feet and whispered something I could not hear.

"It's all right, Sofia. Everyone at some point needs help when things change."

Or when they don't.

"It was the only job I knew," she said. "I didn't have anything else but that. When Papa left, it was all I had."

I patted her hand. "I know."

"I did give tours, you know. I found people every day in the piazzas who needed someone to tell them what they were seeing. I did it quietly. And they paid me nothing. I wasn't doing it for the money. It was never about the money."

"I believe you."

A long stretch of silence followed. I pretended it didn't alarm me a little.

"I don't think I want to know what happened to that other mother," Sofia finally said.

"You don't have to know what happened to her."

For several seconds she was unmoving and silent. Then she shook her head slowly. "Everything I know seems to be disappearing from me," she said softly. "I don't know what I am going to be left with."

I reached into my pants pocket and withdrew the lire coin. I took her hand and placed the coin in her open palm. "You have all of Florence, Sofia. And you have Renata and Lorenzo and me. And your father for a little while. And you have all those wonderful memories and stories and all the things he told you." I closed her fingers around the coin in her hand.

"And what about my book? Do I still have that?" She wouldn't look at me.

My hand still encircled her closed fist. As I looked at my fingers covering hers, an idea sprang to my mind; an idea for a book that would allow Sofia to tell her story—and Nora's—just the way she had told it to me.

"I say you do," I said.

She looked up from our joined hands to study my face, to make sure I was serious or perhaps to convince herself she had heard me say it.

"No one will ever believe that I'm a Medici."

"I can believe it."

She smiled faintly. "Because you want to."

I smiled back. "And there's nothing wrong with that."

Nora

The carriage is waiting for me below, and Maria is already in the court-yard telling the driver that I am coming. But there is one thing I must do before leaving Florence forever.

I make my way to Maria's bedchamber where her looking glass stands near the window. A scarlet sun is slipping into the honeyed horizon as I step toward it. I watch the girl in the glass walk toward me as she matches my tentative steps.

I reach toward her, and she extends her hand toward mine.

Our fingertips meet and we whisper our good-byes.

"Don't forget me," we whisper to each other.

I linger there for a moment with my hand on the glass, at the place where our palms meet, as the sun dips low over Florence and her treasures.

My treasures.

I turn to walk away from her, glancing back just once. She is turned to me as if she knew I would turn to look at her. She is smiling at me—reminding me without a word of who I am and who I can be if I can imagine it.

32

I spent my last day in Florence doing whatever Sofia wanted to do. We awoke on Sunday to cathedral bells and brilliant sunshine. After a breakfast of fruit and cheese and soft-boiled eggs, we attended Mass and then had lunch with Renata and Lorenzo on a lovely hilltop overlooking toast-colored roofs.

In the afternoon we walked through a Sunday market, and I bought a few more gifts to bring home. Linens for my mother. Hand-embossed stationery for Kara. A necklace for myself. A leather hat for Devon and one for my dad too. Sofia walked beside me in the marketplace, but her thoughts seemed far away. She was no longer the talkative tour guide. She was just a kind Florentine friend helping me make change.

The last couple of days had been emotionally draining on her, and I knew events to come would be equally hard. Her father's eventual mental disappearance was one, the sale of the building was another, and the impending sessions with a psychologist was another. I wouldn't be around for any of those things, and Renata and Lorenzo had a busy writing schedule. I hoped that the resiliency and fortitude Sofia had been led to believe were in her blood would carry her through. Part of me wanted to confess to her that I had been the one to convince her father to sign for the sale of the building, and part of me knew there was nothing to be gained from telling her that. Lorenzo, Renata, and I did what we did because we cared for her. It wasn't the first time in her life that had happened.

We came back to the flat in the late afternoon, and Sofia asked if I minded if she wrote for a little while. She wanted to finish what she had started even if the outcome of the book was as uncertain as ever. I had not told her the idea that had come to me as we sat on the floor of the Palatine Gallery at the Pitti Palace. I hadn't told anyone. I wanted to present the idea to Beatriz and Geoffrey at the same time I told them the original plan would not work. If I could get Beatriz and Geoffrey to agree to my new idea, perhaps I could also convince Sofia.

I spent the last remaining daylight hours sipping cappuccino at a bustling café and journaling onto my computer thoughts from my long-awaited trip to Florence in a letter to my father, one that I knew I would never send. As the sun dipped into the horizon, I checked my e-mail one last time. My mother announced that she and Devon had cleaned out my fridge and put in fresh eggs and milk so that I wouldn't starve to death when I got home. Beatriz said I could come in at noon on Tuesday. Kara invited me to a purse party on Friday night. And Gabe confirmed he was still able to pick me up at LAX. He was looking forward to it.

I was too.

When I got back to Sofia's, she was making a salad to take over to Renata and Lorenzo's for our last supper together.

The four of us ate Lorenzo's amazing rack of lamb and homemade gnocchi in cream sauce. Despite the lovely meal, the mood was a bit solemn. I was leaving the next day, and Sofia was about to begin a new chapter of her life with only Renata and Lorenzo for a cheering section.

After the meal, and while Renata and Sofia did the dishes, Lorenzo invited me out for a walk, my last moonlight stroll in Florence.

He took my hand in his as we walked. We arrived at the river, which was as it had been the night I came. Shimmery, silvery, and alive with subtle movement. He put his arm around me.

"Was she everything you had hoped she'd be, cara?" he said. And I knew he spoke of the city. Florence. My Neverland.

I laughed lightly. "It's far more memorable than I ever dreamed it would be."

He laughed too. "But you had a good time, yes? Even though your father did not bring you? Even with all this trouble with Emilio and Sofia?"

I looked out over the water swaying southward on its constant course. "It was amazingly wonderful," I said. "I saw so much, experienced so much." I turned to him. "I've loved every minute of it."

He kissed my forehead. "I think I might want you to stay," he whispered. "I miss you already."

I felt unsteady on my feet with him so close and the romantic pull of Florence all around me. I looked up at him to say something witty, but his lips were on mine before I could think of anything clever.

It was a kiss of sweetness and delight and playful desire. I pulled away gently.

I could imagine Lorenzo being in love with me and marrying me and being a devoted father to our children and faithful lover to me. It was easy to imagine those things with a starry Florentine night shining down on us.

But surely Lorenzo wasn't in love with me. He couldn't be. He wanted me to stay because he enjoyed my company.

"Very sweet. But I have to go home."

"No, you don't."

"Yes, I do."

He pulled me back into his arms. "What for? What do you have back there that you must get back to? Stay."

"I can't stay. I have a job."

"A job is never a reason to live somewhere. Quit the job. Stay here. Renata could get you an editing job. She knows everybody. Stay." He rubbed his thumb across my jaw line, and I backed away before I fell headlong into his charms.

"And have you break my heart? No thanks."

His eyes widened in playful surprise. "I could never break your heart!"

"Oh yes, you could. Come with me to the airport tomorrow and see me off," I said, wanting very much to change the subject.

"Really? That is what you want? You want to go back?"

I thought of my comfortable job where Gabe waited and my cozy borrowed cottage with a view of the ocean if I stood on tiptoe. And I thought of how I felt when I saw Lorenzo with Bianca, and the easy way he kissed her cheek.

"I want Perseus," I barely whispered.

"What?"

"Yes, I want to go back. I can't compete with all the Biancas in Florence."

He laughed. "Bianca?"

"Don't laugh at me. Yes, Bianca. And all the other girls you've dated."

His laugh morphed into a quizzical smile. "Bianca is an old friend, cara. I'm not in love with her. She would break *my* heart. I am not in love with any of those women I have dated."

That's what scares me the most, Lorenzo, I wanted to say, but didn't. "Don't you want to love someone?" I said instead. "Don't you want someone to love you? Don't you want to believe the rules for love are worth embracing?"

"The rules for love," he echoed.

"Yes. What you said at the restaurant the other night. Don't you want the best love has to offer? Don't you think it's worth the struggle?"

He looked off into the distance, thinking. "You can want something that you're not cut out to have," he finally said.

I reached up to his face and turned it toward me. "Who says you're not cut out to have it?"

Lorenzo shrugged effortlessly. "I've never felt like anyone believed I was. I'm pretty sure I'm not."

I said nothing as a thick sadness fell about me. Lorenzo rode no winged horse. For the first time since I arrived, Florence suddenly seemed a lonely place.

"So will you come to the airport with me?" I said quickly.

He frowned, genuinely disappointed. Then he seemed to shake it off, almost as if my staying in Florence would have been too much to hope for. "What, ride the taxi with you? I hate the drive to the airport. Too much traffic."

"Okay, suit yourself." I started to walk on, away from the tension of that moment. He grabbed my arm.

"We have a car, you know. Renata and I. I keep it garaged a couple miles from here at a friend's house. We use it for trips to France and Spain."

"Sounds like you are offering to give me a ride to the airport. All right. I accept."

He grinned. "Let's go get it!"

"What? Now?"

"Yes!"

"Lorenzo, I really was just kidding. I can take a taxi."

He grabbed my hand, and we dashed across the street. Moments later we were in a taxi. And twenty minutes after that, we were in a tiny black Fiat, zipping along the narrow streets, looking for a *gelateria* open late on a Sunday night, both of us pretending that was the only thing we were looking for.

❧

I awoke for the last time in Sofia's bed, and I lay there for several minutes just listening to the waking world outside the window. By the same time tomorrow, I'd be back in the cottage with Findlay's cat pawing at my bedroom door.

I had packed my bags the night before, after Lorenzo and I returned from cruising Florence in his little convertible. I got dressed and pulled my suitcase out to the living room. Sofia was in the kitchen, making us a spinach-and-feta omelet.

We ate on her little balcony as the pink dawn turned golden, struggling to make small talk after all that the last couple of days had been like. Our conversation steered toward her manuscript and what the future held for it.

I told her sometimes a book idea births a second book idea and it's the second idea that gets published.

"I wouldn't know what to write in a second book," she said.

"I'm not talking about a second book. I'm talking about a second idea. A second concept. Your first concept was based on a historical concept: you are a Medici. What if the second idea was based on a twin concept? A concept we don't have to prove?"

"What concept?"

"Nora Orsini's life story."

"Her story?" She looked surprised, as if she hadn't even begun to realize what I had.

"Your stories have Nora's perspective, as you see it, written all over them. It's real. Real enough to allow us to imagine the other parts are all real too. Even the parts we cannot prove."

She sipped her coffee, contemplating my words and looking past me to the spread of Florence awaking. Then she set her coffee cup down and turned her gaze back to me.

"But there's hardly anything written about her. The only things I know are the scattered echoes she left for me. And those ended when she left Florence to marry."

"Which leaves you lots of room for conjecture. If you imagine the missing parts of her life story, no one can say it didn't happen that way. And you can still weave in your own memoir, because your story is wrapped up in hers."

"So...what do you want me to do, exactly?"

"Finish the book. The story of the Medicis and the wonder of Florence is Nora's story too. Go ahead and finish the book." I reached out to squeeze her hand. "And then trust me with it."

At seven thirty, Lorenzo was at the door waiting to take me to the airport. Renata was with him, in a silk nightgown, sleep still in her eyes. She hugged me good-bye, told me to come back next summer and go with them to Morocco. Then she traipsed back across the hall to return to her bed. Lorenzo took my bags and told me he'd wait for me at the curb and not to take too long saying good-bye to Sofia; he was parked illegally.

When he was gone, I turned to my gracious hostess; at once she pulled me into her embrace. "Thank you for spending your week in Florence with me. I hope I did not ruin it for you."

Tears nearly sprang to my eyes. "Oh, Sofia. I can't imagine having seen it any other way. I loved sharing this week with you. You've...you've been such an inspiration to me. I can't even tell you how much."

She pulled back and stared at me, surprised to her wits at what I had said.

"I'm serious," I continued.

"I don't see how," she said, doubt laced in every word.

"I think I will be able to show you—soon. I need to get back and talk to Beatriz and Geoffrey first. In the meantime I want you to keep writing. Promise me you won't stop."

"All right. I promise."

"And promise me you will listen to Renata and Lorenzo. They care very much for you. You can trust them. Will you do that?"

She nodded.

I hugged her again, and she held me tightly. "Will you ever come back?"

"Of course," I said. "Whenever I am homesick."

I turned from her and headed down the stairs to the street.

Lorenzo put down the top on his convertible and held my hand as we flew down the narrow streets. The breeze of the fair city lifted my hair from my neck, nudging me gently to tip my head back and let the Florence sun kiss me good-bye.

At the terminal I instructed Lorenzo to please let me off and leave quickly. But he did not listen. He yanked my bags out of the backseat, set them down beside me, and drew me into his arms. He seemed on the verge of saying something as he released me, but then he kissed me lightly on the cheek, his lips lingering, waiting perhaps to see if I would turn my head and match my lips to his. I pulled away before I had a chance to decide if I would.

33

There's something to be said for a very long plane ride that takes you from a magical place back to the world where your real life waits. I didn't sleep on the flight home. I didn't watch the in-flight movies or lose myself in the pages of a novel. When you are thirty thousand feet above everything that is real, you have a perspective on your life perhaps only a Renaissance artist would understand.

Sometimes you need to stand back to see the vanishing point; that place in the distance where two roads appear to converge. And you have to stand still long enough to realize they only appear to converge. There is a place where what is real meets up with what we can imagine is real. It's actually a black-and-white place, a place of safety. A boundary that gives us a handrail.

I knew I was being catapulted back to all that I had left behind me when I boarded the plane for home. But that didn't mean everything would be the same.

My father was still missing, albeit voluntarily so, and my mother was in a dating relationship I envied, but from my chair in the heavens, that jealousy felt weightless for the first time since I met Devon at the Melting Pot.

I closed my eyes, not to sleep, but to engrave on my mind what it felt like to be far enough away from reality to actually see it.

I had my father's love, and he had mine. I didn't have to search for it in someone like Devon because I already had it. Lorenzo was not far from me even at thirty thousand feet above the ground, but I reasoned that when I saw Gabe waiting for me at the airport, I could lay that temporary distraction to rest. Lorenzo could not save me. He was part of my dream world. Gabe was real.

I landed in Los Angeles a little after six in the evening. My body clock was telling me it was the middle of the night and that I should be sleeping, and my heart was telling me it was the dawn of something new. I made my way through customs, weary but energized to see Gabe and embrace my post-Florence life. Everywhere around me were people dragging suitcases filled with the real-life things they had brought with them, folding themselves back into the fabric of their daily routines, just like I was. I felt a little dizzy. The terminal seemed to swim a little bit as I pushed my way through the mental fog into the sea of people in baggage claim waiting for the travelers they'd come for. They were the first wave of real life, those people standing there.

He saw me first.

I was scanning the messy rows of waiting people, looking for Gabe's curly head, when I suddenly felt him near me.

I turned to my right, and he was just a few feet away, smiling and moving toward me.

His arms were quickly around me in a welcoming embrace, and I smelled ink, oranges, and green tea—all the remnants of his day.

"Welcome home." He stepped back and smiled at me.

I waited for the whoosh of comfort those tried-and-true words should've enveloped me with, but I felt strangely untethered to the ground I stood on. Like I didn't belong here at all.

❧

I tried to stay awake on the drive back to San Diego, but after an hour of sharing my many highlights and the latest on Sofia, I couldn't keep my eyes open.

"You don't have to stay awake, Meg," Gabe said gently, and his voice sounded like a lullaby.

"But I want to," I mumbled.

"I'll get you home safe," I heard him say, and then I gave in to dreamless sleep.

I awoke with a start when the car engine stopped. We were in front of the cottage, and the lights were on. A car was parked in the driveway. Not mine. Devon's.

"Looks like your mom is here to welcome you back." Gabe laughed easily.

"Looks like," I echoed, attempting to match his humor.

We got out of the car. Gabe retrieved my suitcase, and I slung my carry-on over my shoulder. We walked up the steps, and I heard my mom inside say, "She's home."

I opened the door, and there was my mother, ready to wrap her arms around me. Devon was standing a few feet away, smiling. I sensed a small remnant of the strange attraction I had left with the week before, and I found it only a tad difficult to smile back at him.

My mother hugged me tight. "How are you? How was your flight?"

"It was fine." I turned to Gabe who was still just inches away. "Mom, Devon, this is Gabe Robicheau. We work together. He's a graphic artist. Gabe, this is Elaine Pomeroy and Devon…"

I could not remember his last name. I laughed and would have gone on laughing had I not been worried it would seem incredibly rude.

I couldn't remember Devon's last name.

"Sheller." Devon stuck out his hand and Gabe shook it.

"I'm so sorry," I said to Devon, but he smiled my apology away.

"You look tired." My mother patted my arm.

"It's five in the morning in Florence," Devon said good-naturedly. "We should go. She's home."

"Can I make you something to eat?"

"There was food on the plane, Mom. I'm fine, but thanks."

Alex strolled in from wherever he had been napping and meowed a greeting, approaching my legs with a cozy arch to his back. I bent down to pick him up.

"Really? Because I brought stuff to make sandwiches."

Devon took a step forward and put his hand on my mother's shoulder. "Why don't we take off and let her settle in?" He looked at me and smiled that crooked smile of his.

"All right. But first we need to show her the surprise," my mother said urgently. I set the cat down, immediately concerned about what my mother might've done while I was gone. Installed security cameras? Bought me a guard dog? Replaced all my plastic, microwaveable dishes with ceramic?

"Close your eyes!"

My mother took my hand. "Close them!"

I did what she asked.

We walked down the hallway to my bedroom, and it took superhuman strength not to open my eyes to look at what my mother had done to my bedroom—of all places—with Devon at her side.

"Keep them closed," she said.

She positioned me in front of my bed; at least that is what it seemed like. To calm myself I asked her if she had replaced Findlay's four-poster with bunk beds.

She laughed. "Don't open them yet." She moved away from me.

"Okay. Now," she said, softly, almost like a caress.

My eyelids lifted and there on the wall in front of me and hanging over my bed was Andromeda.

I felt my mouth drop open and my breath catch in my lungs. It was my nonna's painting, just as I had remembered it, only smaller. It had seemed so big to me when I was young. Now as it hung above my bed, I could see it was not the sweeping gateway to Florence, it was only a window, no wider than one arm's length.

Andromeda in diamond-white marble was sitting bent-kneed on her rock with her arm stretched out. My nonna, a dark-haired little girl in a pink dress, mimicked the pose, as if she and Andromeda were about to dance. The palette of colors was gold and yellows, scarlets and toasty browns. Cheerful. Hopeful. My great-great-grandfather's paint strokes weren't as precise as those of the artists whose work hung in the Pitti Palace, but they were as purposeful. This canvas told a story, just like the statue that inspired it. Just like all paintings do.

They speak; we listen.

"How did you get it?" I whispered.

My mother put her arm around me. "Your father sent it. It was waiting for you on your doorstep today. I had to open it. But I didn't open this. It came with it."

She reached into her sweater pocket and handed me an envelope, still sealed.

"He must've found the painting at one of his cousins' or something. You'll have to read the note to find out, I guess."

I looked at the envelope in my hand. One word was written across it.

Angel.

Hot tears were forming at my eyes and several slipped out. One landed on the *A*.

"Devon hung it," my mother continued nervously, as if my raw emotion at my father's gift was too much for her too. "I thought you'd like it here. I hope that's okay. I didn't want it to be just sitting propped up against a wall when you got home. I know how much you love it."

More tears slipped out of my eyes, and I fingered them away. I had no words to express what I was feeling.

"Okay, time for us to go," Devon interjected.

"Will you call me?" my mother said over her shoulder as the four of us made our way down the hallway back to the living room.

"Tomorrow," I said, feeling like it already was.

I hugged her good-bye and assured her we'd talk more.

I turned to Devon. "Thank you," I said and he nodded. He seemed to understand I was thanking him for more than just hanging a painting. I stood on tiptoe and kissed his cheek and felt nothing but gratitude. "The porcini mushrooms were divine."

He smiled so wide the crook disappeared.

"Dinner tomorrow?" my mother said as she stepped out on the porch.

"Maybe. I'll call you," I said.

Gabe and I stood at the doorway as my mother and Devon got into his car and closed the doors. They drove away.

Gabe turned to me. "Is there anything else I can do for you?"

Something in the way he said those words that way—as if I was some-one who needed help and his compassion had answered that need—stopped me. I just stood there staring at him, feeling strangely relieved. I felt a place open up inside me where my longings are kept—a vacancy. Gabe was the best kind of friend. A true companion. Dependable.

But I was not in love with him.

I felt a pang of heartache, an itch to see Lorenzo. "You've done so much already," I said quickly as emotion swelled in my throat. "I owe you one."

He waved that idea away. "It really wasn't a big deal. You'd do the same for me."

Because that's what friends do.

"You all set, then?" he asked. "I know you're probably tired."

All set. "Yes, I think I am."

I hugged him good-bye, and he hugged me back.

But he didn't kiss me, and I didn't want him to.

A kiss already lingered within me. And as Gabe drove away, I instinctively reached up and felt for that bit of Florence that still clung hours-old to my cheek, reminding me that the man who gave it to me told me the rules for love are made in heaven. Not here on this broken planet, not here. Here is where we learn how to live them, how to honor them, how to risk loving the way God intended; completely, singularly, and with courage.

After Gabe left I sat in the quiet of my living room and read the letter from my father. I read it three times, amazed by the idea that my love had somehow rescued my father, empowered him to be the man I already believed he was.

I had saved him.

Sometimes Andromeda is the one on the horse.

I reached for my phone to call Lorenzo.

My dear angel,

I trust that you are on your way to Florence while I am writing this letter. I hope you have the time of your life and get to see everything you and Nonna talked about seeing. I hope you will forgive me for not being there with you. It was for your safety that

I sent you away the way I did. I made some bad decisions, angel, and I owed some money. The people I owed aren't patient people. They know I have a daughter in San Diego. I couldn't take the chance that they would use you to get to me. I wanted you far away from here while I settled this. You don't need to worry now that you are home. I've taken care of it.

I've broken a lot of promises in my lifetime. I did not want to break the promise that I'd get you to Florence. I promised my mother I'd take you, but I also promised you. And the most amazing thing to me is, you always believed I would. You've always believed in me, Meg. I owe you so much for that. No one else did. Or does. Not Allison. Not my sisters. Not your mother. Not even my mother. Only you.

I found the painting of the statue at my second cousin Tito's house in Phoenix. His wife was rather attached to it, and I had to pay her off to get her to let it go. Tito said I should just take it; it belonged to my mother, after all, but I paid her anyway.

And about the money. By now you know what I've done. I am not proud of it. I got in over my head, and I needed to get out. Allison and I don't see eye-to-eye on the money thing; we never have. And I know I did wrong by her. I am sorry for that. I'm working on a plan to pay her back. And after I can do that, I will come back.

It might take a while. But I will do it. Knowing you believe in me is what keeps me from cashing it all in, Meg. I want you to know that. You have saved my life so many times.

You are my guardian angel.

I love you, Dad

MEDICI DAUGHTER
by Sofia Borelli

Foreword
by Marguerite Pomeroy DiSantis

The first time I saw Florence, I was a little girl standing in my grandmother's living room looking at a painting of a Renaissance statue of Andromeda. My love for Florence begins there, while standing in sneakers on the tiled floor of my immigrant grandmother's house, more than twenty years before I breathed Florentine air and gazed on her beauty.

Sometimes the memories you make from a place you've longed to visit begin before you ever get there. Sometimes they are meshed with the memories others have of that same place, and sometimes your memories find their meaning only in the memories of others.

Florence is a destination, a landmark, a repository, a window to the past, but it is also the canvas on which I found my childhood dreams coming true in surprising ways, within all the treasures of this city. When you can imagine a reality that transcends ugliness, you nurture the hope it takes to see past what perhaps you cannot change.

Imagine for a moment, that you are Medici-born, that in your veins flows the resilient pulse of the Renaissance. Imagine that you can hear the echoes of Michelangelo's chisel and the pounding of the hammer falls on the sweeping curve of the emerging Duomo, and the tiny whispers of horse-hair brushes dipped in paint.

Imagine that you've been empowered to believe *Renaissance* isn't just a word; it's the essence of rebirth; it's what happens when you dare to believe what is isn't what it has to be; it can be remade.

Medici Daughter is the imagined story of Nora Orsini, about whom so little is known, the granddaughter of the great Cosimo I, but it is also Sofia Borelli's story, and hers and mine together as our stories collided on the streets of this beguiling city. It took two years for this half-memoir, half-fictionalized account to find a publishing home, but I believe the wait was worth it.

I met Sofia Borelli on the pages of her memoir of Florence. And then I met Nora Orsini in the very person of Sofia herself. And while learning their stories, I fell in love with their city and with the man I would marry.

Through these two Medici daughters, I learned to imagine what could be, might be.

And that what might be is worth risking to have.

Marguerite Pomeroy DiSantis
Florence, Italy

Readers Guide

1. Do you think there is significance in Meg's living in a borrowed cottage?

2. Was there a place you wanted to visit since you were a child? What was it like when you finally went? If you haven't been yet, do you think you will go?

3. Meg's connection to her Nonna's painting and that feeling she had in her home fuel a great deal of her emotions connected to Florence as well as a deeper longing. Can you identify a memory from your childhood that invokes in you a response like Meg's?

4. How would you describe Meg's father? Do you think he loves his daughter? If you were Meg, would you have waited as long as she did for her father to take her to Florence?

5. Why was Meg's parents' divorce so devastating? Can you relate to her sense of loss?

6. What did Meg find compelling about Devon? What was the basis of her attraction to him? On the other hand, why do you think Devon was attracted to Meg's mother?

7. Were you surprised or not surprised that Meg's father was not in Florence when Meg arrived? How would her trip have been different had he been there?

8. In Nora Orsini's narrative, the nurse tells Nora, "You see that girl in the glass? You are the one who will say who she is, Nora. You decide who she will be." Was that good advice?

9. Were the actions that Sofia's parents took when she was a child justifiable? Did Sofia's father equip her to deal with heartache and loss, or did his actions merely cripple her ability to deal with reality? How did Nora Orsini deal with life's hardships?

10. At dinner, Lorenzo tells Renata that the rules for love are made in heaven, and Renata responds that is why the rules don't work on Earth. Lorenzo says, "I could not live up to the rules. And you could not. The rules are fine. It's us who are broken." Is Lorenzo right? Why do you think Lorenzo felt that he'd failed at love?

11. Lorenzo tells Meg that it's good there are people like Renata who see everything in black and white because "they remind us of what stays the same, no matter what." Do you agree? Are you a shades-of-gray person, or do you see things as black or white? Are you more like Lorenzo or Renata?

12. When Meg finally sees the statue, she is disappointed that it doesn't match the one she has in her memory. Have you ever visited something that was part of a vivid childhood memory

only to have it seem small and underwhelming when you saw it again as an adult? Why do you think that is?

13. Do you think Sofia should be allowed to keep her delusions? Why or why not?

14. What gave Meg the courage to call Lorenzo after she read her father's letter? How do you think Meg convinced Lorenzo he was worth the risk of being loved?

Author's Note

One of the lovely things about writing fiction is the freedom to manipulate reality, to create people who seem real but aren't, endowing them with a past that doesn't exist and giving them desires that resonate in us even if the people themselves are imaginary. There is much about *The Girl in the Glass* that is real, much that I concocted, and much that is as real as I can imagine it.

Nora Orsini was indeed the granddaughter of the great Cosimo I and the daughter of the murdered Isabella de' Medici Orsini. But there is very little written about Nora in any historical records. While we can't know for certain what her childhood was like after her mother was killed and her father disengaged himself from her, it is possible to imagine it. The narrative in *The Girl in the Glass* is how I imagined it.

Nora did indeed marry Alessandro Sforza, and it was a marriage arranged by her uncle Ferdinando Medici. There is no evidence that she was an artist, that she left behind any paintings, that she had a nurse who was kind to her, that she left Florence believing she could overcome heartache by drawing from wells of inner strength. But there is likewise no evidence to the contrary, which of course allowed me to wonder and speculate and suppose. I attempted to craft as believable and accurate a tale as possible. Any inaccuracies were for the sake of story.

If you get to Florence someday, please do find a trattoria that serves porcini mushrooms. They really are as soft and sweet as marshmallows.

If you would like to know more about the Medici family, or Florence, or Isabella de' Medici, I recommend these books: *The House of Medici—*

Its Rise and Fall by Christopher Hibbert (William Morrow Paperbacks, 1999), *The Stones of Florence* by Mary McCarthy (Mariner Books, 2002), *Brunelleschi's Dome: How a Renaissance Genius Reinvented Architecture* by Ross King (Penguin, 2001), and *Murder of a Medici Princess* by Caroline P. Murphy (Oxford University Press, 2009).

Acknowledgments

A novel is never the work of just one person. I am tremendously grateful to my editorial team at WaterBrook Multnomah Publishing Group, including Shannon Marchese, Lissa Halls Johnson, and Laura K. Wright, for opening my eyes to deeper and grander possibilities with these characters. Their insights sent me back to the drawing board more than once, but I am so glad they did. I am also grateful to my agent, Chip MacGregor, for steady encouragement, especially when the task at hand seemed far bigger than my ability to meet it.

Special thanks to Molly Kim, Emily Cates, Jody Cates, Katie Kuhl, and Jennifer Lyn King for sharing their memories, impressions, and photographs of Florence, and for loving this beautiful city like I do.

My Zip It! Book Club gals, and special friends Kimlee Harper, Pam Ingold, and Kathy Sanders prayed me through the tough days of the writing process. Their cheers from the sidelines kept me going. I am beyond grateful.

Hearty thanks are extended to my mother, Judy Horning, for her proofreading prowess, and to my husband, Bob, for letting me go back to Florence—in my mind—every day for nearly a year without him. Bob, *Sei tutto per me.*

Lastly, I am grateful to God for bestowing on humankind the desire and the vision to imagine jaw-dropping beauty and then the talent to bravely create it.

About the Author

Susan Meissner has been a devotee of the art of story since her earliest pencil-and-paper days. She is the award-winning author of *The Shape of Mercy, Lady in Waiting,* and many other novels. She is also a speaker and writing-workshop leader with a background in community journalism. When she's not writing, Susan directs the Small Groups and Connection Ministries program at The Church at Rancho Bernardo in San Diego. She and her pastor husband are the parents of four young adults. Visit her website at www.susanmeissner.com.

SOMETIMES WE FIND *The* TRUTH ABOUT OURSELVES IN THE LIVES *of* OTHERS.

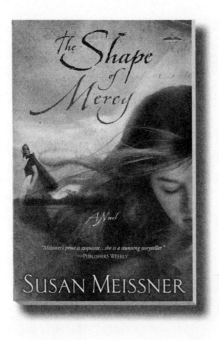

Expected to gracefully embrace a life of privilege, a young woman cuts the purse strings that bind her to plot a new life course. But startling self-realization challenges everything she knows as she begins to study the tragic life of a seventeenth-century victim of the Salem witch trials.

Read an excerpt from this book and more at
WaterBrookMultnomah.com!

An ancient *ring,*

two women separated

by nearly five hundred years,

and the *freedom* to *choose* one's life.

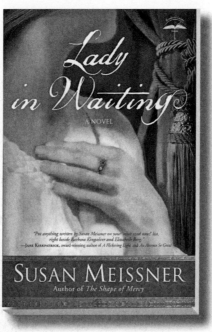

Manhattan antique shop owner, Jane Lindsay is jolted into a new reality when she suddenly has to face the fact that her marriage is crumbling. While she grapples with her husband's abandonment, she comes across an ancient ring that may have belonged to Lady Jane Grey. As she traces the origins of the ring and Lady Grey's story, Jane has to decide whether she will default to habits of powerlessness or whether she will take the first steps towards real truth and happiness.

Read an excerpt from this book and more at
WaterBrookMultnomah.com!

A HOUSE SHROUDED *in* TIME.
A LINE *of* WOMEN WITH
a HERITAGE *of* LOSS.

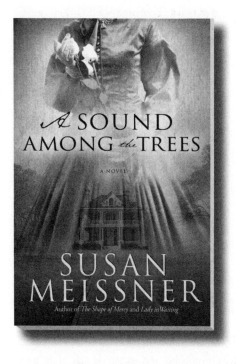

Marielle Bishop marries into an instant family and an antebellum home rumored to be haunted. How can she find the truth without losing herself in the painful past surrounding her?

Read an excerpt from this book and more at
WaterBrookMultnomah.com!

A white picket fence
is no guarantee that all is well.

Amanda's family may look picture-perfect, but it is splintered by
discontent, heartache, and secrets. It isn't until her son, Chase,
and niece, Tally, interview a pair of Holocaust survivors that they
are challenged to face their pain.

Read an excerpt from this book and more at
WaterBrookMultnomah.com!